South Burlington
Public Library
DISCARD

W9-CAE-068

Friday

NOV 0 0 2021

IMAGE COMICS, INC. • **IMAGECOMICS.COM**

Todd McFarlane: President • **Jim Valentino**: Vice President • **Marc Silvestri**: Chief Executive Officer • **Erik Larsen**: Chief Financial Officer • **Robert Kirkman**: Chief Operating Officer • **Eric Stephenson**: Publisher / Chief Creative Officer • **Nicole Lapalme**: Controller • **Leanna Caunter**: Accounting Analyst **Sue Korpela**: Accounting & HR Manager • **Marla Eizik**: Talent Liaison • **Jeff Boison**: Director of Sales & Publishing Planning • **Dirk Wood**: Director of International Sales & Licensing • **Alex Cox**: Director of Direct Market Sales • **Chloe Ramos**: Book Market & Library Sales Manager • **Emilio Bautista**: Digital Sales Coordinator • **Jon Schlaffman**: Specialty Sales Coordinator • **Kat Salazar**: Director of PR & Marketing • **Drew Fitzgerald**: Marketing Content Associate **Heather Doornink**: Production Director • **Drew Gill**: Art Director • **Hilary DiLoreto**: Print Manager • **Tricia Ramos**: Traffic Manager • **Melissa Gifford**: Content Manager • **Erika Schnatz**: Senior Production Artist • **Ryan Brewer**: Production Artist • **Deanna Phelps**: Production Artist

FRIDAY, BOOK ONE: THE FIRST DAY OF CHRISTMAS. First printing. November 2021. Published by Image Comics, Inc. Office of publication: PO BOX 14457, Portland, OR 97293. Copyright © 2021 Basement Gang Inc. and Marcos Martín. All rights reserved. Contains material originally published in single magazine form as FRIDAY #1-3. "Friday," its logos, and the likenesses of all characters herein are trademarks of Basement Gang Inc. and Marcos Martín, unless otherwise noted. "Image" and the Image Comics logos are registered trademarks of Image Comics, Inc. No part of this publication may be reproduced or transmitted, in any form or by any means (except for short excerpts for journalistic or review purposes), without the express written permission of Basement Gang Inc. and Marcos Martín, or Image Comics, Inc. All names, characters, events, and locales in this publication are entirely fictional. Any resemblance to actual persons (living or dead), events, or places, without satirical intent, is coincidental. Printed in the USA. For international rights, contact: foreignlicensing@imagecomics.com. ISBN: 978-1-5343-2058-1.

FRIDAY

✤

Ed Brubaker & Marcos Martín
with
Muntsa Vicente

Book One

Chapter One
The Girl in the Trees

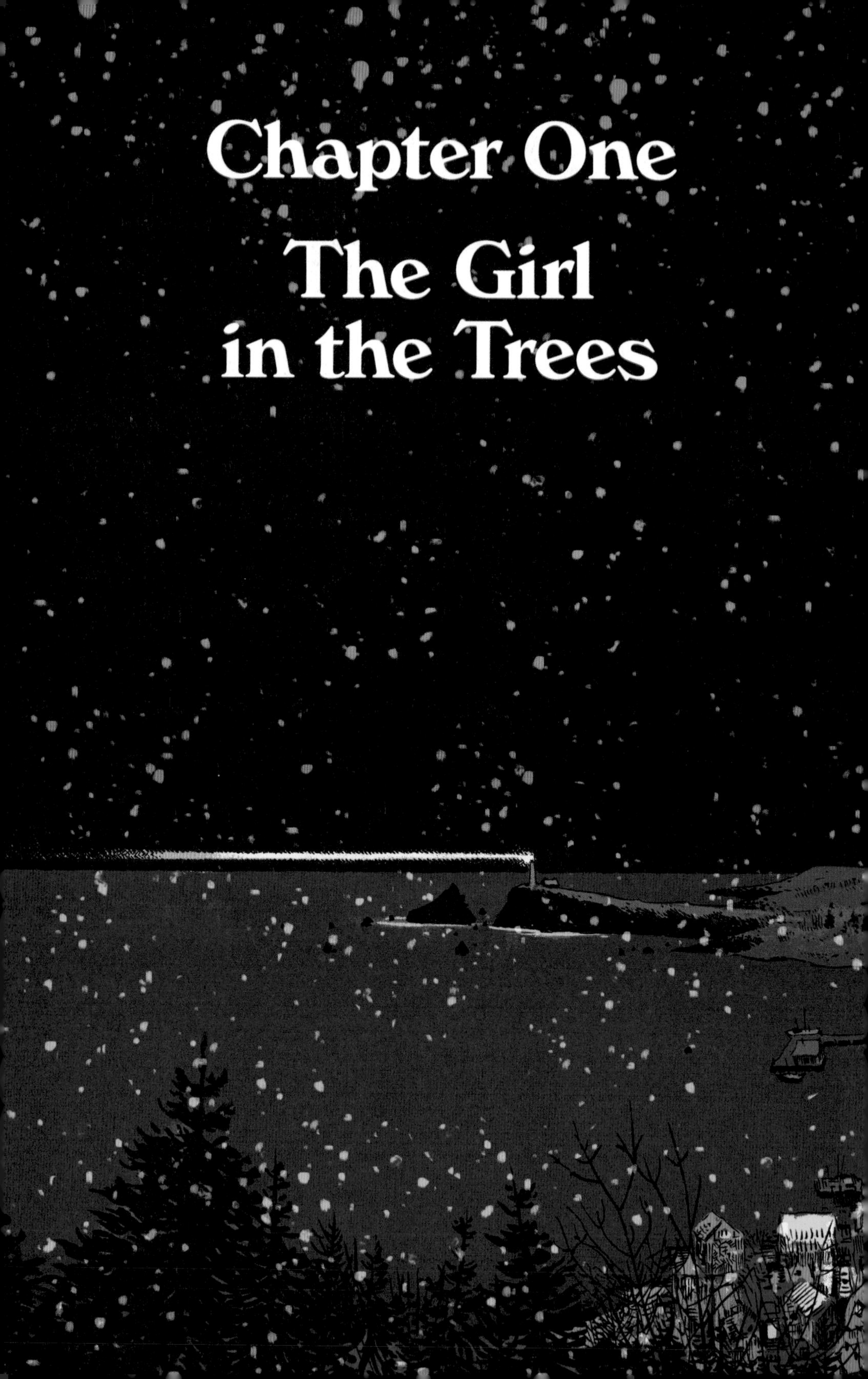

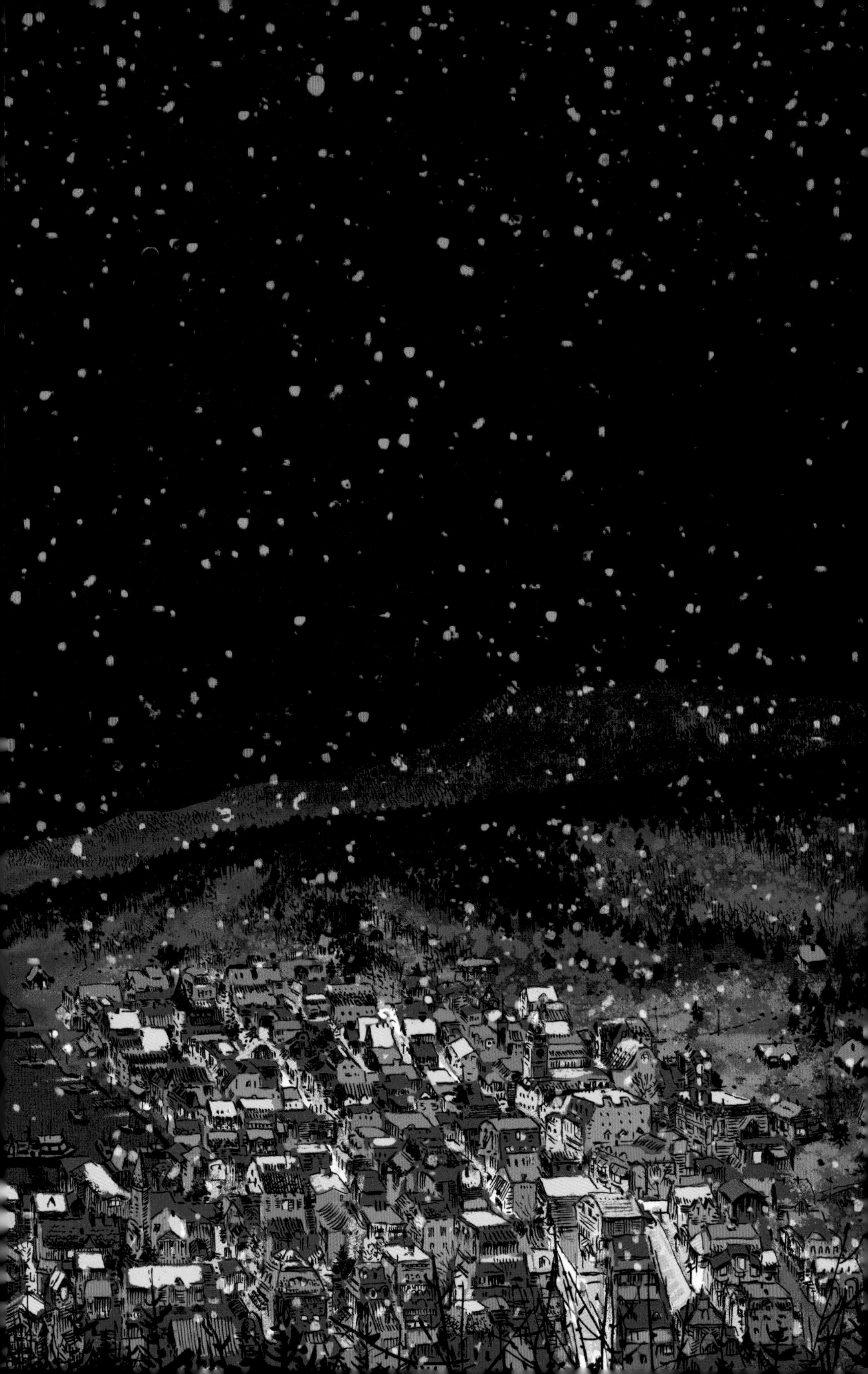

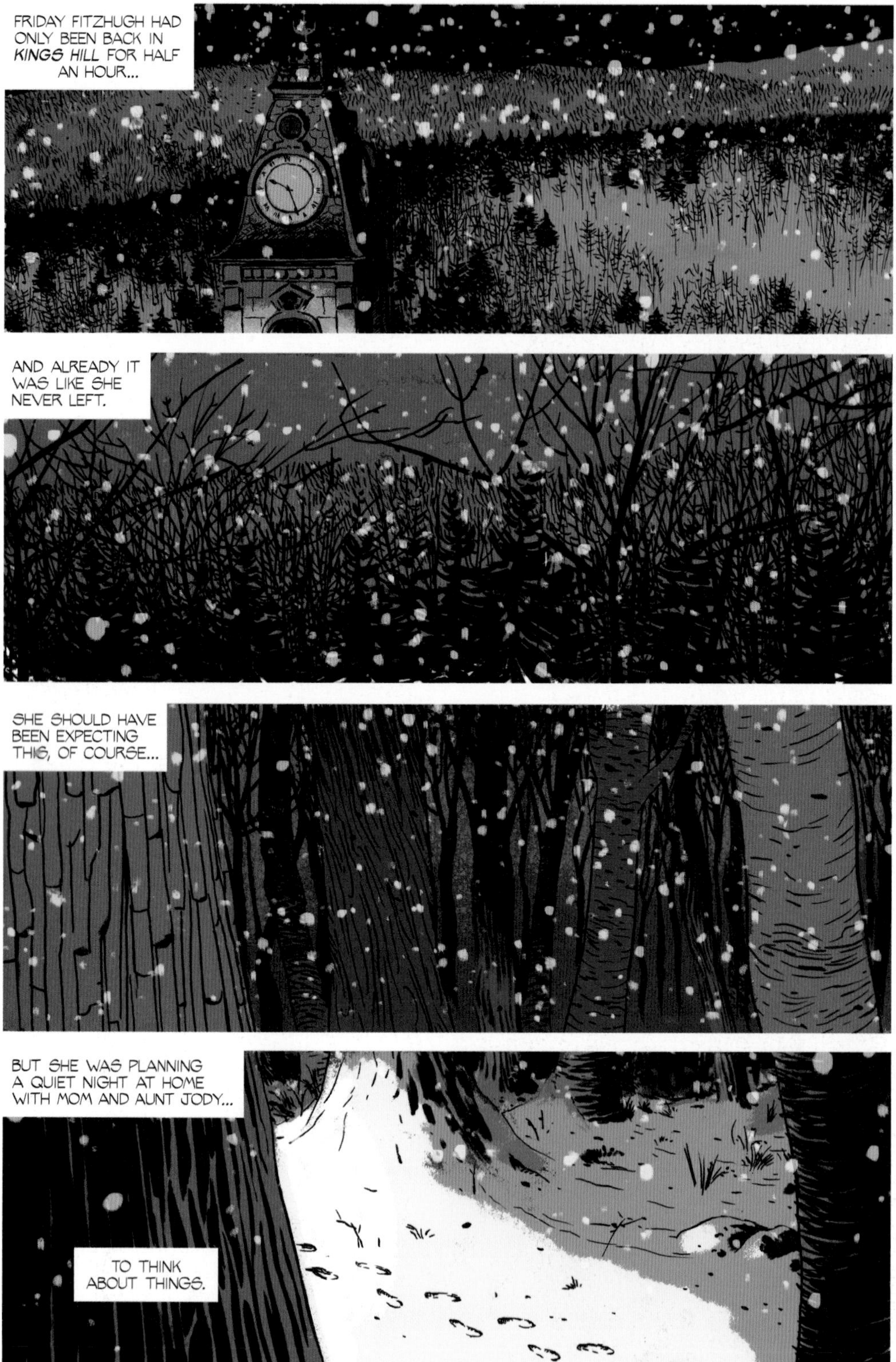
FRIDAY FITZHUGH HAD ONLY BEEN BACK IN KINGS HILL FOR HALF AN HOUR...
AND ALREADY IT WAS LIKE SHE NEVER LEFT.
SHE SHOULD HAVE BEEN EXPECTING THIS, OF COURSE...
BUT SHE WAS PLANNING A QUIET NIGHT AT HOME WITH MOM AND AUNT JODY...
TO THINK ABOUT THINGS.

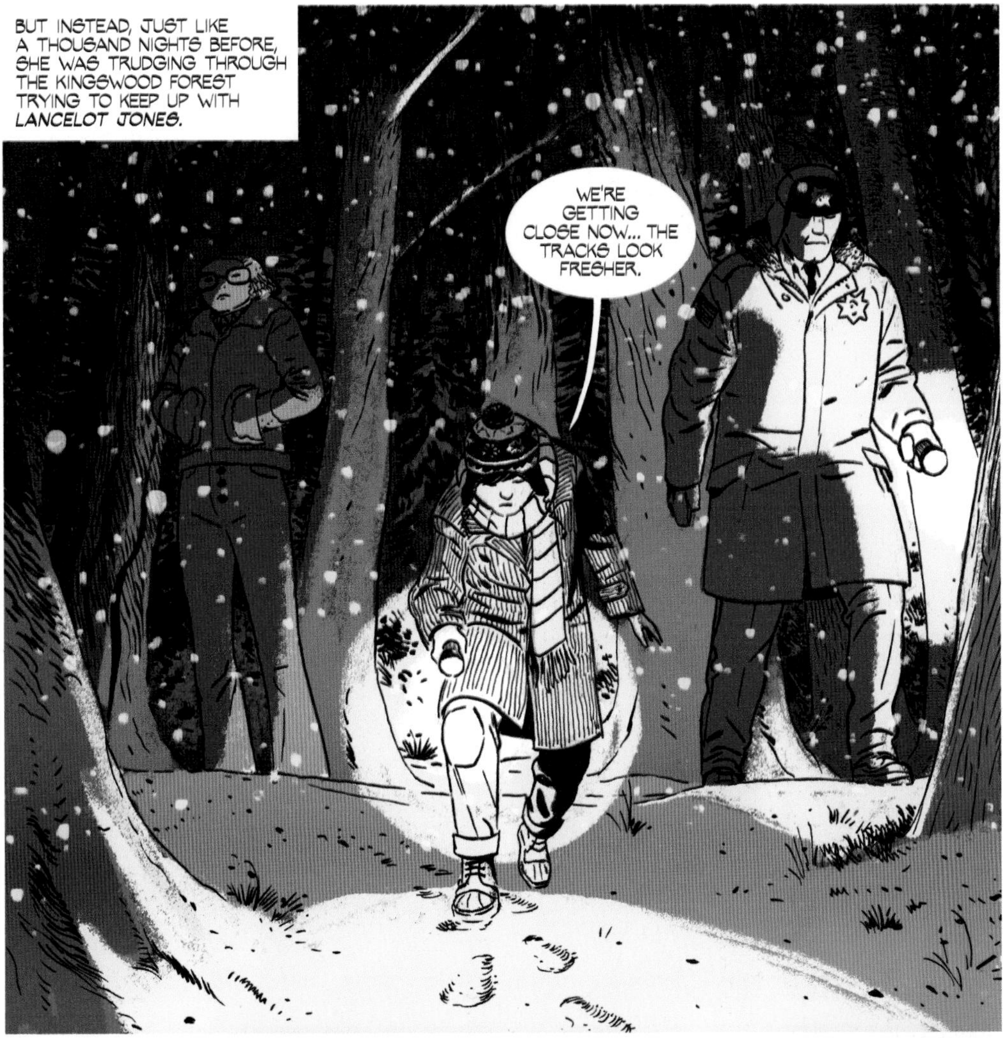
BUT INSTEAD, JUST LIKE A THOUSAND NIGHTS BEFORE, SHE WAS TRUDGING THROUGH THE KINGSWOOD FOREST TRYING TO KEEP UP WITH LANCELOT JONES.
WE'RE GETTING CLOSE NOW... THE TRACKS LOOK FRESHER.

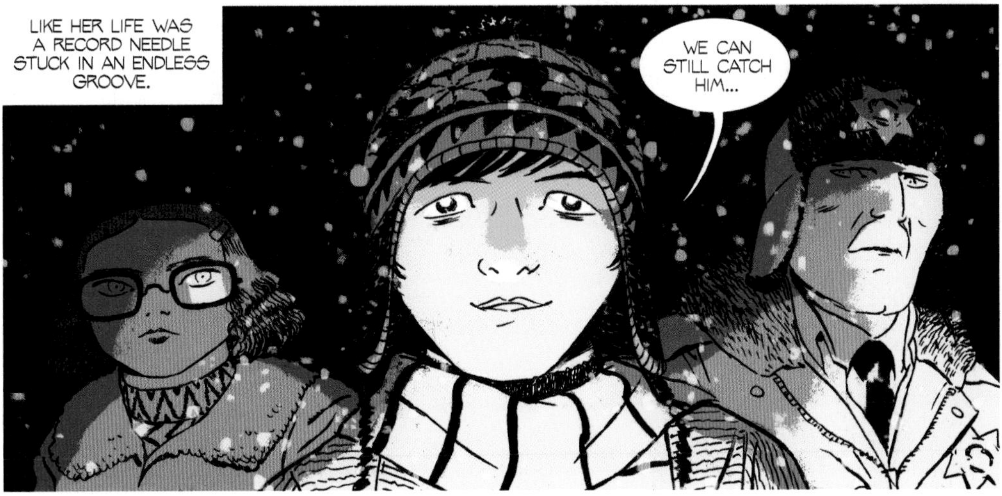
LIKE HER LIFE WAS A RECORD NEEDLE STUCK IN AN ENDLESS GROOVE.
WE CAN STILL CATCH HIM...

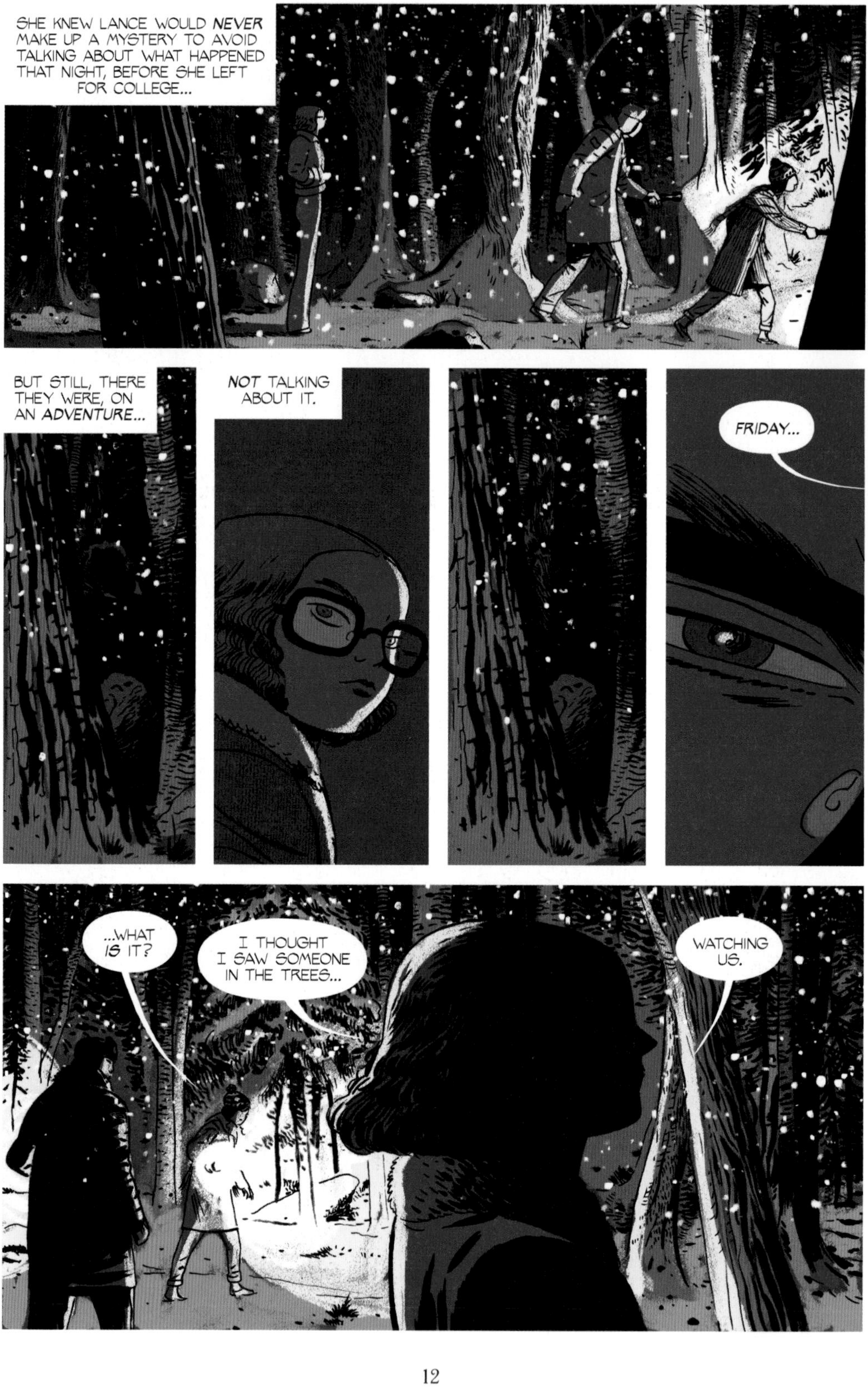
SHE KNEW LANCE WOULD NEVER MAKE UP A MYSTERY TO AVOID TALKING ABOUT WHAT HAPPENED THAT NIGHT, BEFORE SHE LEFT FOR COLLEGE...
BUT STILL, THERE THEY WERE, ON AN ADVENTURE...
NOT TALKING ABOUT IT.
FRIDAY...
...WHAT IS IT?
I THOUGHT I SAW SOMEONE IN THE TREES...
WATCHING US.

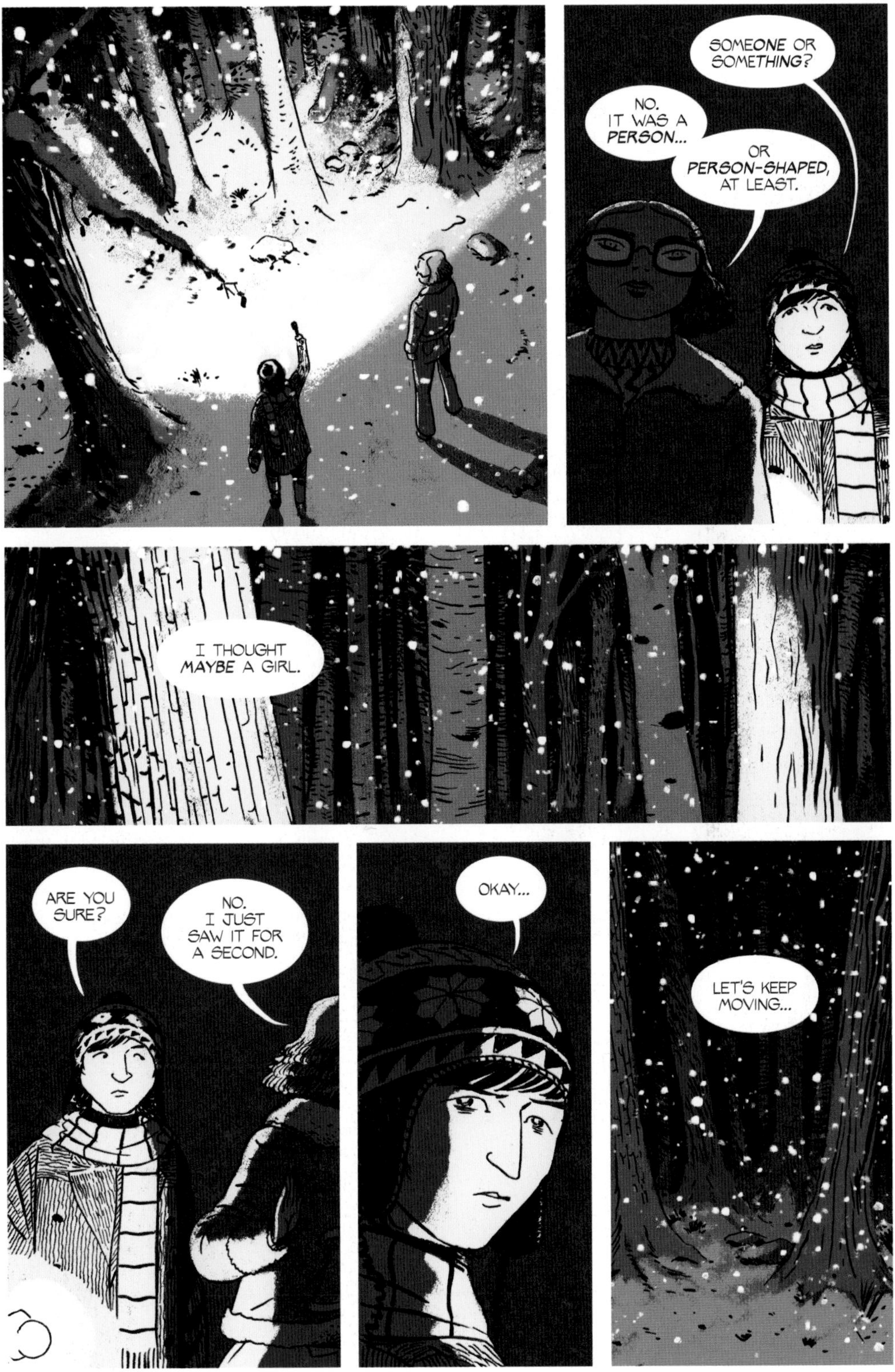
SOMEONE OR SOMETHING?
NO. IT WAS A PERSON...
OR PERSON-SHAPED, AT LEAST.
I THOUGHT MAYBE A GIRL.
ARE YOU SURE?
NO. I JUST SAW IT FOR A SECOND.
OKAY...
LET'S KEEP MOVING...

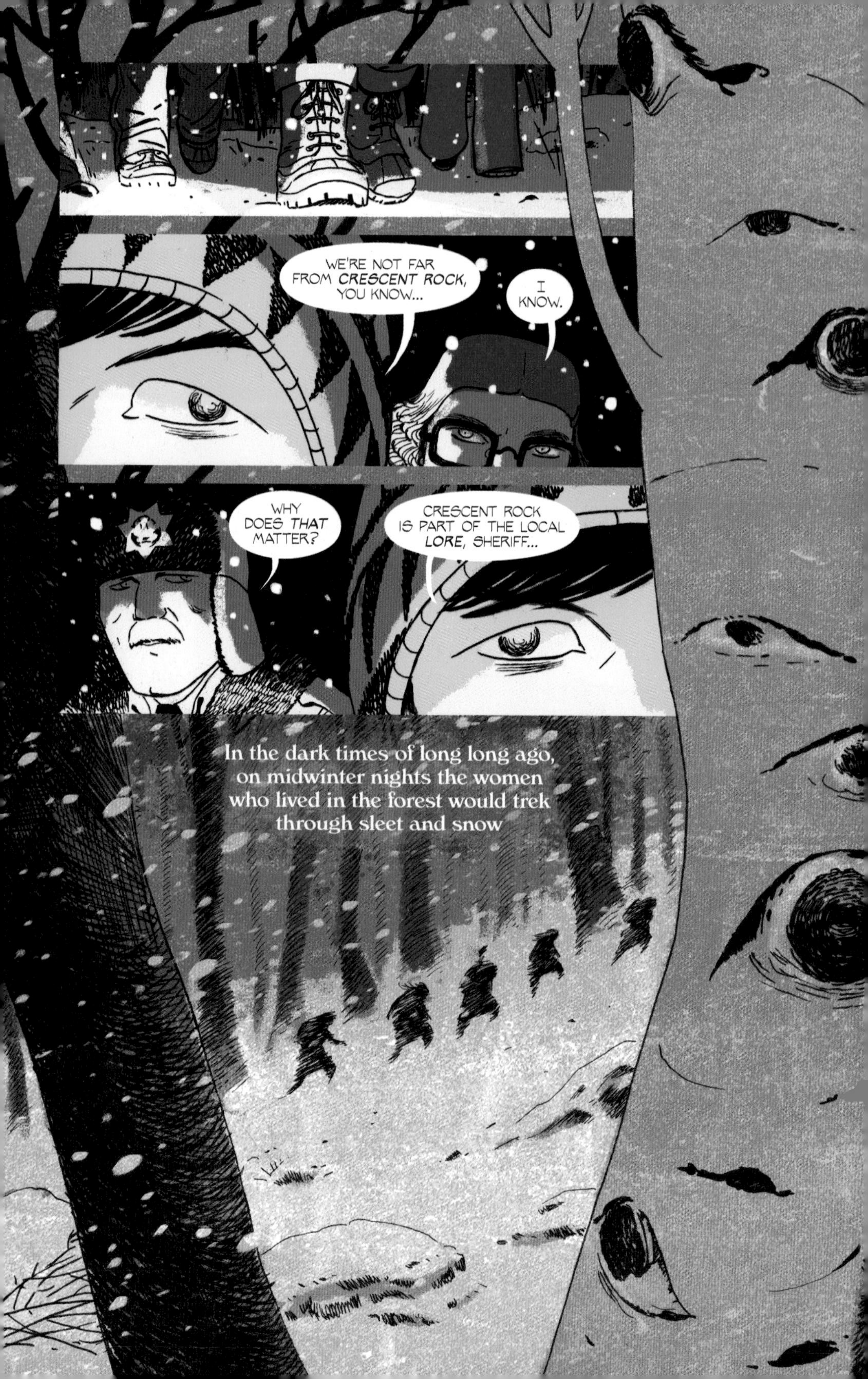
WE'RE NOT FAR FROM CRESCENT ROCK, YOU KNOW...
I KNOW.
WHY DOES THAT MATTER?
CRESCENT ROCK IS PART OF THE LOCAL LORE, SHERIFF...
In the dark times of long long ago, on midwinter nights the women who lived in the forest would trek through sleet and snow

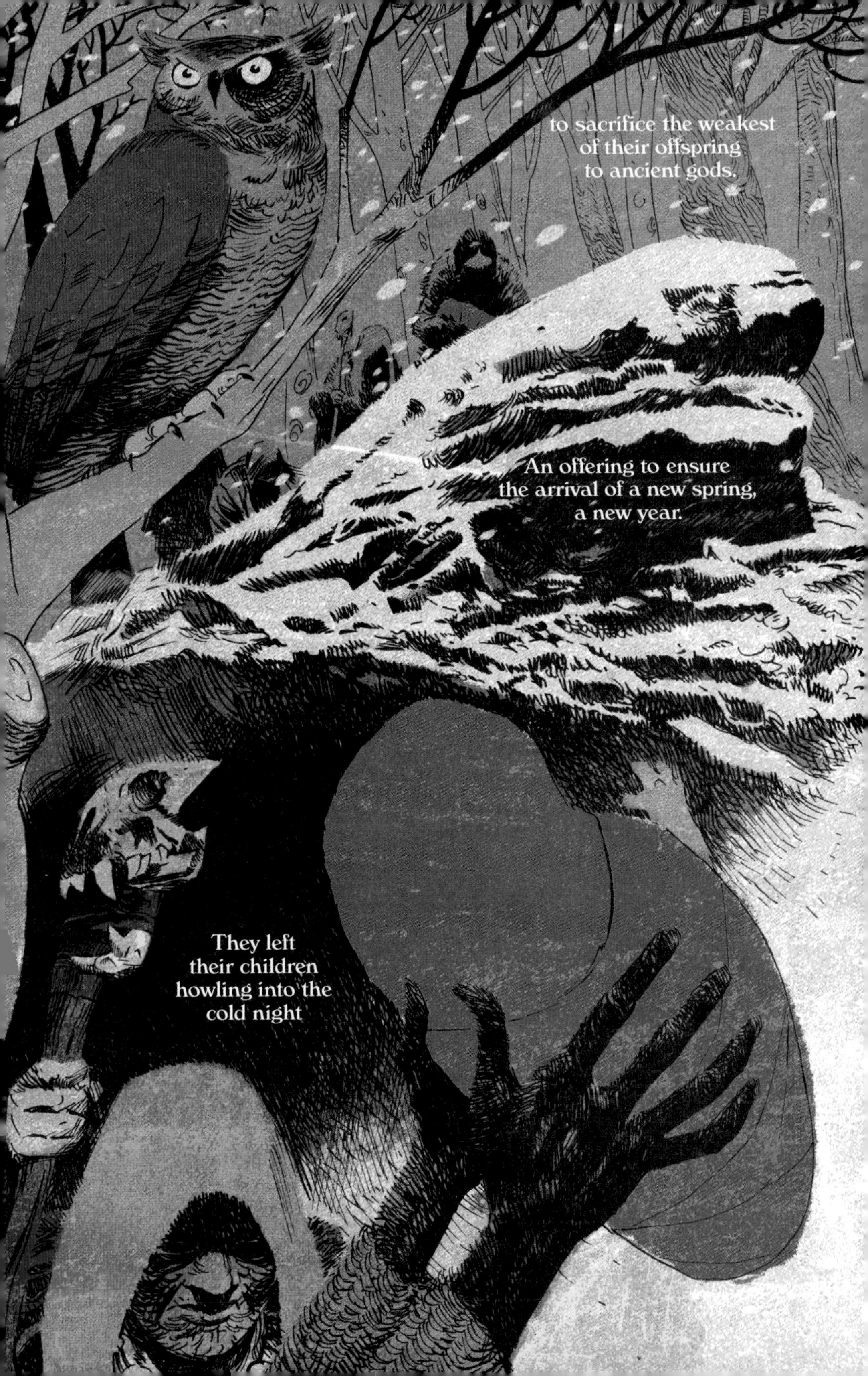
to sacrifice the weakest of their offspring to ancient gods.
An offering to ensure the arrival of a new spring, a new year.
They left their children howling into the cold night

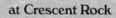
at Crescent Rock

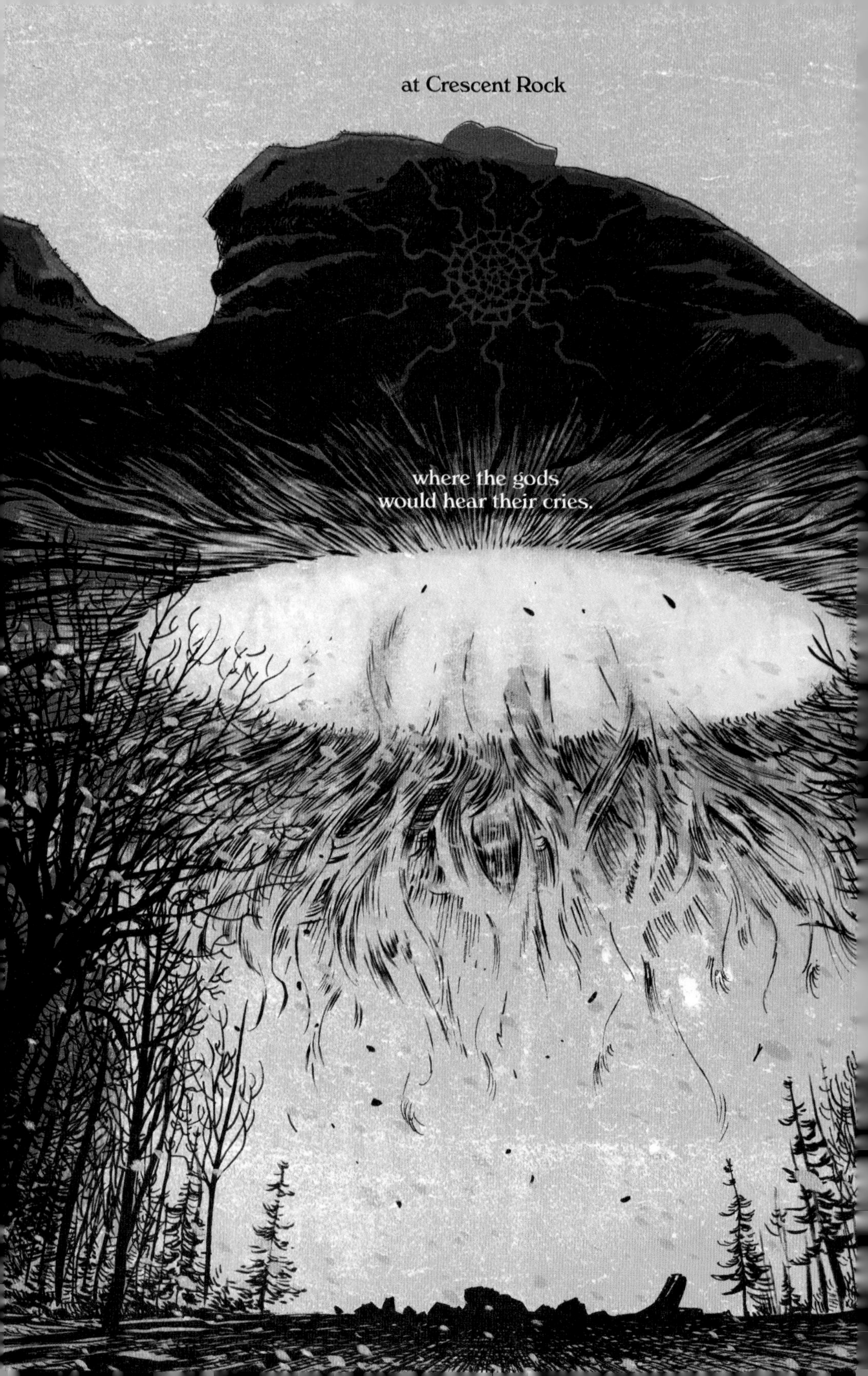

where the gods
would hear their cries.

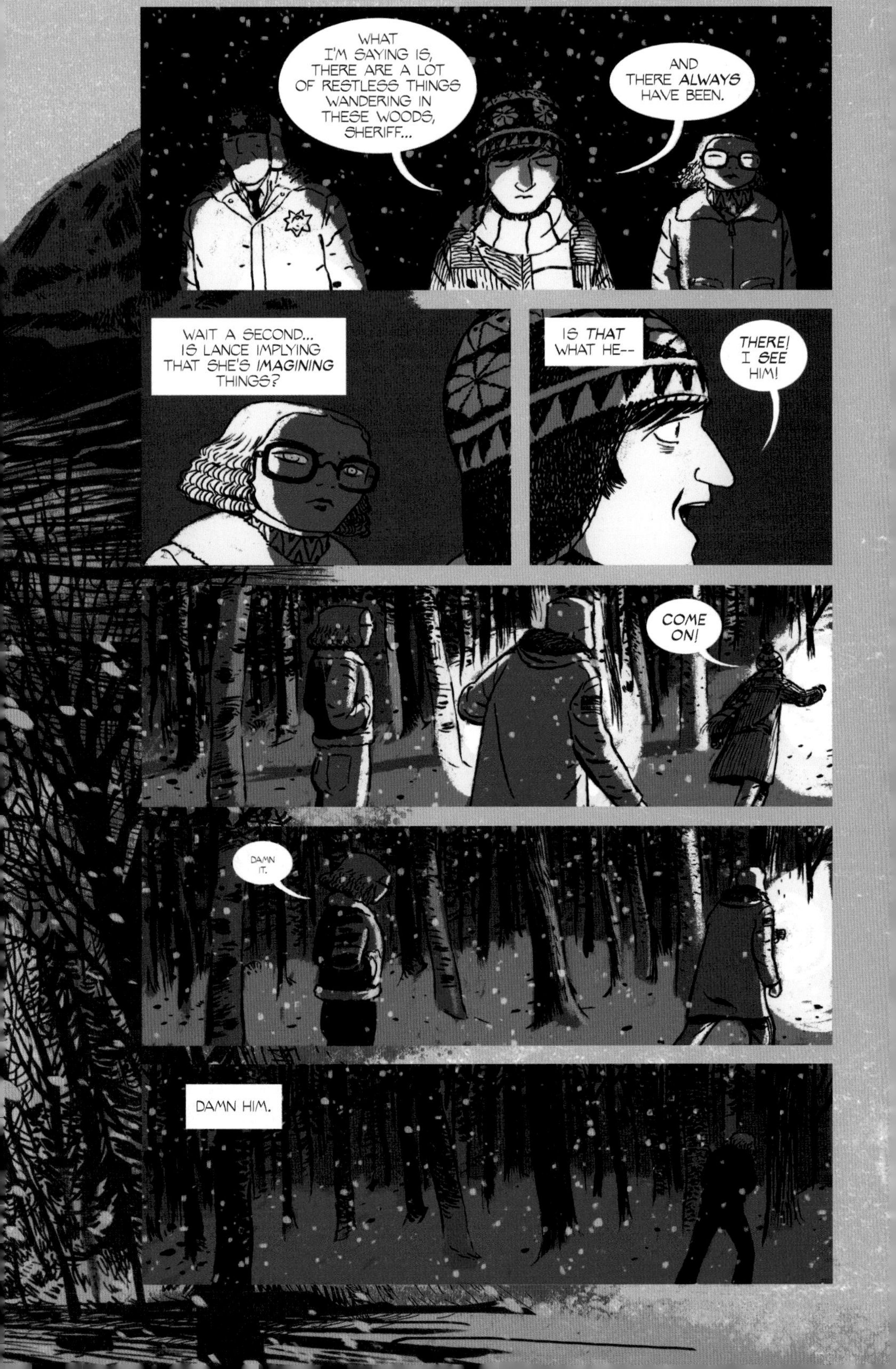
WHAT I'M SAYING IS, THERE ARE A LOT OF RESTLESS THINGS WANDERING IN THESE WOODS, SHERIFF...
AND THERE ALWAYS HAVE BEEN.
WAIT A SECOND... IS LANCE IMPLYING THAT SHE'S IMAGINING THINGS?
IS THAT WHAT HE--
THERE! I SEE HIM!
COME ON!
DAMN IT.
DAMN HIM.

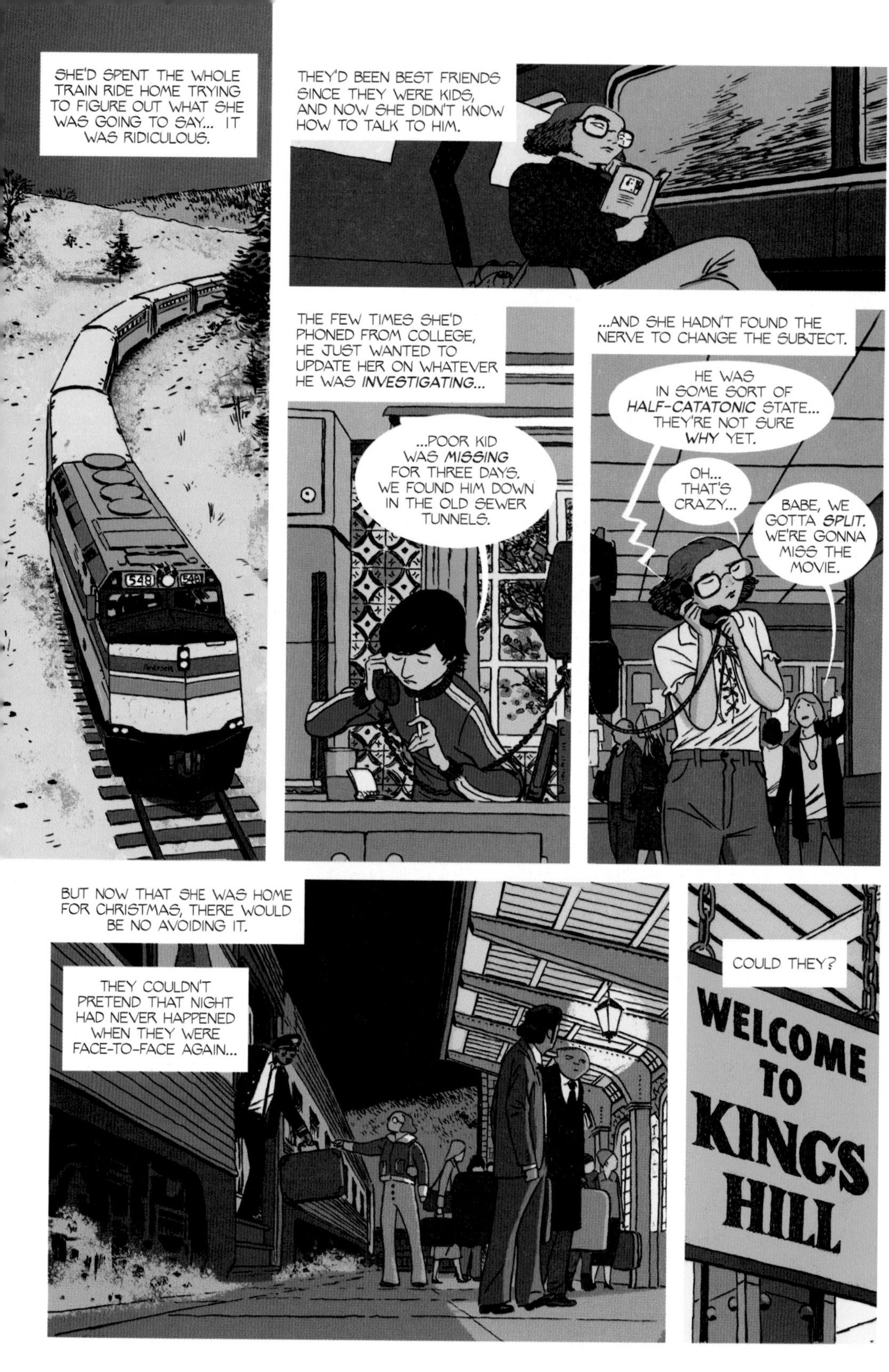

SHE'D SPENT THE WHOLE TRAIN RIDE HOME TRYING TO FIGURE OUT WHAT SHE WAS GOING TO SAY... IT WAS RIDICULOUS.
THEY'D BEEN BEST FRIENDS SINCE THEY WERE KIDS, AND NOW SHE DIDN'T KNOW HOW TO TALK TO HIM.
THE FEW TIMES SHE'D PHONED FROM COLLEGE, HE JUST WANTED TO UPDATE HER ON WHATEVER HE WAS *INVESTIGATING*...
...POOR KID WAS *MISSING* FOR THREE DAYS. WE FOUND HIM DOWN IN THE OLD SEWER TUNNELS.
...AND SHE HADN'T FOUND THE NERVE TO CHANGE THE SUBJECT.
HE WAS IN SOME SORT OF *HALF-CATATONIC* STATE... THEY'RE NOT SURE *WHY* YET.
OH... THAT'S CRAZY...
BABE, WE GOTTA *SPLIT*. WE'RE GONNA MISS THE MOVIE.
BUT NOW THAT SHE WAS HOME FOR CHRISTMAS, THERE WOULD BE NO AVOIDING IT.
THEY COULDN'T PRETEND THAT NIGHT HAD NEVER HAPPENED WHEN THEY WERE FACE-TO-FACE AGAIN...
COULD THEY?
WELCOME TO KINGS HILL

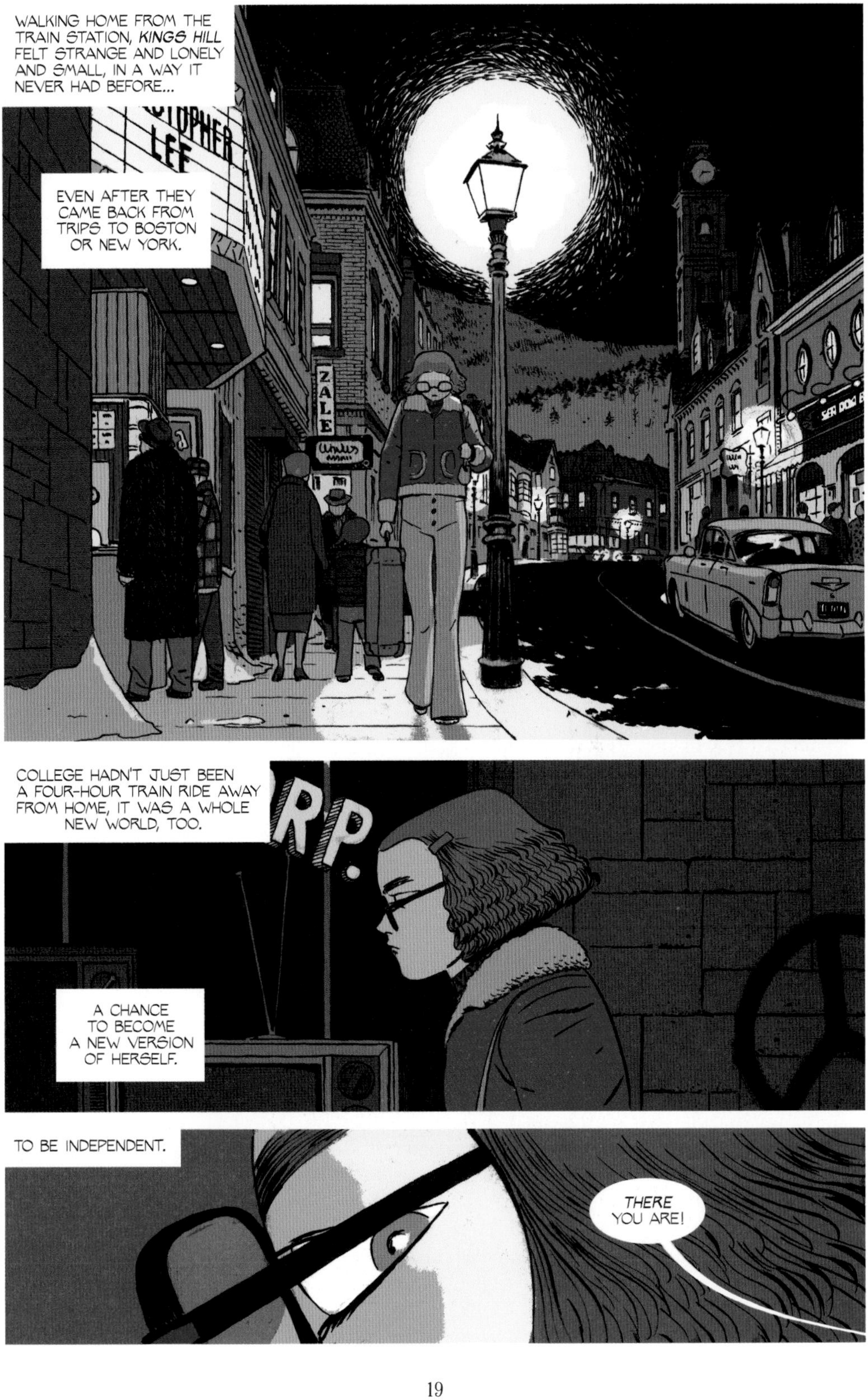
WALKING HOME FROM THE TRAIN STATION, *KINGS HILL* FELT STRANGE AND LONELY AND SMALL, IN A WAY IT NEVER HAD BEFORE...
EVEN AFTER THEY CAME BACK FROM TRIPS TO BOSTON OR NEW YORK.
COLLEGE HADN'T JUST BEEN A FOUR-HOUR TRAIN RIDE AWAY FROM HOME, IT WAS A WHOLE NEW WORLD, TOO.
A CHANCE TO BECOME A NEW VERSION OF HERSELF.
TO BE INDEPENDENT.
THERE YOU ARE!

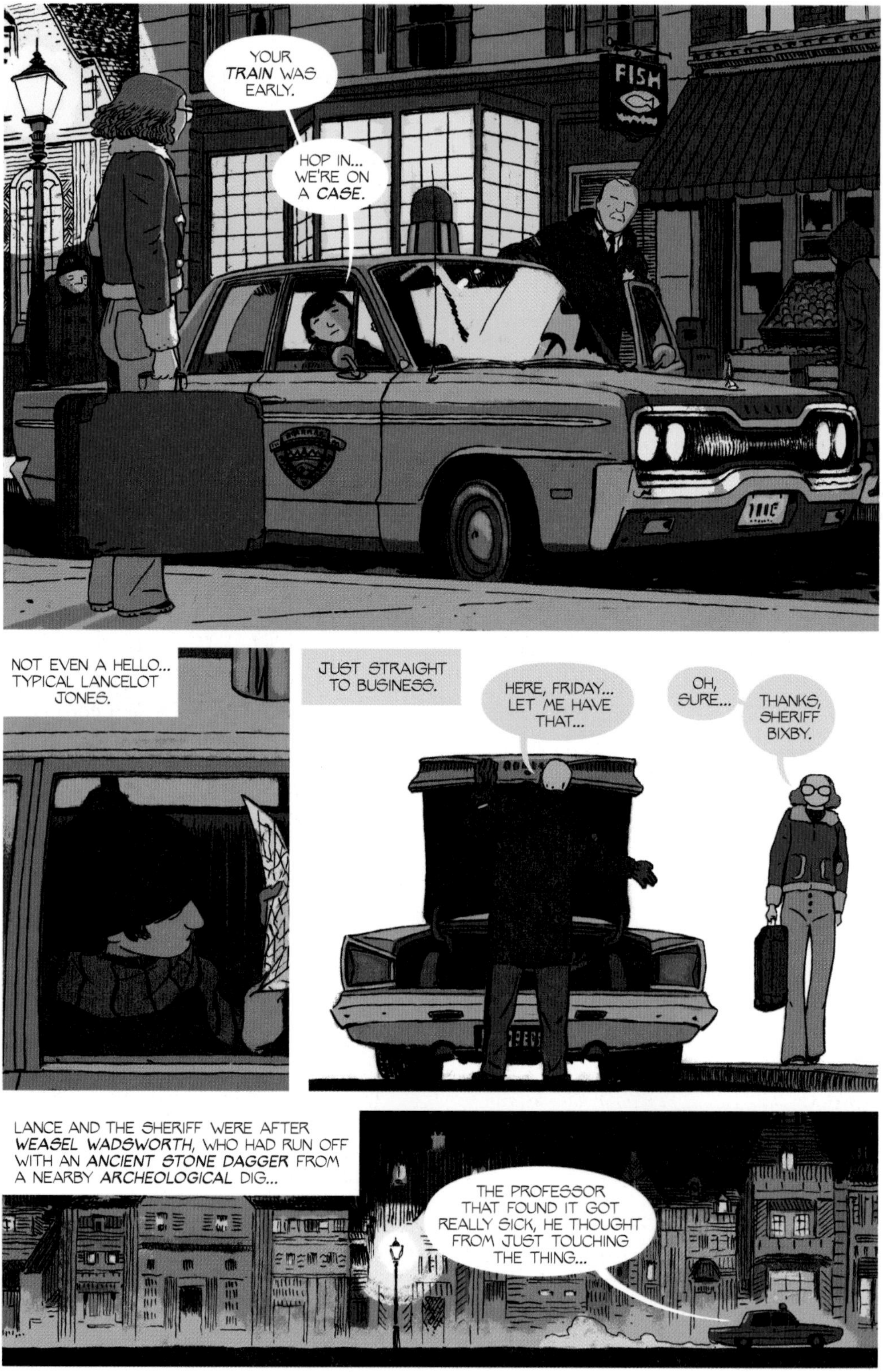
FISH
YOUR TRAIN WAS EARLY.
HOP IN... WE'RE ON A CASE.
NOT EVEN A HELLO... TYPICAL LANCELOT JONES.
JUST STRAIGHT TO BUSINESS.
HERE, FRIDAY... LET ME HAVE THAT...
OH, SURE...
THANKS, SHERIFF BIXBY.
LANCE AND THE SHERIFF WERE AFTER WEASEL WADSWORTH, WHO HAD RUN OFF WITH AN ANCIENT STONE DAGGER FROM A NEARBY ARCHEOLOGICAL DIG...
THE PROFESSOR THAT FOUND IT GOT REALLY SICK, HE THOUGHT FROM JUST TOUCHING THE THING...

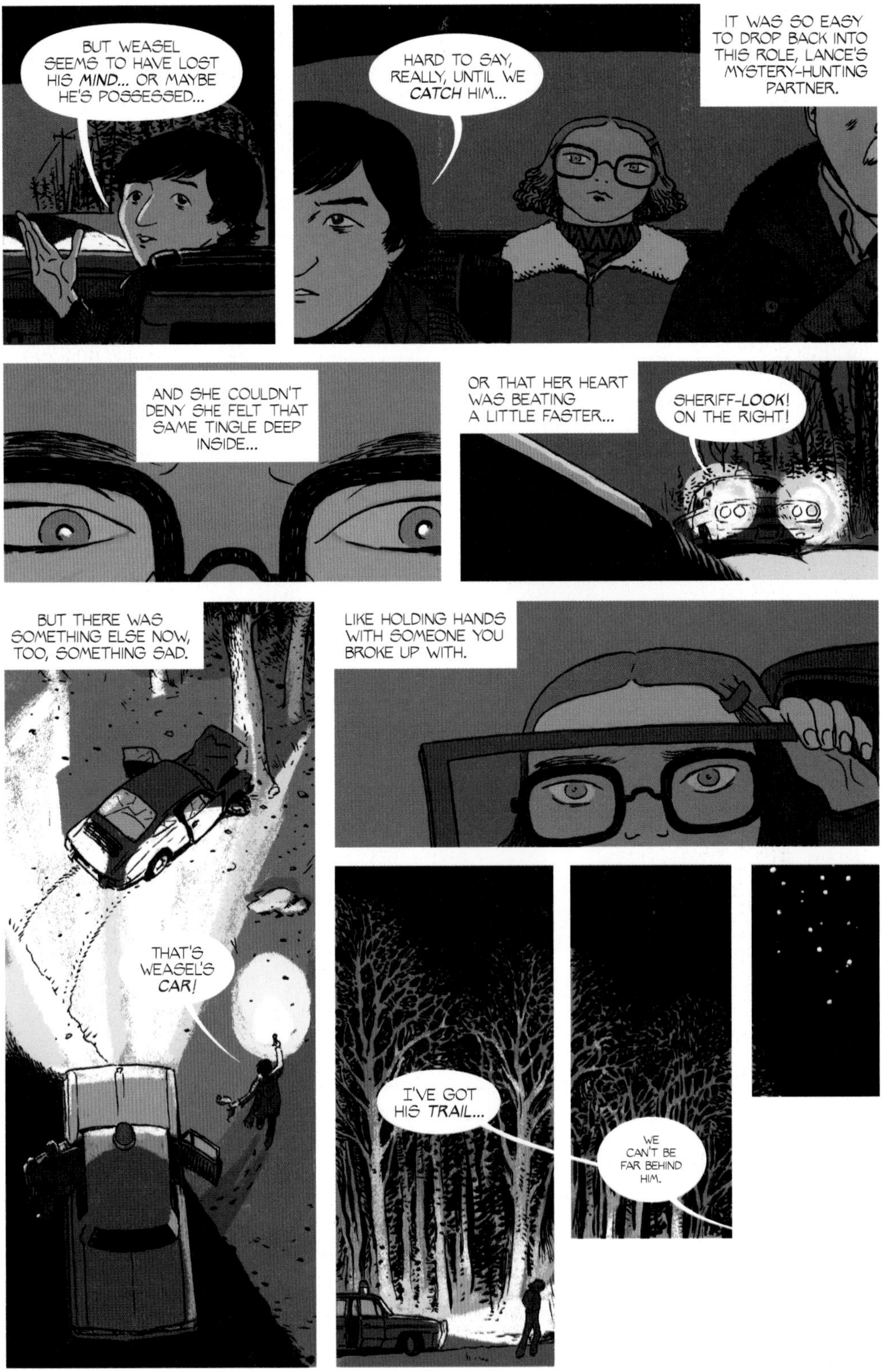
BUT WEASEL SEEMS TO HAVE LOST HIS *MIND*... OR MAYBE HE'S POSSESSED...
HARD TO SAY, REALLY, UNTIL WE *CATCH* HIM...
IT WAS SO EASY TO DROP BACK INTO THIS ROLE, LANCE'S MYSTERY-HUNTING PARTNER.
AND SHE COULDN'T DENY SHE FELT THAT SAME TINGLE DEEP INSIDE...
OR THAT HER HEART WAS BEATING A LITTLE FASTER...
SHERIFF-*LOOK*! ON THE RIGHT!
BUT THERE WAS SOMETHING ELSE NOW, TOO, SOMETHING SAD.
THAT'S WEASEL'S *CAR*!
LIKE HOLDING HANDS WITH SOMEONE YOU BROKE UP WITH.
I'VE GOT HIS *TRAIL*...
WE CAN'T BE FAR BEHIND HIM.

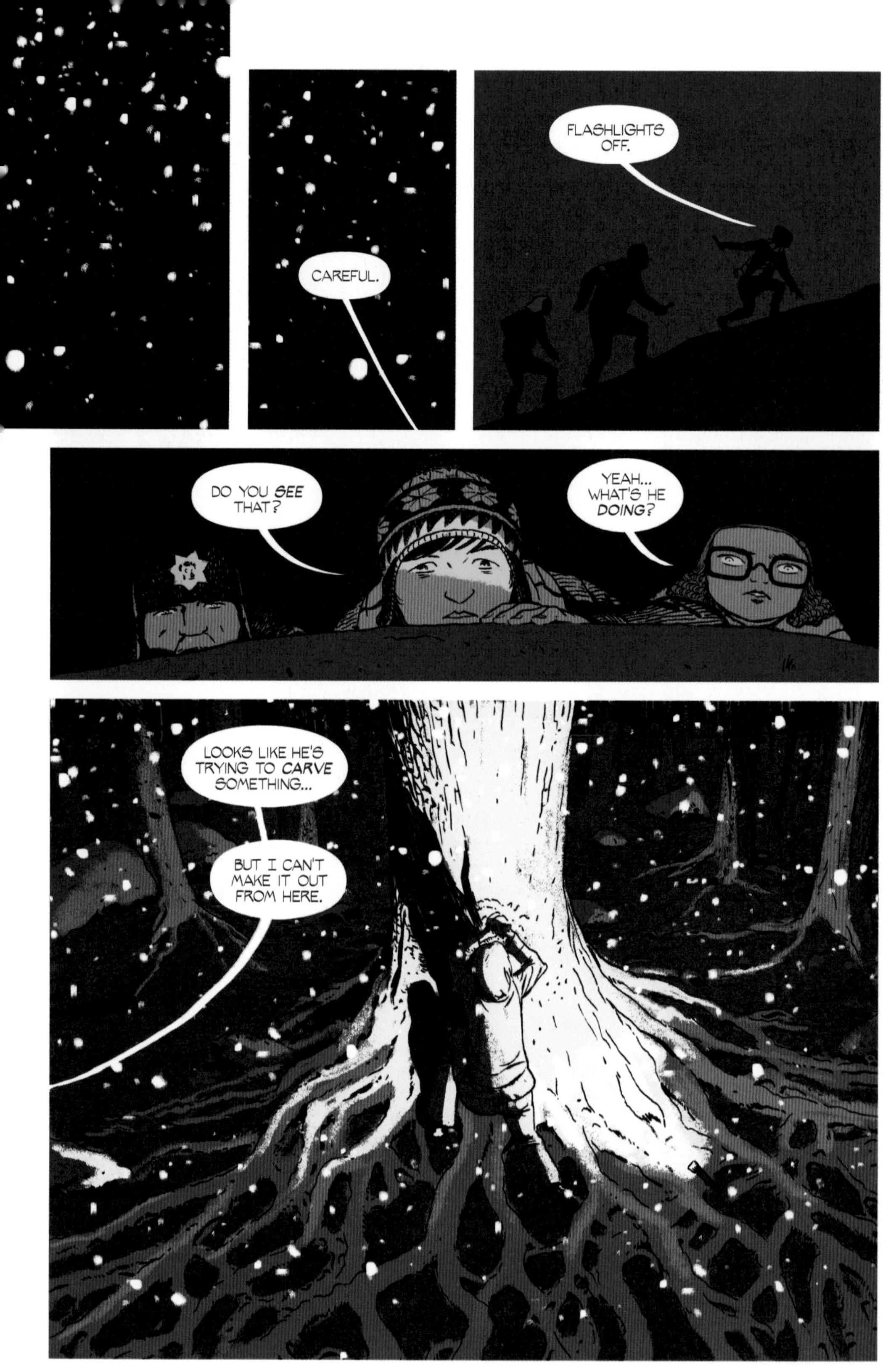
CAREFUL.
FLASHLIGHTS OFF.
DO YOU SEE THAT?
YEAH... WHAT'S HE DOING?
LOOKS LIKE HE'S TRYING TO CARVE SOMETHING...
BUT I CAN'T MAKE IT OUT FROM HERE.

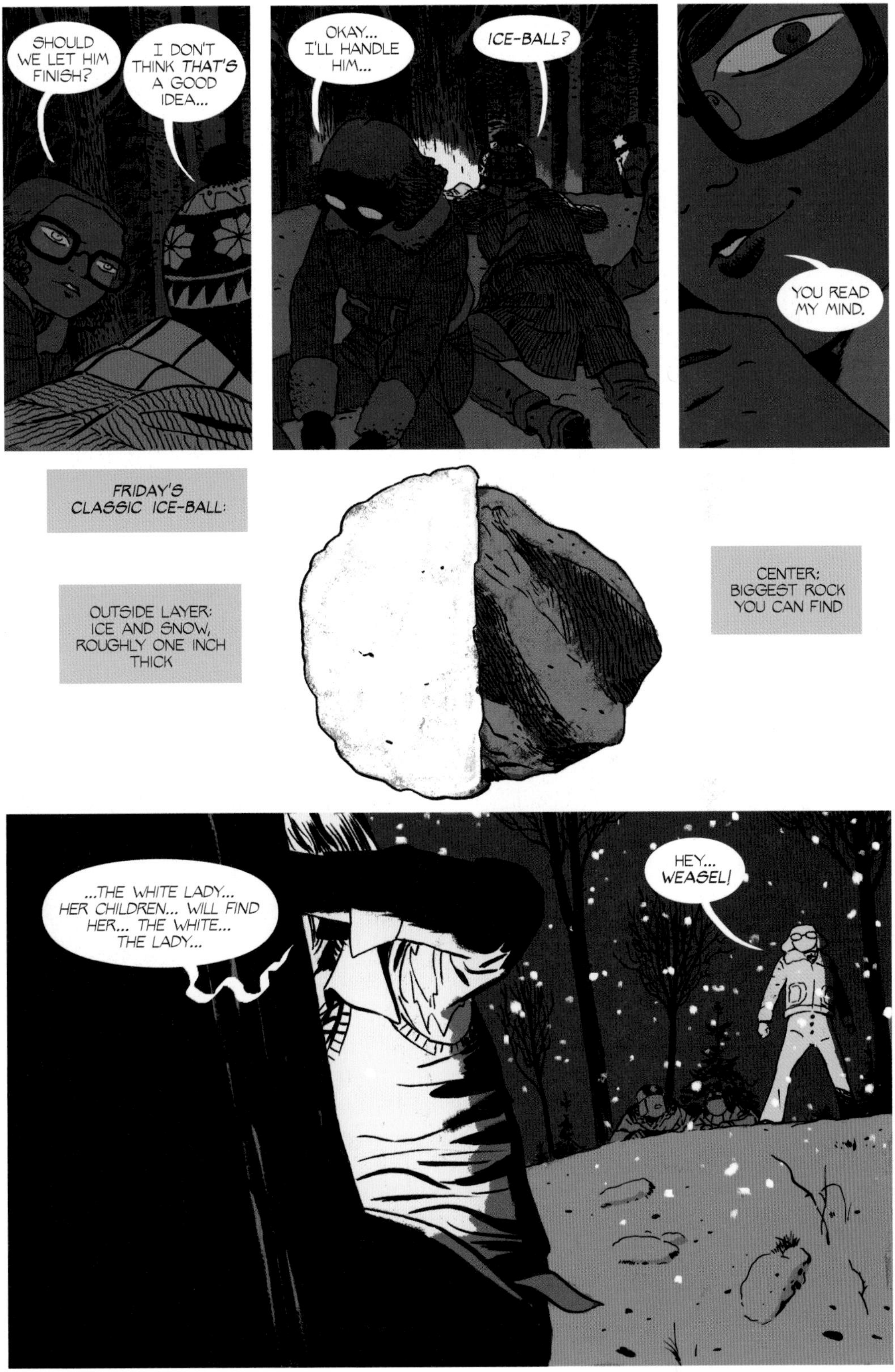
SHOULD WE LET HIM FINISH?
I DON'T THINK *THAT'S* A GOOD IDEA...
OKAY... I'LL HANDLE HIM...
ICE-BALL?
YOU READ MY MIND.
FRIDAY'S CLASSIC ICE-BALL:
OUTSIDE LAYER: ICE AND SNOW, ROUGHLY ONE INCH THICK
CENTER: BIGGEST ROCK YOU CAN FIND
...THE WHITE LADY... HER CHILDREN... WILL FIND HER... THE WHITE... THE LADY...
HEY... **WEASEL!**

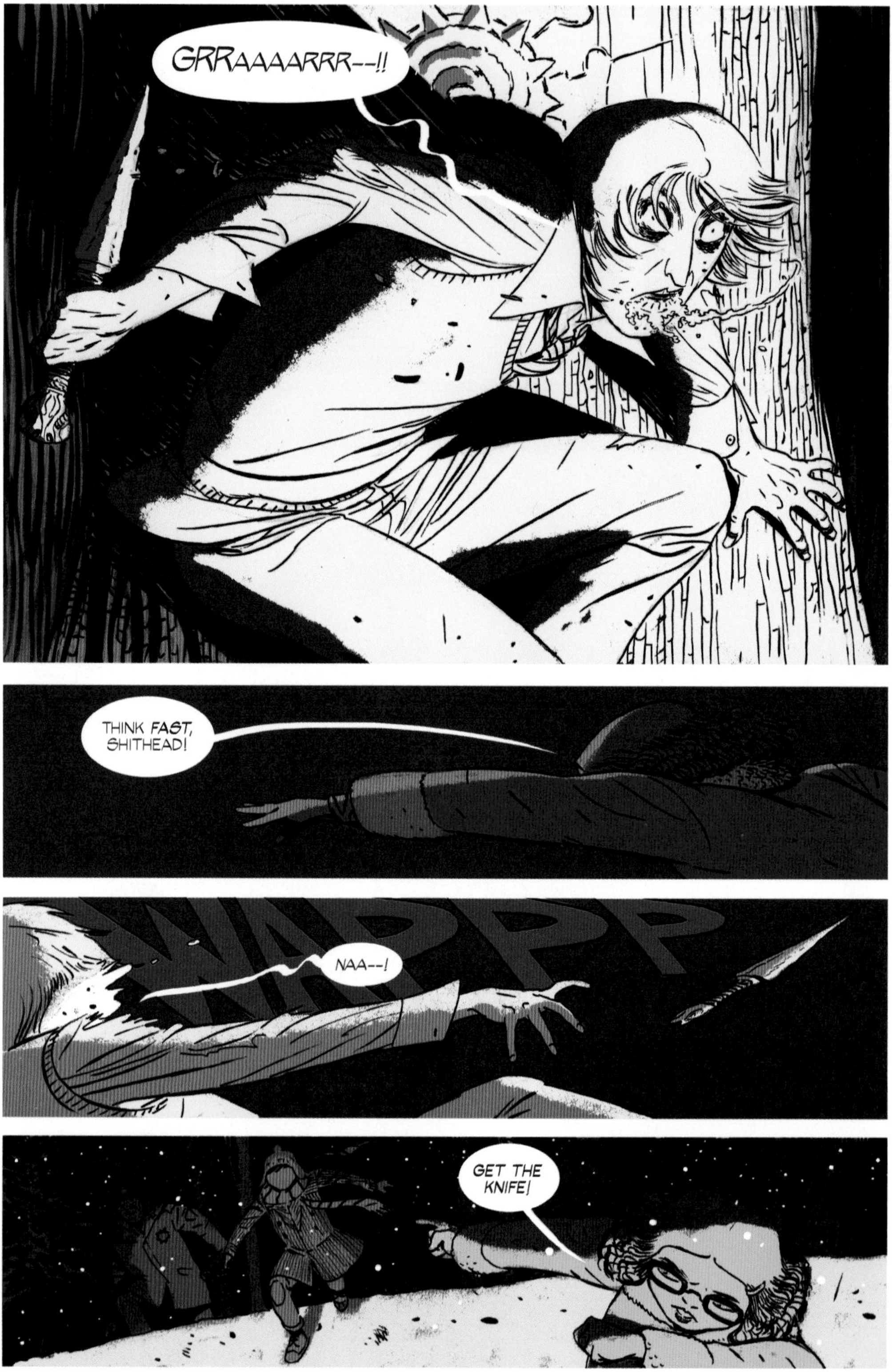
GRRAAAARRR--!!
THINK FAST, SHITHEAD!
WAPPP
NAA--!
GET THE KNIFE!

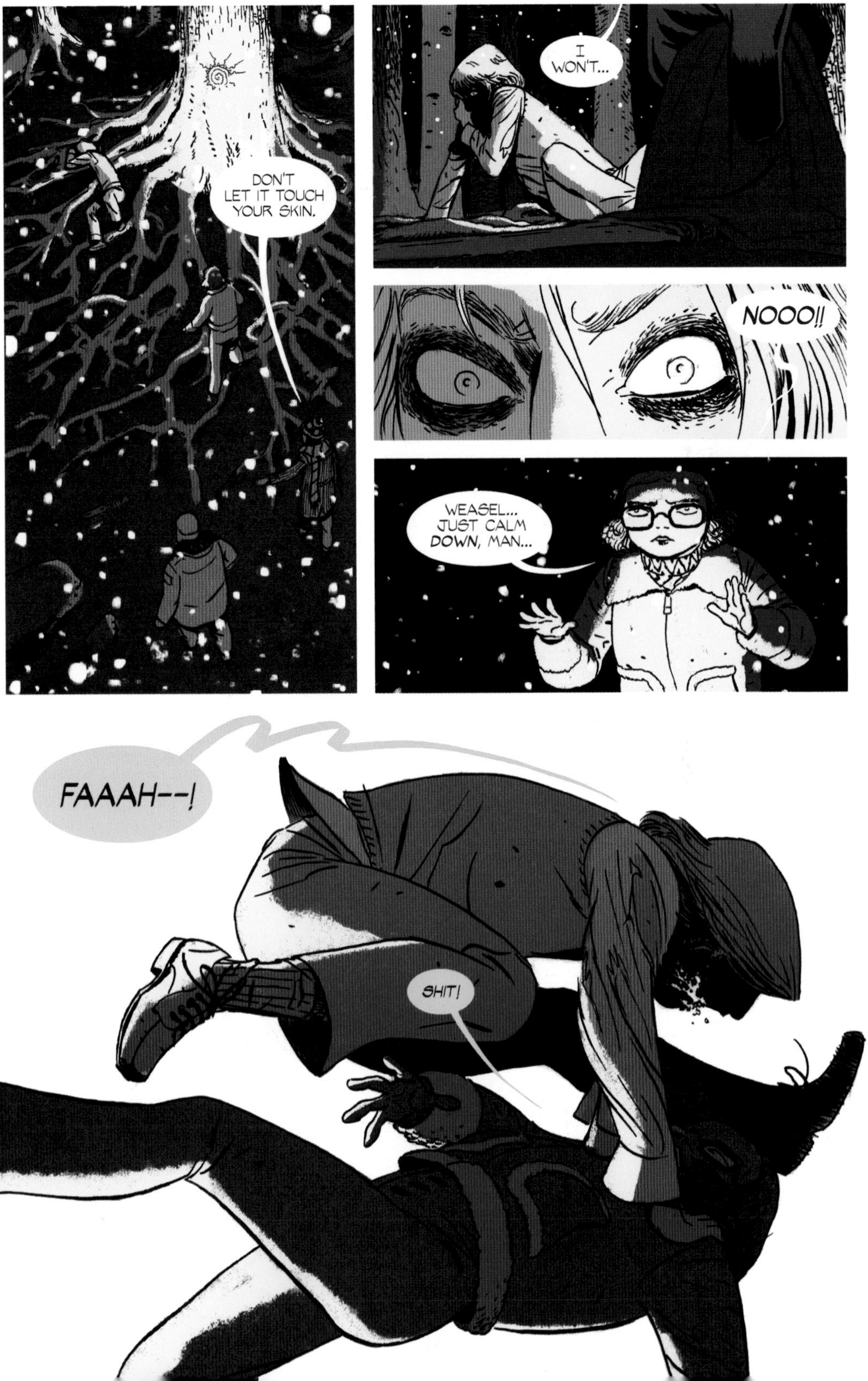
DON'T LET IT TOUCH YOUR SKIN.
I WON'T...
NOOO!!
WEASEL... JUST CALM DOWN, MAN...
FAAAH--!
SHIT!

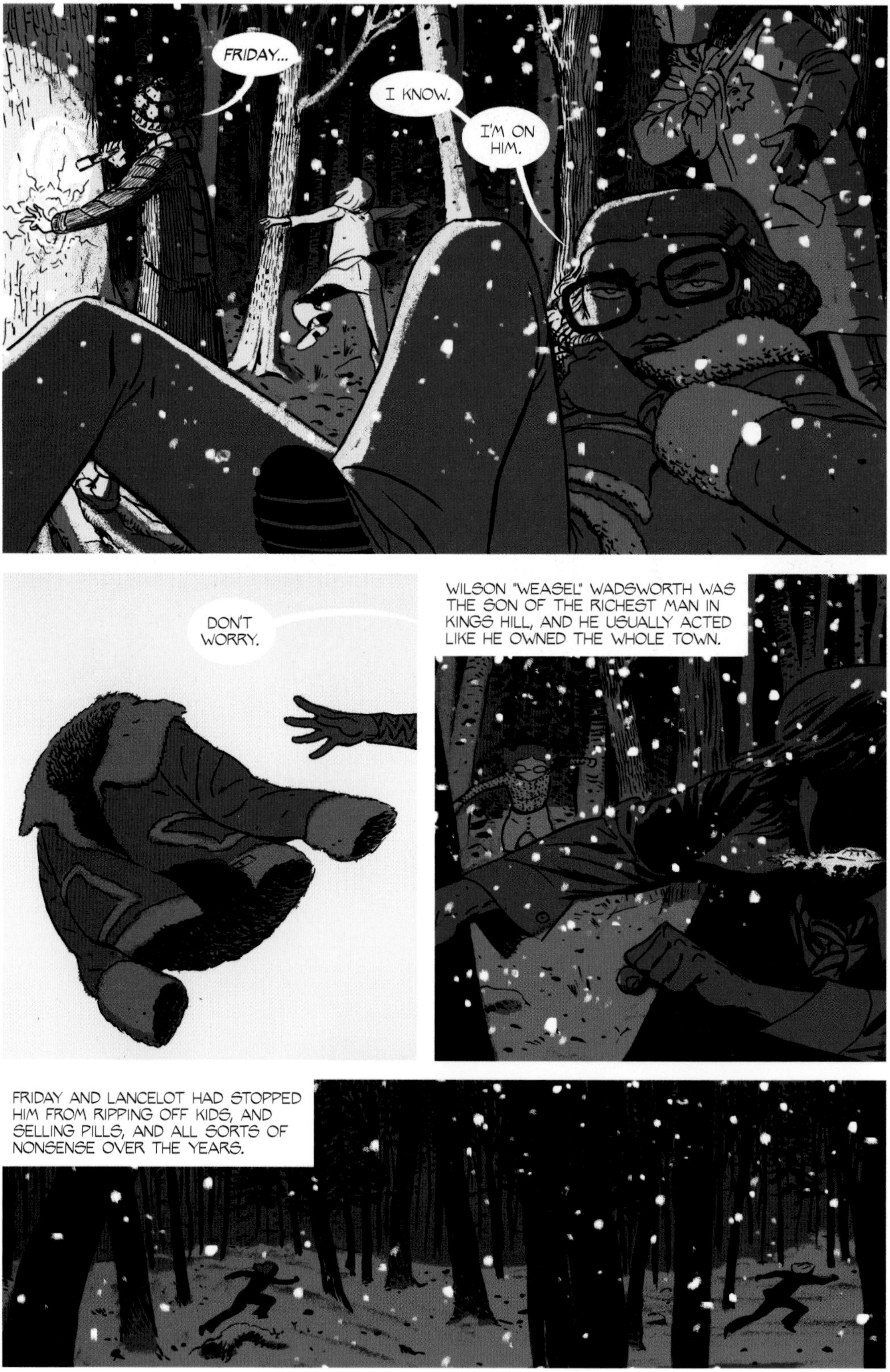
FRIDAY...
I KNOW.
I'M ON HIM.
DON'T WORRY.
WILSON "WEASEL" WADSWORTH WAS THE SON OF THE RICHEST MAN IN KINGS HILL, AND HE USUALLY ACTED LIKE HE OWNED THE WHOLE TOWN.
FRIDAY AND LANCELOT HAD STOPPED HIM FROM RIPPING OFF KIDS, AND SELLING PILLS, AND ALL SORTS OF NONSENSE OVER THE YEARS.

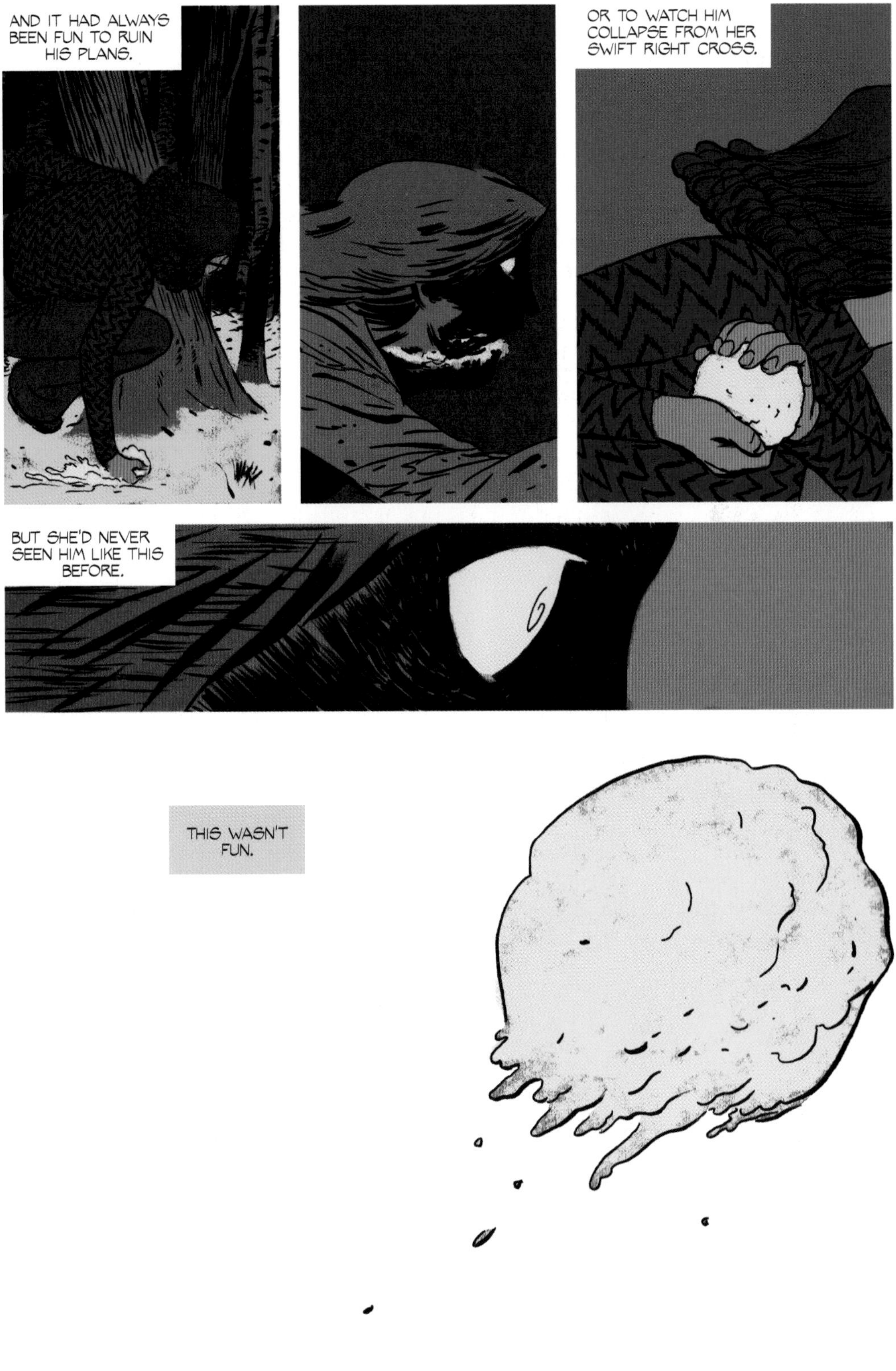
AND IT HAD ALWAYS BEEN FUN TO RUIN HIS PLANS.
OR TO WATCH HIM COLLAPSE FROM HER SWIFT RIGHT CROSS.
BUT SHE'D NEVER SEEN HIM LIKE THIS BEFORE.
THIS WASN'T FUN.

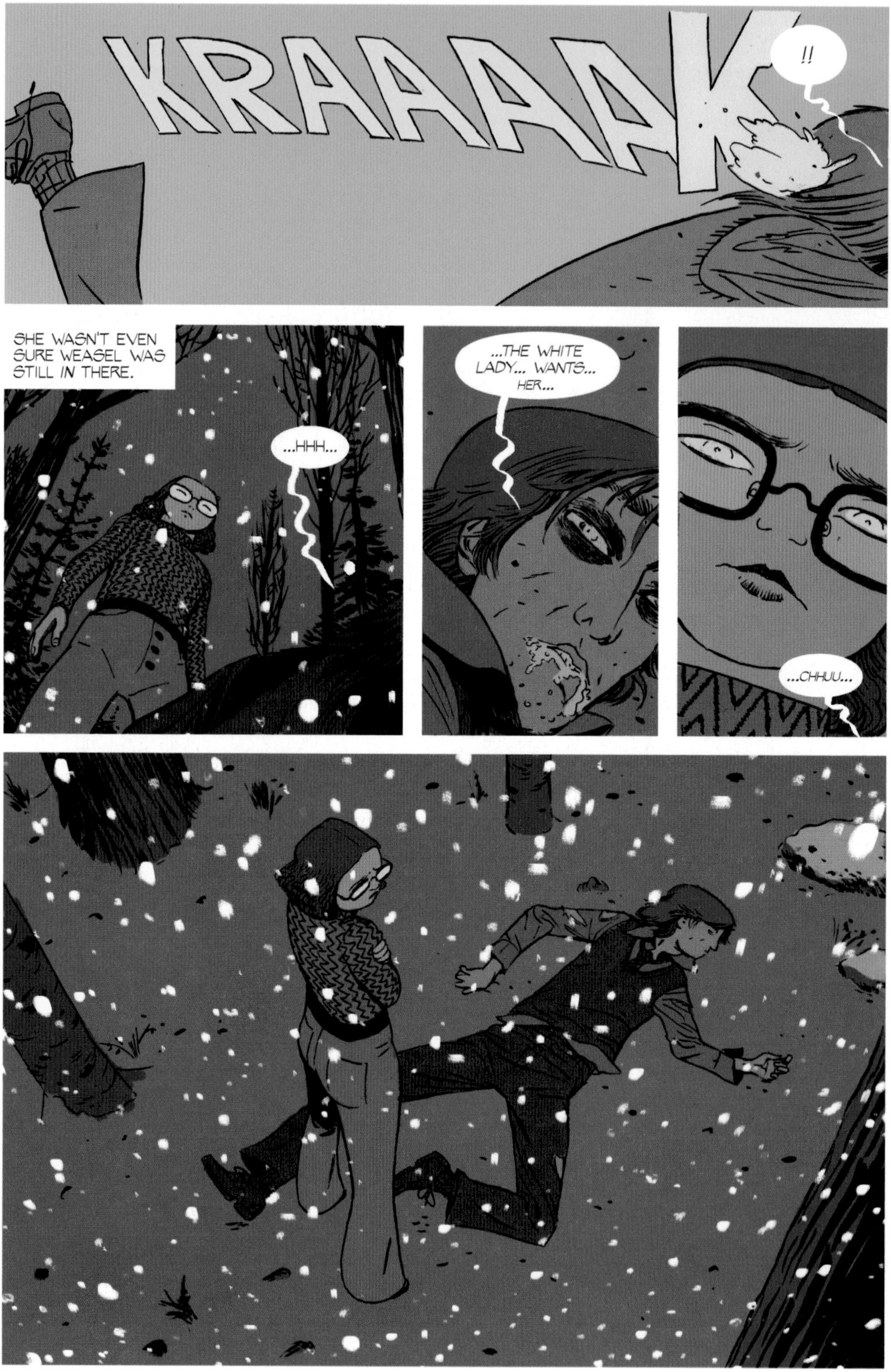
KRAAAAK
!!
SHE WASN'T EVEN SURE WEASEL WAS STILL IN THERE.
...HHH...
...THE WHITE LADY... WANTS... HER...
...CHHUU...

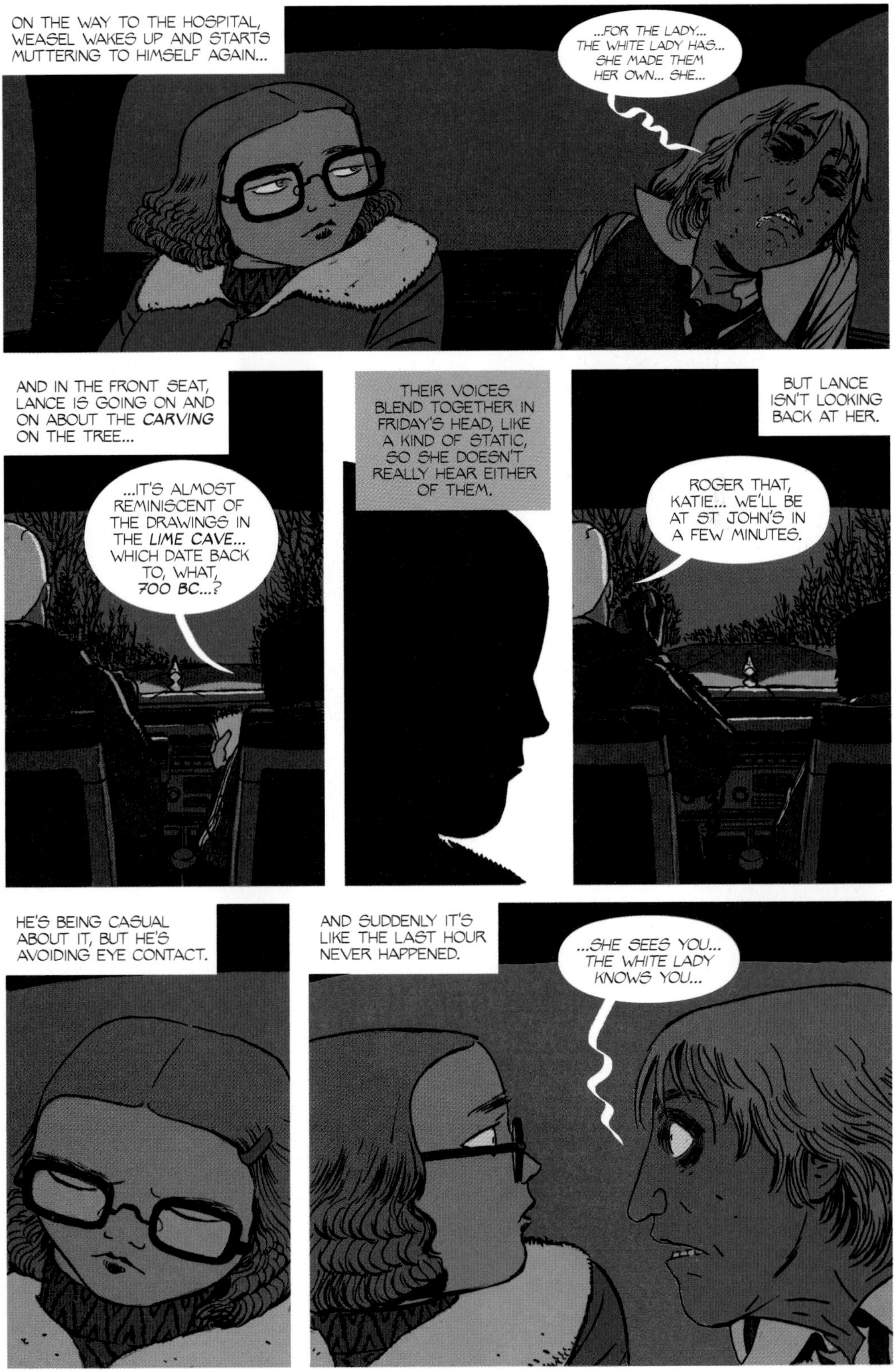

ON THE WAY TO THE HOSPITAL, WEASEL WAKES UP AND STARTS MUTTERING TO HIMSELF AGAIN...
...FOR THE LADY... THE WHITE LADY HAS... SHE MADE THEM HER OWN... SHE...
AND IN THE FRONT SEAT, LANCE IS GOING ON AND ON ABOUT THE CARVING ON THE TREE...
...IT'S ALMOST REMINISCENT OF THE DRAWINGS IN THE LIME CAVE... WHICH DATE BACK TO, WHAT, 700 BC...?
THEIR VOICES BLEND TOGETHER IN FRIDAY'S HEAD, LIKE A KIND OF STATIC, SO SHE DOESN'T REALLY HEAR EITHER OF THEM.
BUT LANCE ISN'T LOOKING BACK AT HER.
ROGER THAT, KATIE... WE'LL BE AT ST JOHN'S IN A FEW MINUTES.
HE'S BEING CASUAL ABOUT IT, BUT HE'S AVOIDING EYE CONTACT.
AND SUDDENLY IT'S LIKE THE LAST HOUR NEVER HAPPENED.
...SHE SEES YOU... THE WHITE LADY KNOWS YOU...

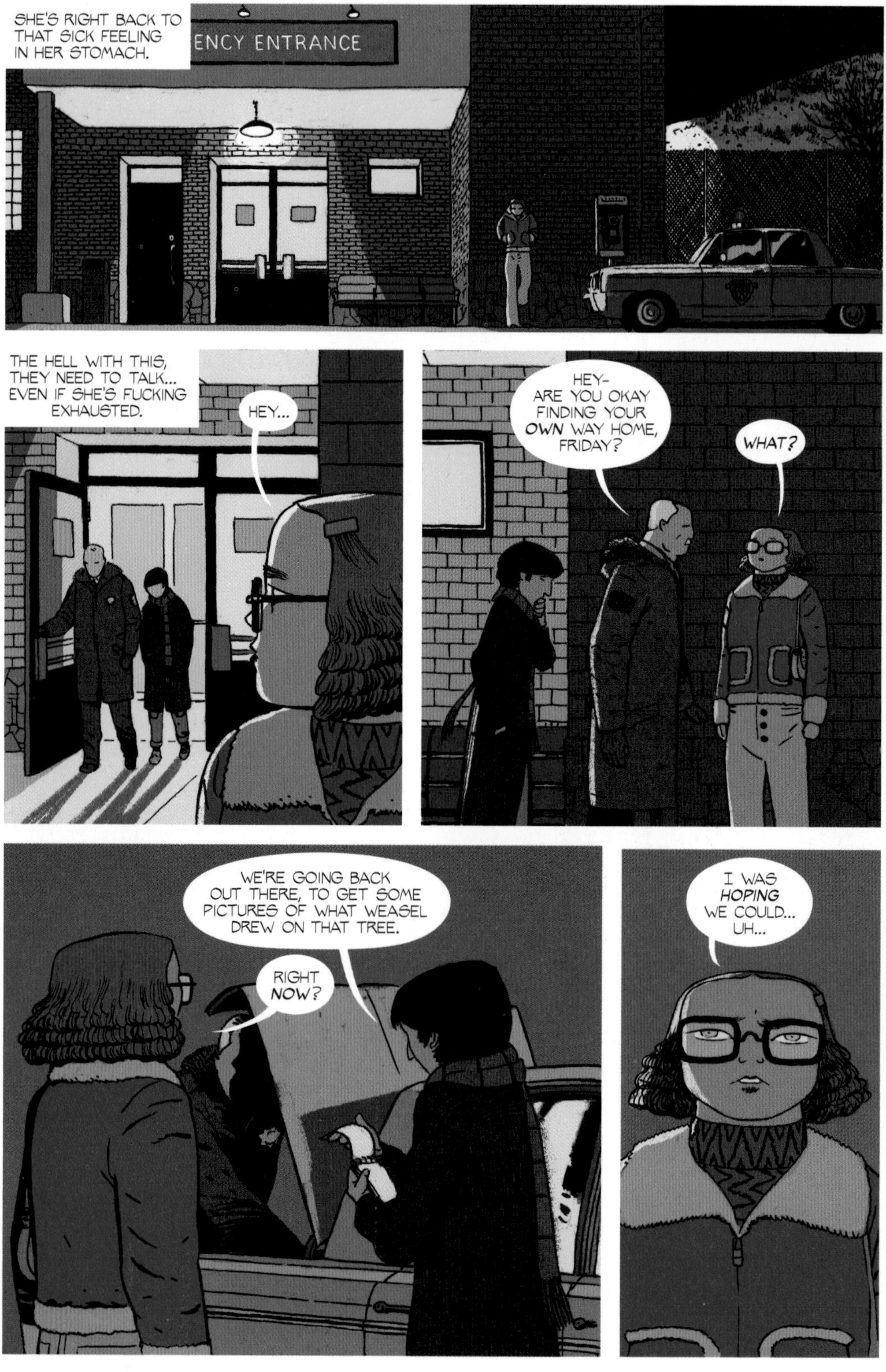
SHE'S RIGHT BACK TO THAT SICK FEELING IN HER STOMACH.
ENCY ENTRANCE
THE HELL WITH THIS, THEY NEED TO TALK... EVEN IF SHE'S FUCKING EXHAUSTED.
HEY...
HEY- ARE YOU OKAY FINDING YOUR OWN WAY HOME, FRIDAY?
WHAT?
WE'RE GOING BACK OUT THERE, TO GET SOME PICTURES OF WHAT WEASEL DREW ON THAT TREE.
RIGHT NOW?
I WAS HOPING WE COULD... UH...

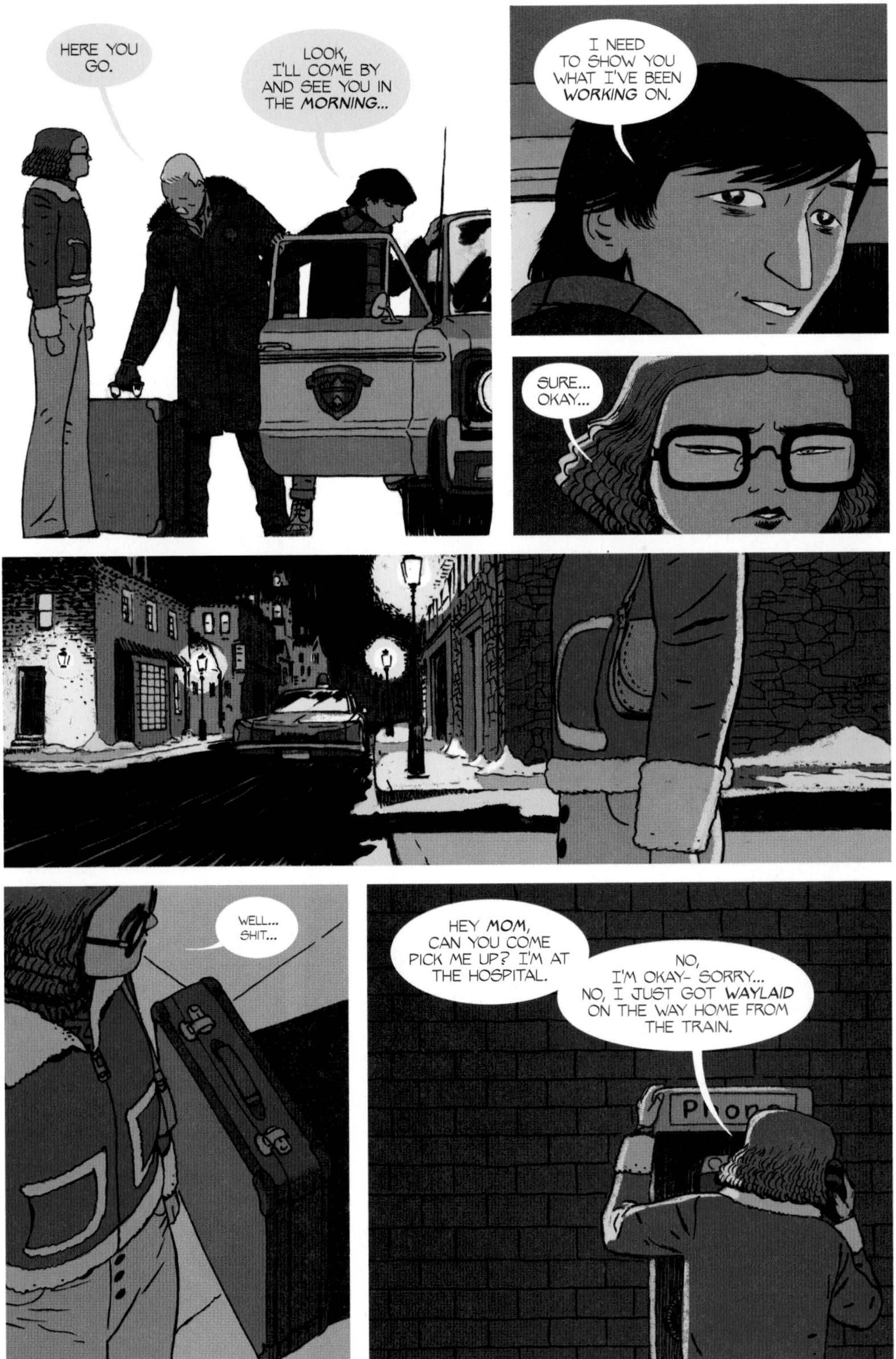
HERE YOU GO.
LOOK, I'LL COME BY AND SEE YOU IN THE MORNING...
I NEED TO SHOW YOU WHAT I'VE BEEN WORKING ON.
SURE... OKAY...
WELL... SHIT...
HEY MOM, CAN YOU COME PICK ME UP? I'M AT THE HOSPITAL.
NO, I'M OKAY- SORRY... NO, I JUST GOT WAYLAID ON THE WAY HOME FROM THE TRAIN.
Phone

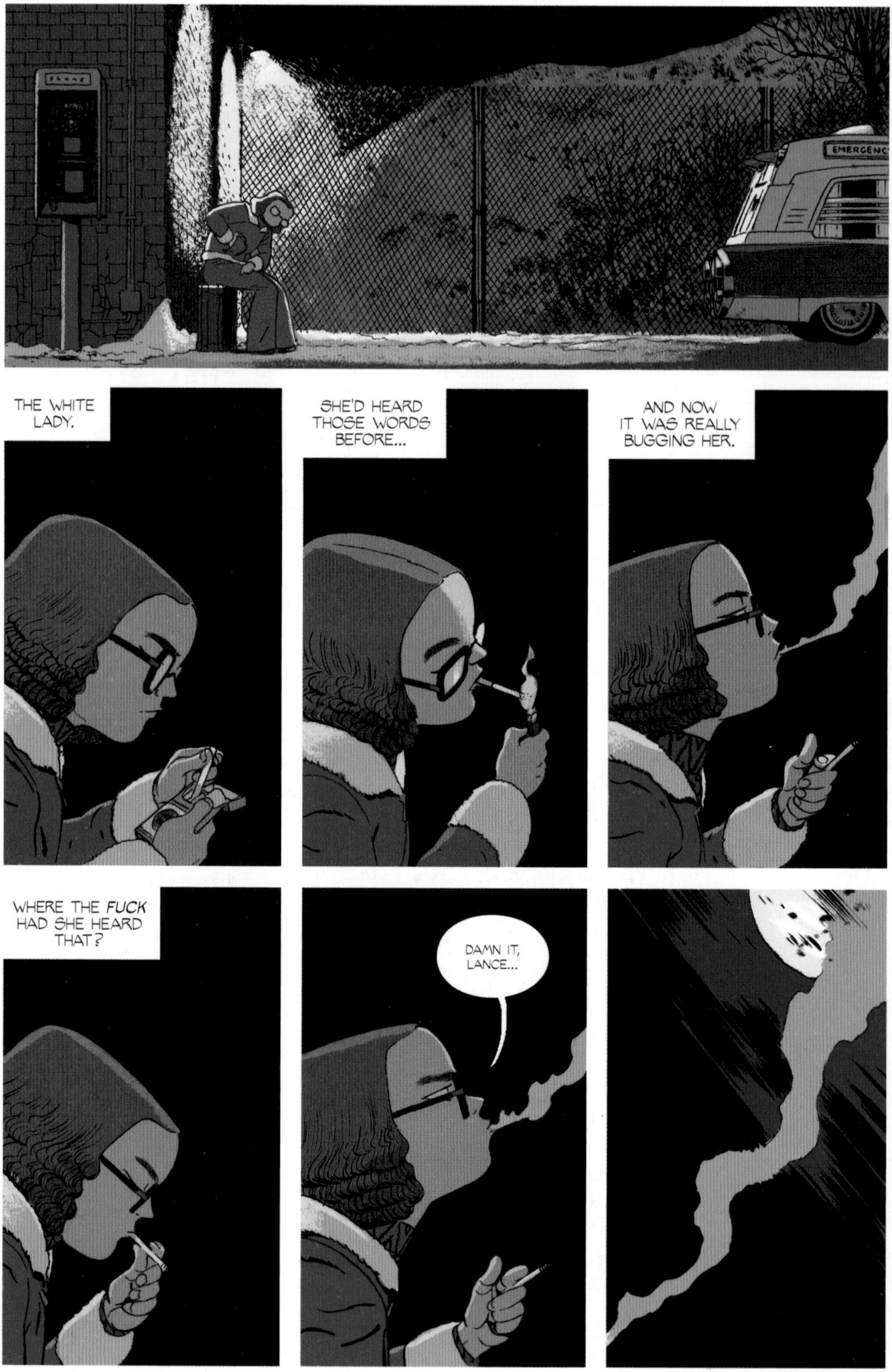
THE WHITE LADY.
SHE'D HEARD THOSE WORDS BEFORE...
AND NOW IT WAS REALLY BUGGING HER.
WHERE THE *FUCK* HAD SHE HEARD THAT?
DAMN IT, LANCE...

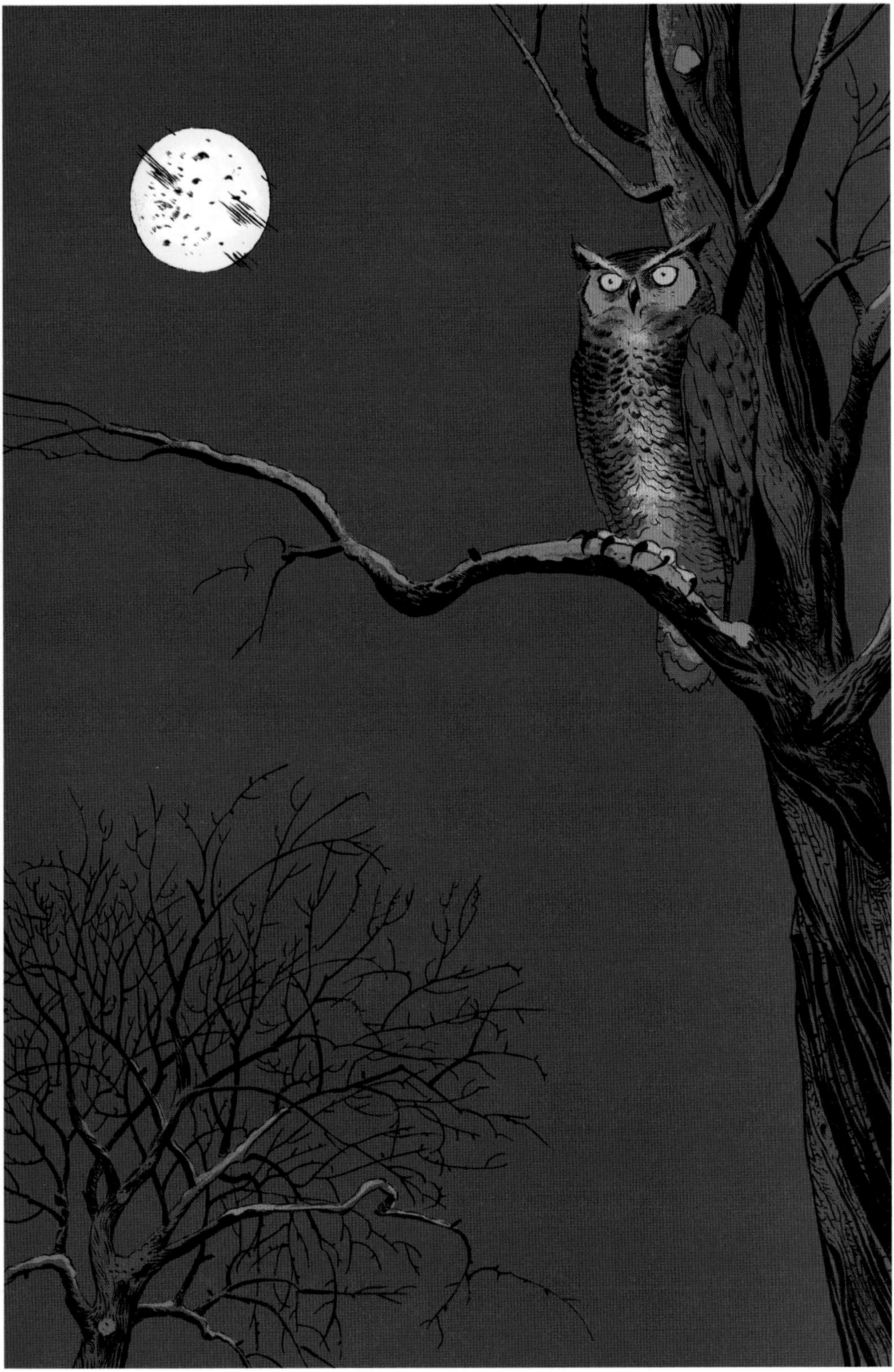

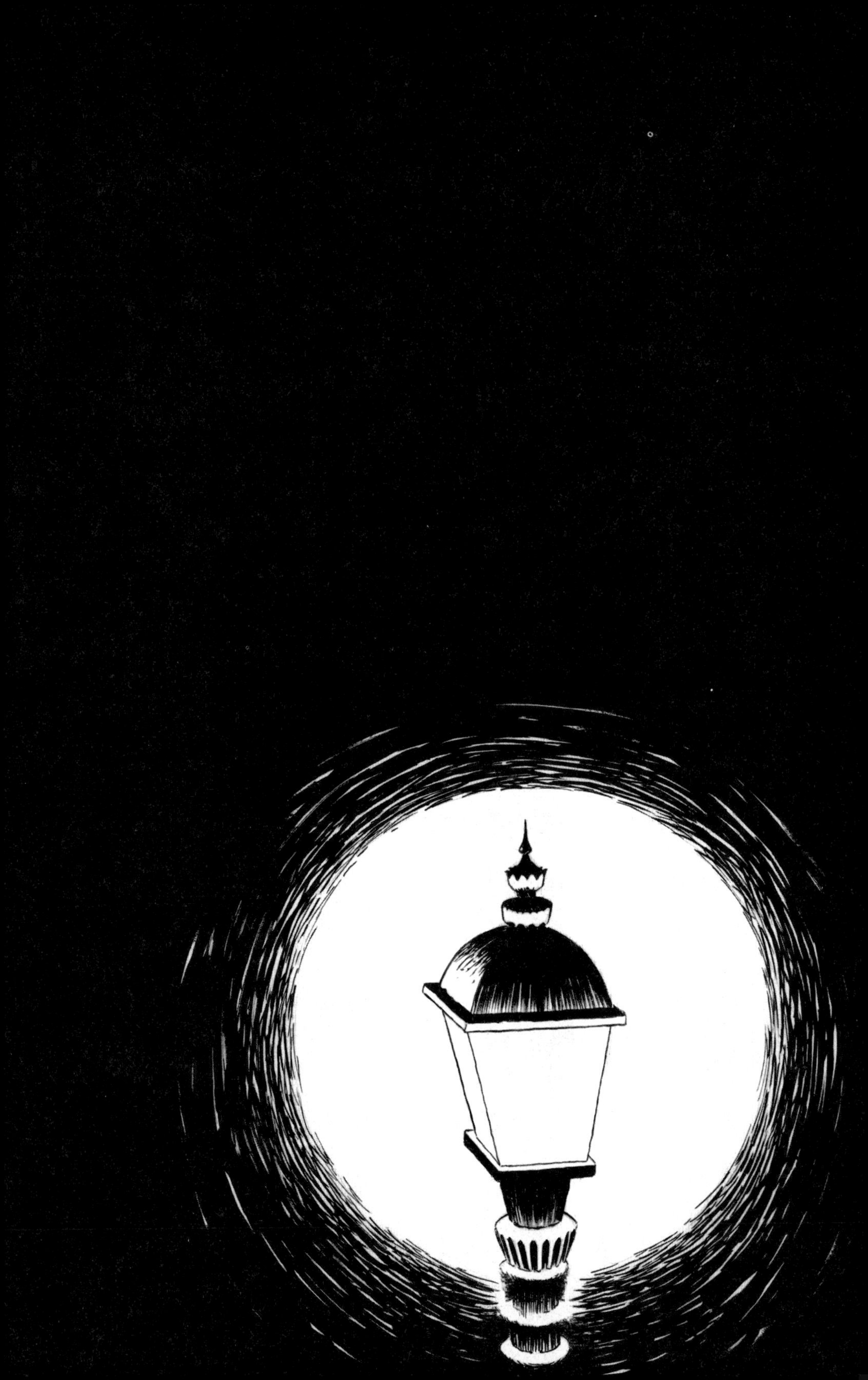

Chapter Two

The Night Before She Left

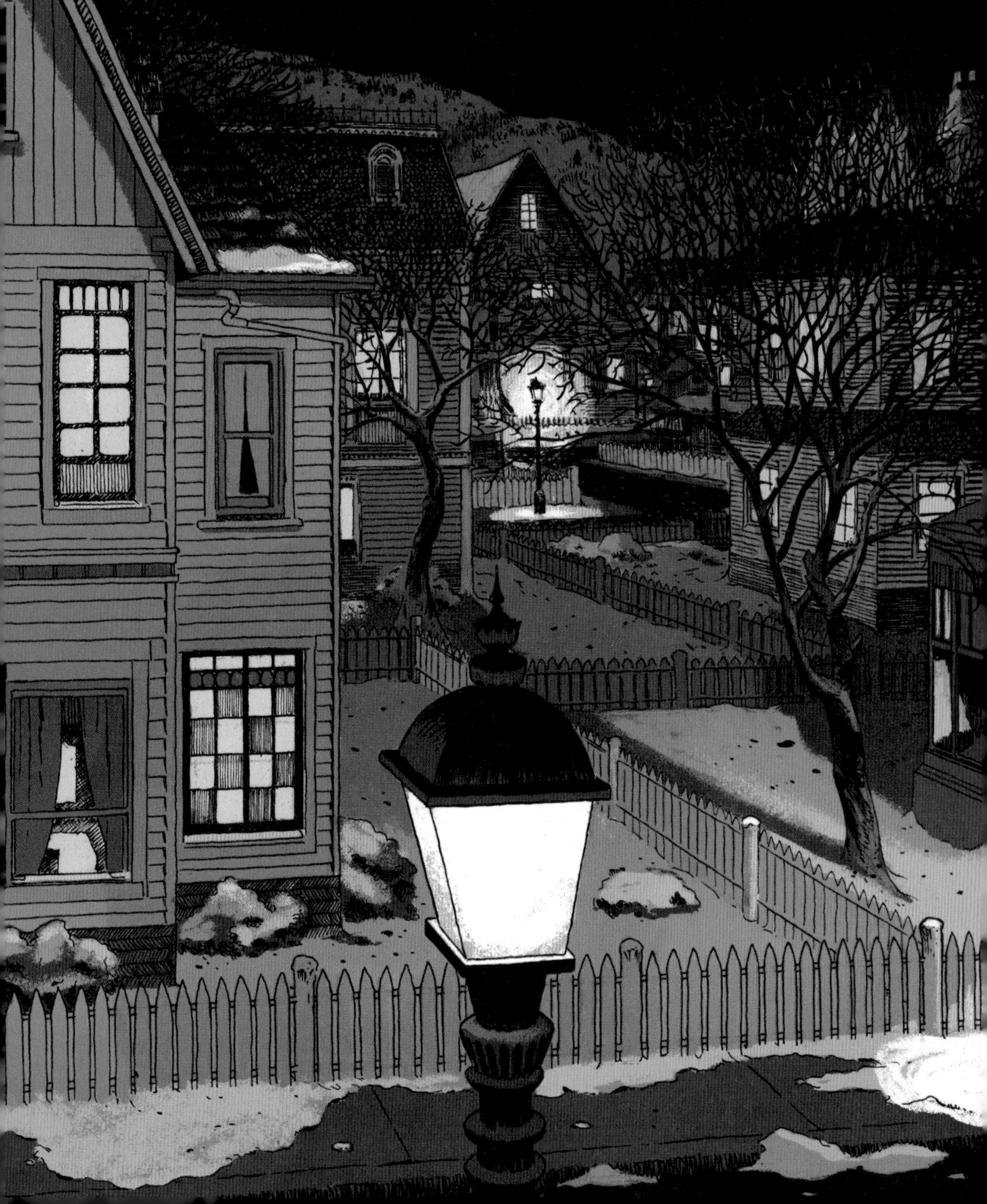

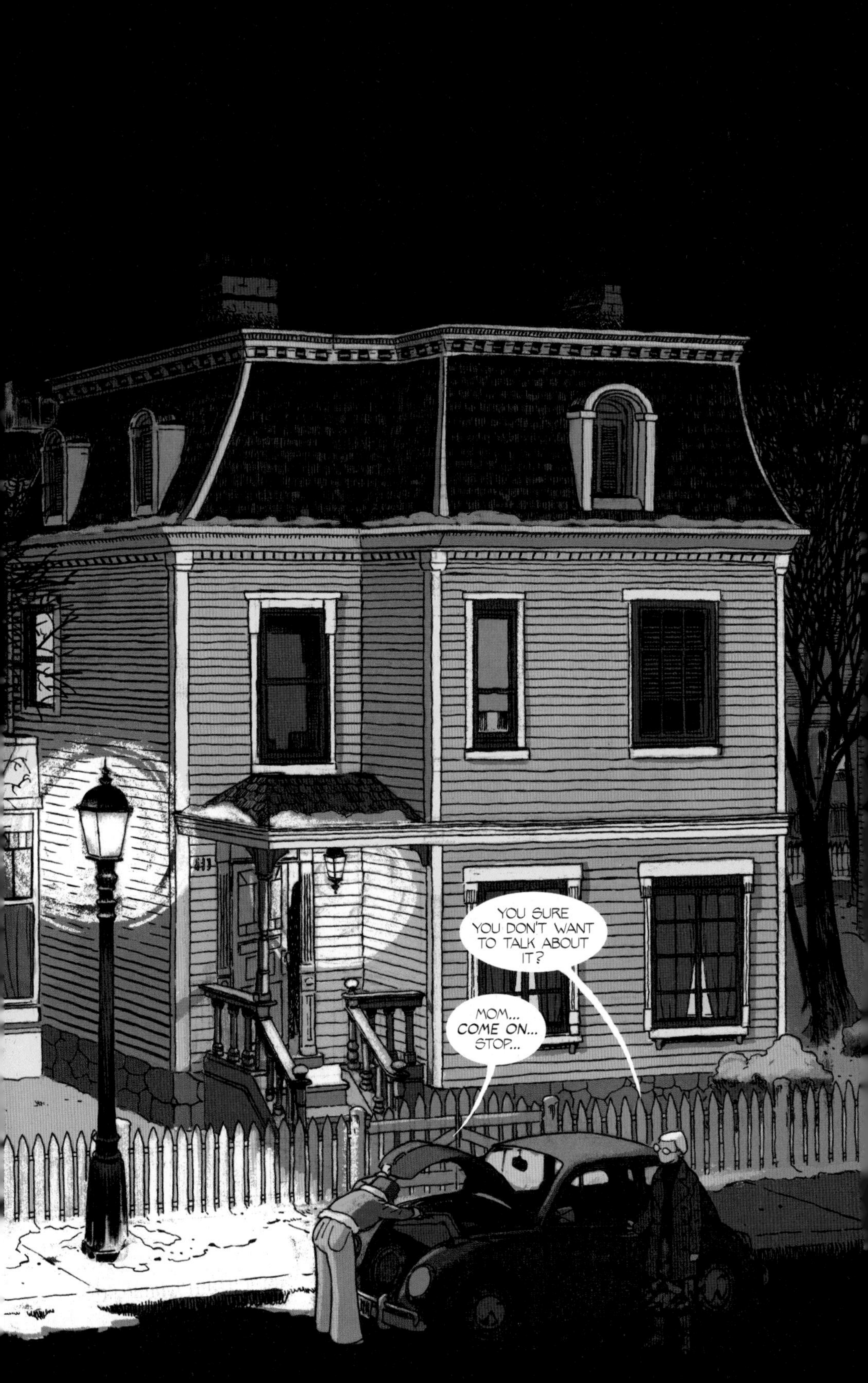
YOU SURE YOU DON'T WANT TO TALK ABOUT IT?
MOM... COME ON... STOP...

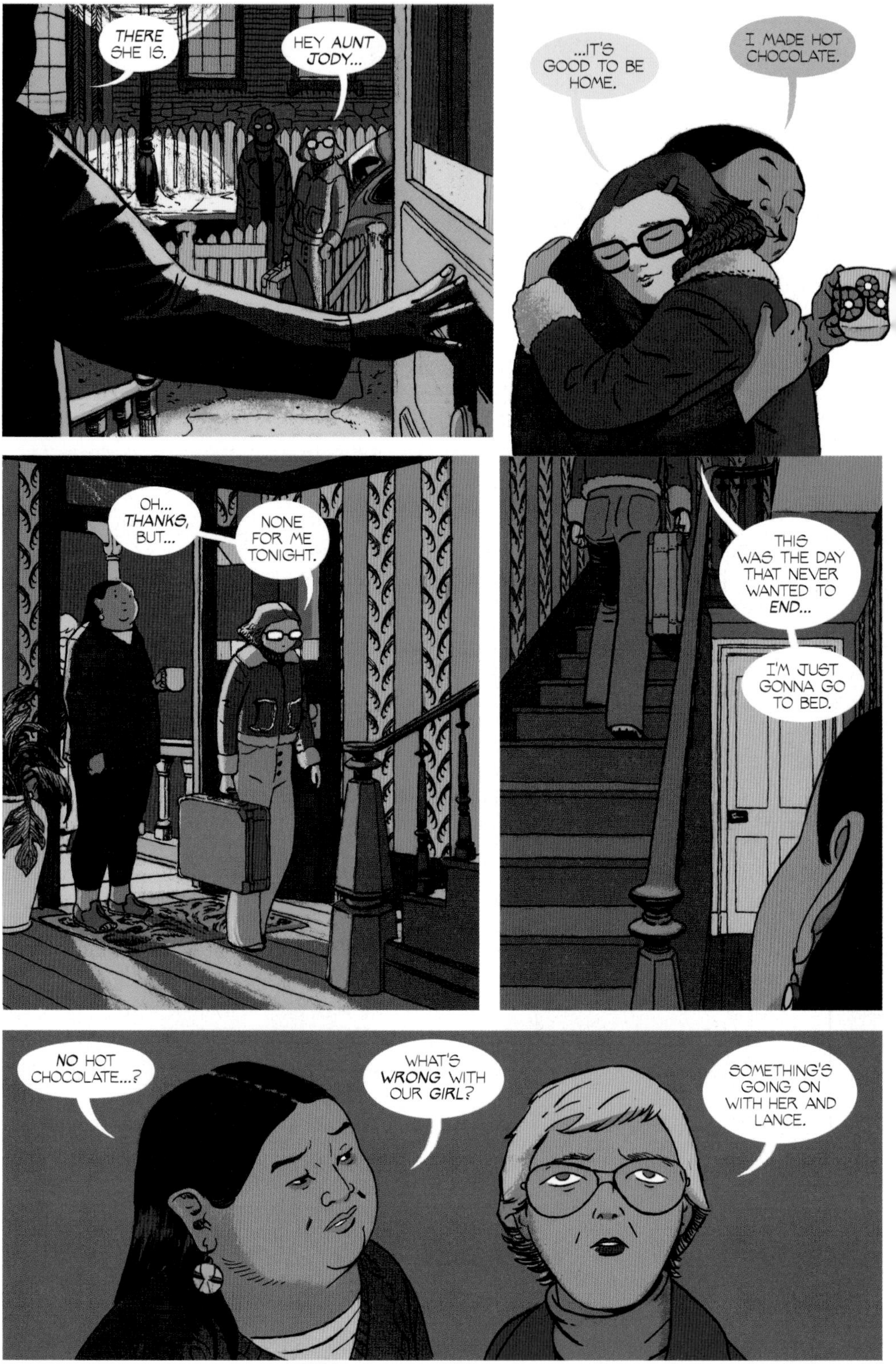
THERE SHE IS.
HEY AUNT JODY...
...IT'S GOOD TO BE HOME.
I MADE HOT CHOCOLATE.
OH... THANKS, BUT...
NONE FOR ME TONIGHT.
THIS WAS THE DAY THAT NEVER WANTED TO END...
I'M JUST GONNA GO TO BED.
NO HOT CHOCOLATE...?
WHAT'S WRONG WITH OUR GIRL?
SOMETHING'S GOING ON WITH HER AND LANCE.

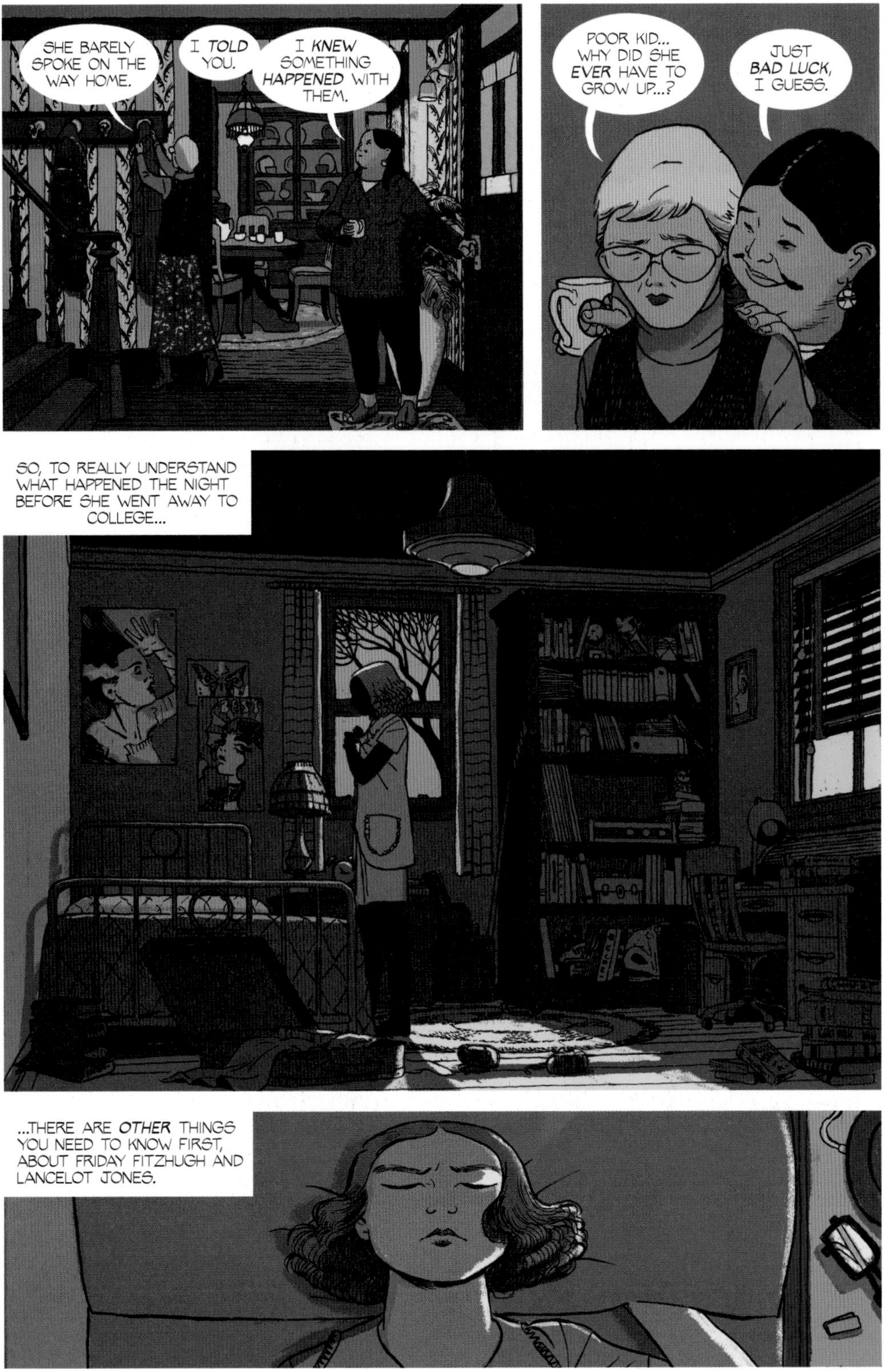
SHE BARELY SPOKE ON THE WAY HOME.
I TOLD YOU.
I KNEW SOMETHING HAPPENED WITH THEM.
POOR KID... WHY DID SHE EVER HAVE TO GROW UP...?
JUST BAD LUCK, I GUESS.
SO, TO REALLY UNDERSTAND WHAT HAPPENED THE NIGHT BEFORE SHE WENT AWAY TO COLLEGE...
...THERE ARE OTHER THINGS YOU NEED TO KNOW FIRST, ABOUT FRIDAY FITZHUGH AND LANCELOT JONES.

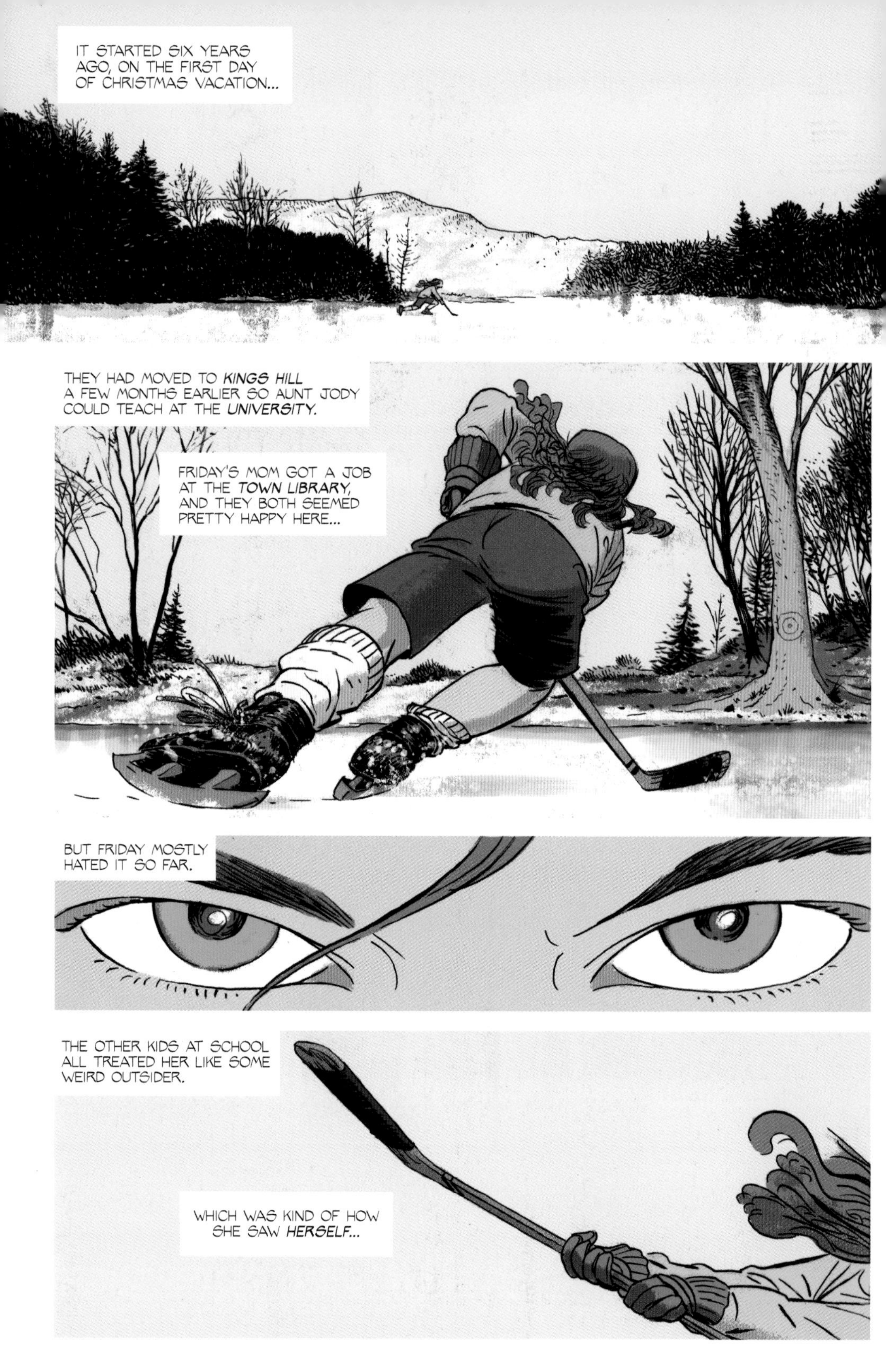
IT STARTED SIX YEARS AGO, ON THE FIRST DAY OF CHRISTMAS VACATION...
THEY HAD MOVED TO *KINGS HILL* A FEW MONTHS EARLIER SO AUNT JODY COULD TEACH AT THE *UNIVERSITY.*
FRIDAY'S MOM GOT A JOB AT THE *TOWN LIBRARY,* AND THEY BOTH SEEMED PRETTY HAPPY HERE...
BUT FRIDAY MOSTLY HATED IT SO FAR.
THE OTHER KIDS AT SCHOOL ALL TREATED HER LIKE SOME WEIRD OUTSIDER.
WHICH WAS KIND OF HOW SHE SAW *HERSELF...*

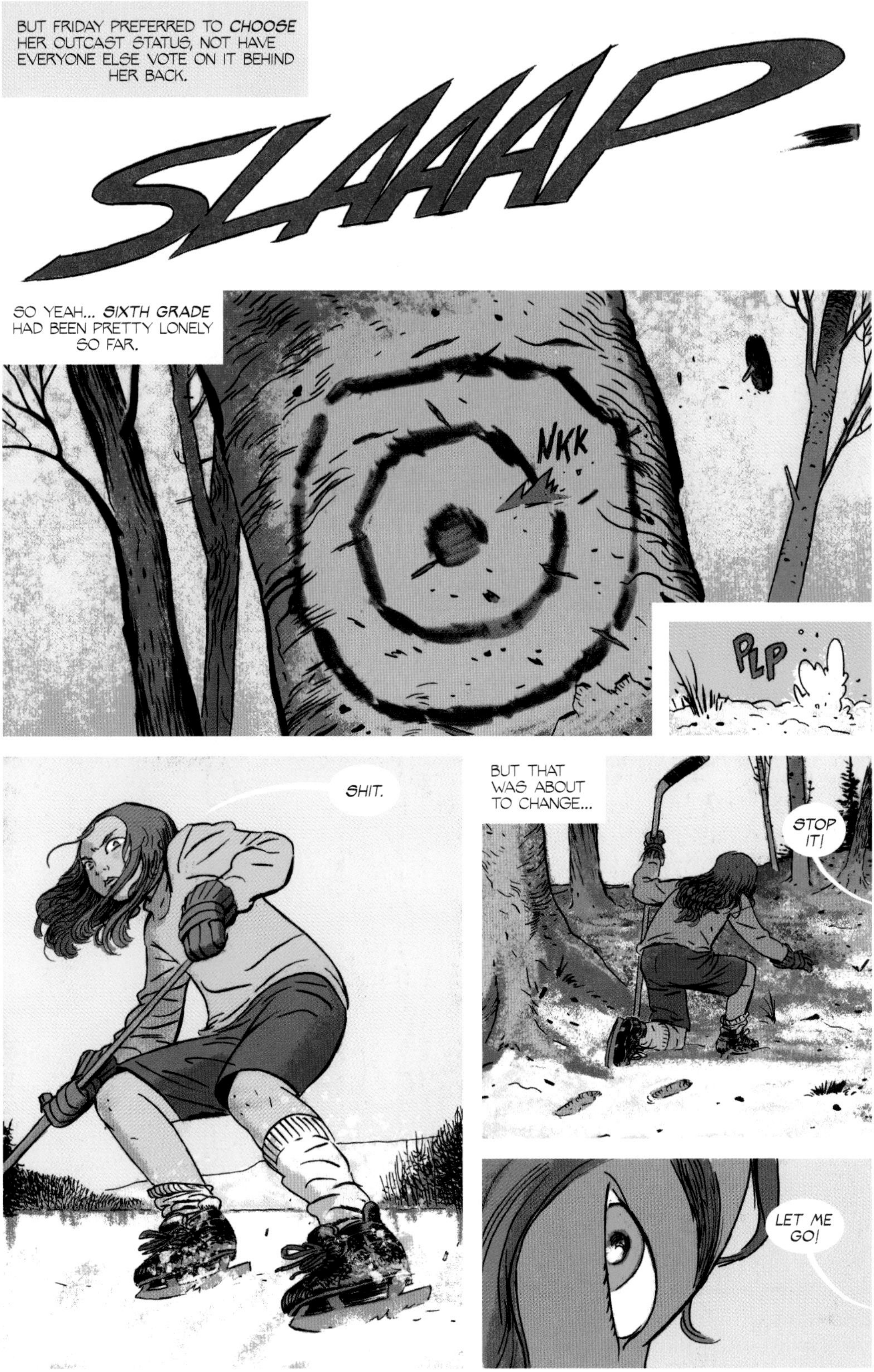
BUT FRIDAY PREFERRED TO *CHOOSE* HER OUTCAST STATUS, NOT HAVE EVERYONE ELSE VOTE ON IT BEHIND HER BACK.
SLAAAP-
SO YEAH... *SIXTH GRADE* HAD BEEN PRETTY LONELY SO FAR.
NKK
PLP
SHIT.
BUT THAT WAS ABOUT TO CHANGE...
STOP IT!
LET ME GO!

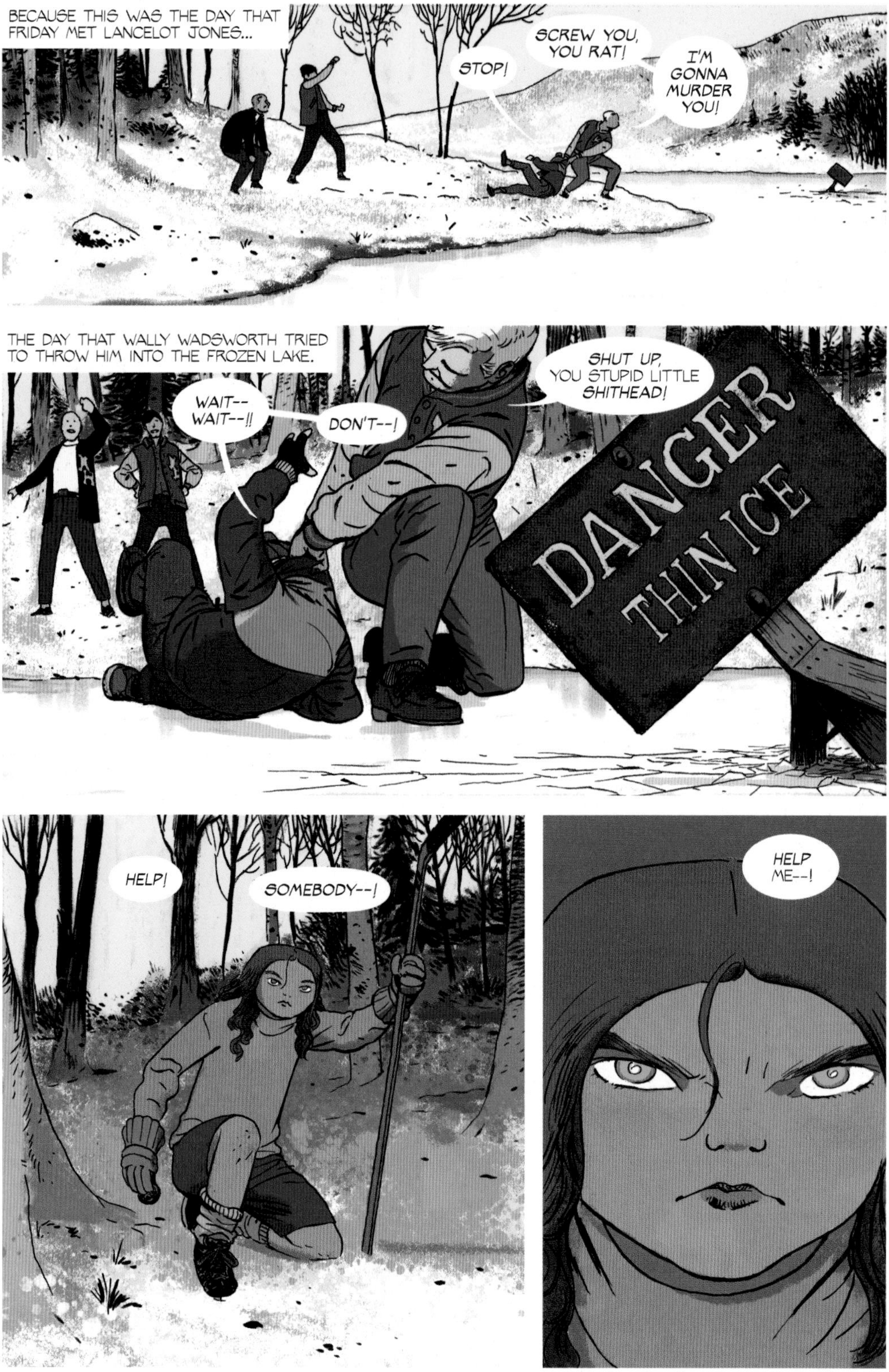
BECAUSE THIS WAS THE DAY THAT FRIDAY MET LANCELOT JONES...
STOP!
SCREW YOU, YOU RAT!
I'M GONNA MURDER YOU!
THE DAY THAT WALLY WADSWORTH TRIED TO THROW HIM INTO THE FROZEN LAKE.
WAIT-- WAIT--!!
DON'T--!
SHUT UP, YOU STUPID LITTLE SHITHEAD!
DANGER THIN ICE
HELP!
SOMEBODY--!
HELP ME--!

FRIDAY RECOGNIZED LANCE FROM SCHOOL. HE WAS TWO GRADES AHEAD OF HER, EVEN THOUGH SHE WAS OLDER THAN HIM.

BUT SHE'D HEARD HE WAS SOME KIND OF PRODIGY... THE TOWN GENIUS.

THE KIND OF LABEL THAT USUALLY MAKES YOU A TARGET FOR THE *LESS-THAN-GENIUS* KIDS.

WALLY WADSWORTH, OF COURSE, WAS WEASEL'S OLDER *BROTHER*... AND EVERYONE IN TOWN KNEW WALLY...

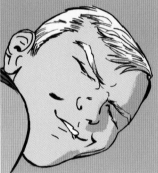

STAR QUARTERBACK...

HOMECOMING KING...

COMPLETE ASSHOLE.

HEY WALLY--

--SLAP SHOT!!

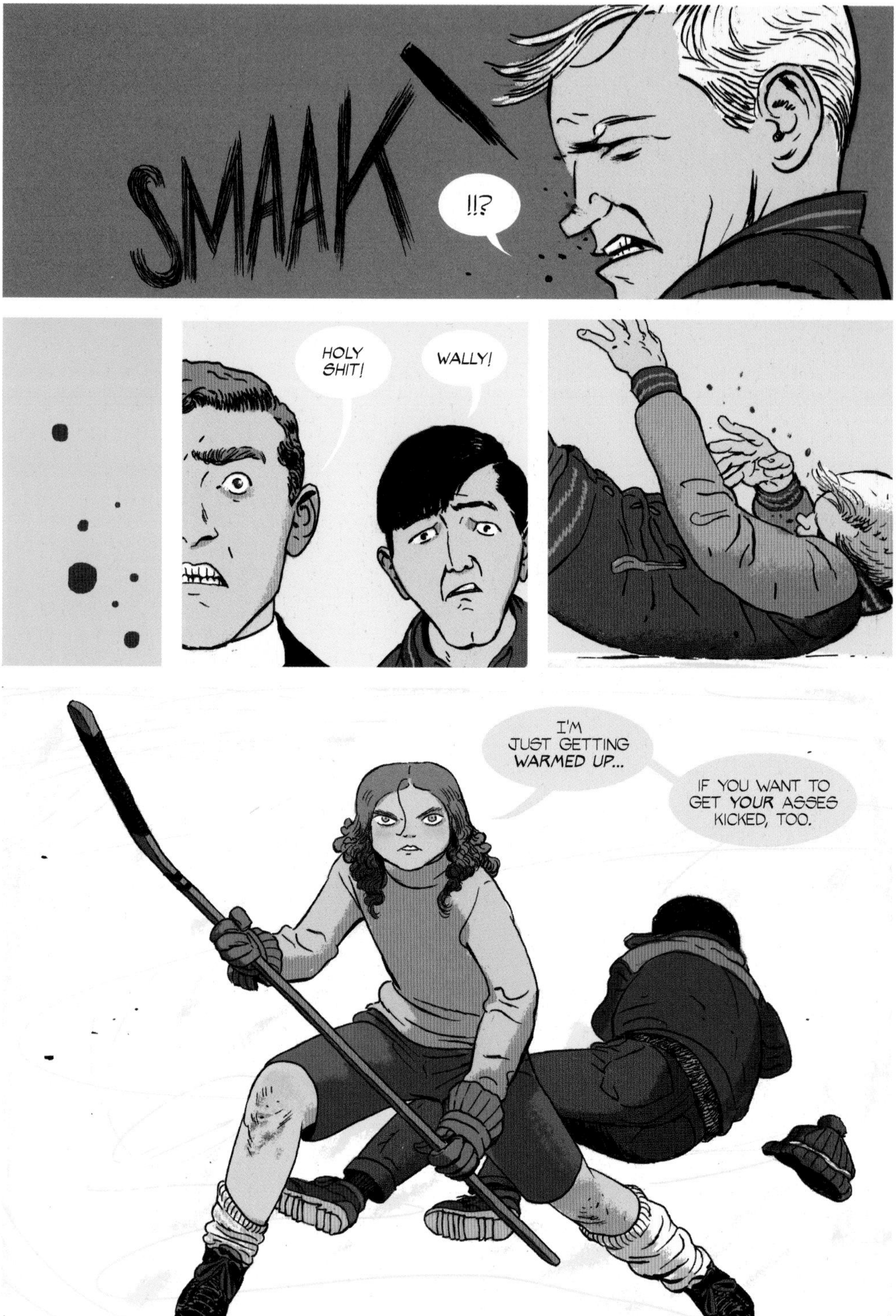
SMAAK
!!?
HOLY SHIT!
WALLY!
I'M JUST GETTING WARMED UP...
IF YOU WANT TO GET YOUR ASSES KICKED, TOO.

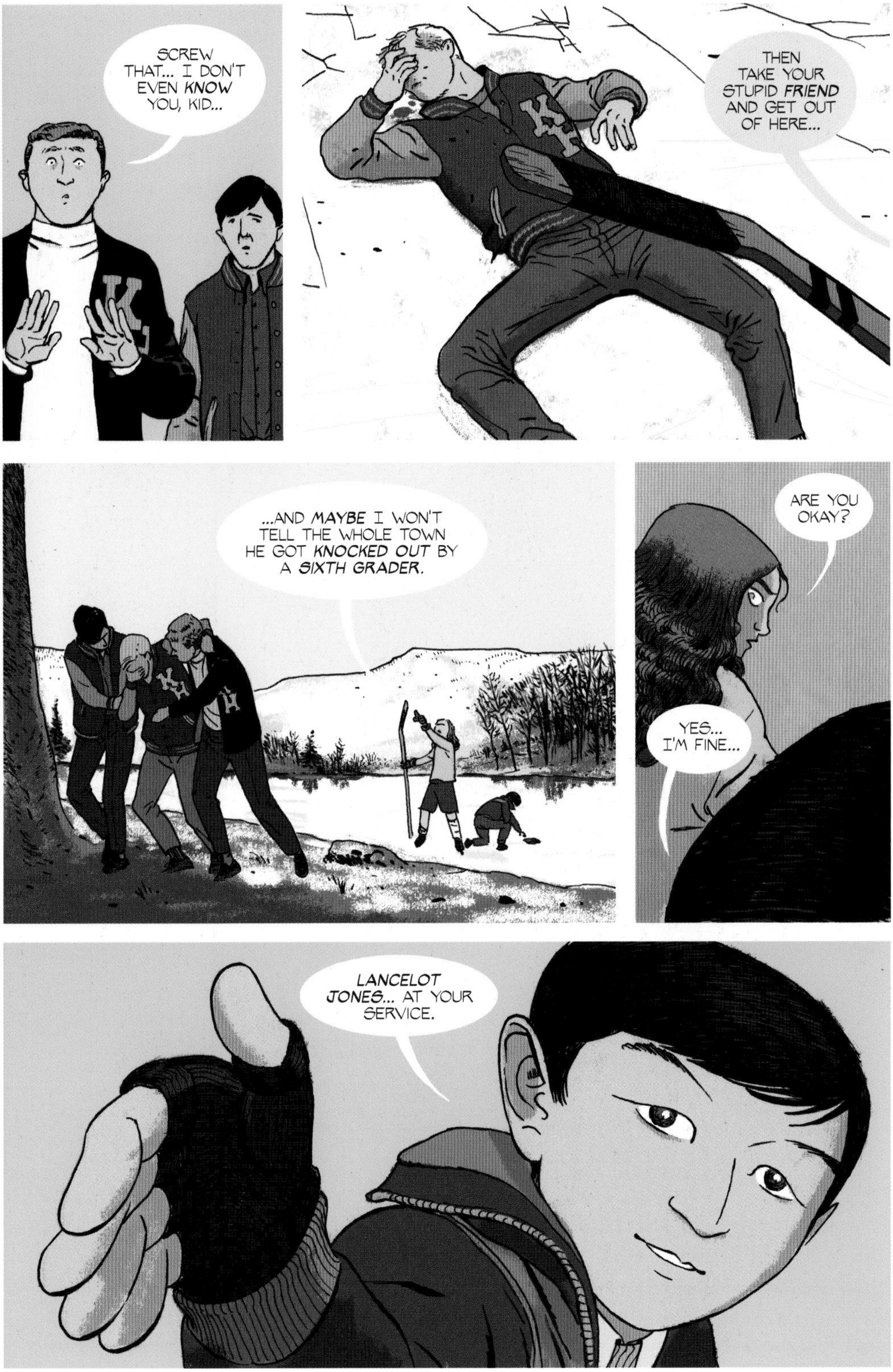
SCREW THAT... I DON'T EVEN KNOW YOU, KID...
THEN TAKE YOUR STUPID FRIEND AND GET OUT OF HERE...
...AND MAYBE I WON'T TELL THE WHOLE TOWN HE GOT KNOCKED OUT BY A SIXTH GRADER.
ARE YOU OKAY?
YES... I'M FINE...
LANCELOT JONES... AT YOUR SERVICE.

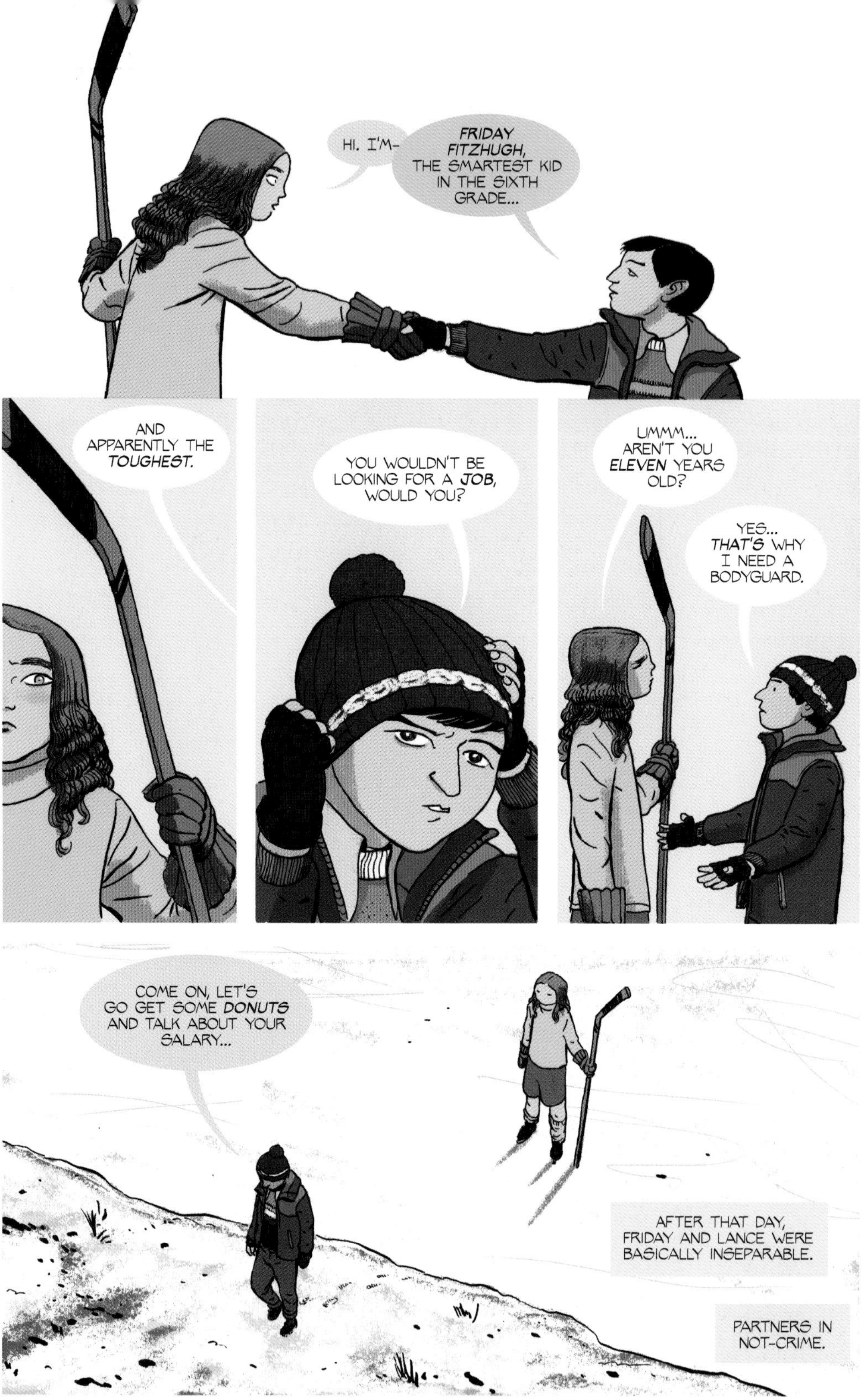
HI. I'M–
FRIDAY FITZHUGH, THE SMARTEST KID IN THE SIXTH GRADE...
AND APPARENTLY THE TOUGHEST.
YOU WOULDN'T BE LOOKING FOR A JOB, WOULD YOU?
UMMM... AREN'T YOU ELEVEN YEARS OLD?
YES... THAT'S WHY I NEED A BODYGUARD.
COME ON, LET'S GO GET SOME DONUTS AND TALK ABOUT YOUR SALARY...
AFTER THAT DAY, FRIDAY AND LANCE WERE BASICALLY INSEPARABLE.
PARTNERS IN NOT-CRIME.

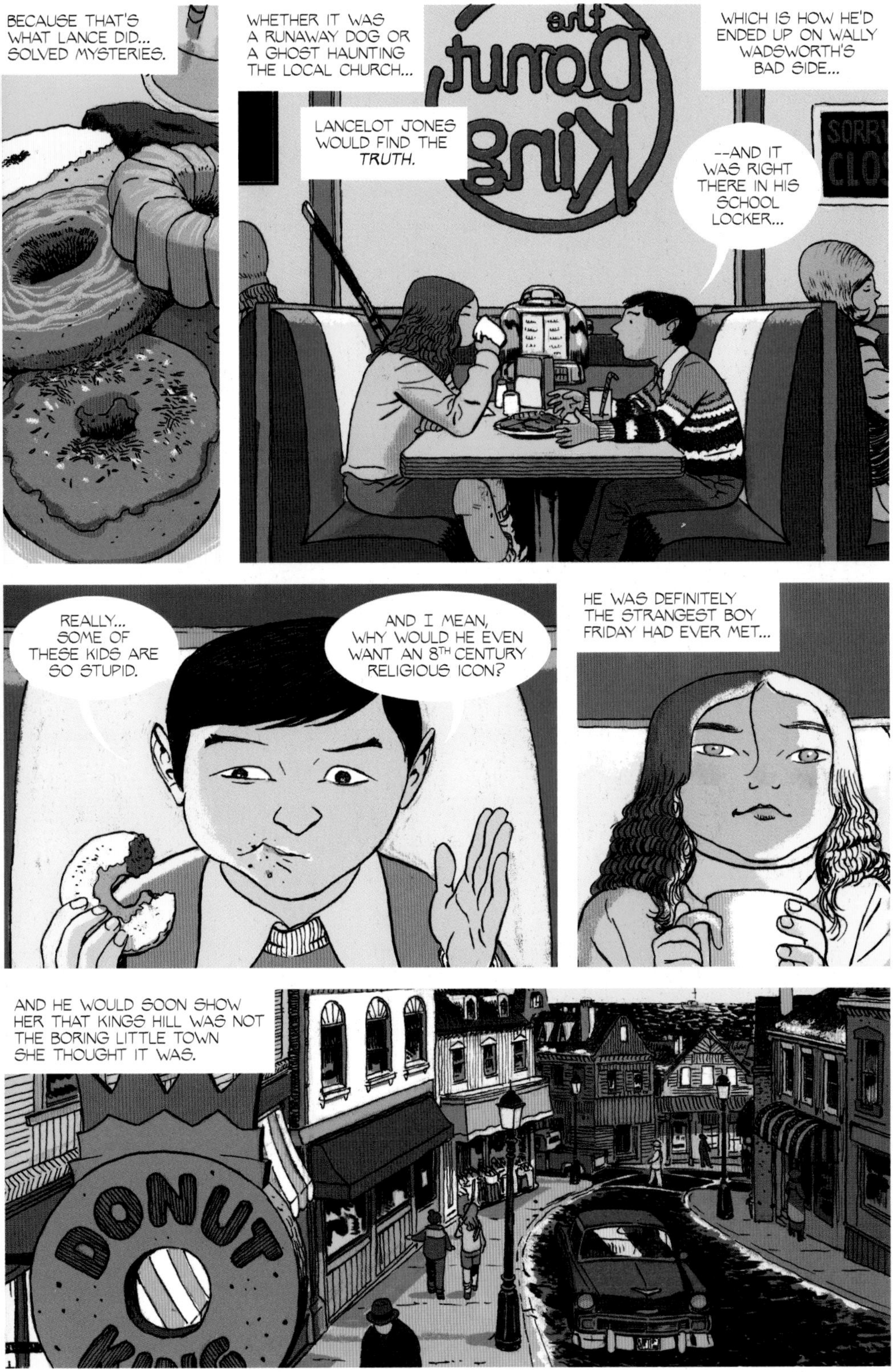
BECAUSE THAT'S WHAT LANCE DID... SOLVED MYSTERIES.
WHETHER IT WAS A RUNAWAY DOG OR A GHOST HAUNTING THE LOCAL CHURCH...
LANCELOT JONES WOULD FIND THE *TRUTH.*
the Donut King
WHICH IS HOW HE'D ENDED UP ON WALLY WADSWORTH'S BAD SIDE...
--AND IT WAS RIGHT THERE IN HIS SCHOOL LOCKER...
REALLY... SOME OF THESE KIDS ARE SO STUPID.
AND I MEAN, WHY WOULD HE EVEN WANT AN 8TH CENTURY RELIGIOUS ICON?
HE WAS DEFINITELY THE STRANGEST BOY FRIDAY HAD EVER MET...
AND HE WOULD SOON SHOW HER THAT KINGS HILL WAS NOT THE BORING LITTLE TOWN SHE THOUGHT IT WAS.
DONUT

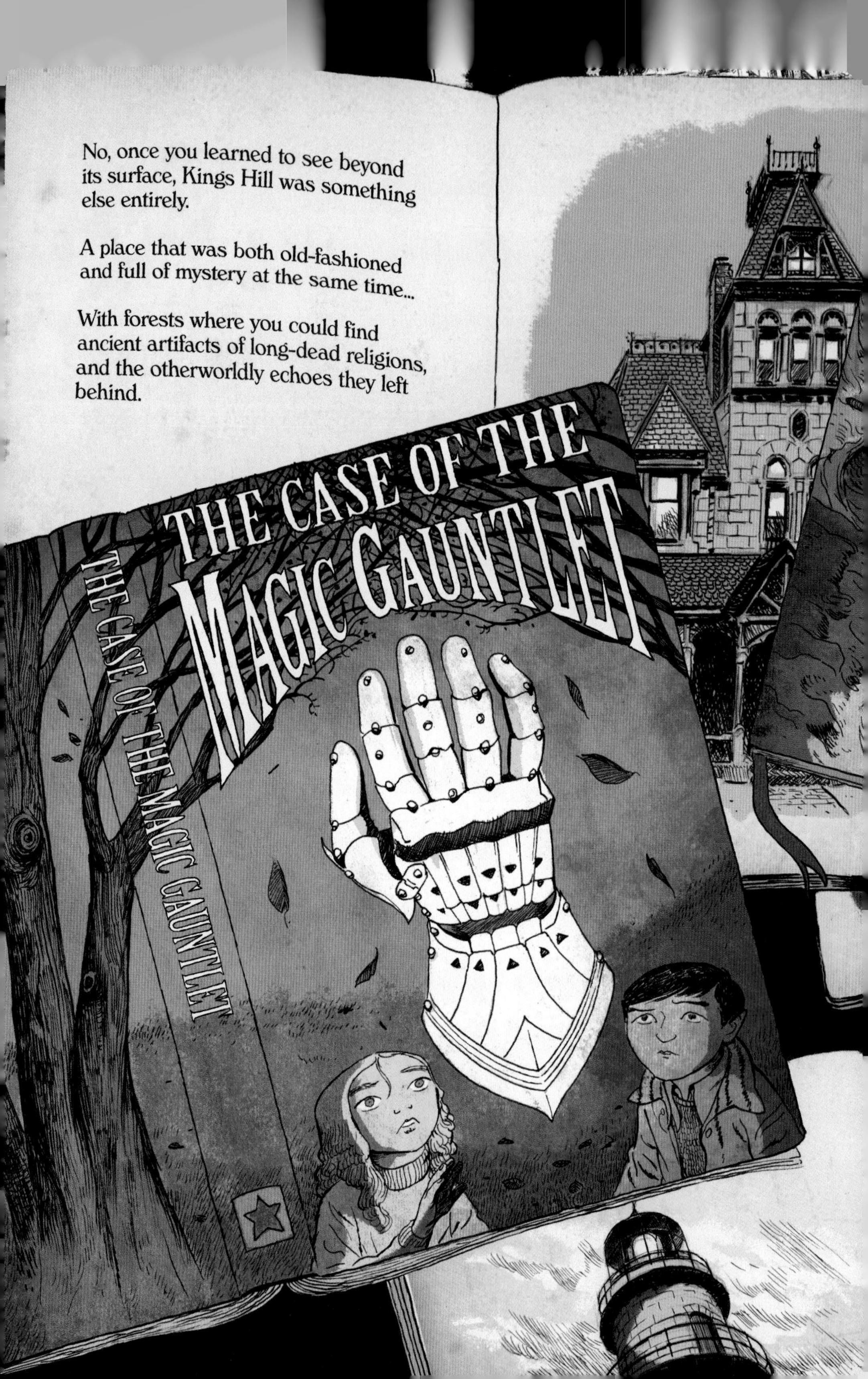
No, once you learned to see beyond its surface, Kings Hill was something else entirely.
A place that was both old-fashioned and full of mystery at the same time...
With forests where you could find ancient artifacts of long-dead religions, and the otherworldly echoes they left behind.
THE CASE OF THE MAGIC GAUNTLET
THE CASE OF THE MAGIC GAUNTLET

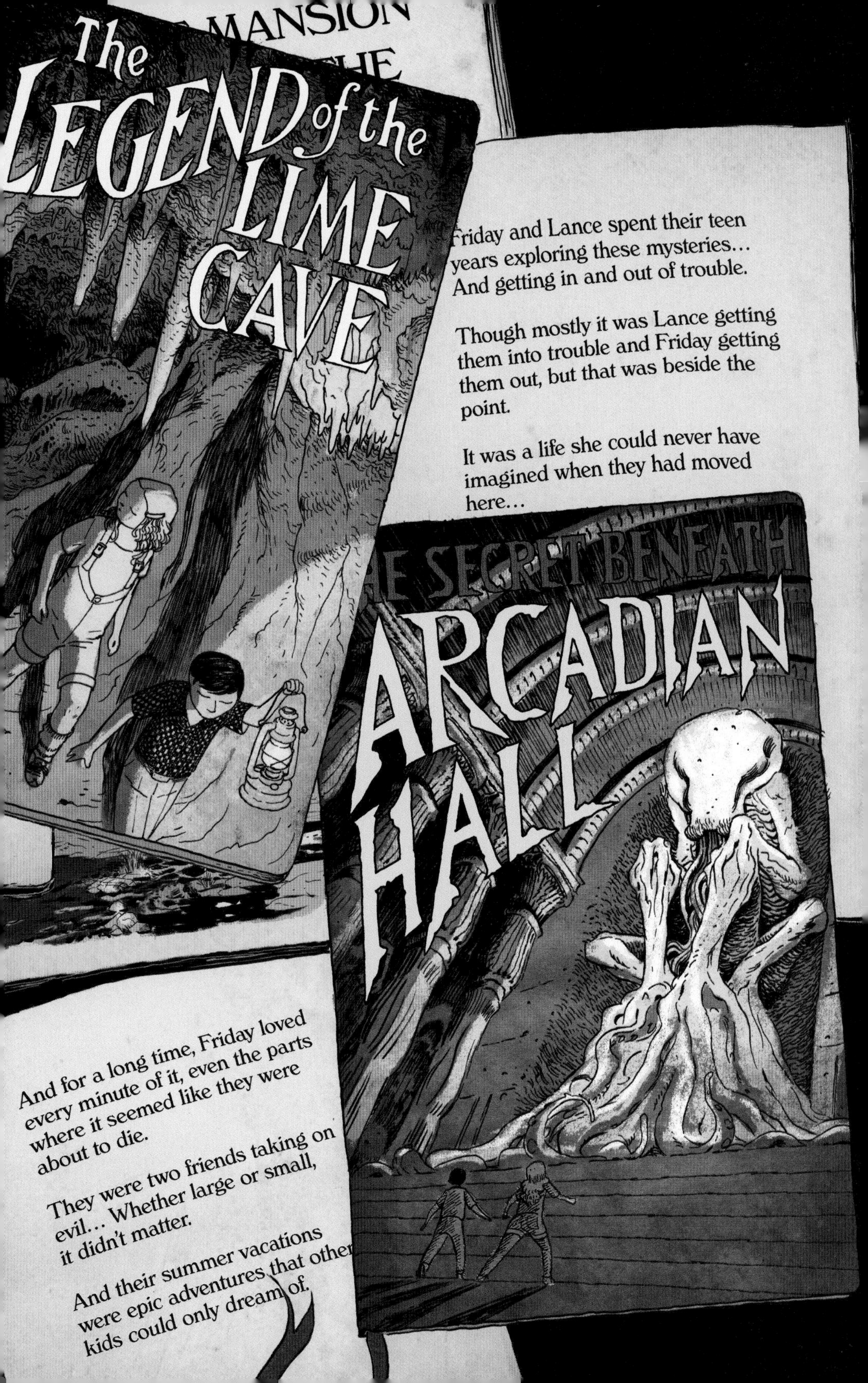
MANSION
The LEGEND of the LIME CAVE
Friday and Lance spent their teen years exploring these mysteries… And getting in and out of trouble.
Though mostly it was Lance getting them into trouble and Friday getting them out, but that was beside the point.
It was a life she could never have imagined when they had moved here…
E SECRET BENEATH
ARCADIAN HALL
And for a long time, Friday loved every minute of it, even the parts where it seemed like they were about to die.
They were two friends taking on evil… Whether large or small, it didn't matter.
And their summer vacations were epic adventures that other kids could only dream of.

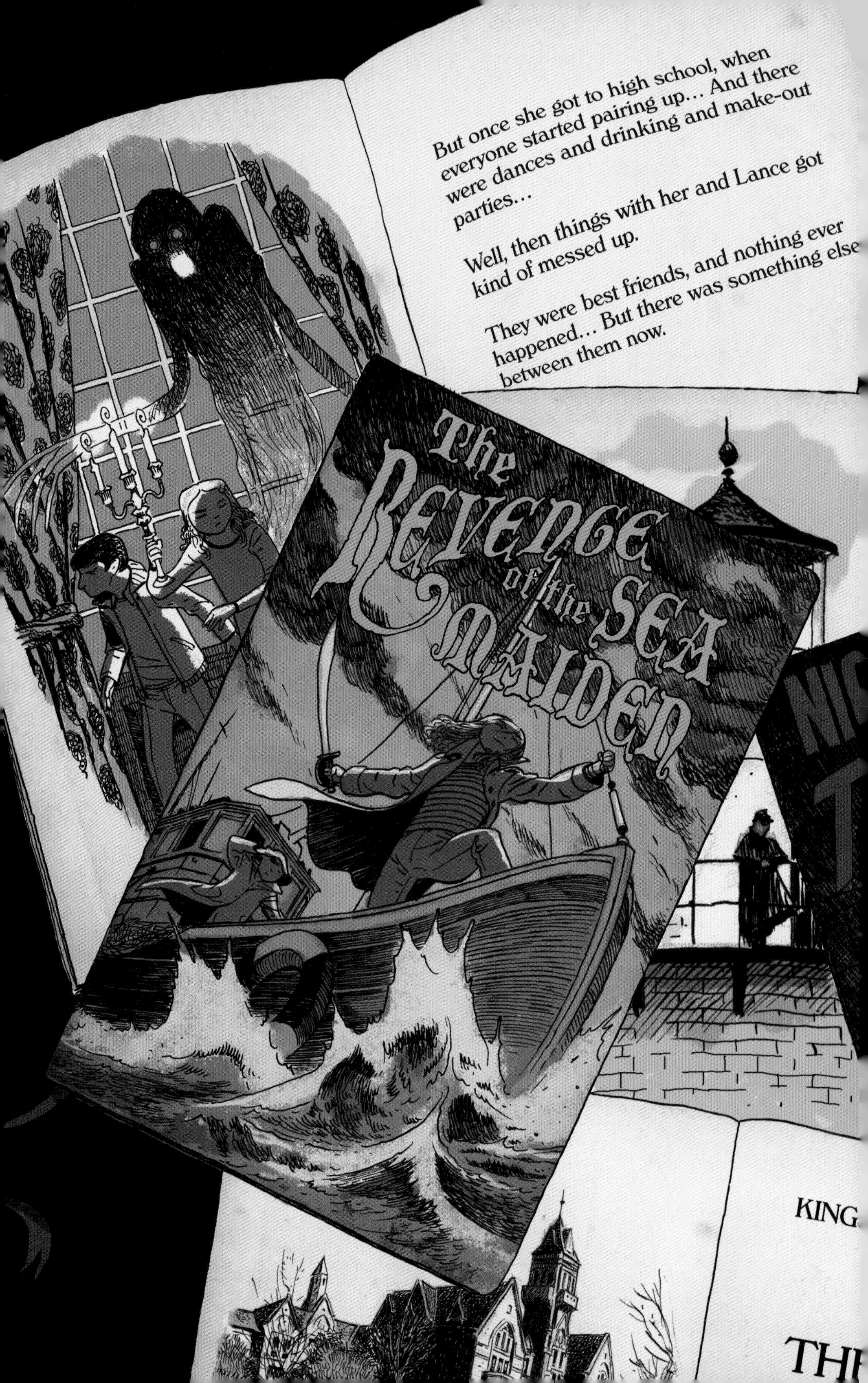
But once she got to high school, when everyone started pairing up… And there were dances and drinking and make-out parties…
Well, then things with her and Lance got kind of messed up.
They were best friends, and nothing ever happened… But there was something else between them now.
The Revenge of the Sea Maiden

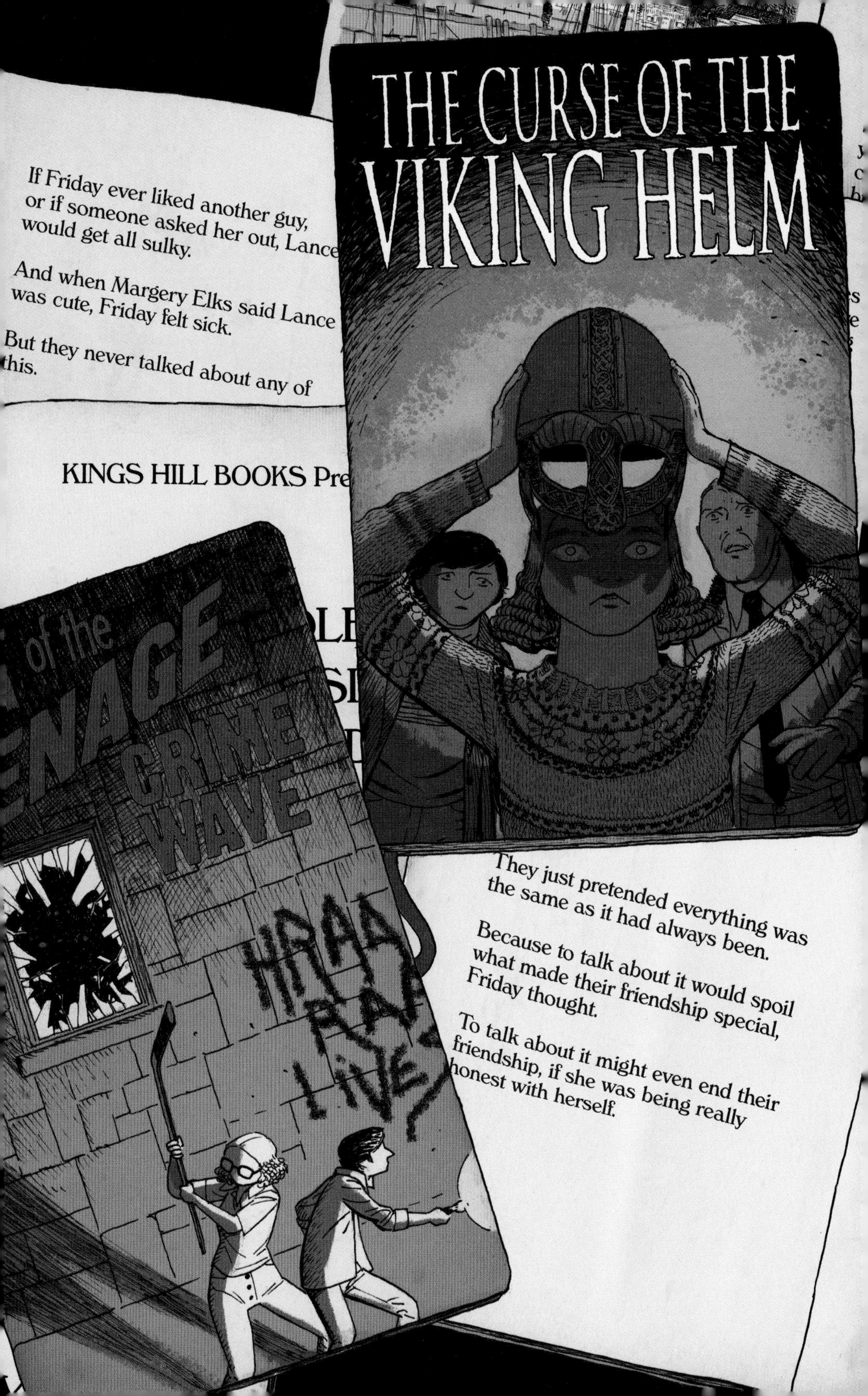
If Friday ever liked another guy, or if someone asked her out, Lance would get all sulky.
And when Margery Elks said Lance was cute, Friday felt sick.
But they never talked about any of this.
THE CURSE OF THE VIKING HELM
KINGS HILL BOOKS Pre
of the
NAGE
CRIME WAVE
They just pretended everything was the same as it had always been.
Because to talk about it would spoil what made their friendship special, Friday thought.
To talk about it might even end their friendship, if she was being really honest with herself.

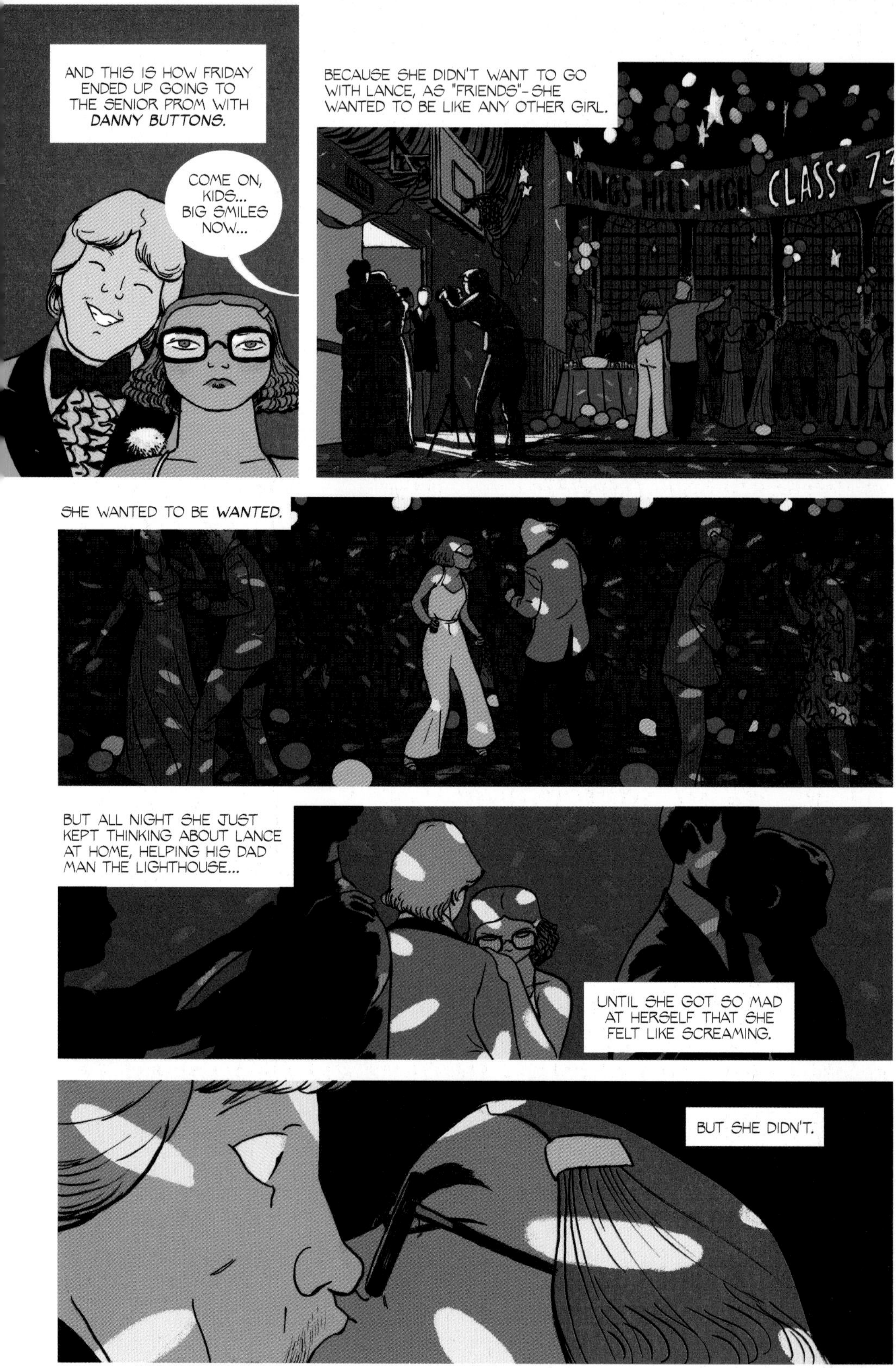
AND THIS IS HOW FRIDAY ENDED UP GOING TO THE SENIOR PROM WITH *DANNY BUTTONS.*
COME ON, KIDS... BIG SMILES NOW...
BECAUSE SHE DIDN'T WANT TO GO WITH LANCE, AS "FRIENDS"- SHE WANTED TO BE LIKE ANY OTHER GIRL.
KINGS HILL HIGH CLASS OF 73
SHE WANTED TO BE *WANTED.*
BUT ALL NIGHT SHE JUST KEPT THINKING ABOUT LANCE AT HOME, HELPING HIS DAD MAN THE LIGHTHOUSE...
UNTIL SHE GOT SO MAD AT HERSELF THAT SHE FELT LIKE SCREAMING.
BUT SHE DIDN'T.

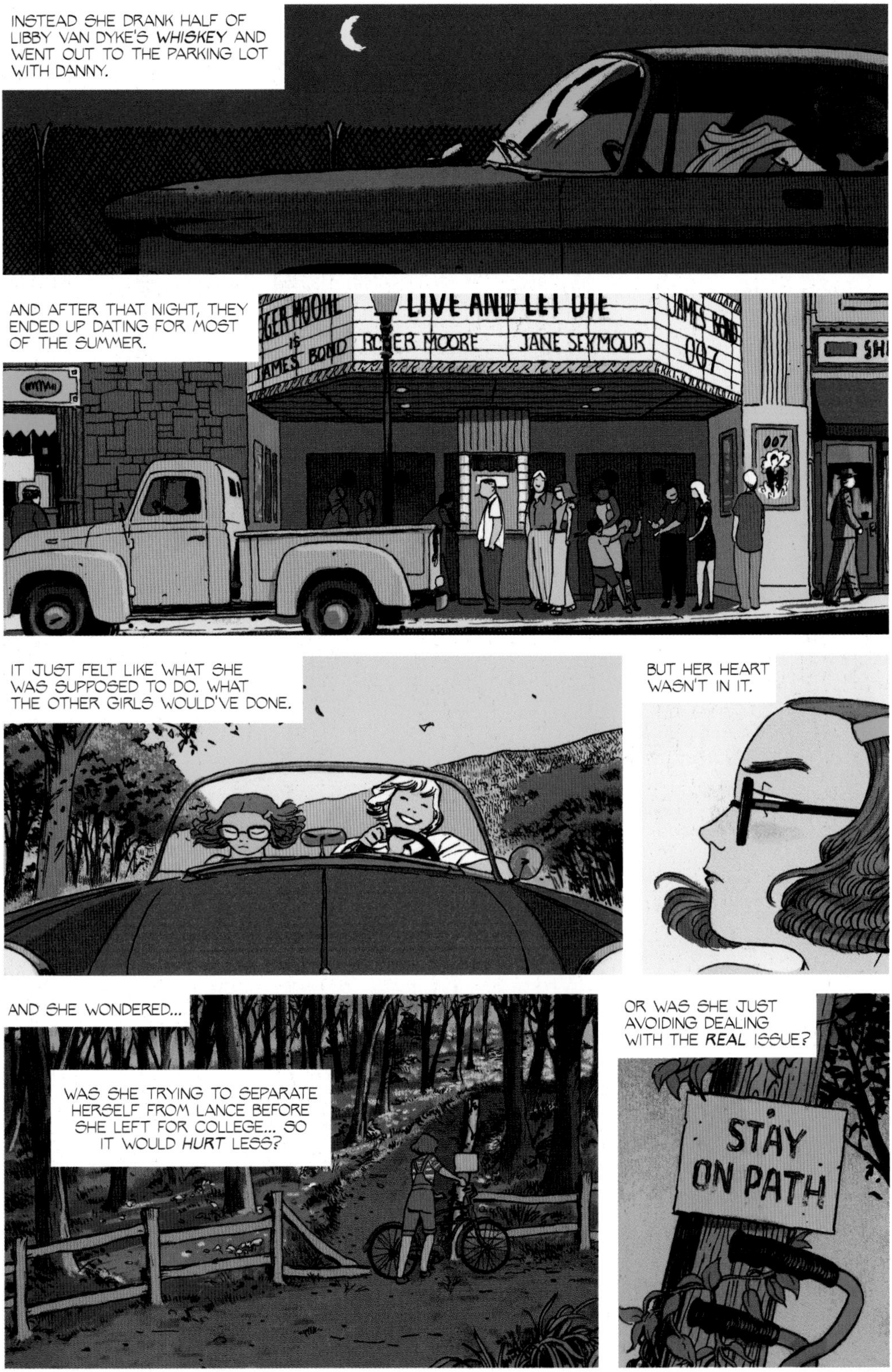

INSTEAD SHE DRANK HALF OF LIBBY VAN DYKE'S *WHISKEY* AND WENT OUT TO THE PARKING LOT WITH DANNY.
AND AFTER THAT NIGHT, THEY ENDED UP DATING FOR MOST OF THE SUMMER.
LIVE AND LET DIE
ROGER MOORE JANE SEYMOUR
JAMES BOND 007
007
IT JUST FELT LIKE WHAT SHE WAS SUPPOSED TO DO. WHAT THE OTHER GIRLS WOULD'VE DONE.
BUT HER HEART WASN'T IN IT.
AND SHE WONDERED...
WAS SHE TRYING TO SEPARATE HERSELF FROM LANCE BEFORE SHE LEFT FOR COLLEGE... SO IT WOULD *HURT* LESS?
OR WAS SHE JUST AVOIDING DEALING WITH THE *REAL* ISSUE?
STAY ON PATH

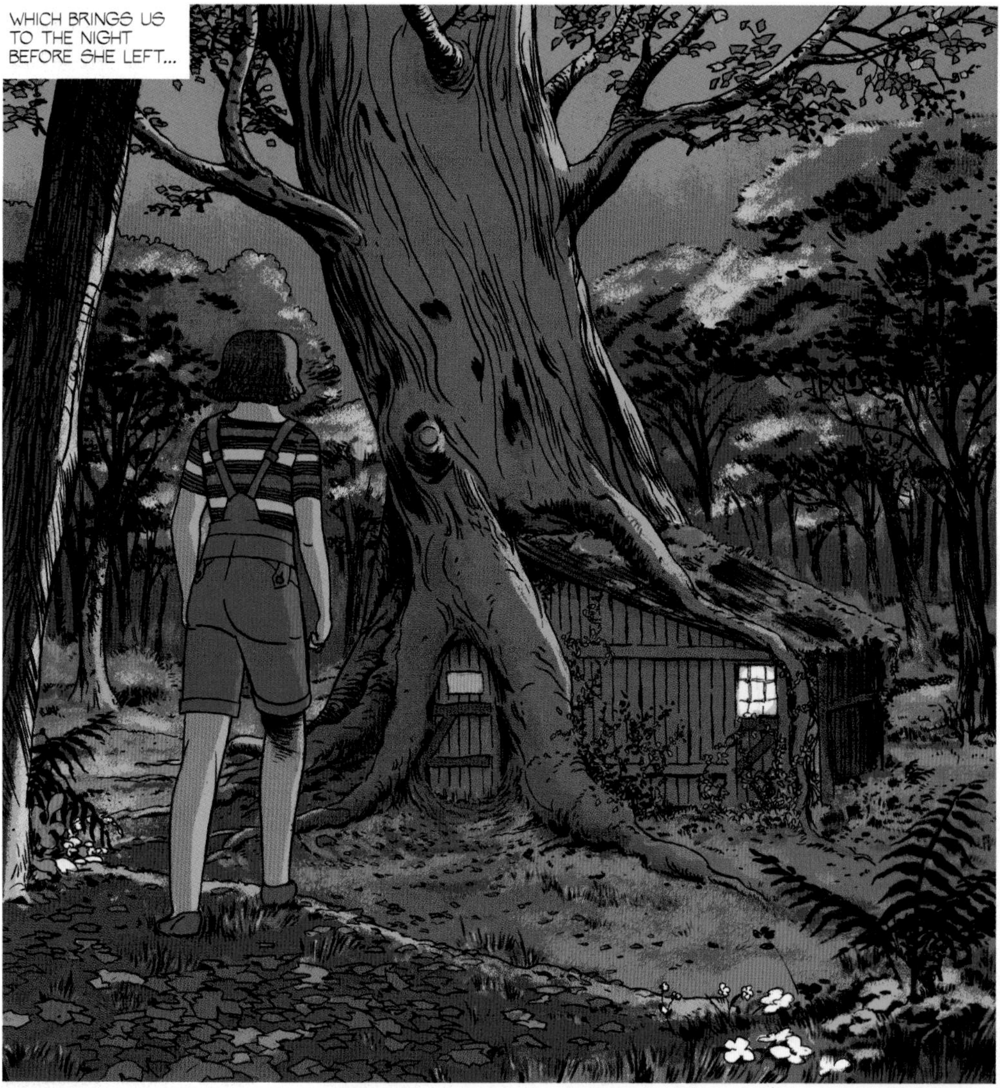
WHICH BRINGS US TO THE NIGHT BEFORE SHE LEFT...

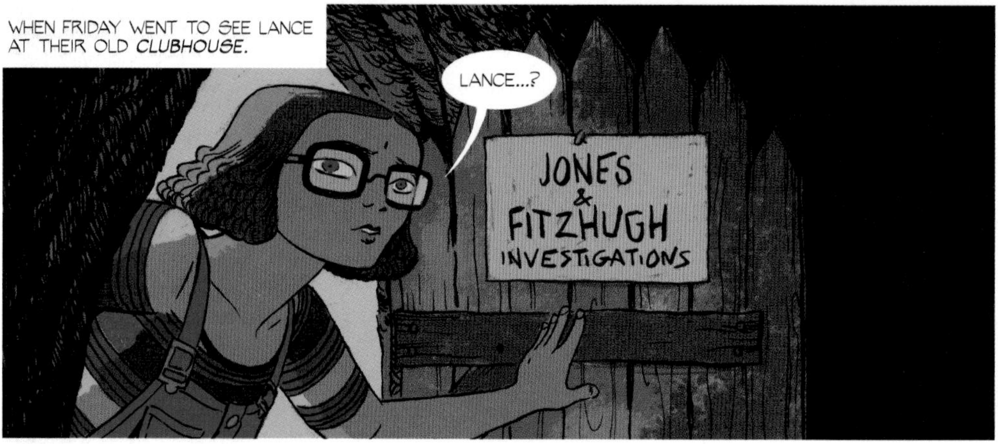
WHEN FRIDAY WENT TO SEE LANCE AT THEIR OLD *CLUBHOUSE*.
LANCE...?
JONES & FITZHUGH INVESTIGATIONS

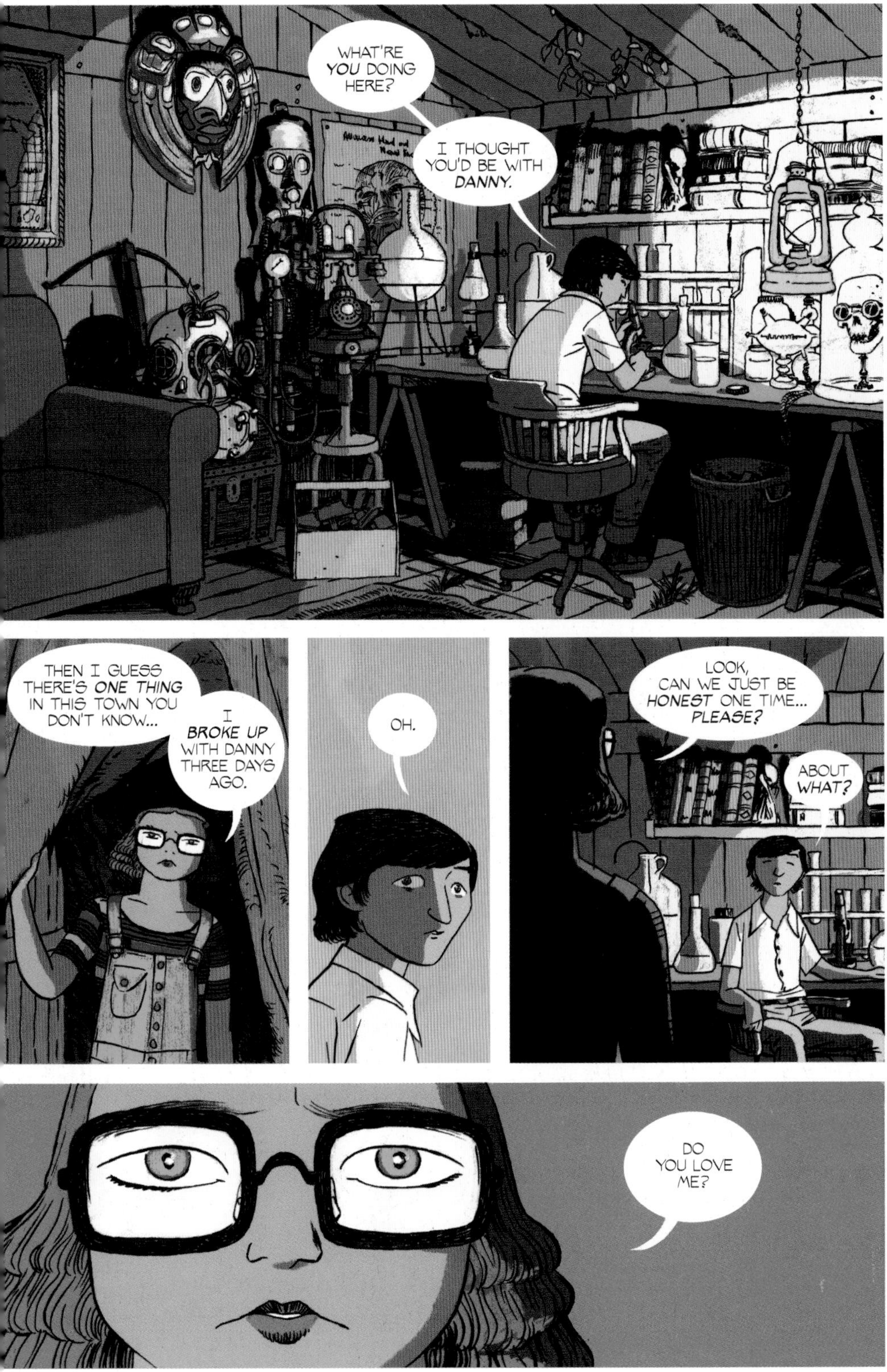
WHAT'RE YOU DOING HERE?
I THOUGHT YOU'D BE WITH DANNY.
THEN I GUESS THERE'S ONE THING IN THIS TOWN YOU DON'T KNOW...
I BROKE UP WITH DANNY THREE DAYS AGO.
OH.
LOOK, CAN WE JUST BE HONEST ONE TIME... PLEASE?
ABOUT WHAT?
DO YOU LOVE ME?

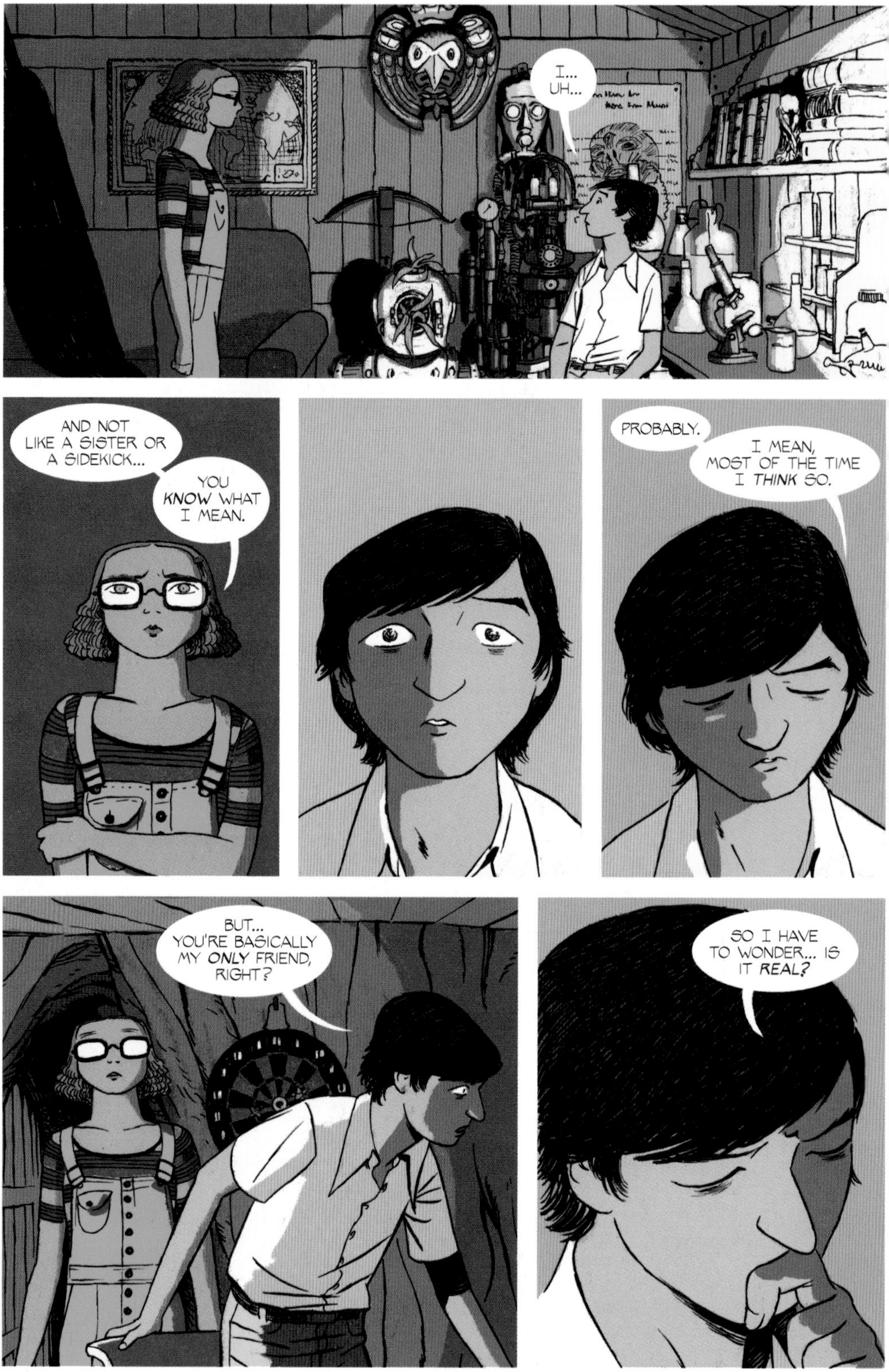
I... UH...
AND NOT LIKE A SISTER OR A SIDEKICK...
YOU *KNOW* WHAT I MEAN.
PROBABLY.
I MEAN, MOST OF THE TIME I *THINK* SO.
BUT... YOU'RE BASICALLY MY *ONLY* FRIEND, RIGHT?
SO I HAVE TO WONDER... IS IT *REAL?*

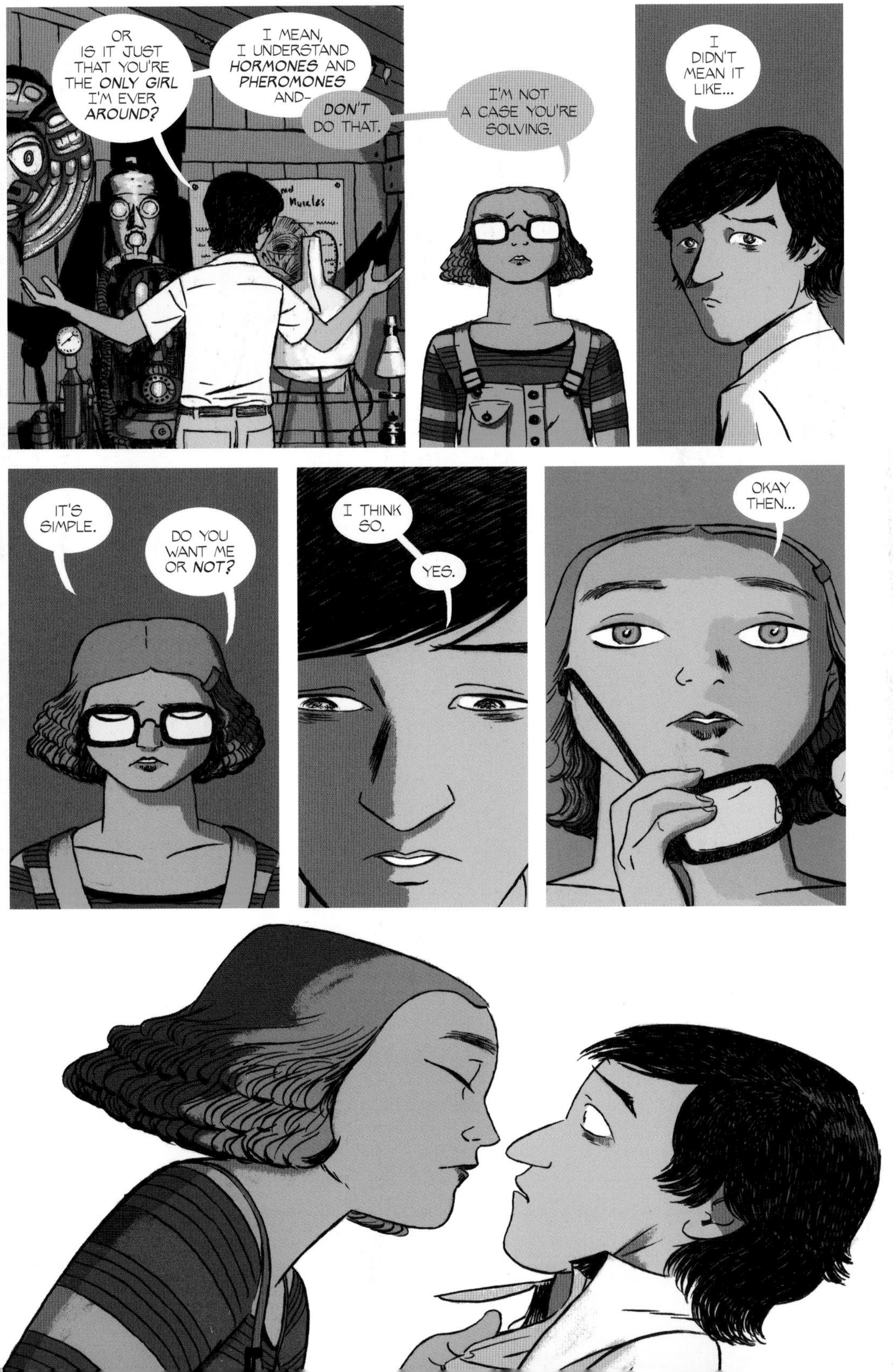
OR IS IT JUST THAT YOU'RE THE ONLY GIRL I'M EVER AROUND?
I MEAN, I UNDERSTAND HORMONES AND PHEROMONES AND-
DON'T DO THAT.
I'M NOT A CASE YOU'RE SOLVING.
I DIDN'T MEAN IT LIKE...
IT'S SIMPLE.
DO YOU WANT ME OR NOT?
I THINK SO.
YES.
OKAY THEN...

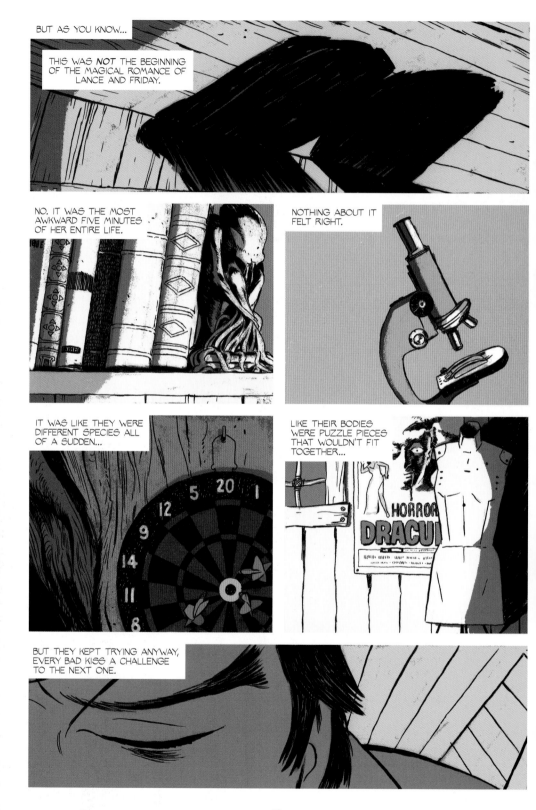

BUT AS YOU KNOW...

THIS WAS *NOT* THE BEGINNING OF THE MAGICAL ROMANCE OF LANCE AND FRIDAY.

NO. IT WAS THE MOST AWKWARD FIVE MINUTES OF HER ENTIRE LIFE.

NOTHING ABOUT IT FELT RIGHT.

IT WAS LIKE THEY WERE DIFFERENT SPECIES ALL OF A SUDDEN...

LIKE THEIR BODIES WERE PUZZLE PIECES THAT WOULDN'T FIT TOGETHER...

BUT THEY KEPT TRYING ANYWAY, EVERY BAD KISS A CHALLENGE TO THE NEXT ONE.

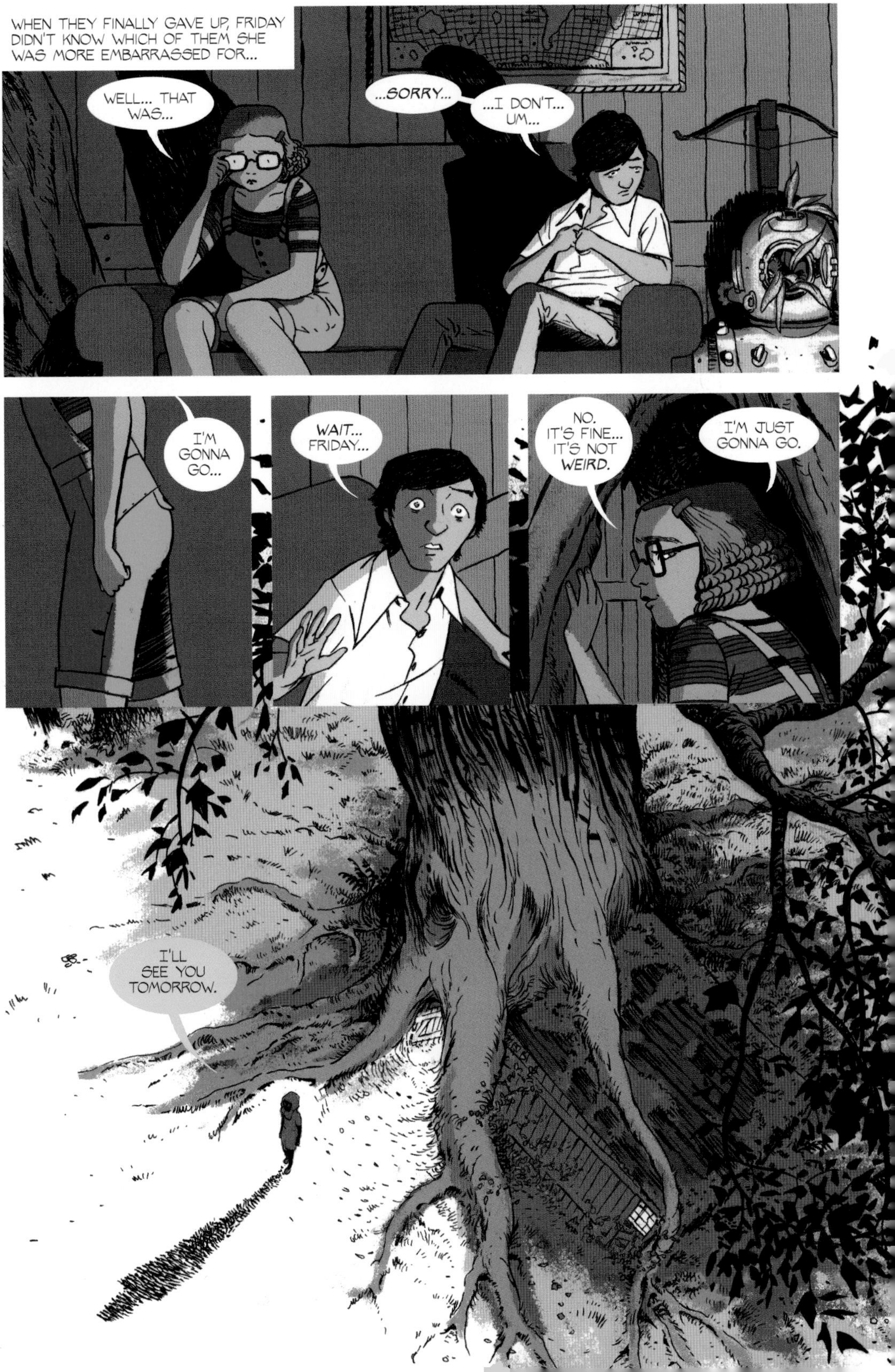
WHEN THEY FINALLY GAVE UP, FRIDAY DIDN'T KNOW WHICH OF THEM SHE WAS MORE EMBARRASSED FOR...
WELL... THAT WAS...
...SORRY...
...I DON'T... UM...
I'M GONNA GO...
WAIT... FRIDAY...
NO. IT'S FINE... IT'S NOT WEIRD.
I'M JUST GONNA GO.
I'LL SEE YOU TOMORROW.

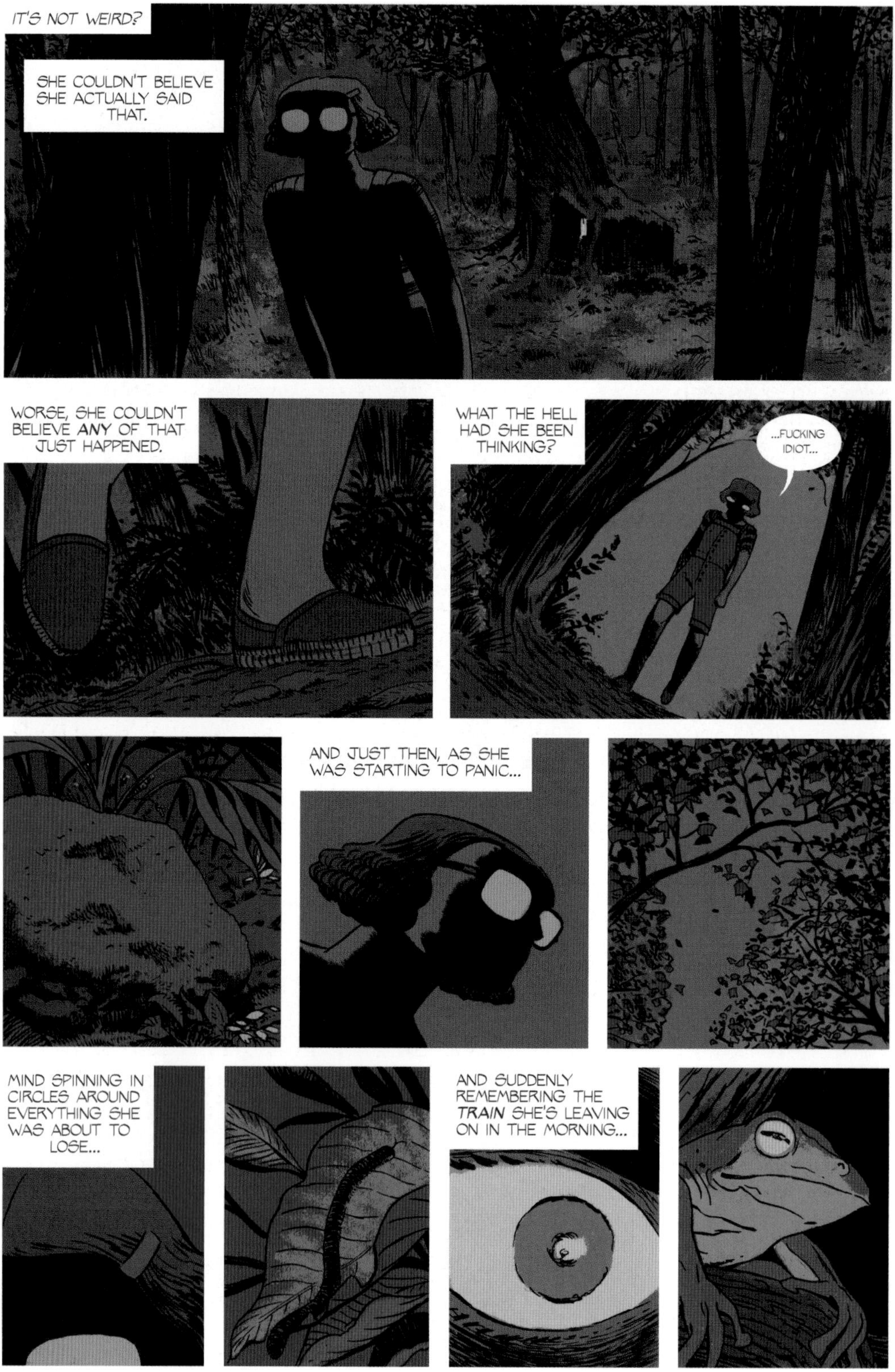
IT'S NOT WEIRD?
SHE COULDN'T BELIEVE SHE ACTUALLY SAID THAT.
WORSE, SHE COULDN'T BELIEVE ANY OF THAT JUST HAPPENED.
WHAT THE HELL HAD SHE BEEN THINKING?
...FUCKING IDIOT...
AND JUST THEN, AS SHE WAS STARTING TO PANIC...
MIND SPINNING IN CIRCLES AROUND EVERYTHING SHE WAS ABOUT TO LOSE...
AND SUDDENLY REMEMBERING THE TRAIN SHE'S LEAVING ON IN THE MORNING...

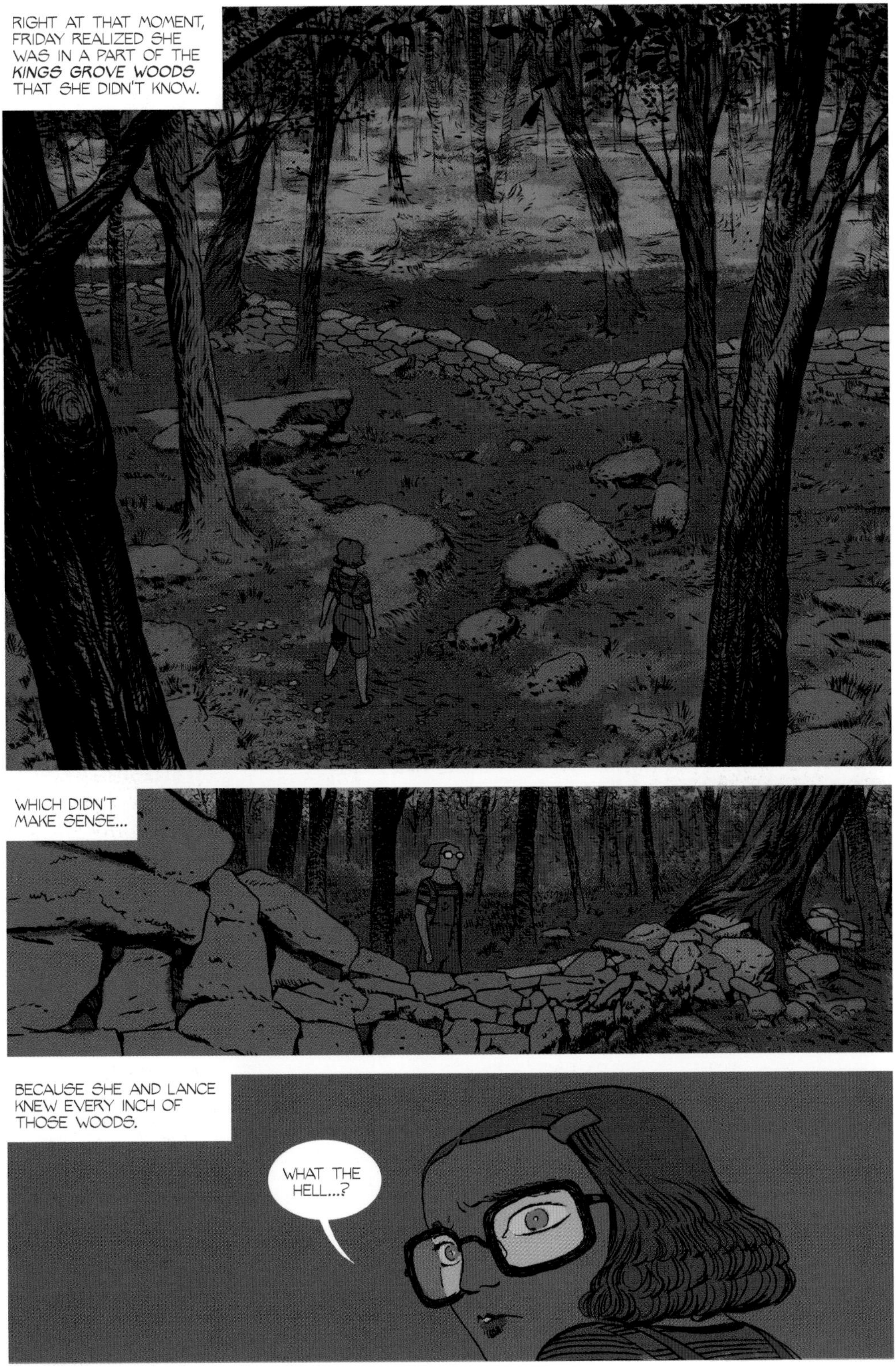
RIGHT AT THAT MOMENT, FRIDAY REALIZED SHE WAS IN A PART OF THE ***KINGS GROVE WOODS*** THAT SHE DIDN'T KNOW.
WHICH DIDN'T MAKE SENSE...
BECAUSE SHE AND LANCE KNEW EVERY INCH OF THOSE WOODS.
WHAT THE HELL...?

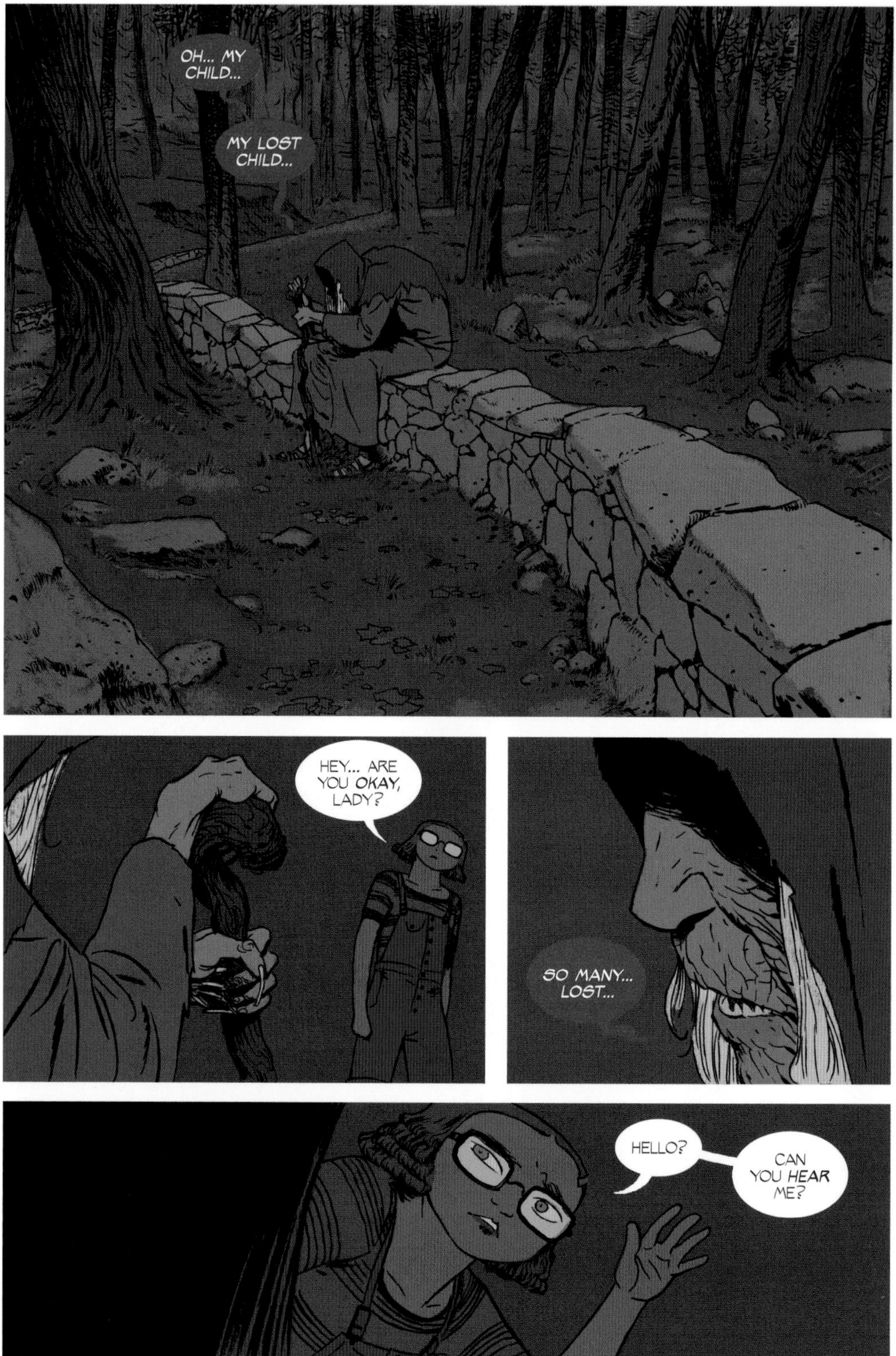
OH... MY CHILD...
MY LOST CHILD...
HEY... ARE YOU OKAY, LADY?
SO MANY... LOST...
HELLO?
CAN YOU HEAR ME?

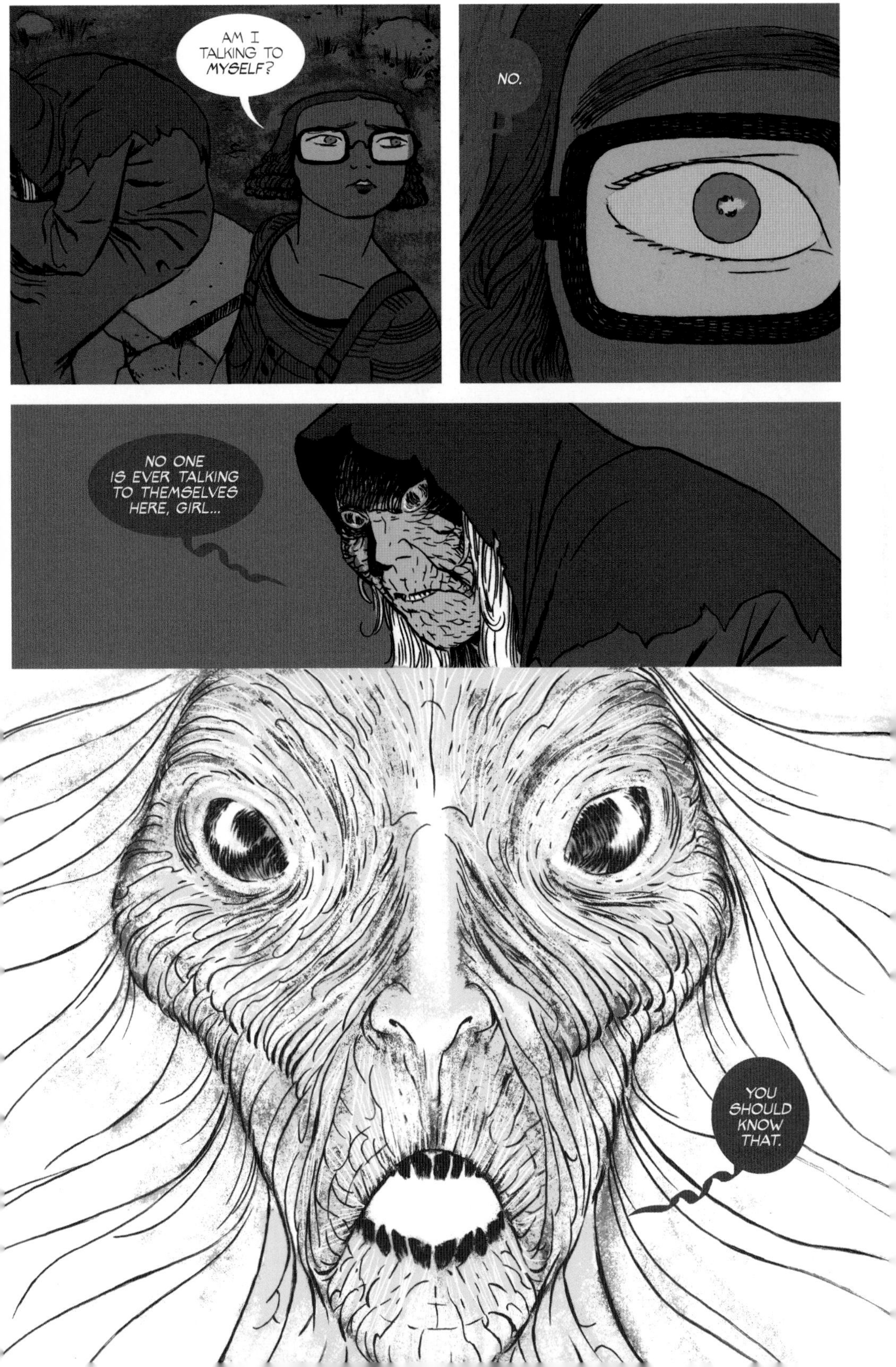
AM I TALKING TO MYSELF?
NO.
NO ONE IS EVER TALKING TO THEMSELVES HERE, GIRL...
YOU SHOULD KNOW THAT.

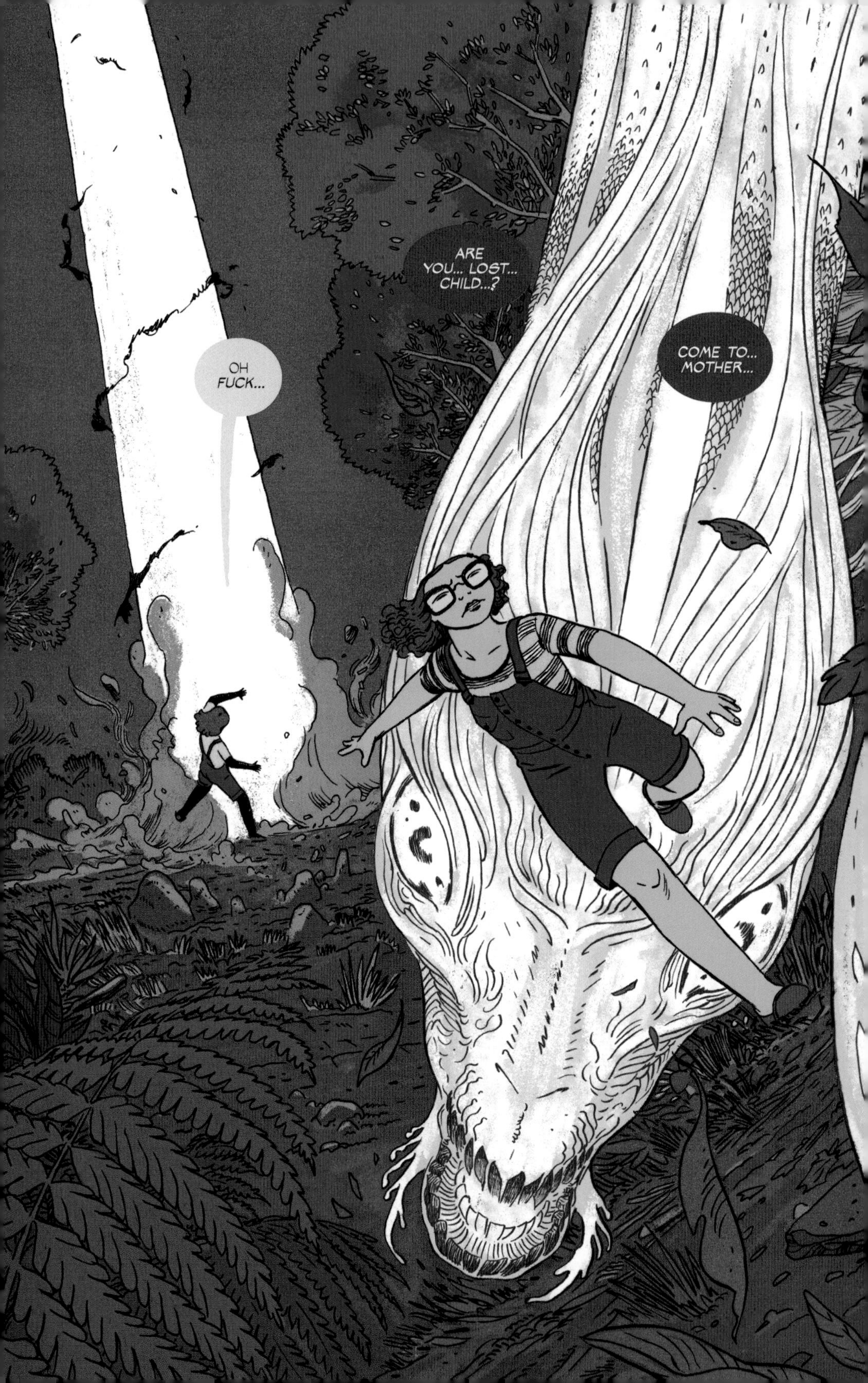
OH FUCK...
ARE YOU... LOST... CHILD...?
COME TO... MOTHER...

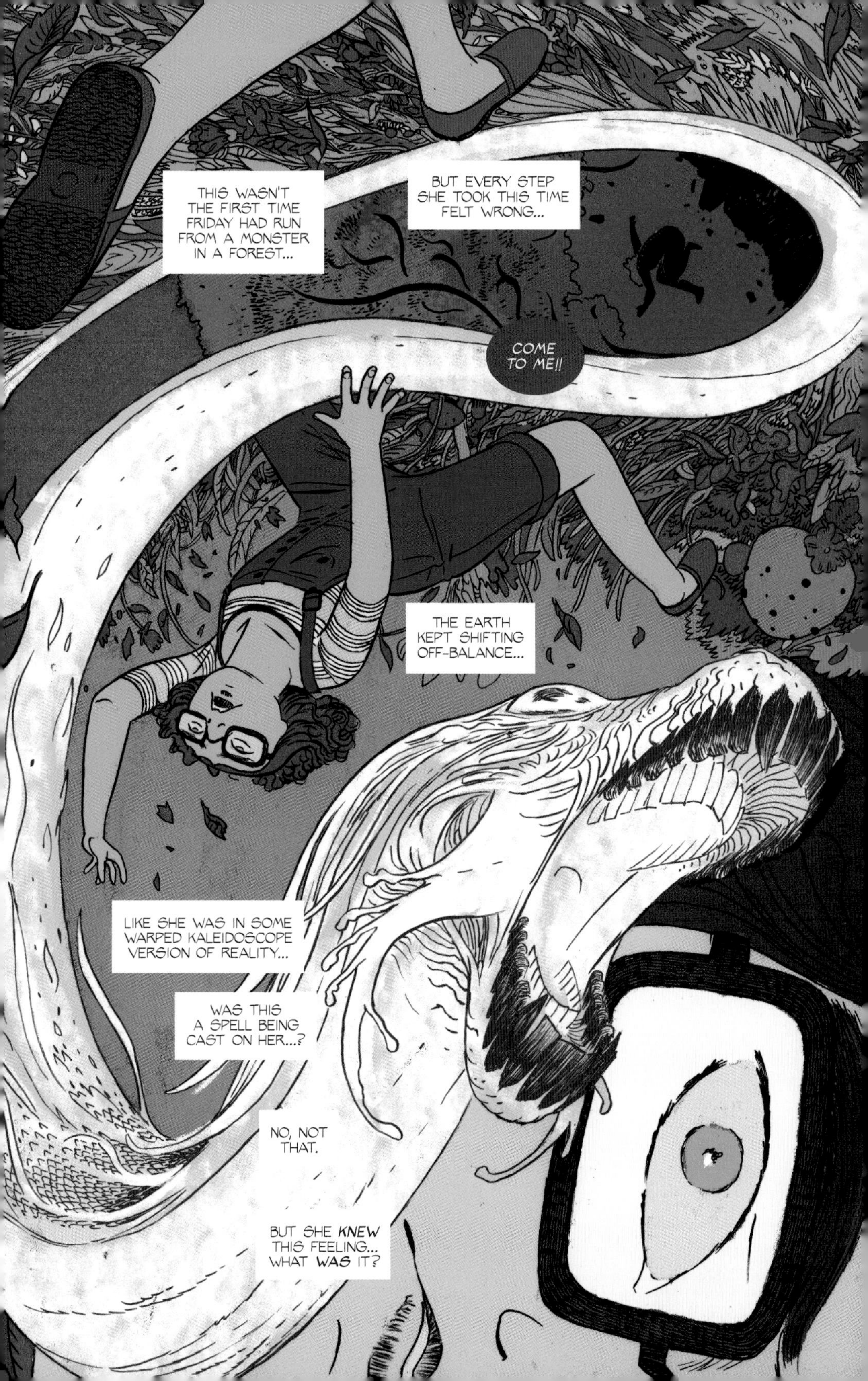
THIS WASN'T THE FIRST TIME FRIDAY HAD RUN FROM A MONSTER IN A FOREST...
BUT EVERY STEP SHE TOOK THIS TIME FELT WRONG...
COME TO ME!!
THE EARTH KEPT SHIFTING OFF-BALANCE...
LIKE SHE WAS IN SOME WARPED KALEIDOSCOPE VERSION OF REALITY...
WAS THIS A SPELL BEING CAST ON HER...?
NO, NOT THAT.
BUT SHE **KNEW** THIS FEELING... WHAT **WAS** IT?

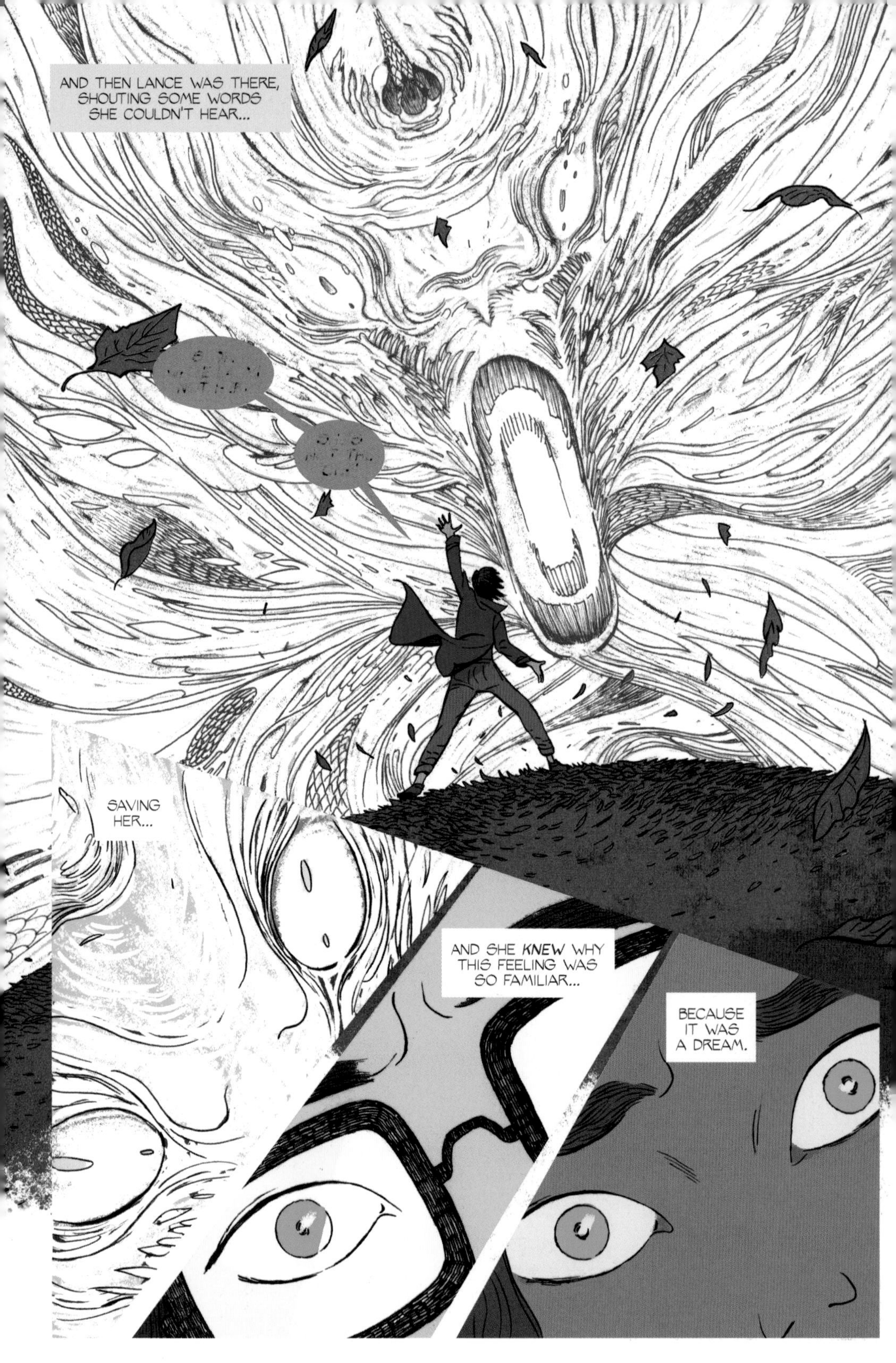
AND THEN LANCE WAS THERE, SHOUTING SOME WORDS SHE COULDN'T HEAR...
SAVING HER...
AND SHE KNEW WHY THIS FEELING WAS SO FAMILIAR...
BECAUSE IT WAS A DREAM.

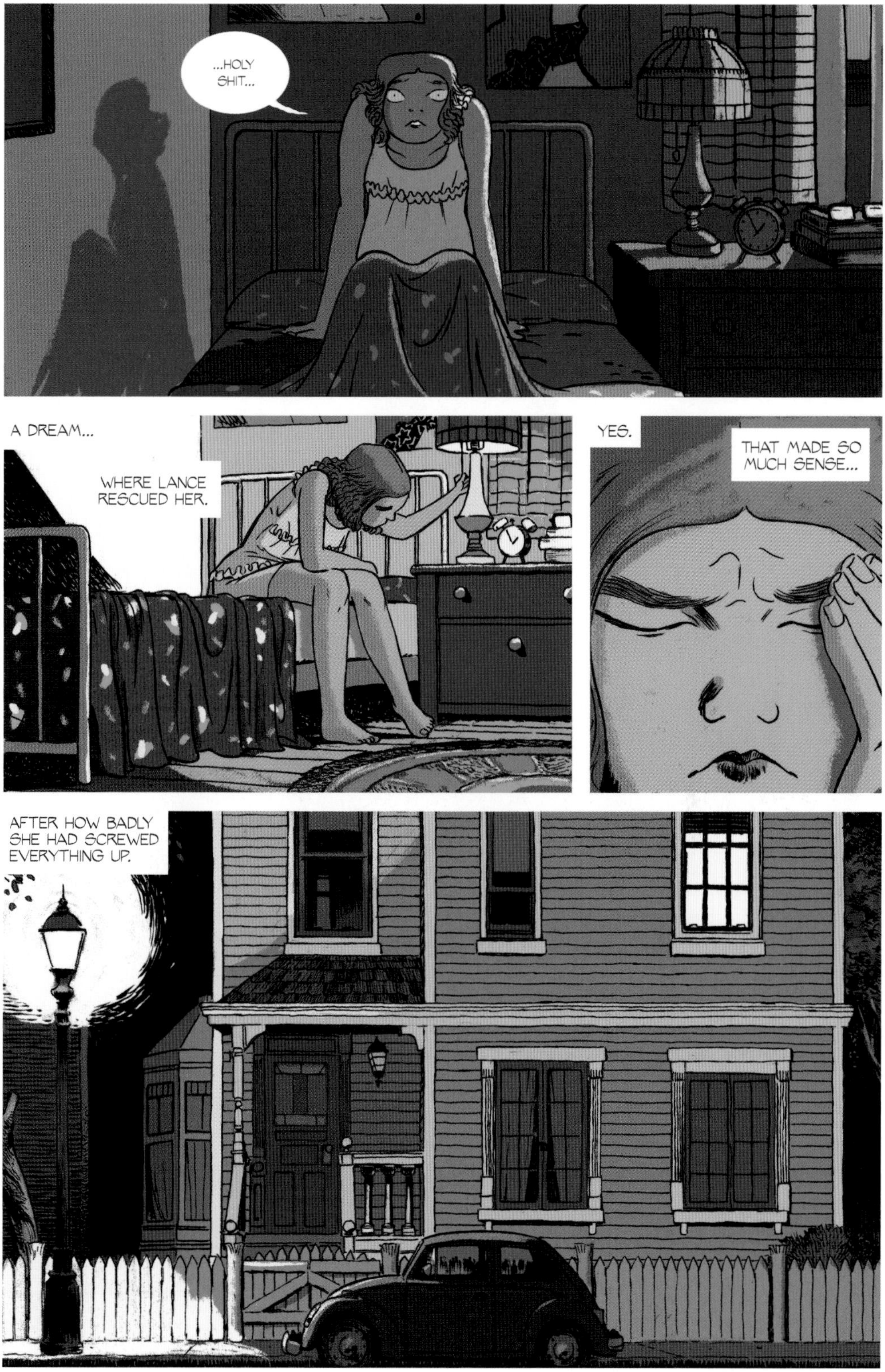

...HOLY SHIT...
A DREAM...
WHERE LANCE RESCUED HER.
YES.
THAT MADE SO MUCH SENSE...
AFTER HOW BADLY SHE HAD SCREWED EVERYTHING UP.

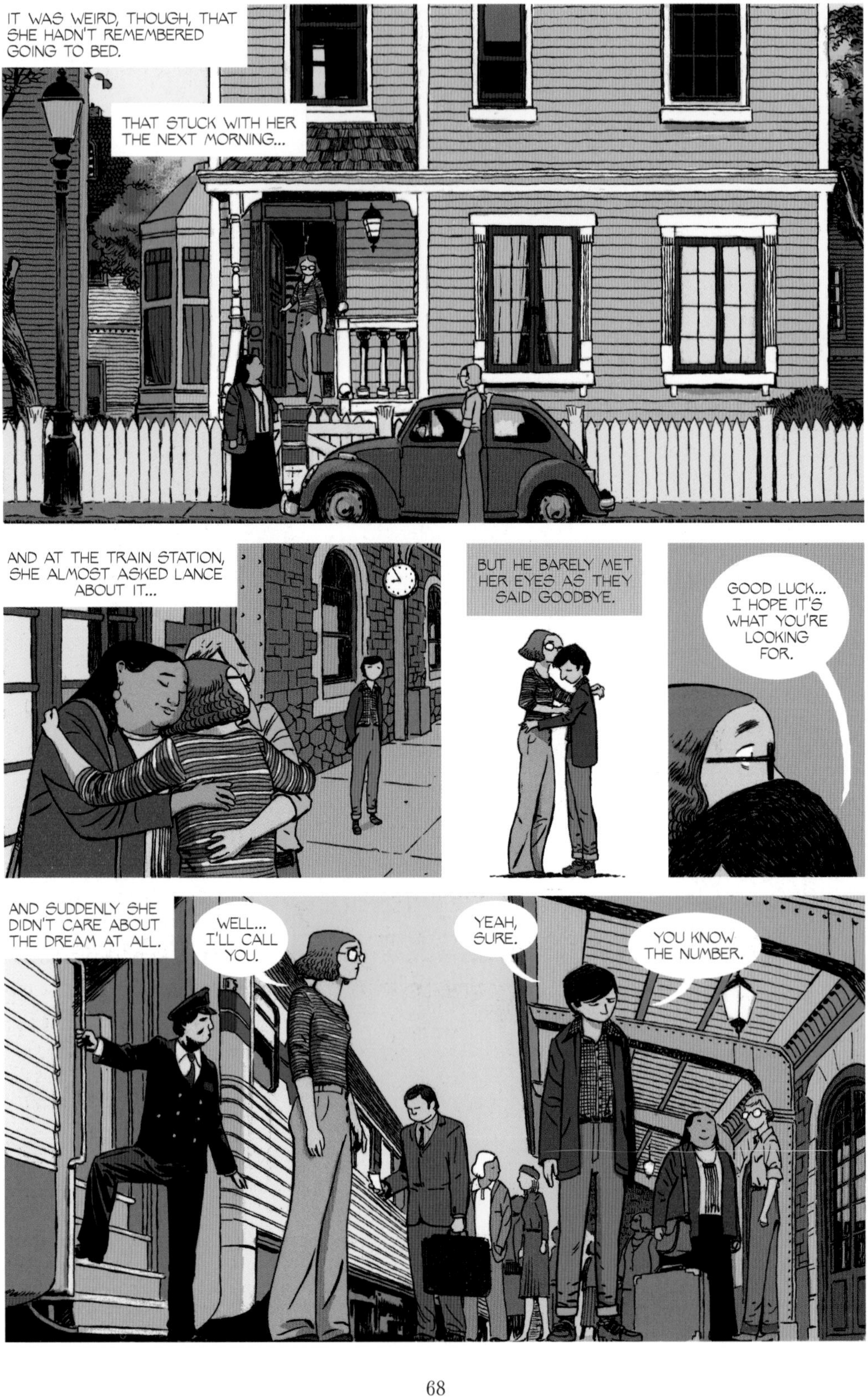
IT WAS WEIRD, THOUGH, THAT SHE HADN'T REMEMBERED GOING TO BED.
THAT STUCK WITH HER THE NEXT MORNING...
AND AT THE TRAIN STATION, SHE ALMOST ASKED LANCE ABOUT IT...
BUT HE BARELY MET HER EYES AS THEY SAID GOODBYE.
GOOD LUCK... I HOPE IT'S WHAT YOU'RE LOOKING FOR.
AND SUDDENLY SHE DIDN'T CARE ABOUT THE DREAM AT ALL.
WELL... I'LL CALL YOU.
YEAH, SURE.
YOU KNOW THE NUMBER.

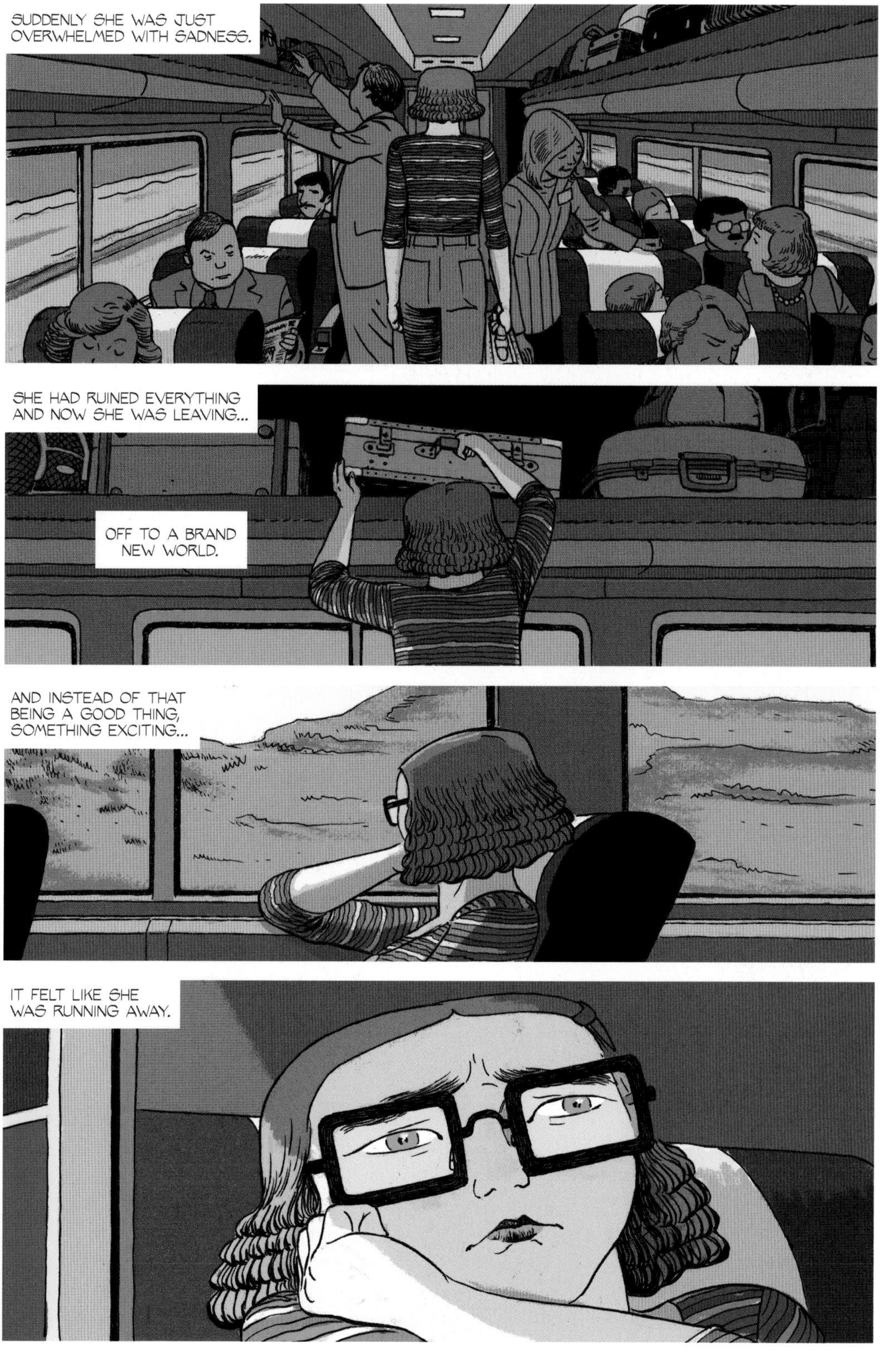
SUDDENLY SHE WAS JUST OVERWHELMED WITH SADNESS.
SHE HAD RUINED EVERYTHING AND NOW SHE WAS LEAVING...
OFF TO A BRAND NEW WORLD.
AND INSTEAD OF THAT BEING A GOOD THING, SOMETHING EXCITING...
IT FELT LIKE SHE WAS RUNNING AWAY.

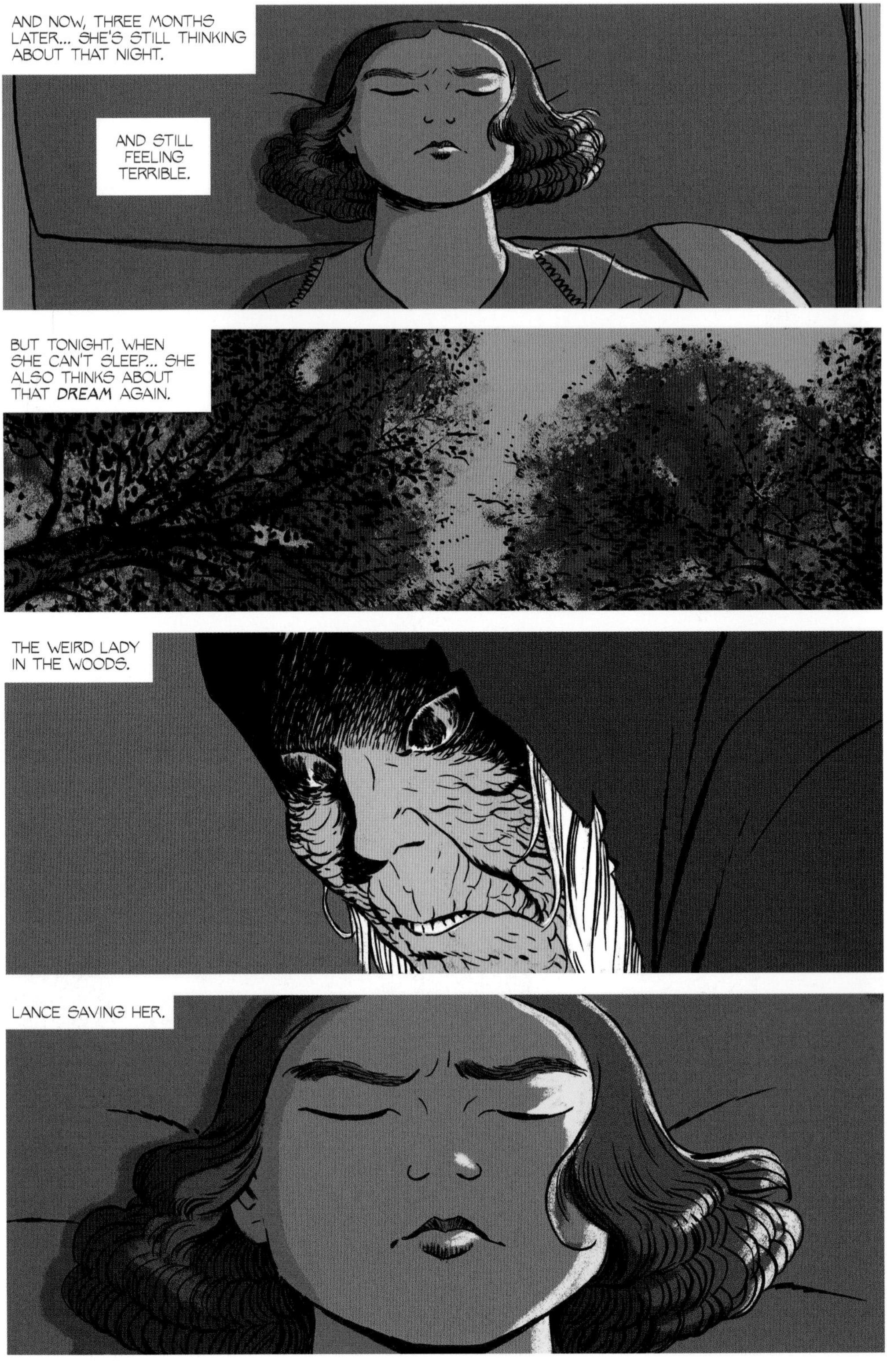
AND NOW, THREE MONTHS LATER... SHE'S STILL THINKING ABOUT THAT NIGHT.
AND STILL FEELING TERRIBLE.
BUT TONIGHT, WHEN SHE CAN'T SLEEP... SHE ALSO THINKS ABOUT THAT DREAM AGAIN.
THE WEIRD LADY IN THE WOODS.
LANCE SAVING HER.

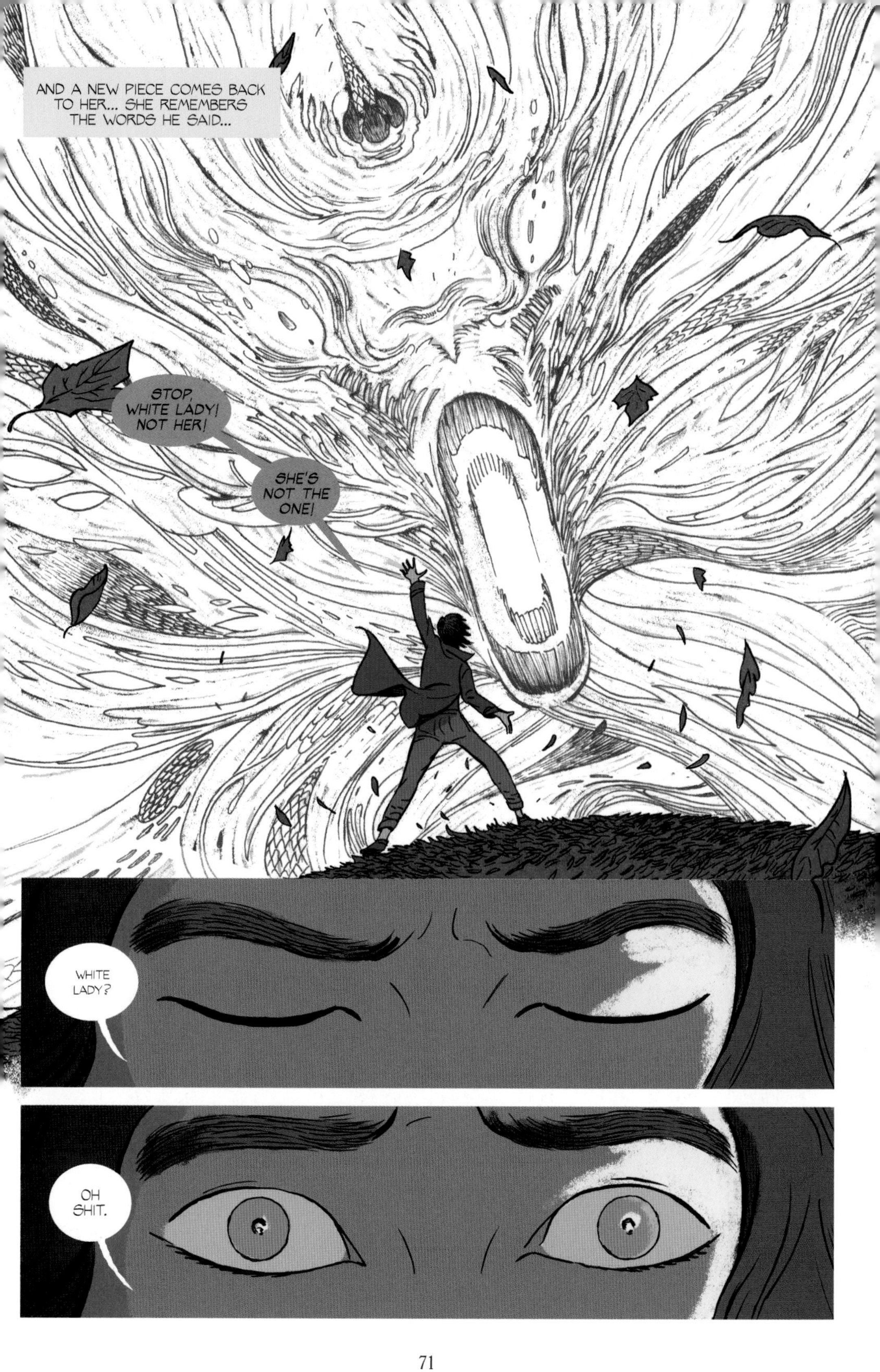
AND A NEW PIECE COMES BACK TO HER... SHE REMEMBERS THE WORDS HE SAID...
STOP, WHITE LADY! NOT HER!
SHE'S NOT THE ONE!
WHITE LADY?
OH SHIT.

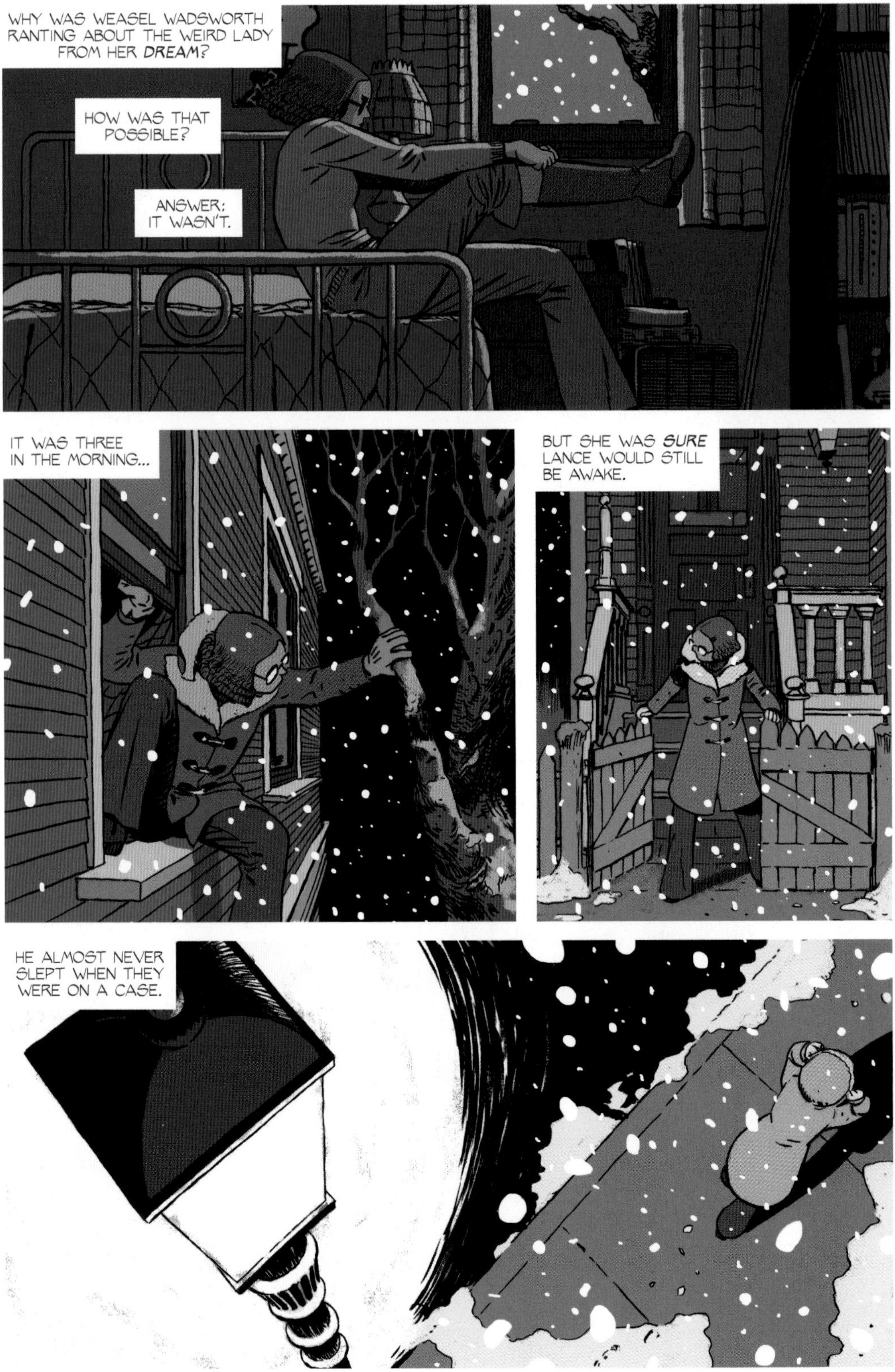
WHY WAS WEASEL WADSWORTH RANTING ABOUT THE WEIRD LADY FROM HER DREAM?
HOW WAS THAT POSSIBLE?
ANSWER: IT WASN'T.
IT WAS THREE IN THE MORNING...
BUT SHE WAS SURE LANCE WOULD STILL BE AWAKE.
HE ALMOST NEVER SLEPT WHEN THEY WERE ON A CASE.

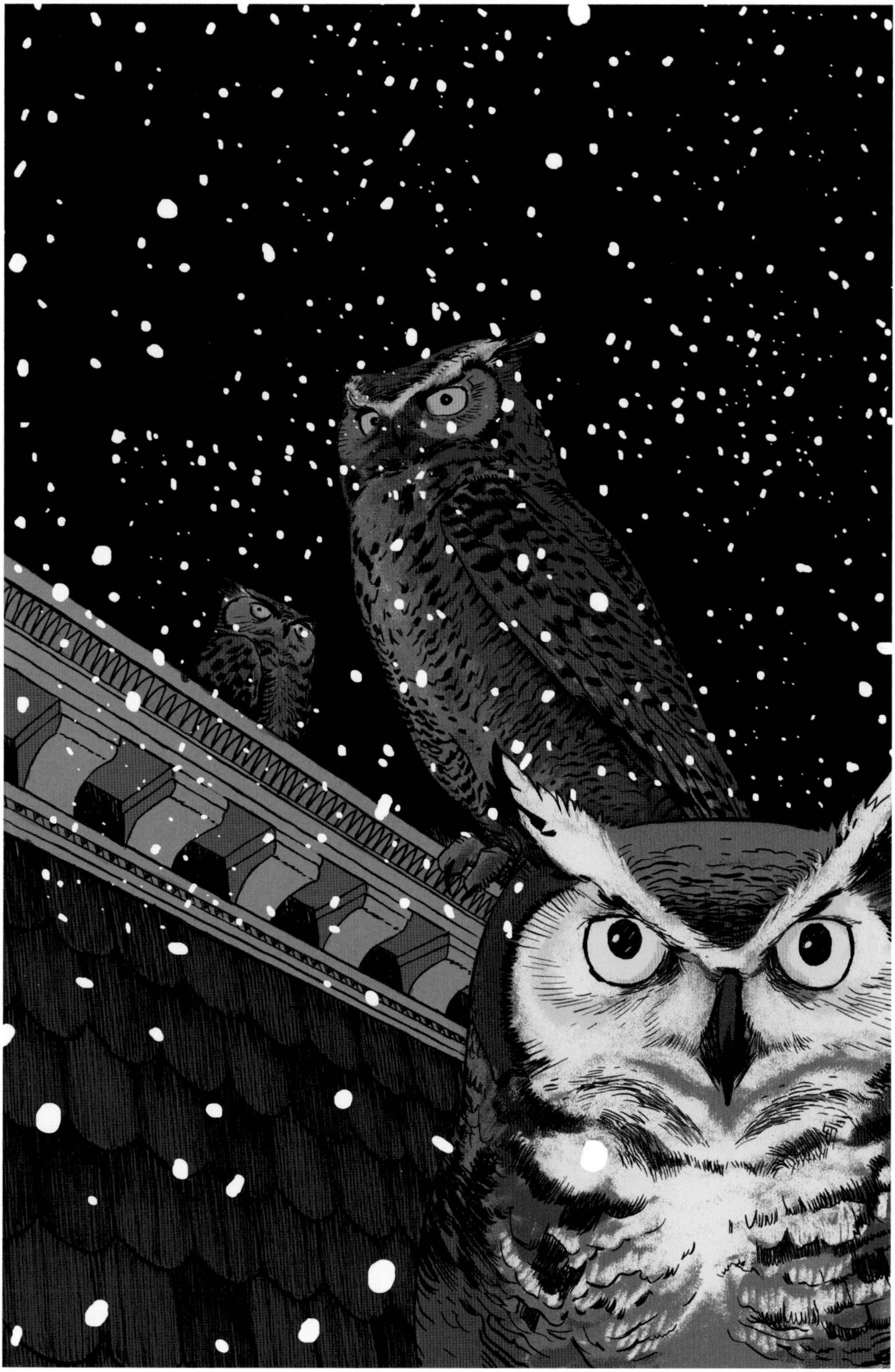

Chapter Three
Shadows in the Storm

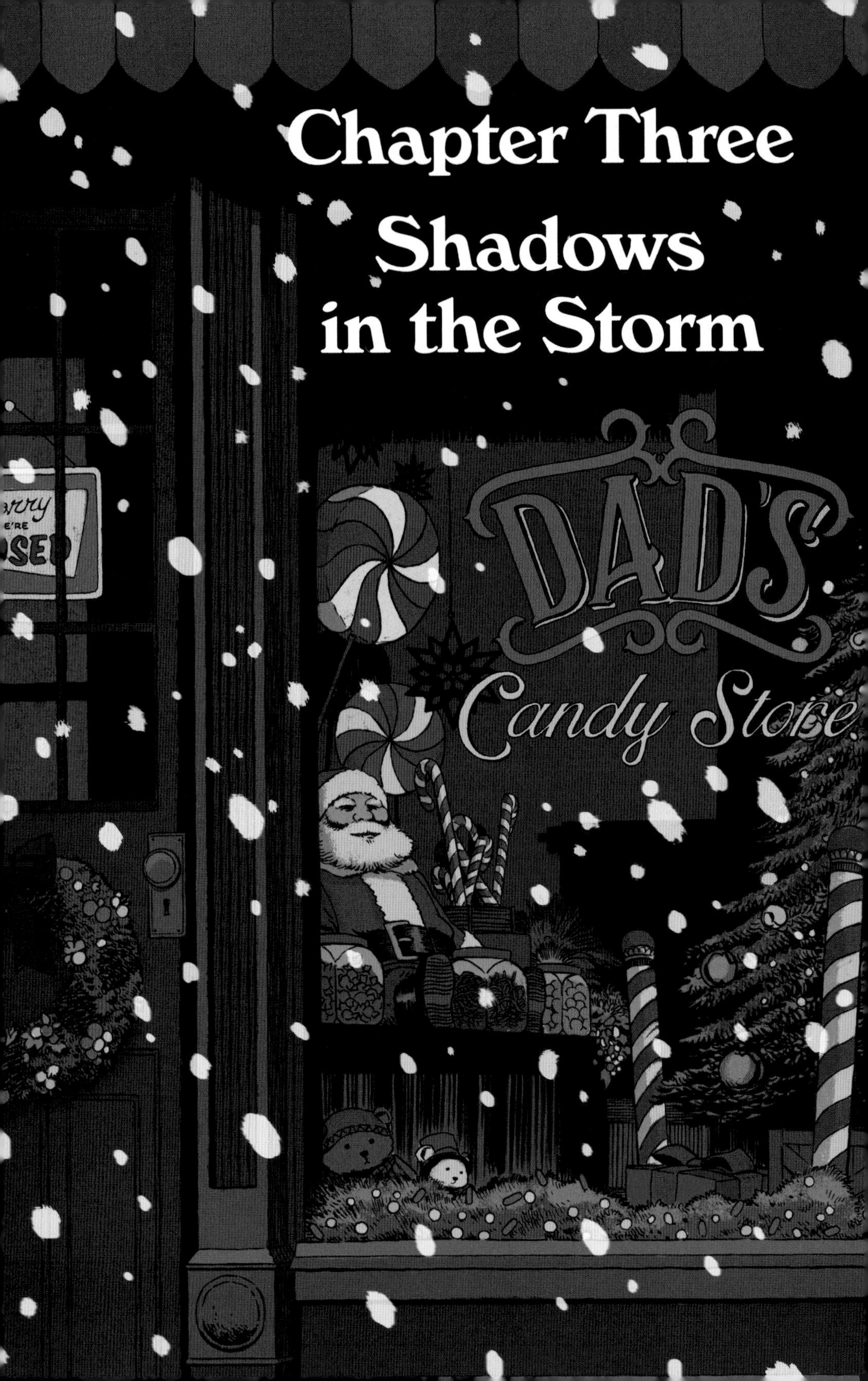
DAD'S
Candy Store

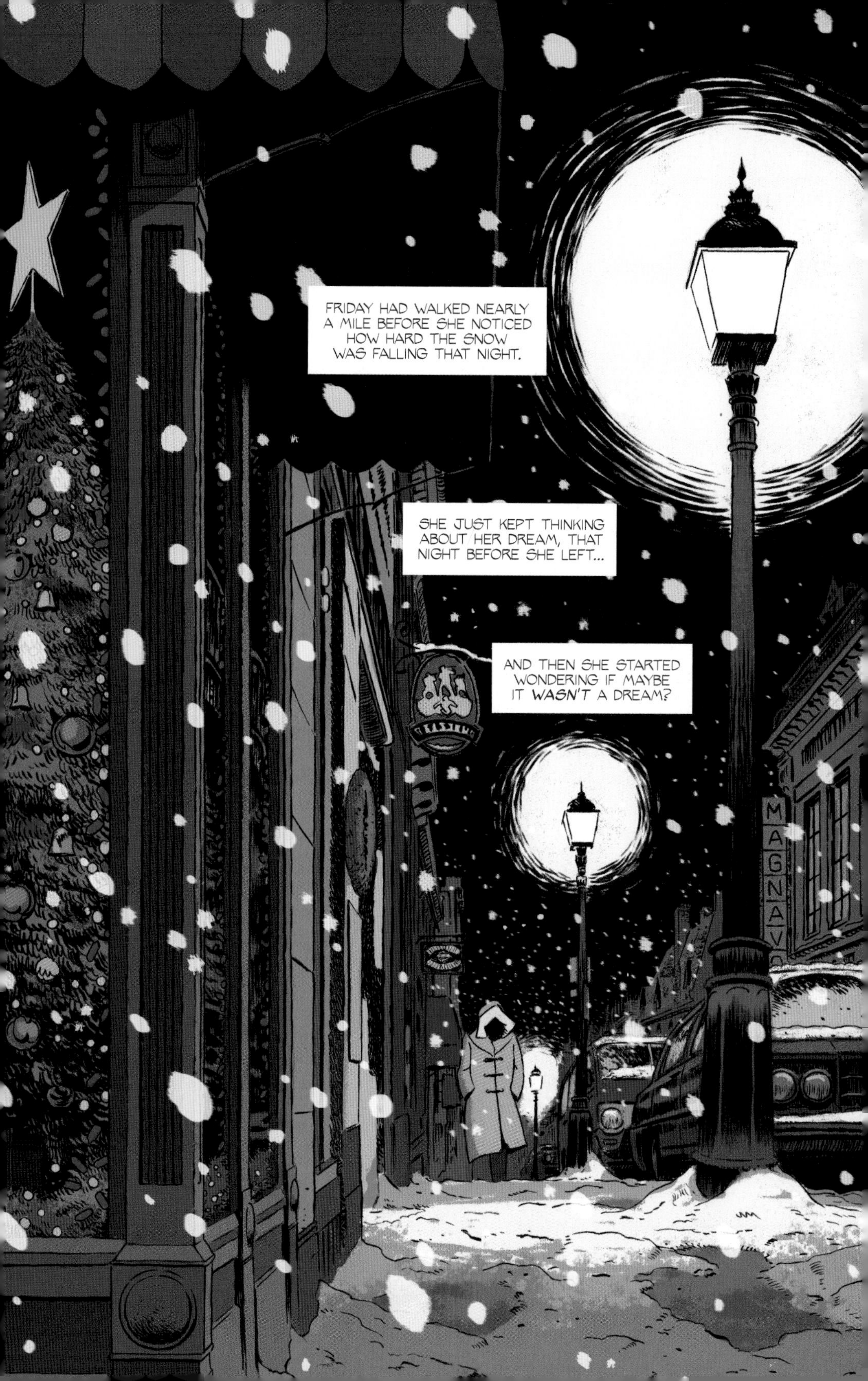
FRIDAY HAD WALKED NEARLY A MILE BEFORE SHE NOTICED HOW HARD THE SNOW WAS FALLING THAT NIGHT.
SHE JUST KEPT THINKING ABOUT HER DREAM, THAT NIGHT BEFORE SHE LEFT...
AND THEN SHE STARTED WONDERING IF MAYBE IT *WASN'T* A DREAM?
MAGNAV

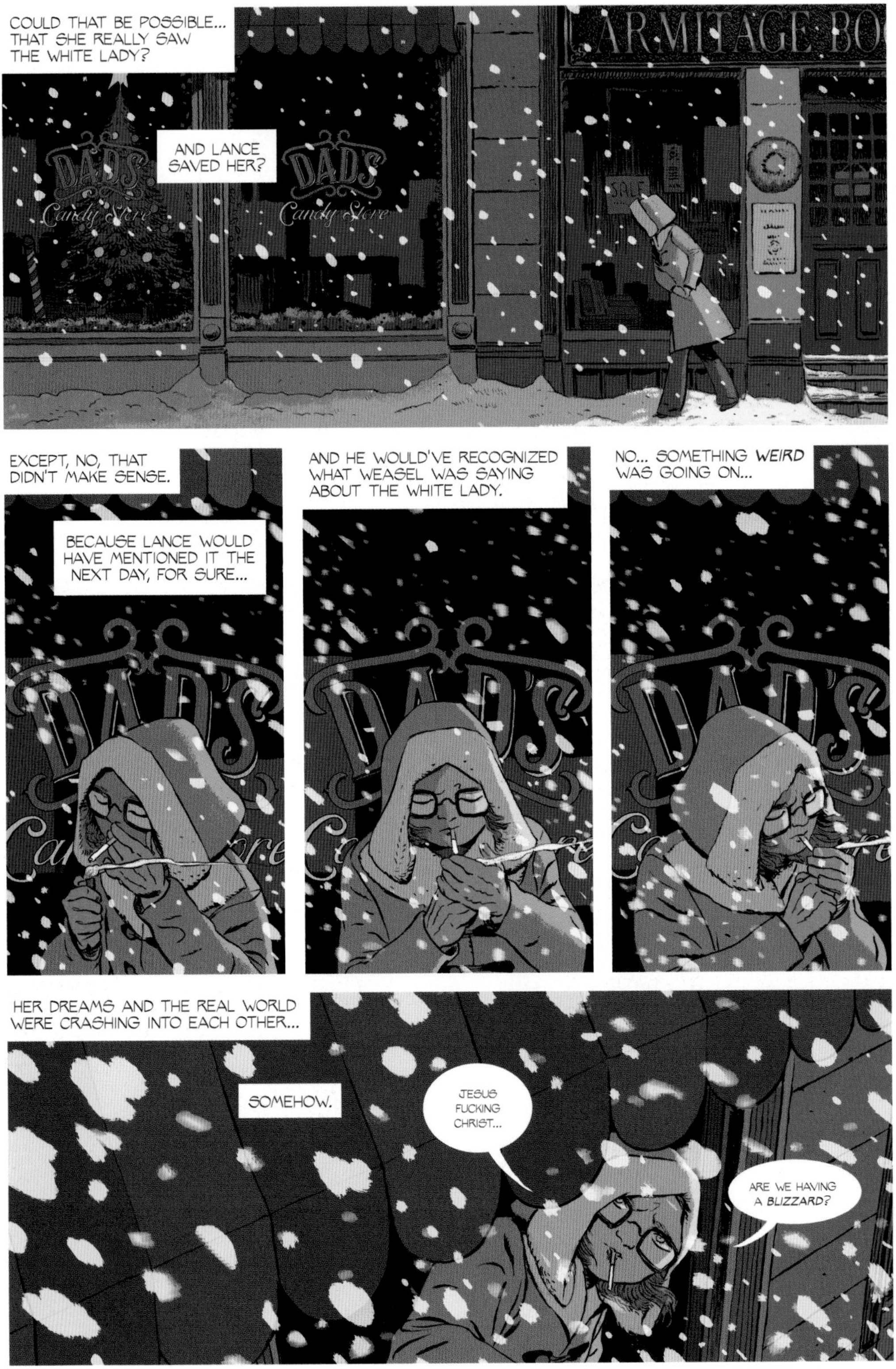
COULD THAT BE POSSIBLE... THAT SHE REALLY SAW THE WHITE LADY?
AND LANCE SAVED HER?
ARMITAGE BO
DAD'S Candy Store
EXCEPT, NO, THAT DIDN'T MAKE SENSE.
BECAUSE LANCE WOULD HAVE MENTIONED IT THE NEXT DAY, FOR SURE...
AND HE WOULD'VE RECOGNIZED WHAT WEASEL WAS SAYING ABOUT THE WHITE LADY.
NO... SOMETHING *WEIRD* WAS GOING ON...
HER DREAMS AND THE REAL WORLD WERE CRASHING INTO EACH OTHER...
SOMEHOW.
JESUS FUCKING CHRIST...
ARE WE HAVING A *BLIZZARD*?

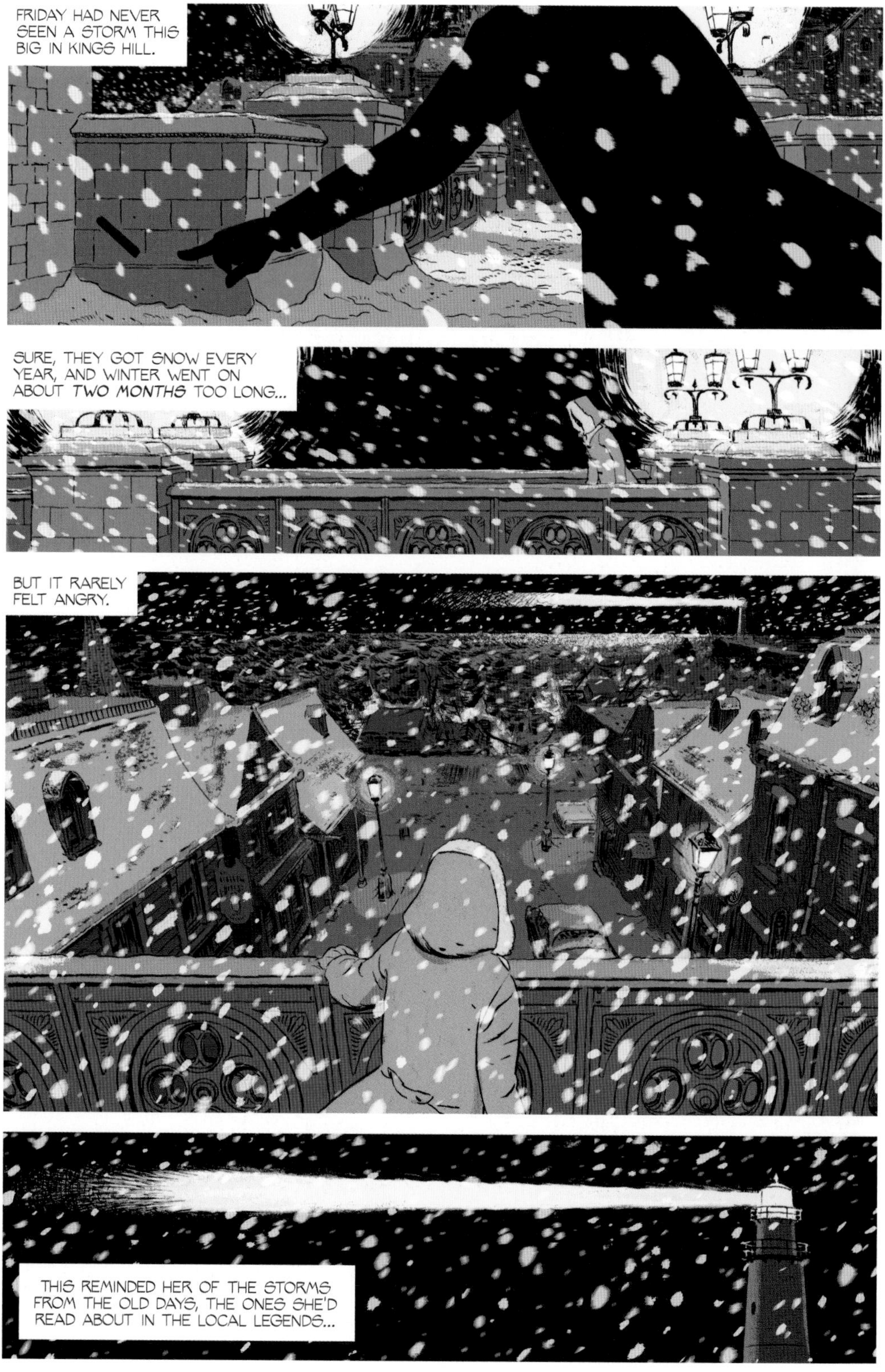
FRIDAY HAD NEVER SEEN A STORM THIS BIG IN KINGS HILL.
SURE, THEY GOT SNOW EVERY YEAR, AND WINTER WENT ON ABOUT *TWO MONTHS* TOO LONG...
BUT IT RARELY FELT ANGRY.
THIS REMINDED HER OF THE STORMS FROM THE OLD DAYS, THE ONES SHE'D READ ABOUT IN THE LOCAL LEGENDS...

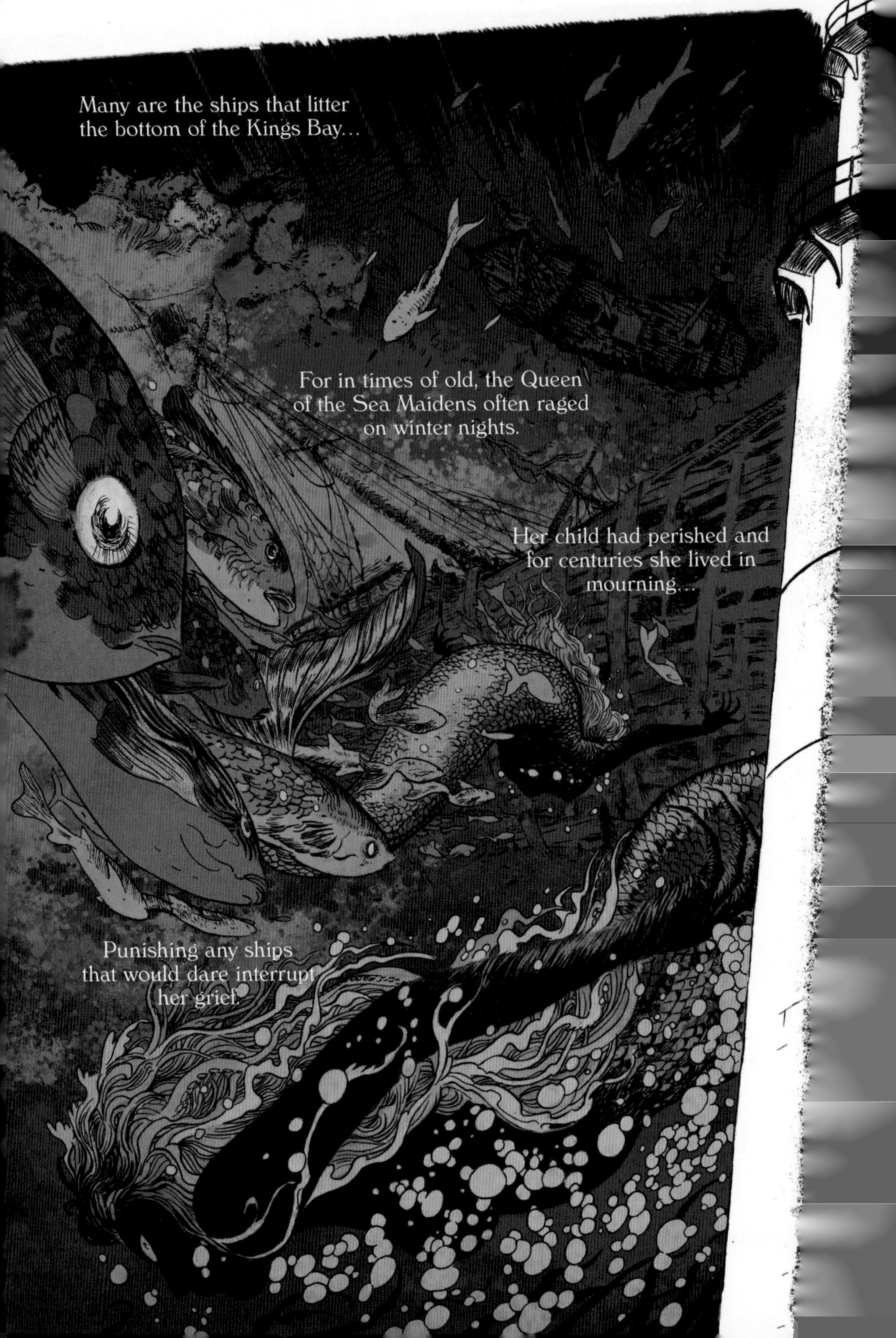
Many are the ships that litter the bottom of the Kings Bay...
For in times of old, the Queen of the Sea Maidens often raged on winter nights.
Her child had perished and for centuries she lived in mourning...
Punishing any ships that would dare interrupt her grief.

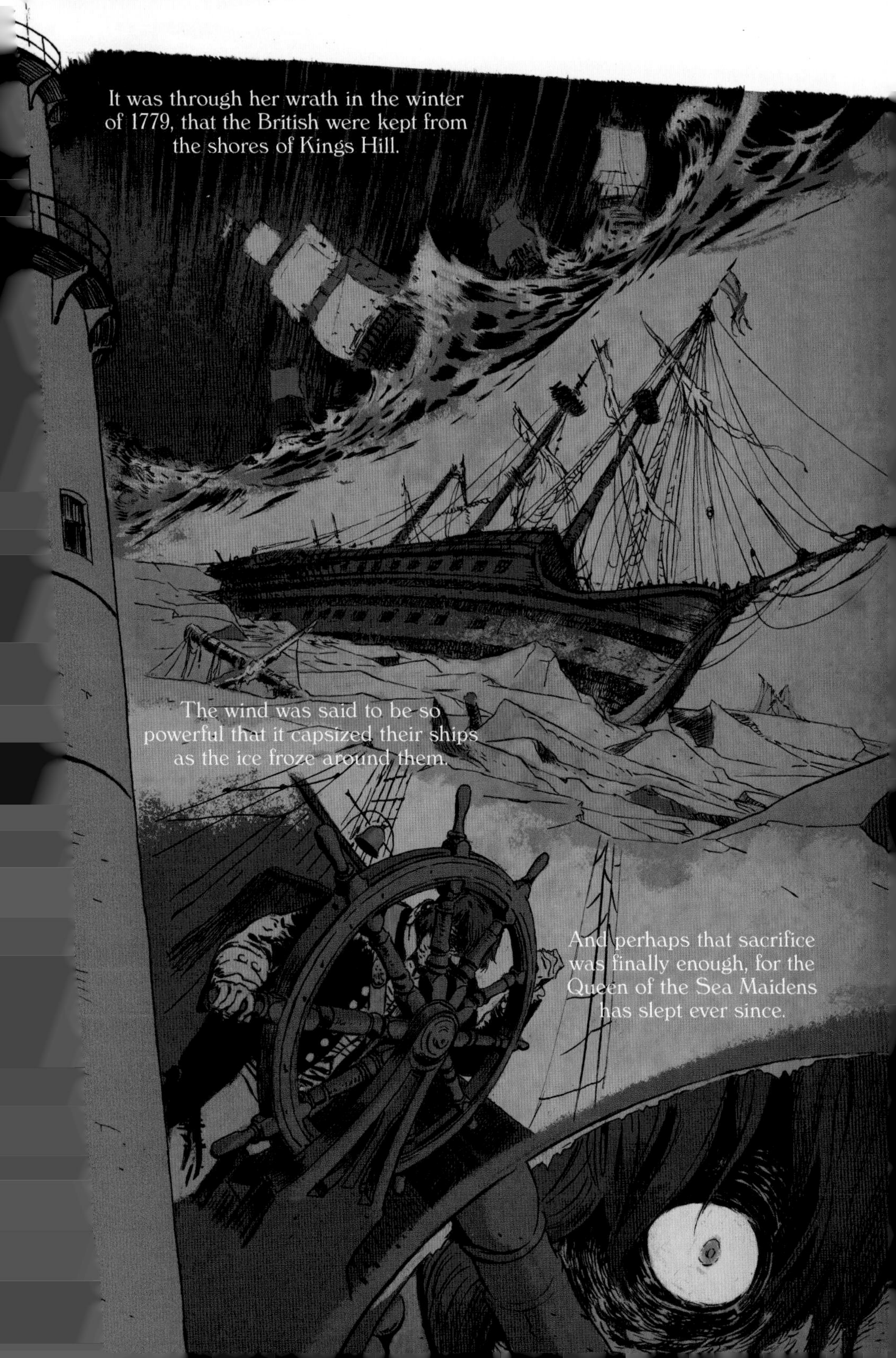
It was through her wrath in the winter of 1779, that the British were kept from the shores of Kings Hill.
The wind was said to be so powerful that it capsized their ships as the ice froze around them.
And perhaps that sacrifice was finally enough, for the Queen of the Sea Maidens has slept ever since.

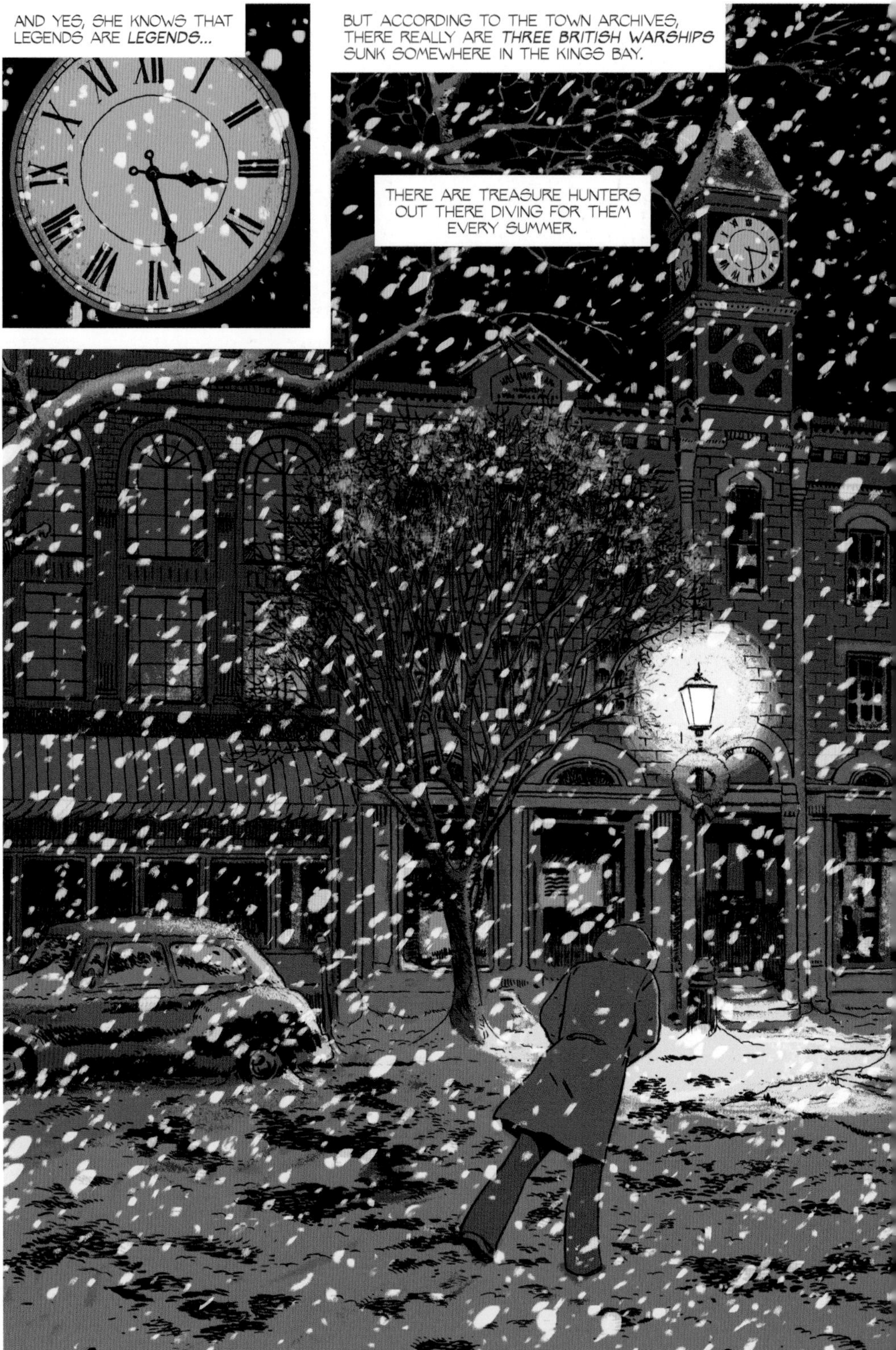
AND YES, SHE KNOWS THAT LEGENDS ARE *LEGENDS*...
BUT ACCORDING TO THE TOWN ARCHIVES, THERE REALLY ARE *THREE BRITISH WARSHIPS* SUNK SOMEWHERE IN THE KINGS BAY.
THERE ARE TREASURE HUNTERS OUT THERE DIVING FOR THEM EVERY SUMMER.

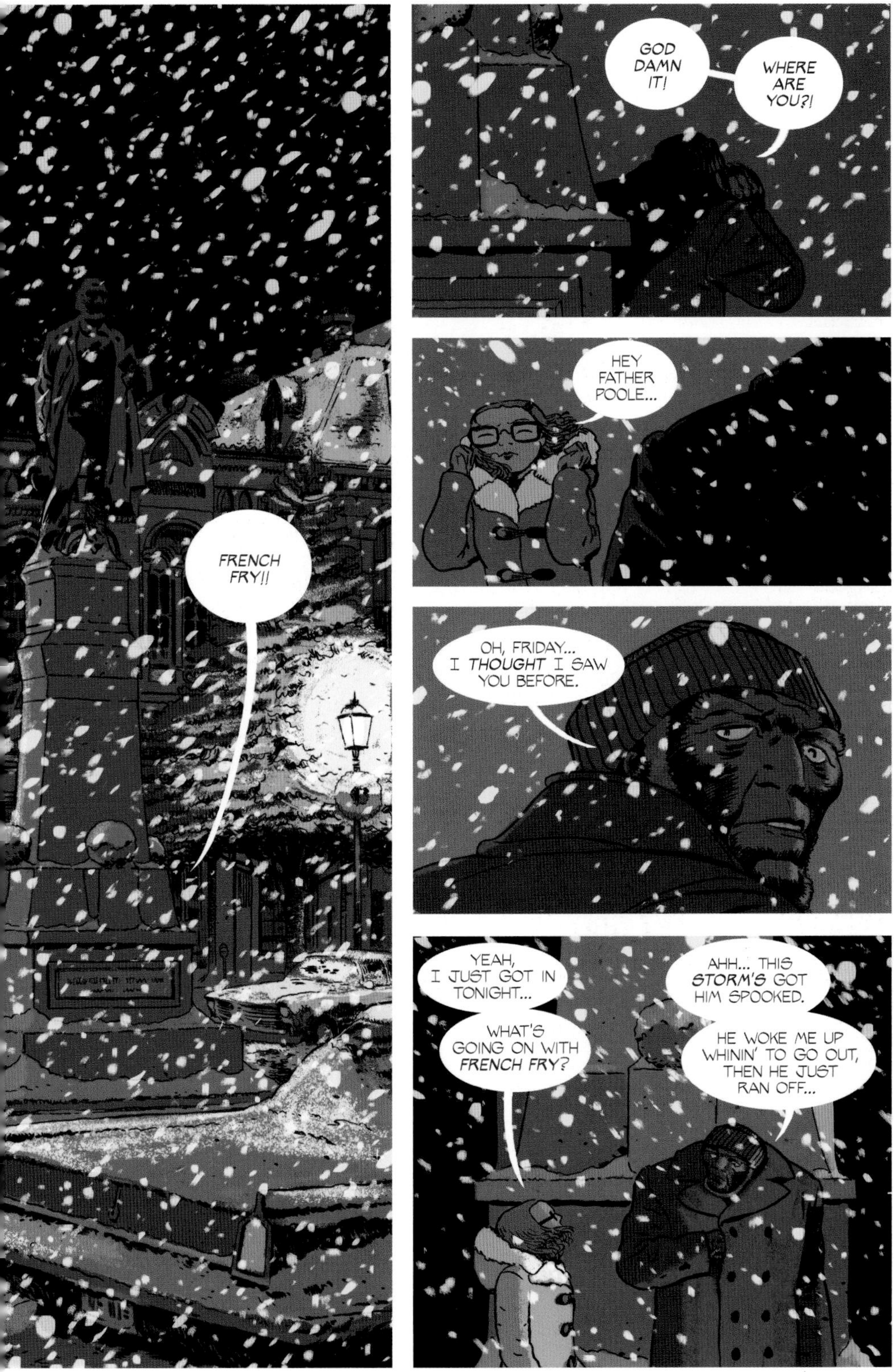
FRENCH FRY!!
GOD DAMN IT!
WHERE ARE YOU?!
HEY FATHER POOLE...
OH, FRIDAY... I *THOUGHT* I SAW YOU BEFORE.
YEAH, I JUST GOT IN TONIGHT...
WHAT'S GOING ON WITH *FRENCH FRY*?
AHH... THIS *STORM'S* GOT HIM SPOOKED.
HE WOKE ME UP WHININ' TO GO OUT, THEN HE JUST RAN OFF...

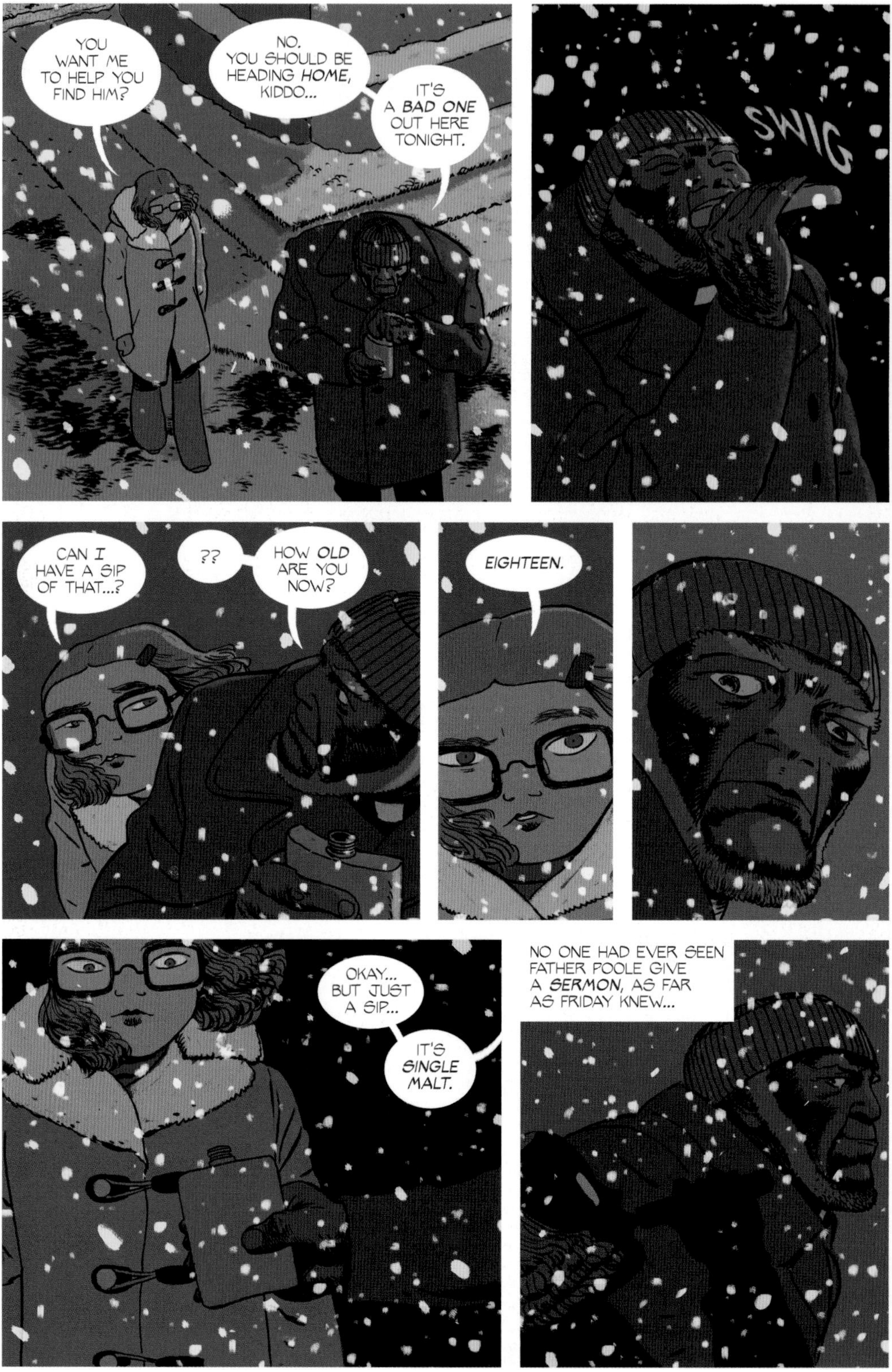
YOU WANT ME TO HELP YOU FIND HIM?
NO. YOU SHOULD BE HEADING HOME, KIDDO...
IT'S A BAD ONE OUT HERE TONIGHT.
SWIG
CAN I HAVE A SIP OF THAT...?
??
HOW OLD ARE YOU NOW?
EIGHTEEN.
OKAY... BUT JUST A SIP...
IT'S SINGLE MALT.
NO ONE HAD EVER SEEN FATHER POOLE GIVE A SERMON, AS FAR AS FRIDAY KNEW...

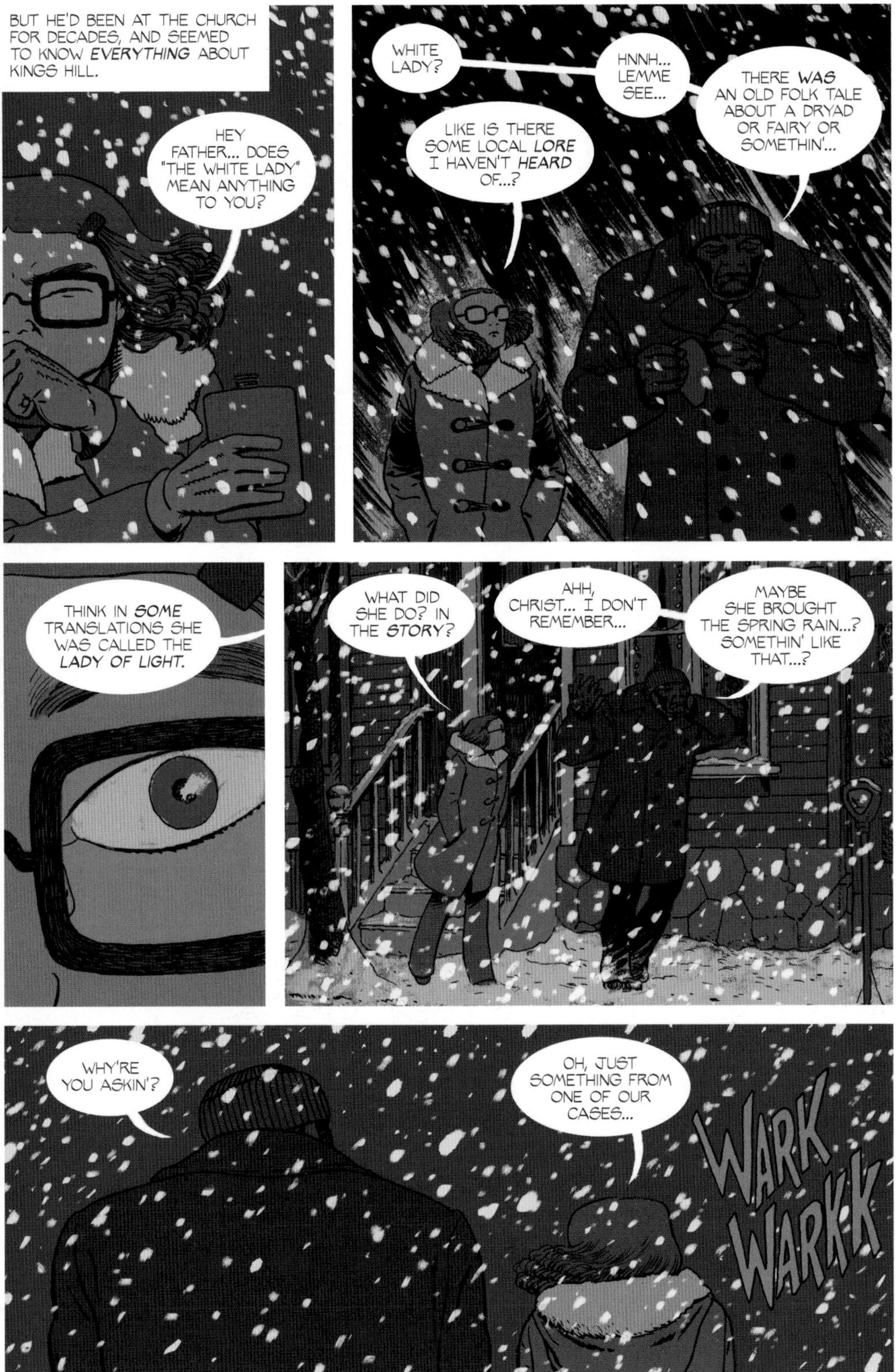
BUT HE'D BEEN AT THE CHURCH FOR DECADES, AND SEEMED TO KNOW EVERYTHING ABOUT KINGS HILL.
HEY FATHER... DOES "THE WHITE LADY" MEAN ANYTHING TO YOU?
WHITE LADY?
LIKE IS THERE SOME LOCAL LORE I HAVEN'T HEARD OF...?
HNNH... LEMME SEE...
THERE WAS AN OLD FOLK TALE ABOUT A DRYAD OR FAIRY OR SOMETHIN'...
THINK IN SOME TRANSLATIONS SHE WAS CALLED THE LADY OF LIGHT.
WHAT DID SHE DO? IN THE STORY?
AHH, CHRIST... I DON'T REMEMBER...
MAYBE SHE BROUGHT THE SPRING RAIN...? SOMETHIN' LIKE THAT...?
WHY'RE YOU ASKIN'?
OH, JUST SOMETHING FROM ONE OF OUR CASES...
WARK WARKK

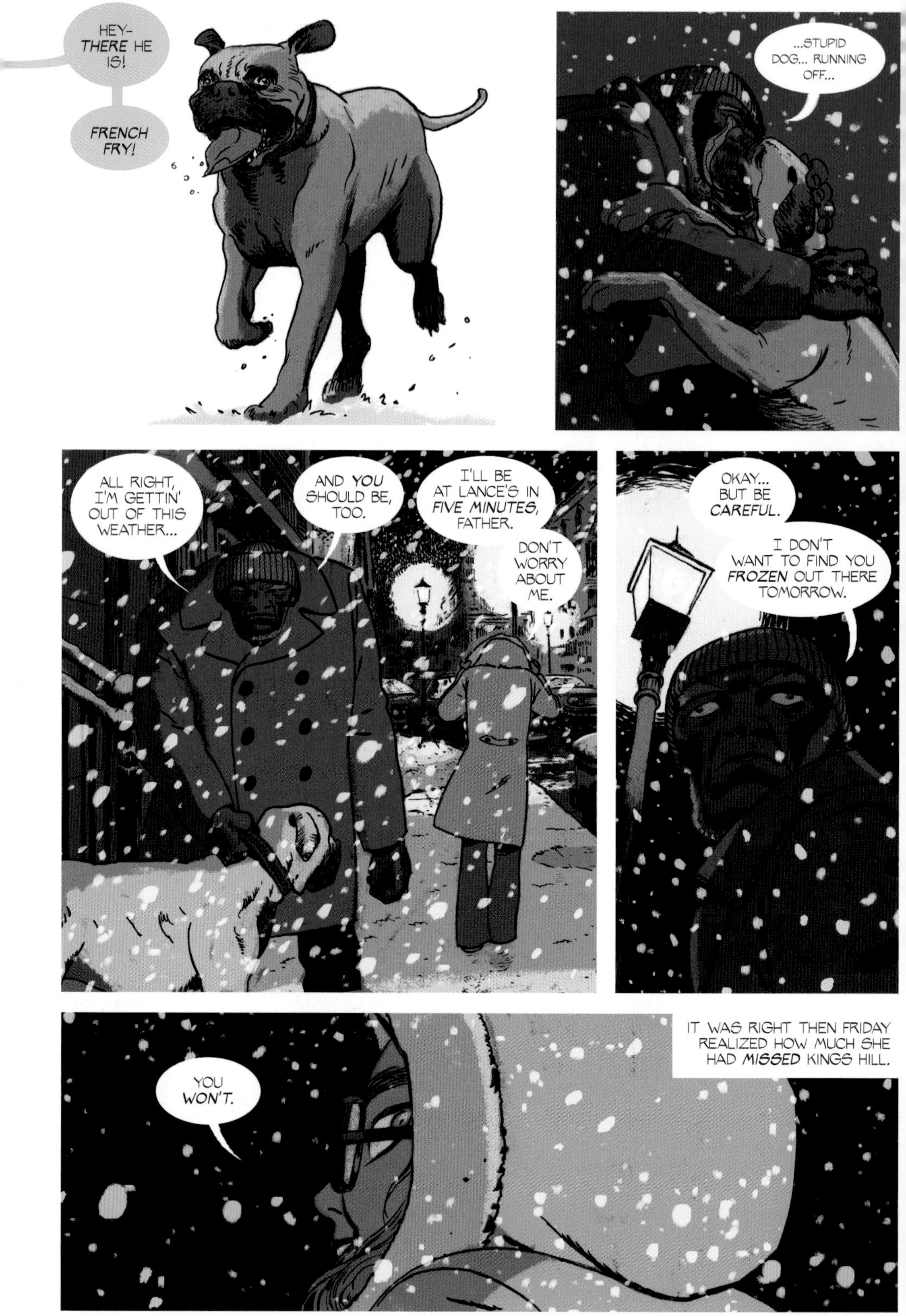
HEY- THERE HE IS!
FRENCH FRY!
...STUPID DOG... RUNNING OFF...
ALL RIGHT, I'M GETTIN' OUT OF THIS WEATHER...
AND YOU SHOULD BE, TOO.
I'LL BE AT LANCE'S IN FIVE MINUTES, FATHER.
DON'T WORRY ABOUT ME.
OKAY... BUT BE CAREFUL.
I DON'T WANT TO FIND YOU FROZEN OUT THERE TOMORROW.
IT WAS RIGHT THEN FRIDAY REALIZED HOW MUCH SHE HAD MISSED KINGS HILL.
YOU WON'T.

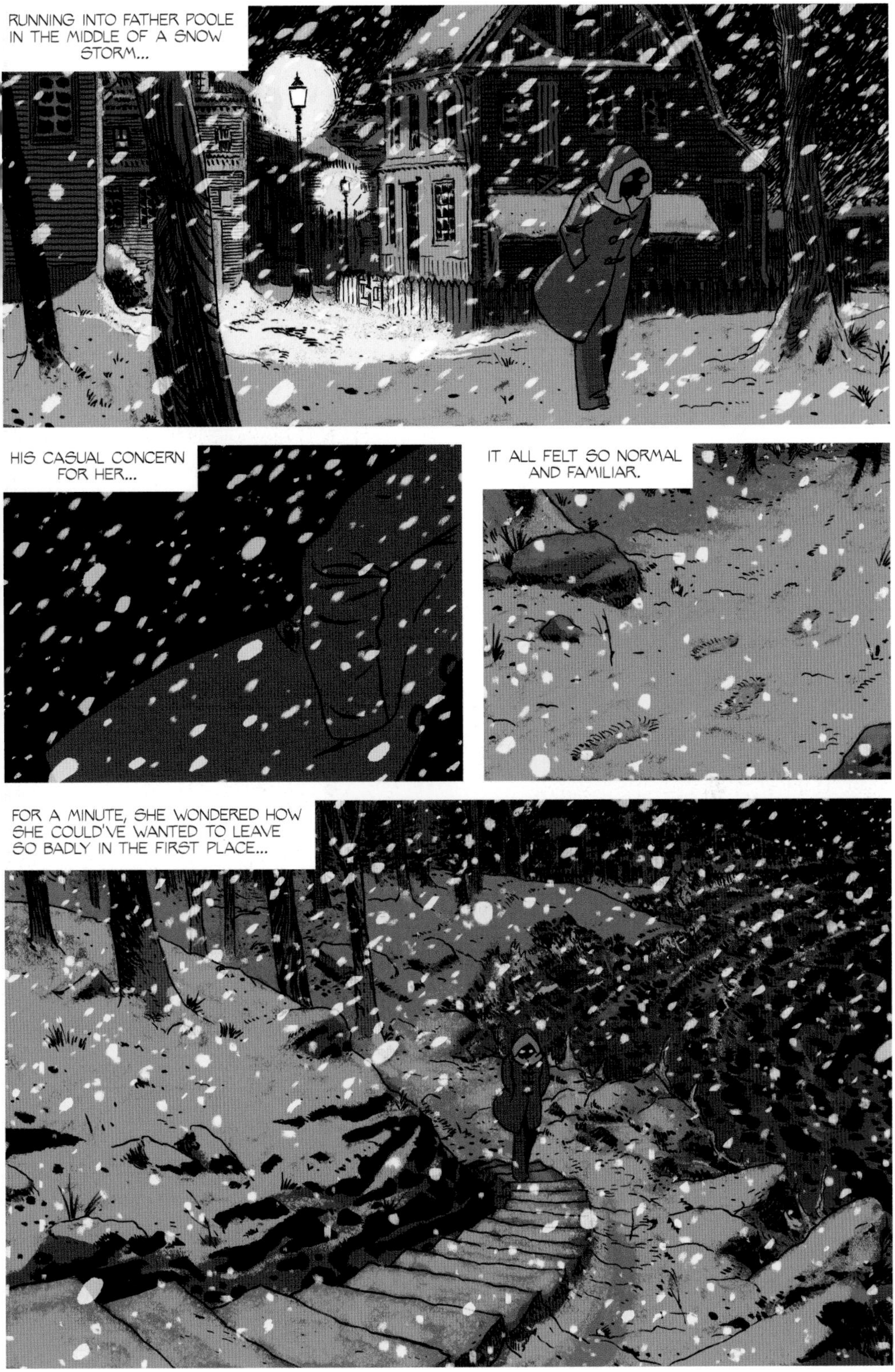
RUNNING INTO FATHER POOLE IN THE MIDDLE OF A SNOW STORM...
HIS CASUAL CONCERN FOR HER...
IT ALL FELT SO NORMAL AND FAMILIAR.
FOR A MINUTE, SHE WONDERED HOW SHE COULD'VE WANTED TO LEAVE SO BADLY IN THE FIRST PLACE...

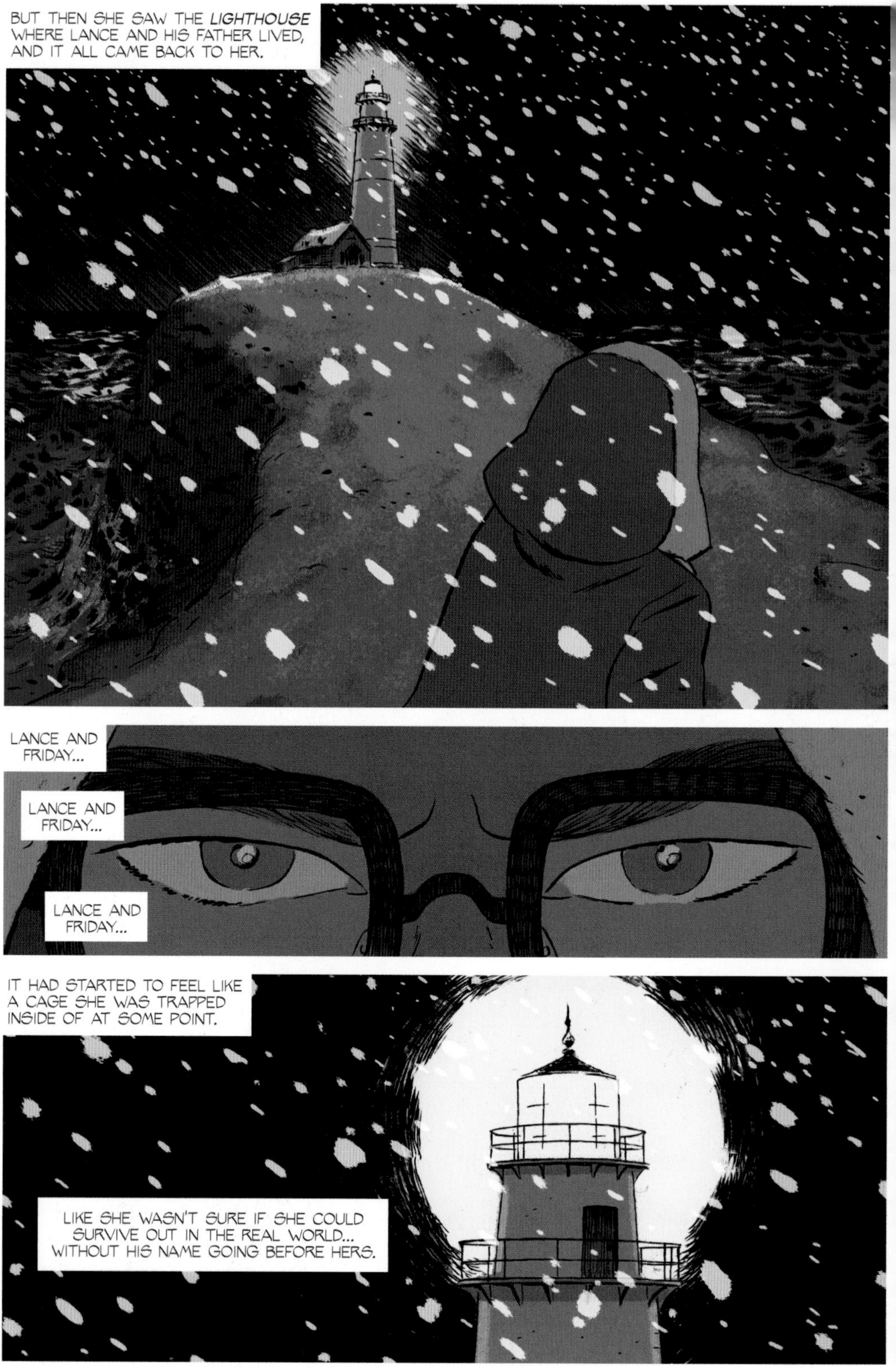
BUT THEN SHE SAW THE *LIGHTHOUSE* WHERE LANCE AND HIS FATHER LIVED, AND IT ALL CAME BACK TO HER.
LANCE AND FRIDAY...
LANCE AND FRIDAY...
LANCE AND FRIDAY...
IT HAD STARTED TO FEEL LIKE A CAGE SHE WAS TRAPPED INSIDE OF AT SOME POINT.
LIKE SHE WASN'T SURE IF SHE COULD SURVIVE OUT IN THE REAL WORLD... WITHOUT HIS NAME GOING BEFORE HERS.

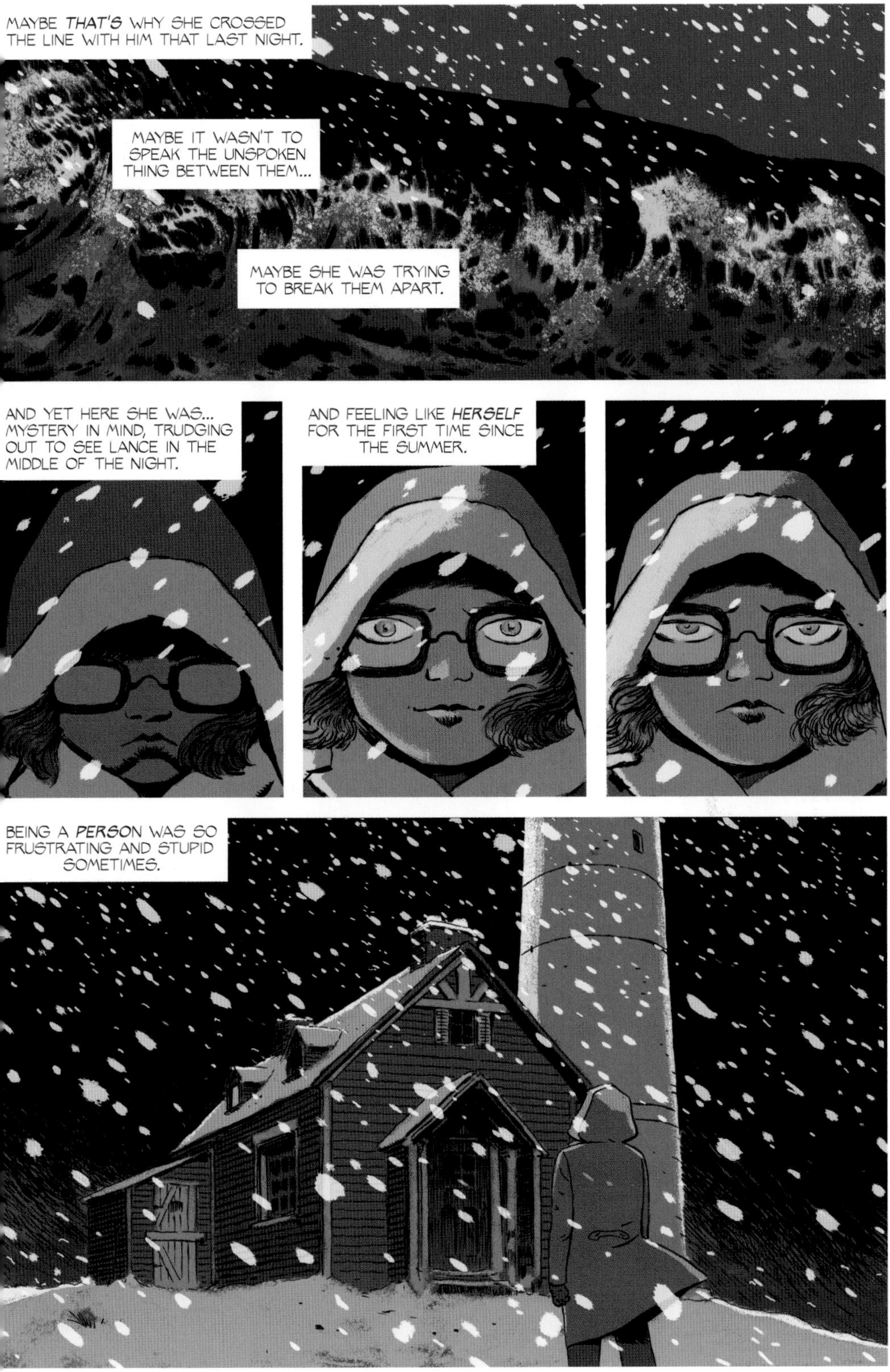
MAYBE *THAT'S* WHY SHE CROSSED THE LINE WITH HIM THAT LAST NIGHT.
MAYBE IT WASN'T TO SPEAK THE UNSPOKEN THING BETWEEN THEM...
MAYBE SHE WAS TRYING TO BREAK THEM APART.
AND YET HERE SHE WAS... MYSTERY IN MIND, TRUDGING OUT TO SEE LANCE IN THE MIDDLE OF THE NIGHT.
AND FEELING LIKE *HERSELF* FOR THE FIRST TIME SINCE THE SUMMER.
BEING A *PERSON* WAS SO FRUSTRATING AND STUPID SOMETIMES.

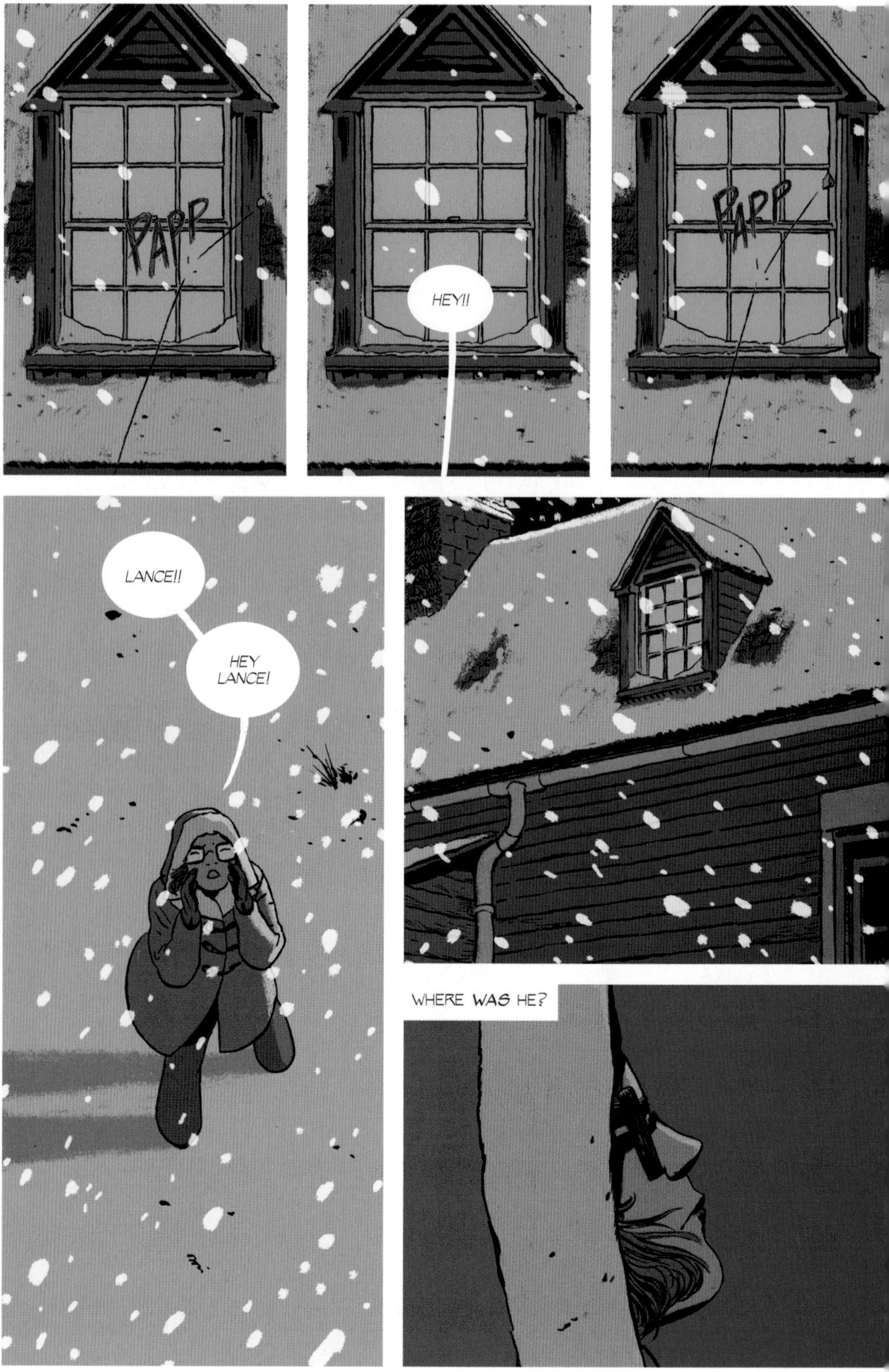
PAPP
HEY!!
PAPP
LANCE!!
HEY LANCE!
WHERE WAS HE?

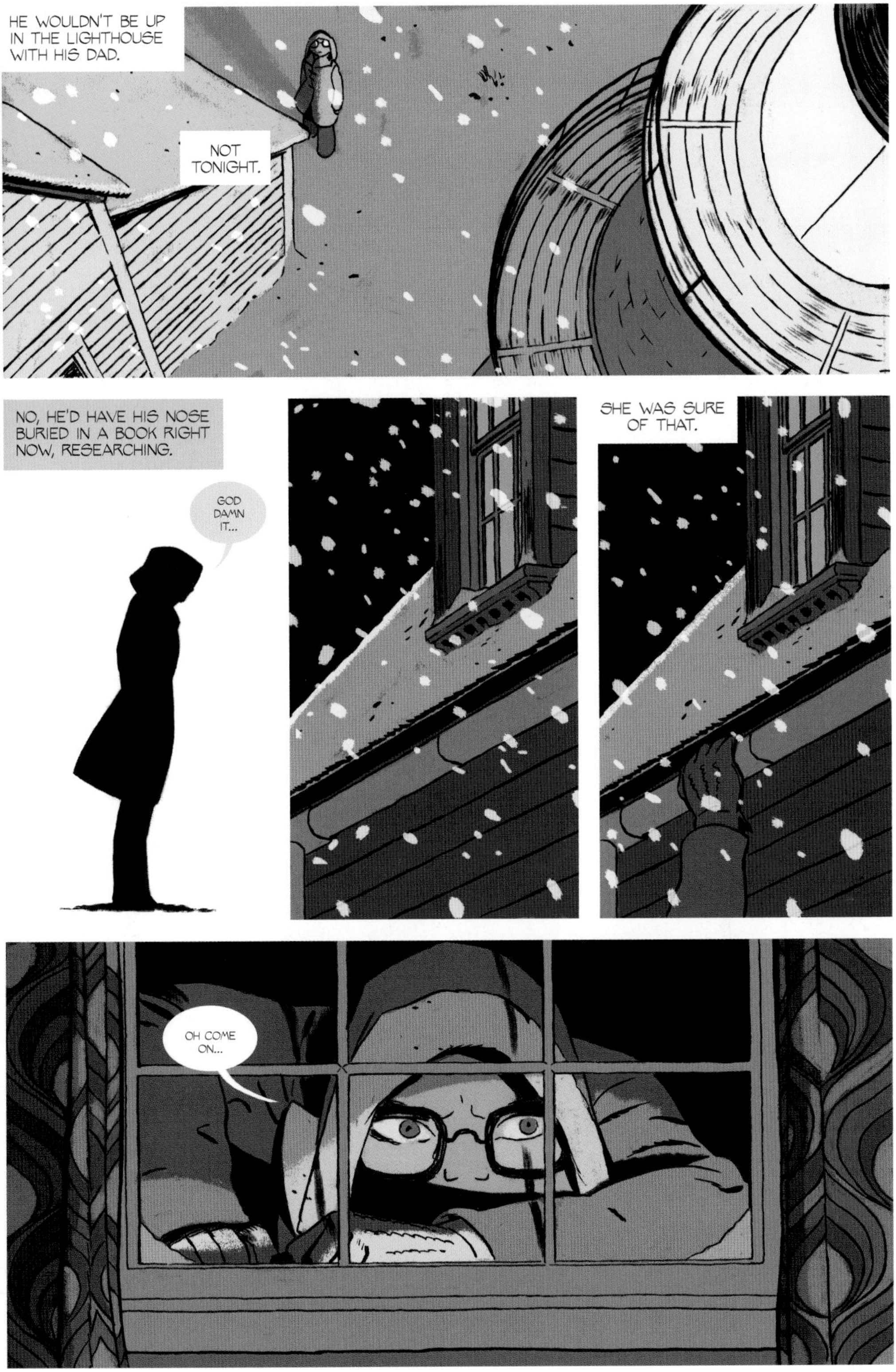
HE WOULDN'T BE UP IN THE LIGHTHOUSE WITH HIS DAD.
NOT TONIGHT.
NO, HE'D HAVE HIS NOSE BURIED IN A BOOK RIGHT NOW, RESEARCHING.
GOD DAMN IT...
SHE WAS SURE OF THAT.
OH COME ON...

LANCE WENT OUT INTO THIS BLIZZARD, TOO?

...YOU'VE GOT TO BE *KIDDING* ME.

WHY? WHAT WAS *HIS* BRAINSTORM?

MAYBE HIS RESEARCH WOULD GIVE HER A CLUE...

X-RAY

OR...

THAT *PRESUMPTUOUS* FUCKER...

Friday

OF COURSE.

OF COURSE IT COULDN'T BE *EASY*.

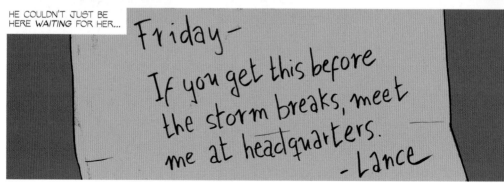

HE COULDN'T JUST BE HERE *WAITING* FOR HER...

Friday—
If you get this before
the storm breaks, meet
me at headquarters.
—Lance

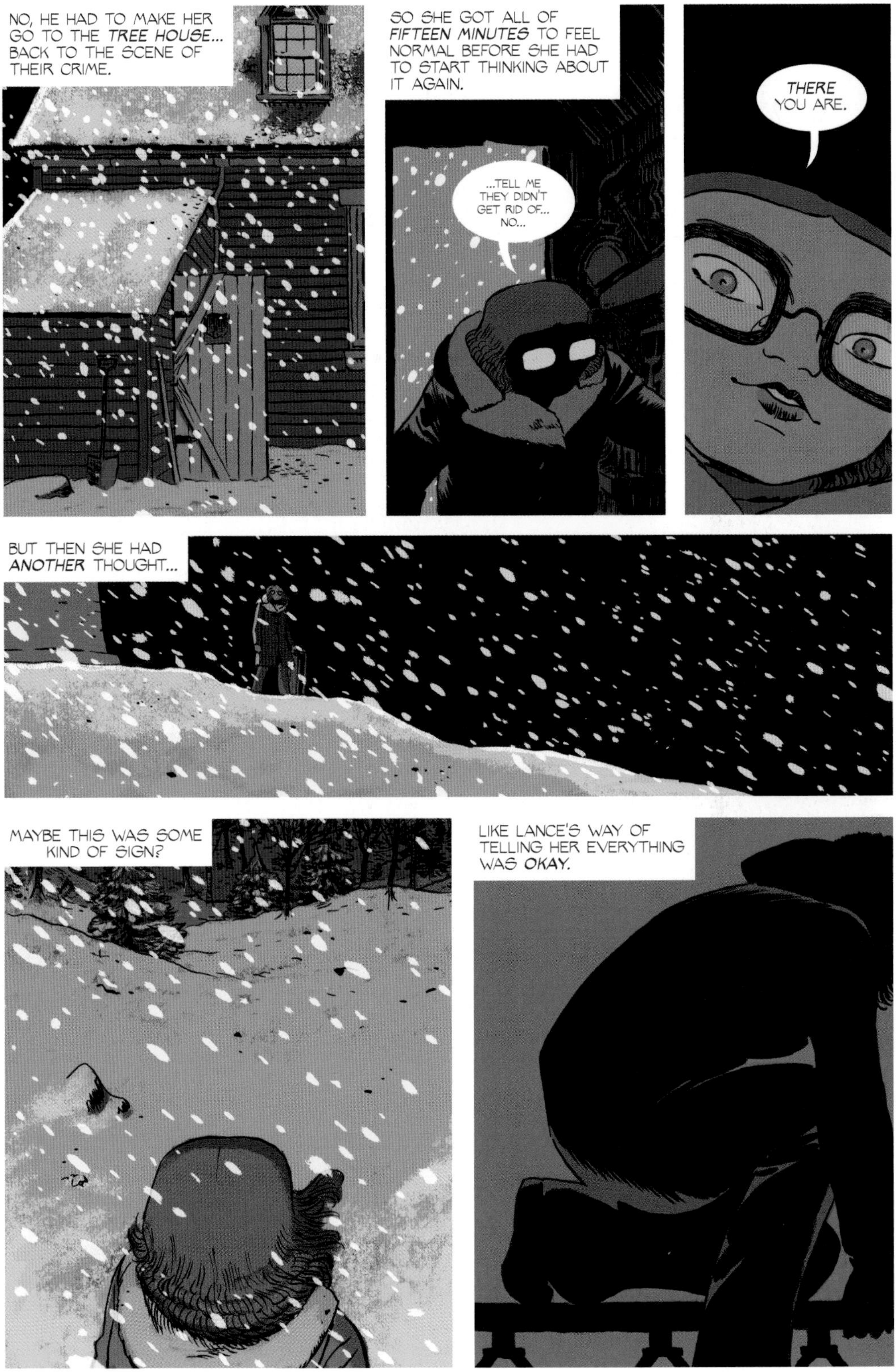

NO, HE HAD TO MAKE HER GO TO THE TREE HOUSE... BACK TO THE SCENE OF THEIR CRIME.
SO SHE GOT ALL OF FIFTEEN MINUTES TO FEEL NORMAL BEFORE SHE HAD TO START THINKING ABOUT IT AGAIN.
...TELL ME THEY DIDN'T GET RID OF... NO...
THERE YOU ARE.
BUT THEN SHE HAD ANOTHER THOUGHT...
MAYBE THIS WAS SOME KIND OF SIGN?
LIKE LANCE'S WAY OF TELLING HER EVERYTHING WAS OKAY.

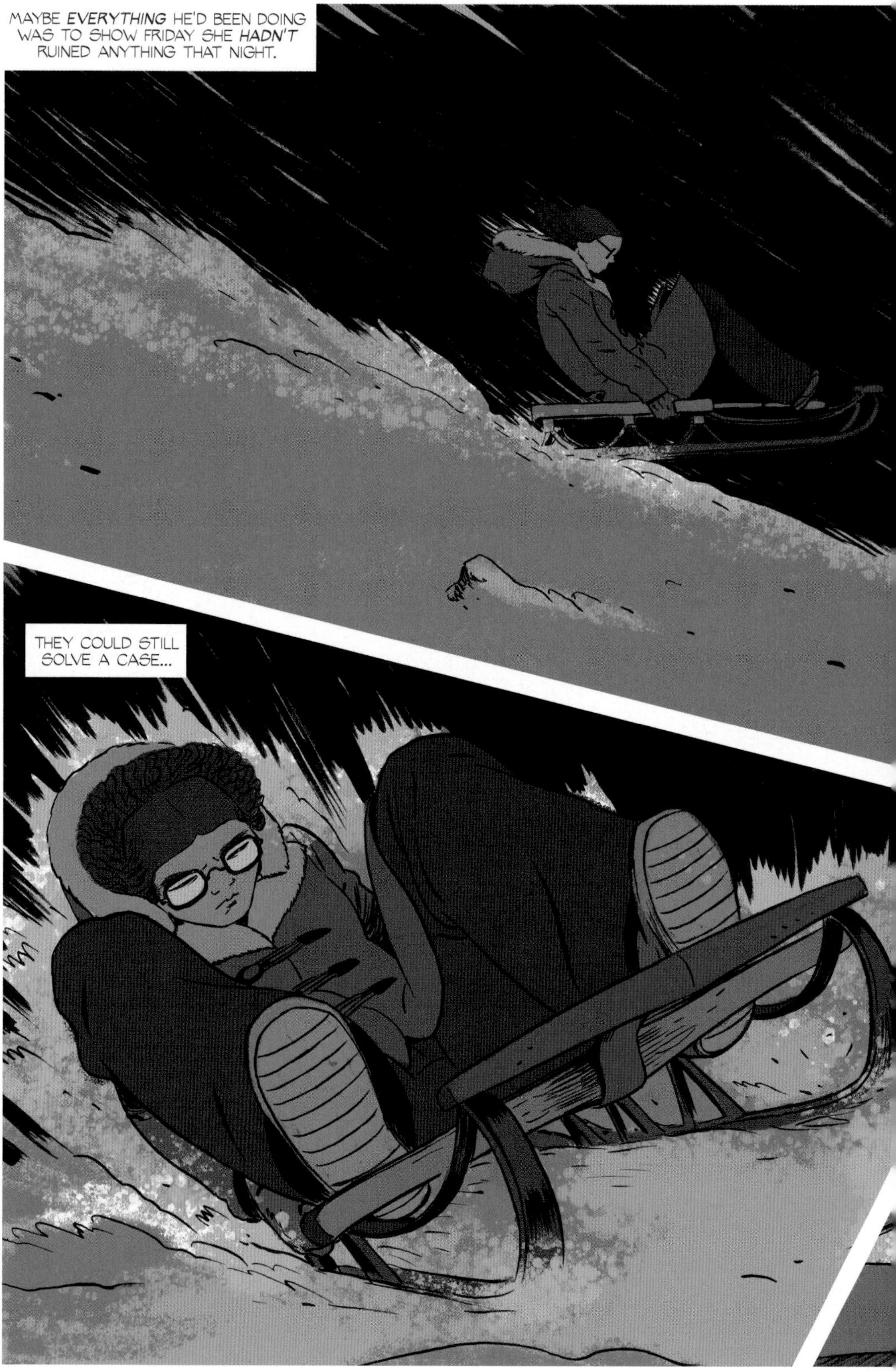
MAYBE *EVERYTHING* HE'D BEEN DOING WAS TO SHOW FRIDAY SHE *HADN'T* RUINED ANYTHING THAT NIGHT.
THEY COULD STILL SOLVE A CASE...

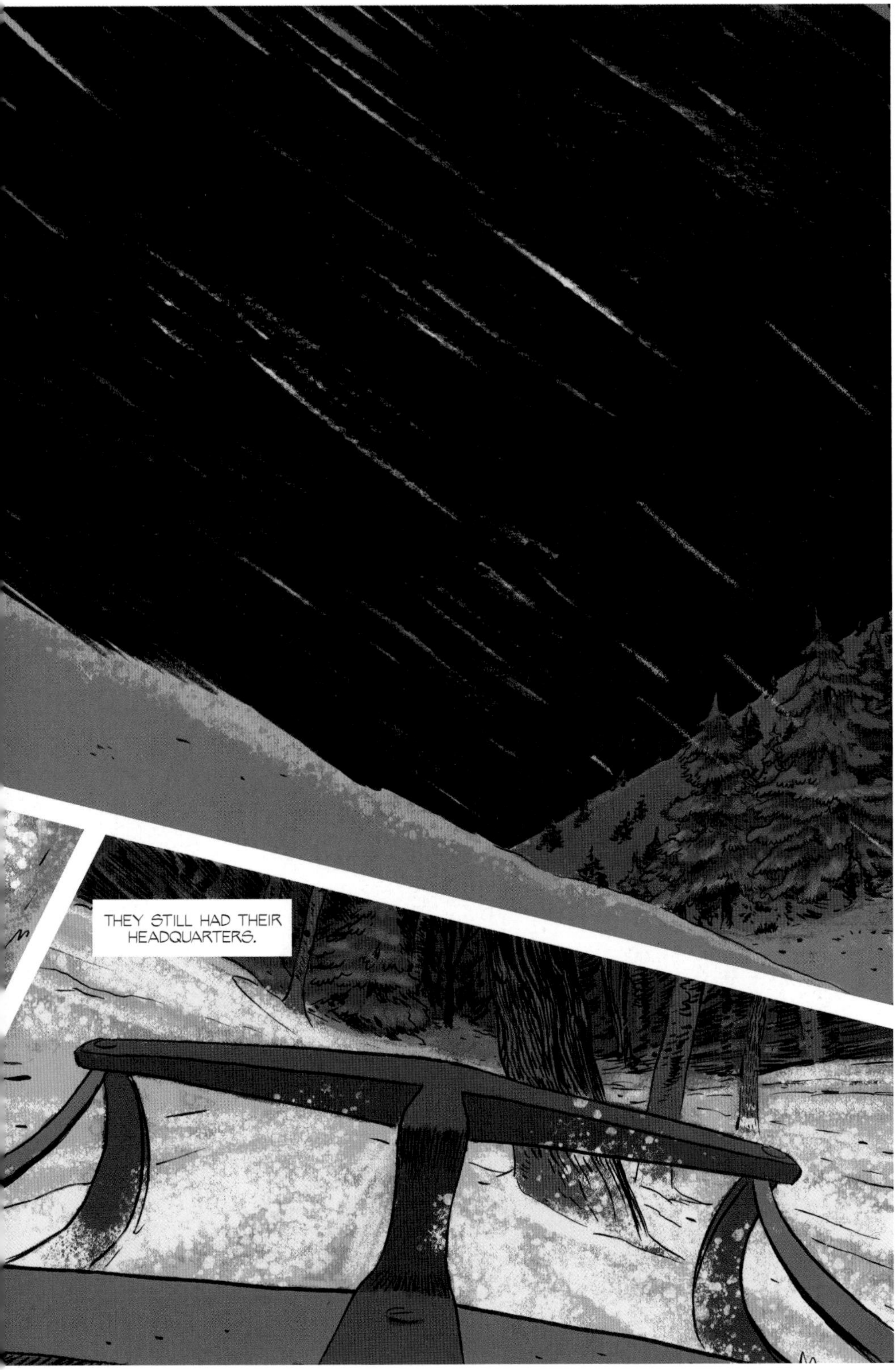
THEY STILL HAD THEIR HEADQUARTERS.

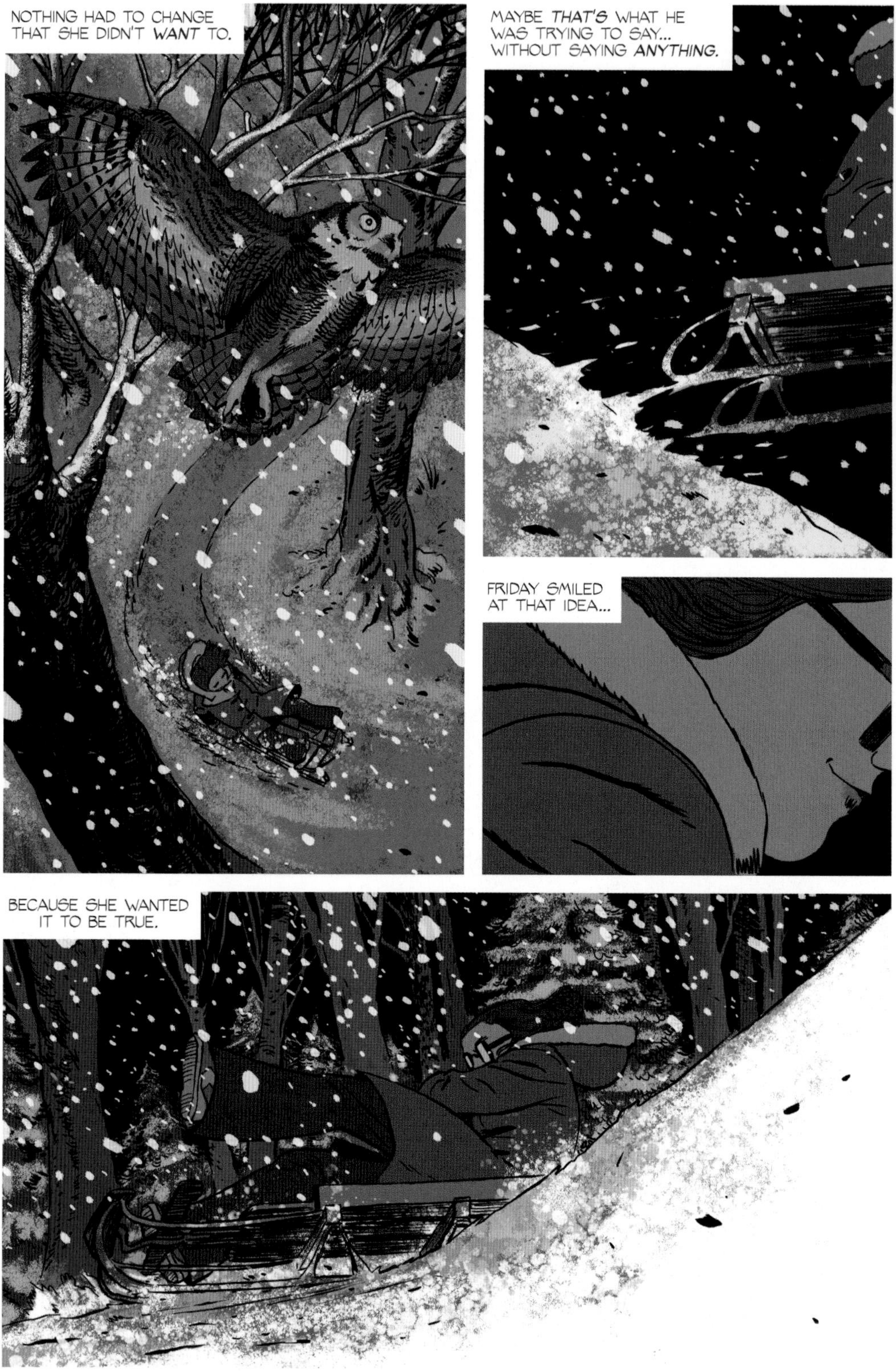
NOTHING HAD TO CHANGE THAT SHE DIDN'T *WANT* TO.
MAYBE *THAT'S* WHAT HE WAS TRYING TO SAY... WITHOUT SAYING *ANYTHING.*
FRIDAY SMILED AT THAT IDEA...
BECAUSE SHE WANTED IT TO BE TRUE.

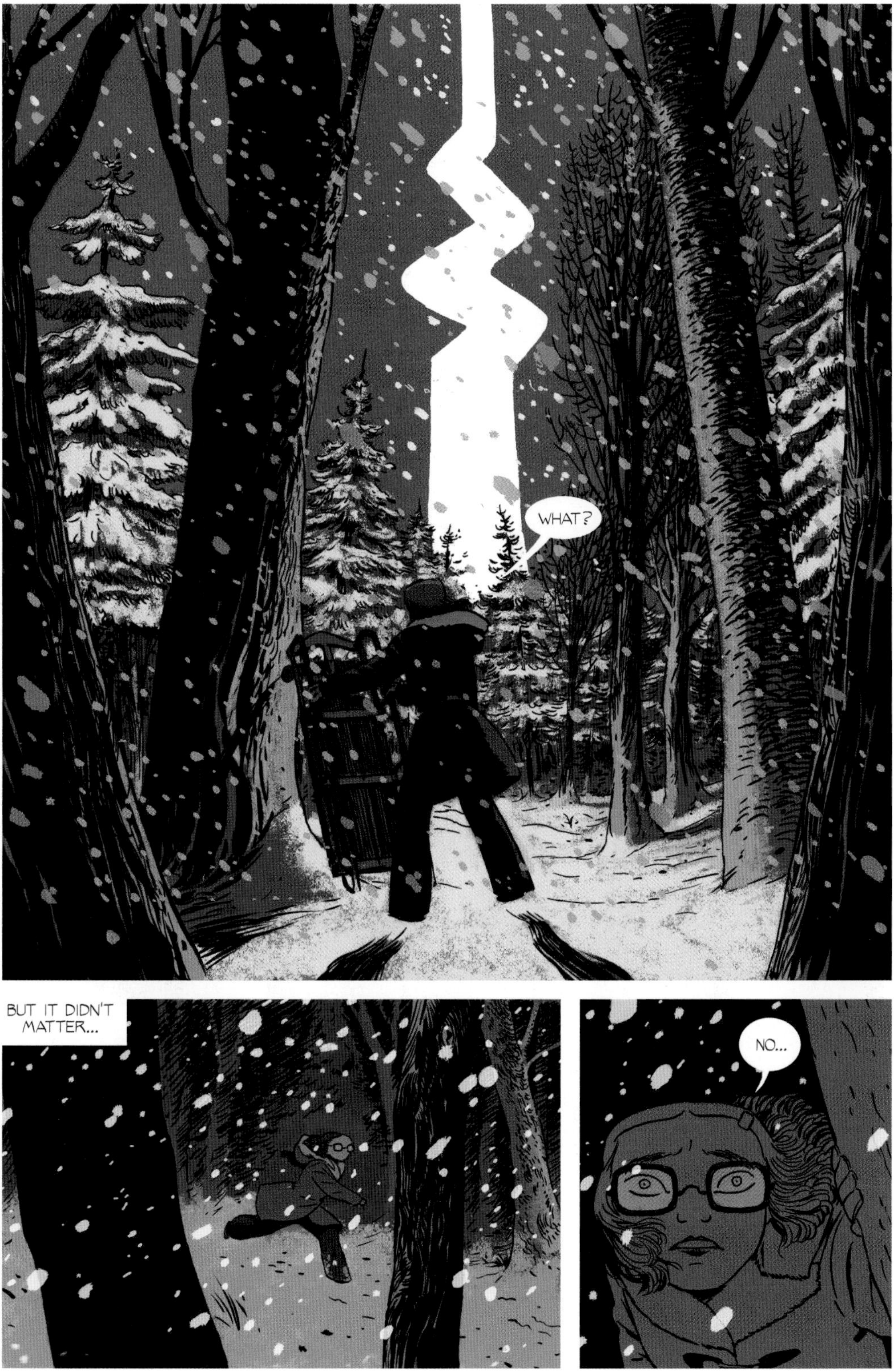
WHAT?
BUT IT DIDN'T MATTER...
NO...

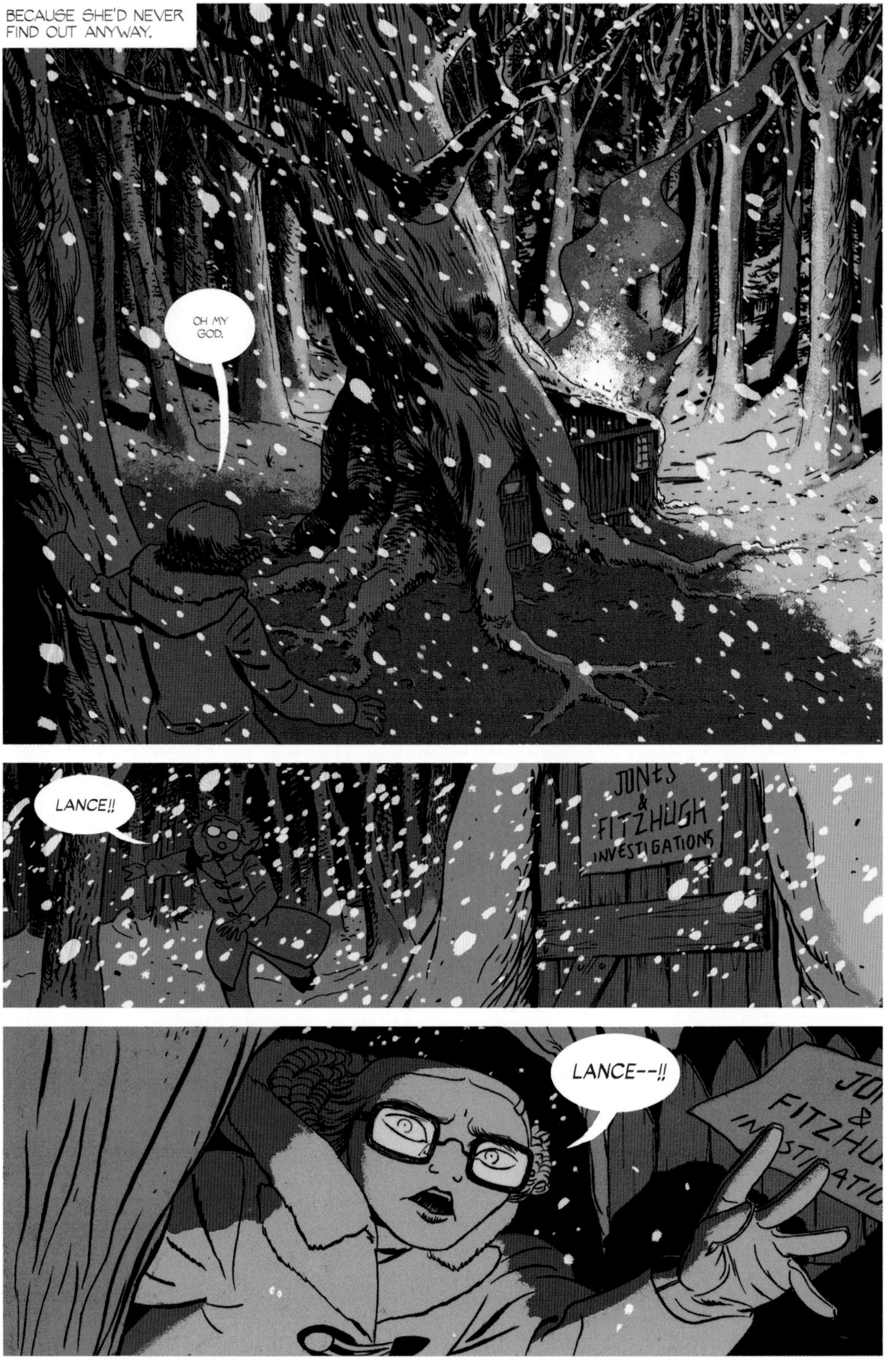
BECAUSE SHE'D NEVER FIND OUT ANYWAY.
OH MY GOD.
LANCE!!
JONES & FITZHUGH INVESTIGATIONS
LANCE--!!

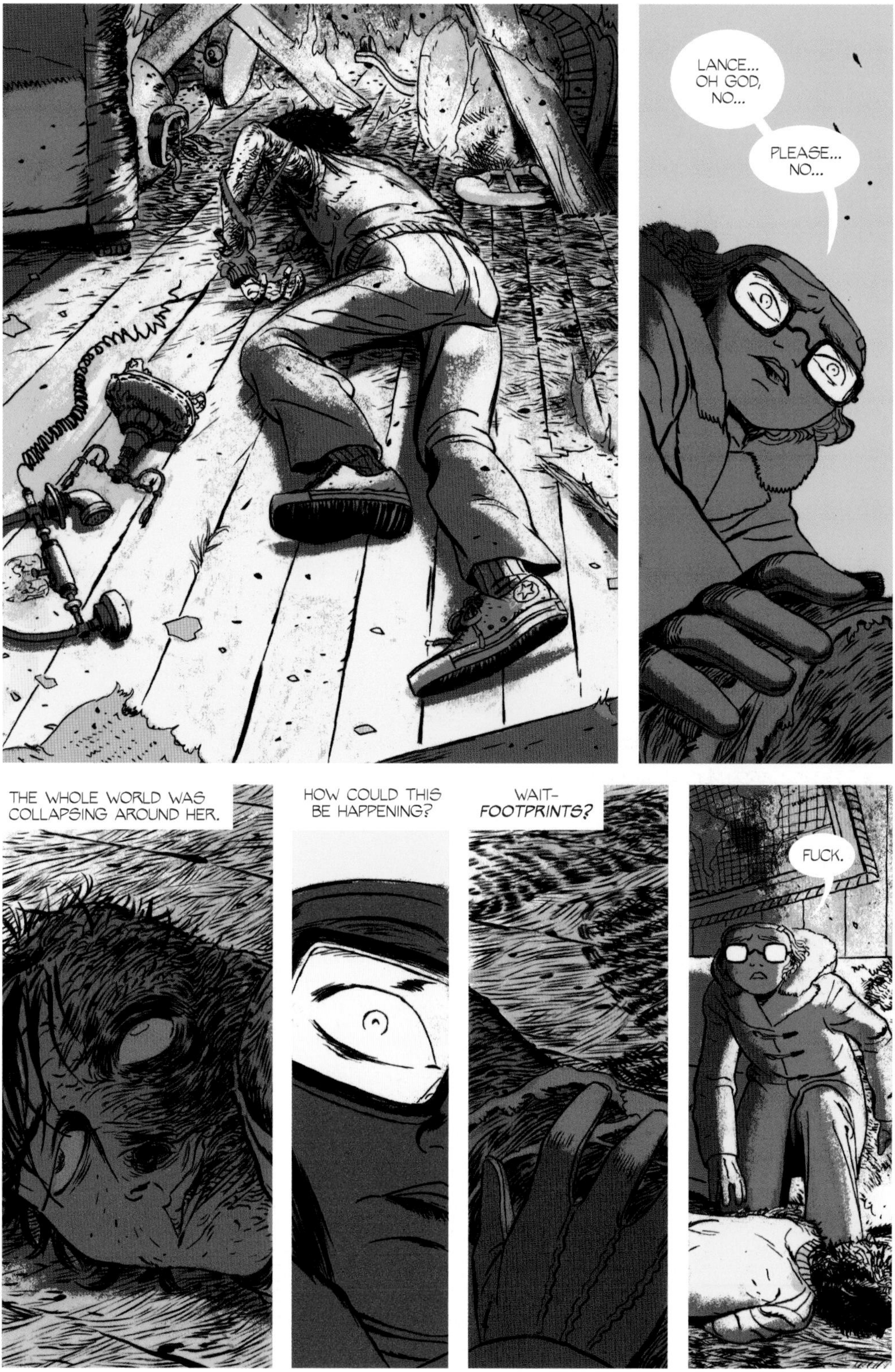
LANCE... OH GOD, NO...
PLEASE... NO...
THE WHOLE WORLD WAS COLLAPSING AROUND HER.
HOW COULD THIS BE HAPPENING?
WAIT- *FOOTPRINTS?*
FUCK.

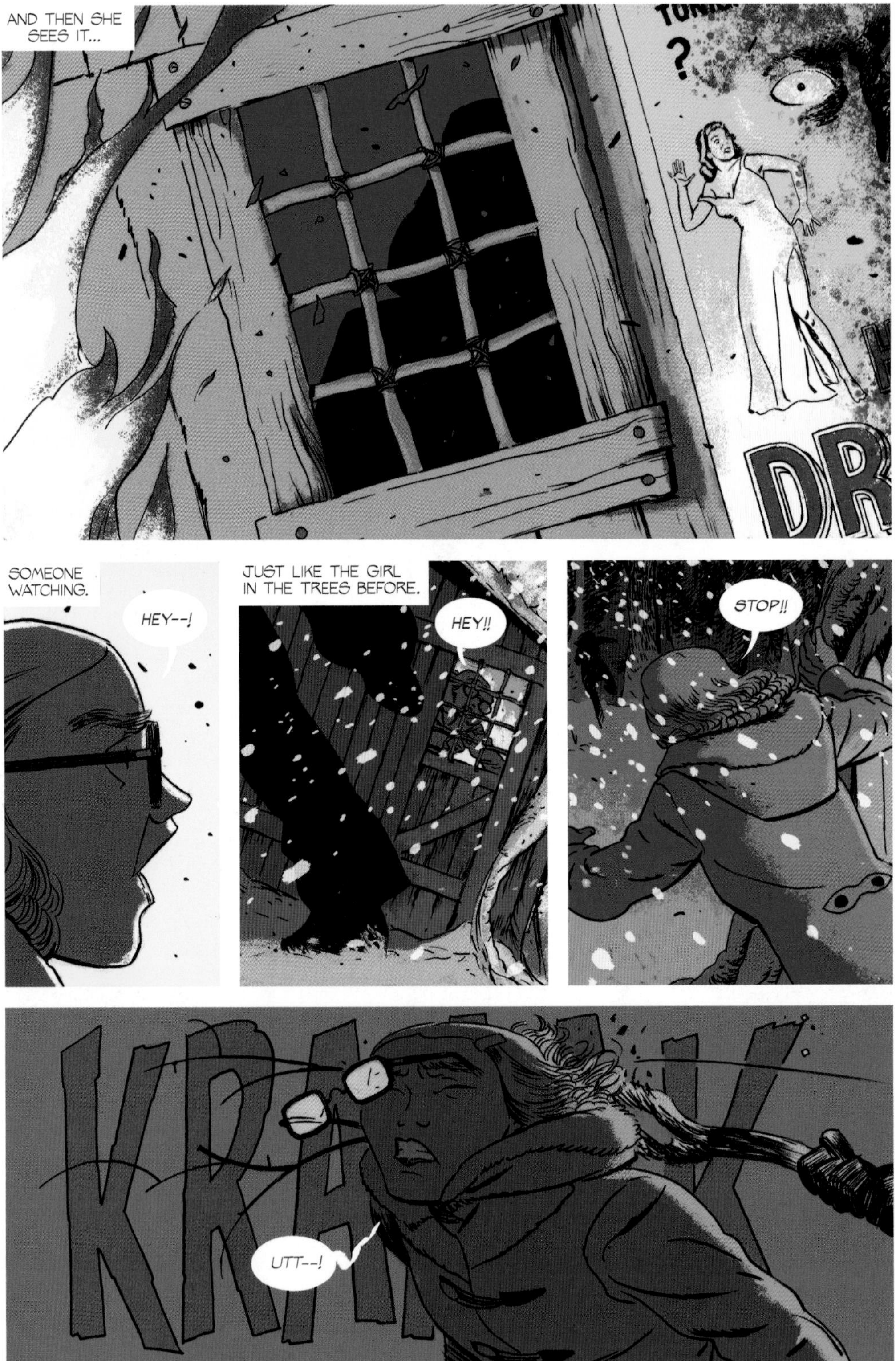
AND THEN SHE SEES IT...
SOMEONE WATCHING.
HEY--!
JUST LIKE THE GIRL IN THE TREES BEFORE.
HEY!!
STOP!!
UTT--!

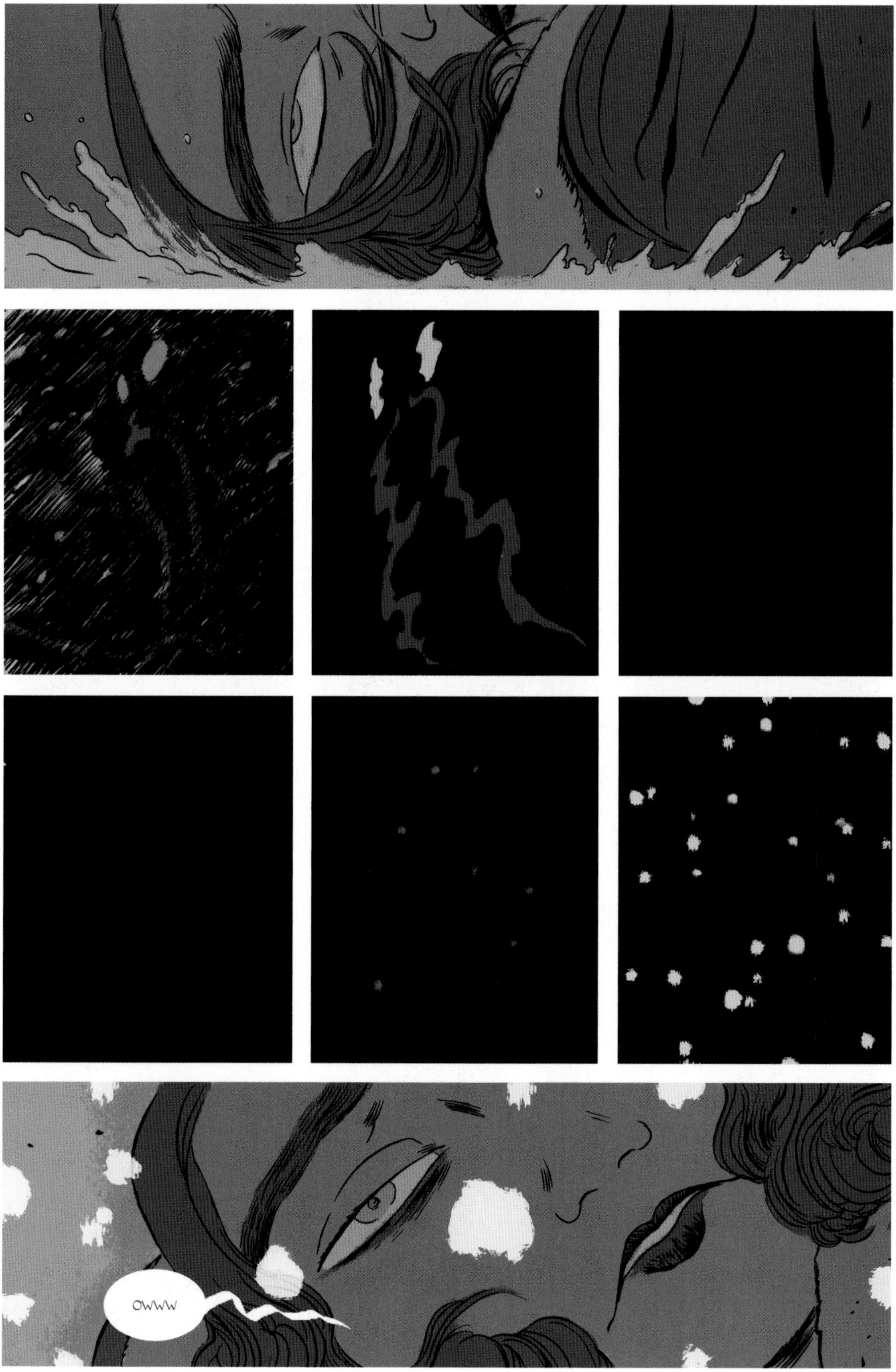
OWWW

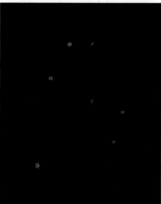

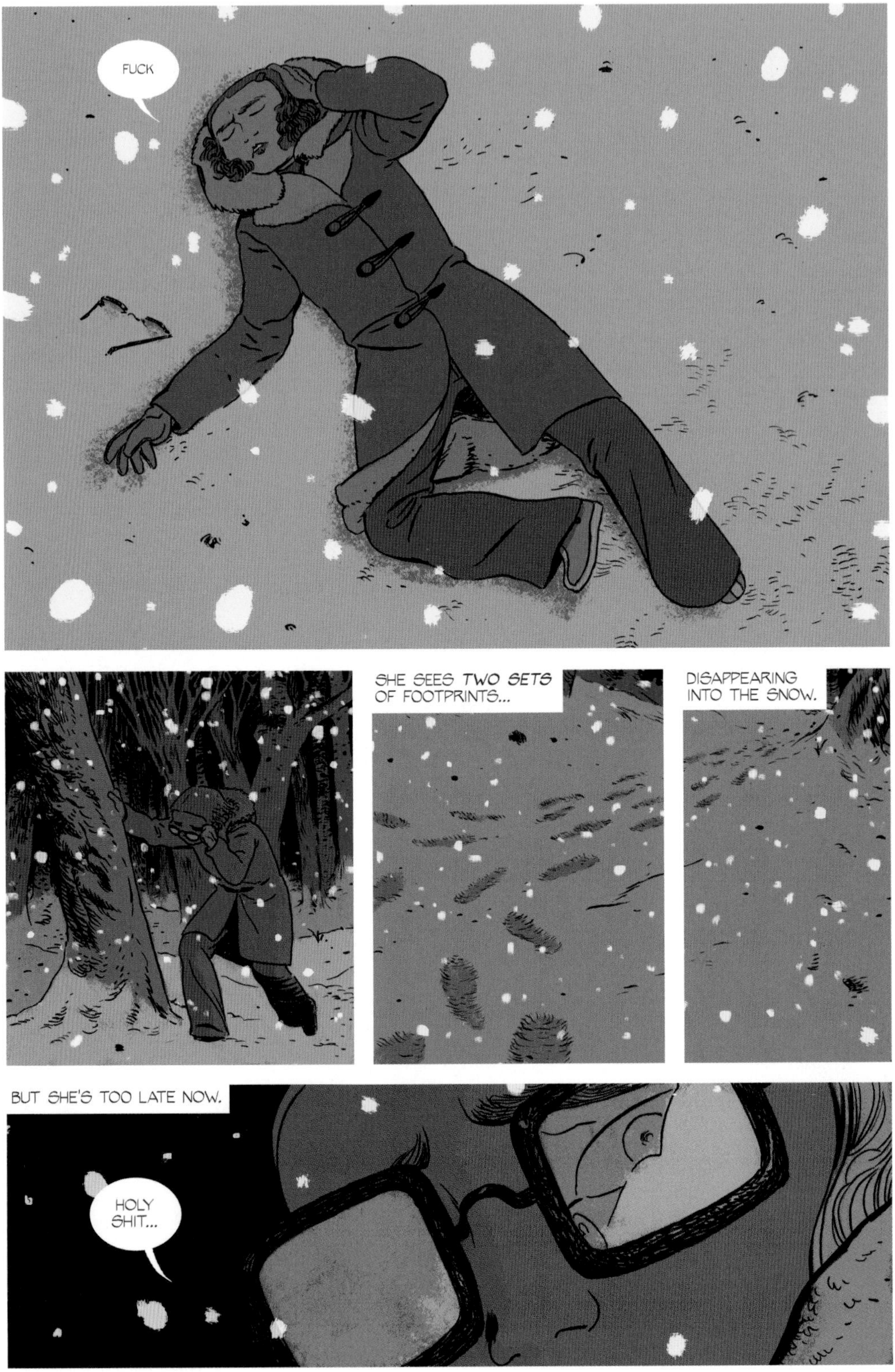
FUCK
SHE SEES **TWO SETS** OF FOOTPRINTS...
DISAPPEARING INTO THE SNOW.
BUT SHE'S TOO LATE NOW.
HOLY SHIT...

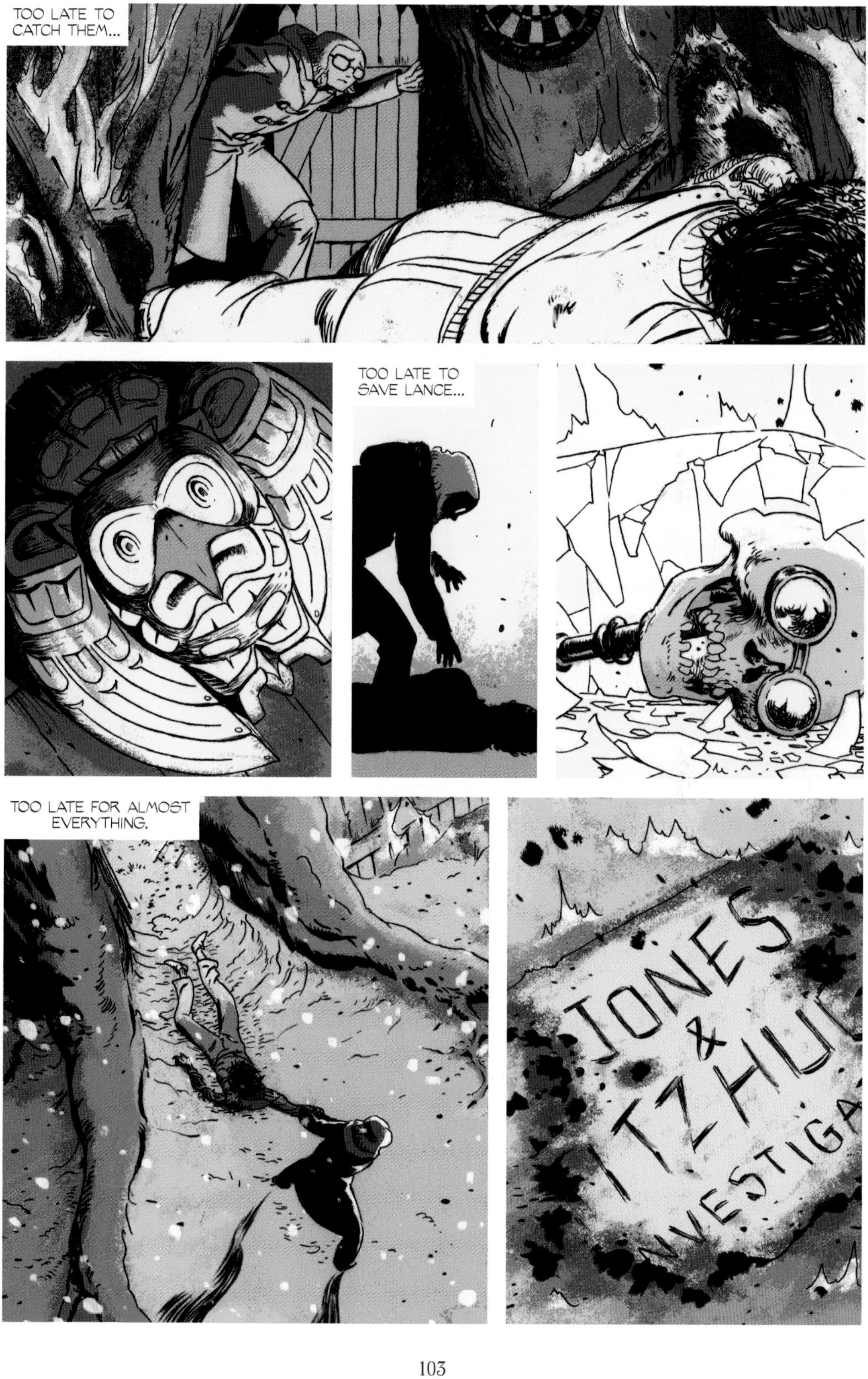

TOO LATE TO CATCH THEM...
TOO LATE TO SAVE LANCE...
TOO LATE FOR ALMOST EVERYTHING.
JONES & ITZHU
NVESTIGA

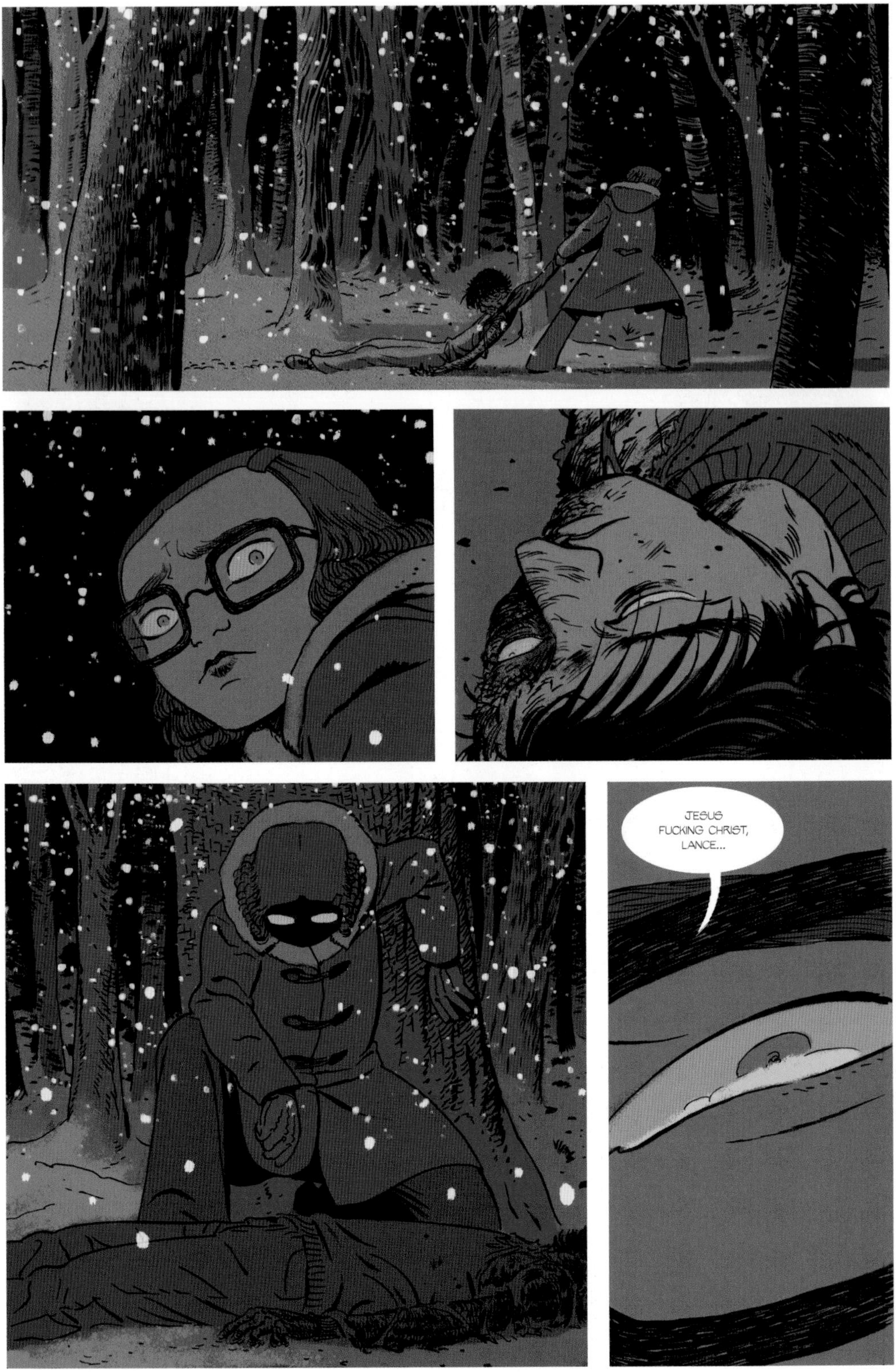
JESUS FUCKING CHRIST, LANCE...

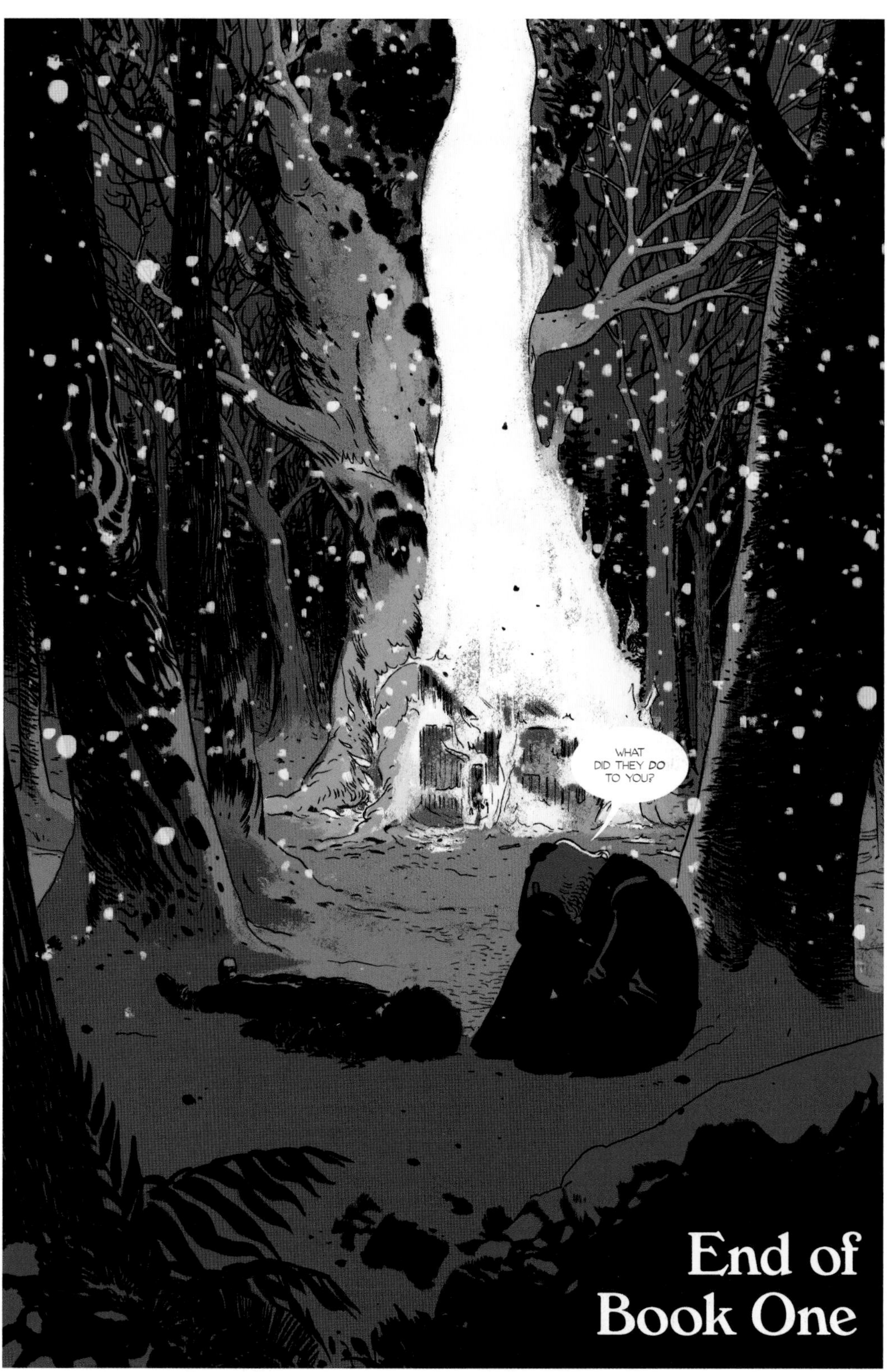
WHAT DID THEY DO TO YOU?
End of Book One

SO WHERE DID FRIDAY COME FROM…?

The short answer is that FRIDAY exists because a while back, Marcos asked if I wanted to write something for him. I thought about it for maybe one minute, then wrote back with the basic pitch for this book, which seemingly came to me in one quick burst of inspiration, as I was trying to picture what I most wanted to see Marcos Martin draw next.

But the long answer is more complicated. Because FRIDAY is something that's been building in the back of my mind for probably half my life, that I was starting to think I'd never actually get to write. From the time I was 25 or so, I had this vague dream of writing a book like this… Something that felt gothic but grounded, like a post-YA book, where the kids that solved mysteries and confronted ghosts and monsters also grew up and had the same problems we all do, the same struggles, and bad habits.

See, when I was young and barely scraping by as a cartoonist, I lived around the corner from a Public Library and when I'd get depressed, I'd go over and dig through their young adult section. It started because I saw a stack of **Great Brain** books waiting to be reshelved. I remembered them from when I was like 10 or 11, so I checked them all out and read them in two days, and it was like a time machine. After that, for about a year I was I checking out books like that all the time – Encyclopedia Brown, The Egypt Game, Roald Dahl books, a bunch of the John Bellairs series like **The House with the Clock in its Walls**, or Daniel Pinkwater's **Snarkout Boys** series, and my favorite YA books of all time, **Harriet the Spy** and its sequel **The Long Secret**.

At some point I drifted down to the mystery section and started rereading Jim Thompson books and Raymond Chandler, and that stuff spoke to me too, obviously, and led me to pursuing a whole other career… but that year of reading and rereading those 60s and 70s YA novels always stuck in the back of my mind.

Sometimes I'd jot down notes – trying to blend Lovecraft's New England and Edward Gorey's, playing with fairy tales and occult conspiracy theories – but nothing ever came of it. I was busy writing crime comics and superhero comics that were sort of like crime comics, and somehow building a side career as a YA (or post-YA) novelist just seemed like one of those "if only I'd taken a different path" kind of things. Here I was buried in deadlines, dreaming of this other life where I sat by a fire with a notebook, writing the continuing adventures of some teen detectives in the timeless 1970s of my youth. It was never going to happen.

But then I got Marcos's email and it all fell together.

I knew the look and the mood this story had to have, and here was the perfect artist to bring it all to life, and someone who was one of my favorite storytellers, on top of it. And suddenly all those years of circling what this project might be paid off, because when I saw Marcos's sketches of Friday, I knew exactly who she was, and what her story would be. And then watching him and Muntsa bring it all to life as each chapter came together was an even more magical experience. Kings Hill feels alive and full of mystery and nostalgia at the same time, and I promise you, we've barely scratched the surface of it so far. I can't wait for you all to read what's coming in the next two books.

--Ed Brubaker

PS - On the following pages, you'll find some of Marcos's sketches and my early ideas about the characters and the town, from our initial emails about the project.

SKETCHBOOK

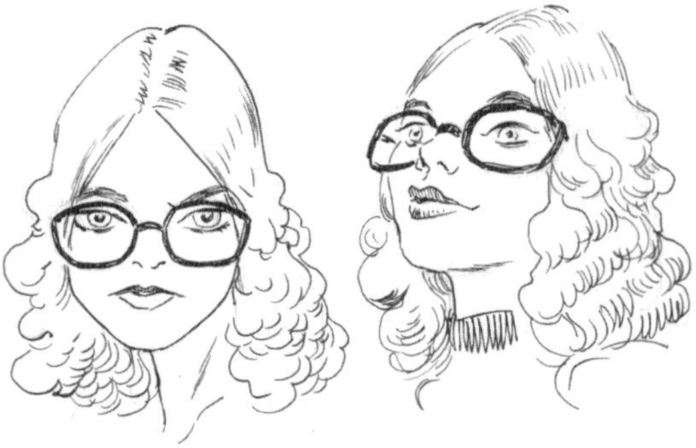

FRIDAY FITZHUGH

An 18 year old girl, in her first year at college. Since she was 12 years old she has been the partner and bodyguard of Lancelot Jones, teen detective. Friday is a tomboy who's starting to wear skirts and lipstick. She has glasses and red hair. She's a great hockey player in the winter when the lake freezes over, and she can beat up most of the boys in her grade and even older.

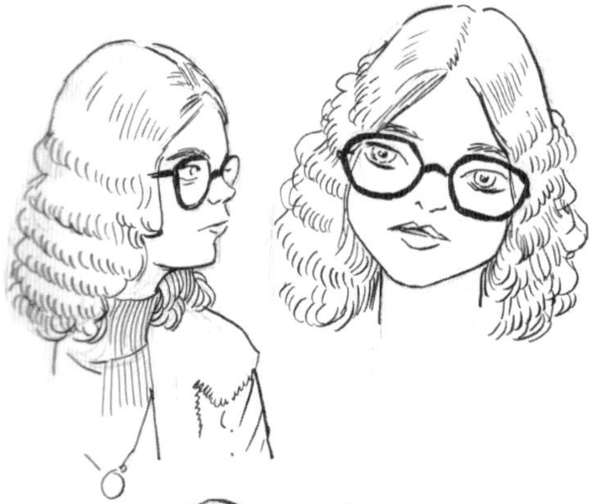

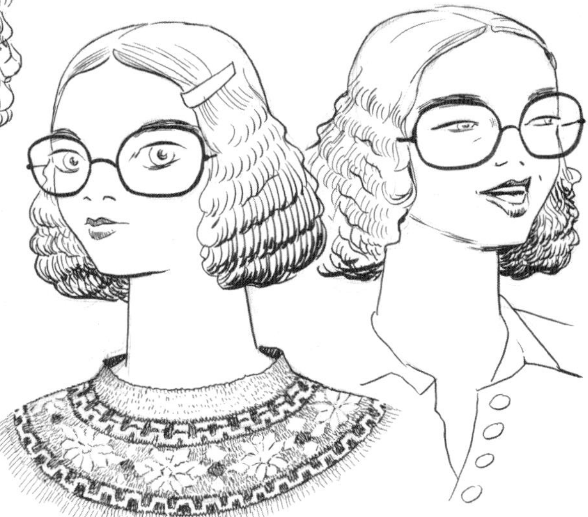

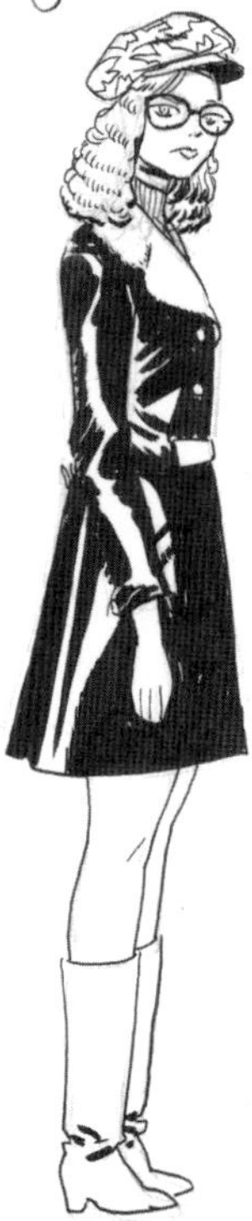

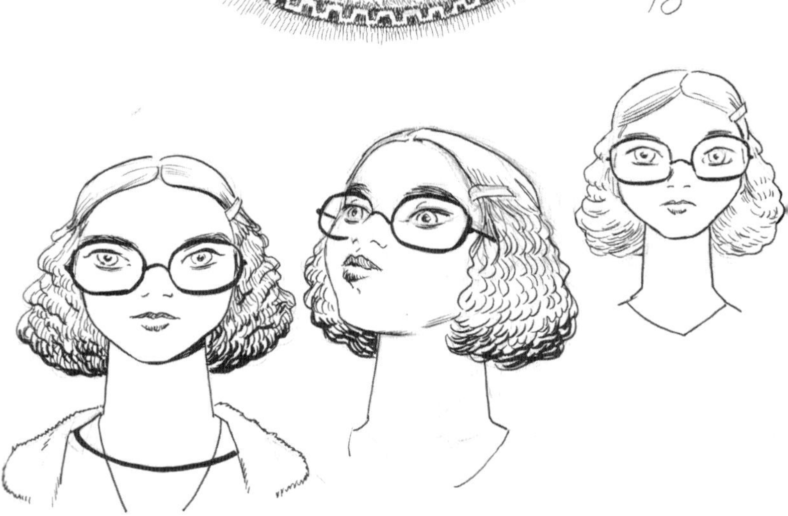

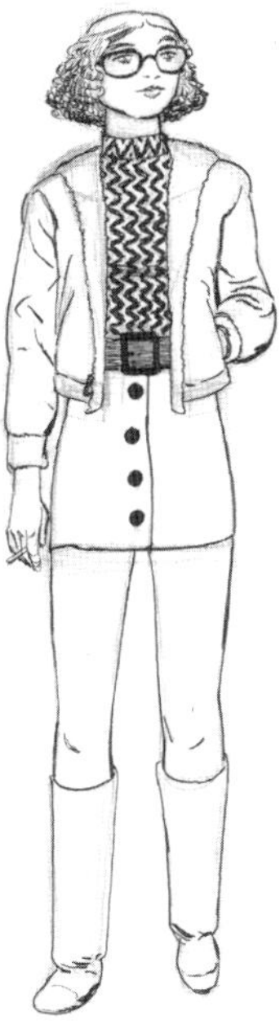

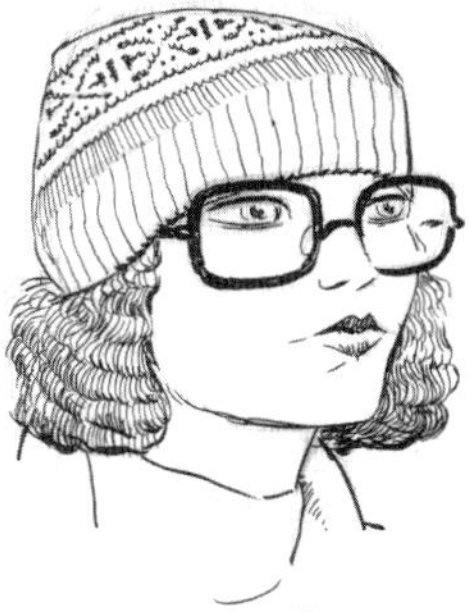

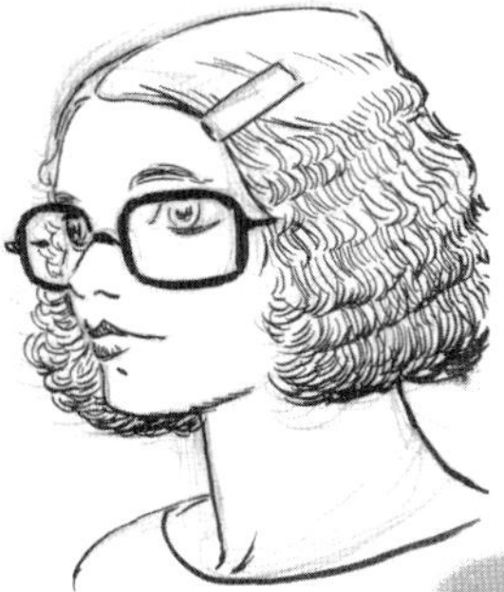

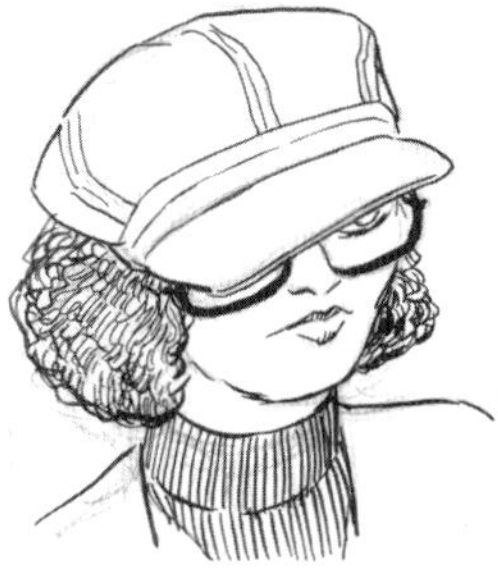

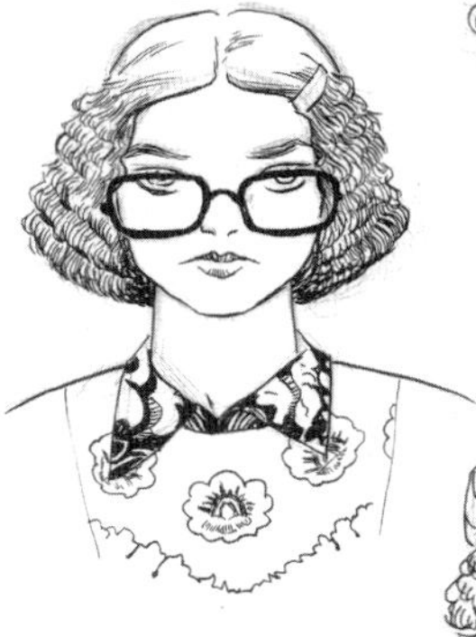

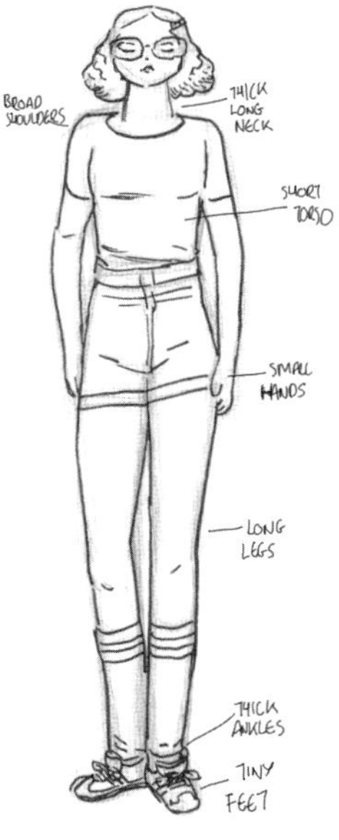
BROAD SHOULDERS
THICK LONG NECK
SHORT TORSO
SMALL HANDS
LONG LEGS
THICK ANKLES
TINY FEET

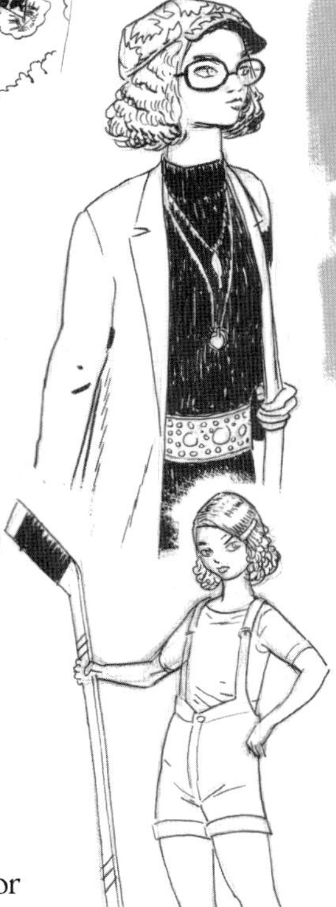

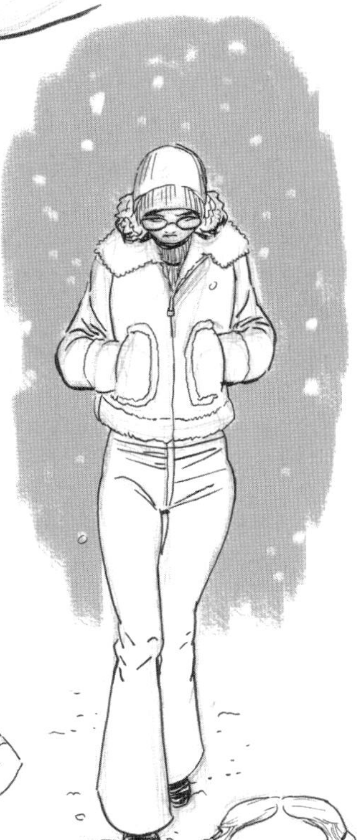

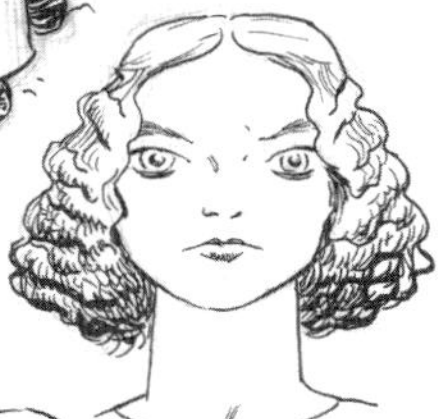

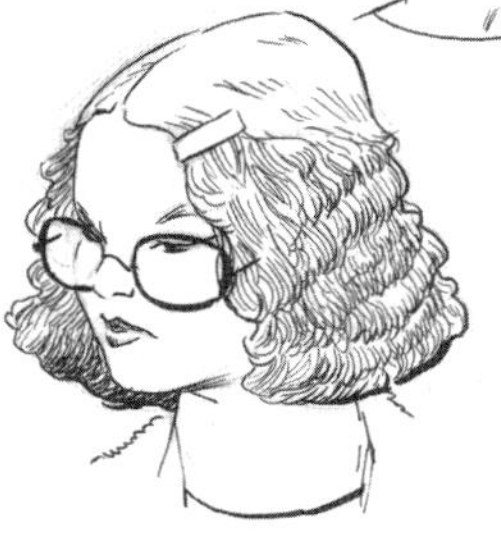

Her clothes should be hip and cool for us to look at, but not goth or steampunk or anything like that. More like a character from a Kubrick or Wes Anderson movie, with that New England in the 70s vibe. She's on the skinny side, but strong and tall. Often wears hi-top tennis shoes and jeans that are rolled up, especially in flashback scenes to the early years of them as teen detectives.

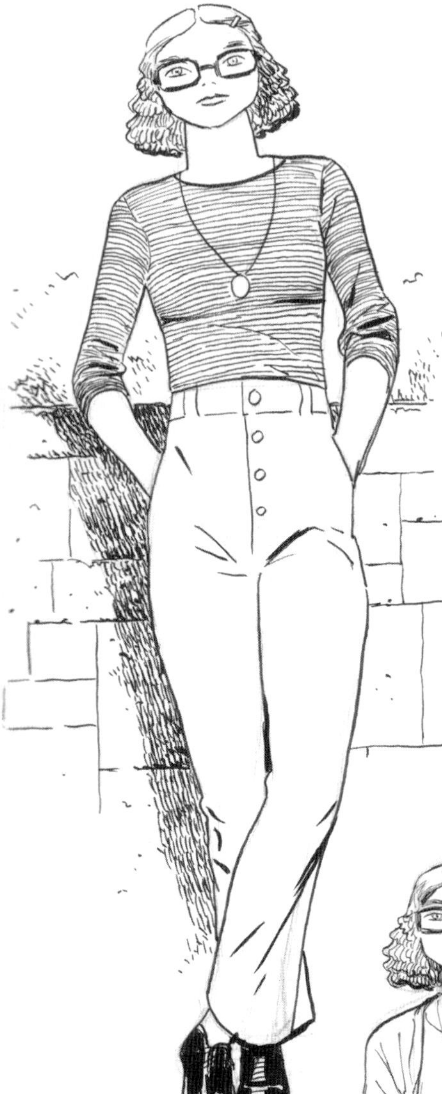
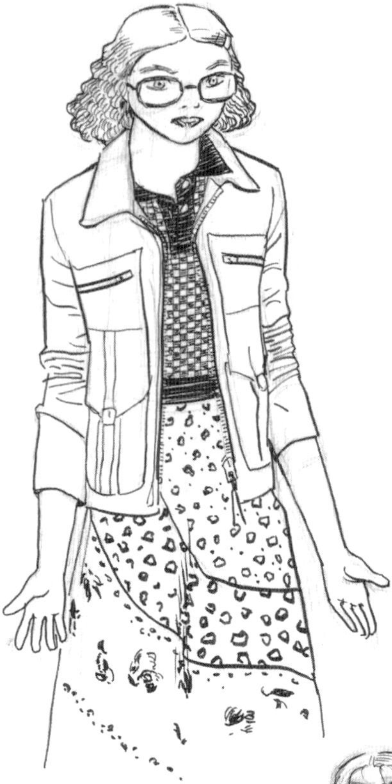
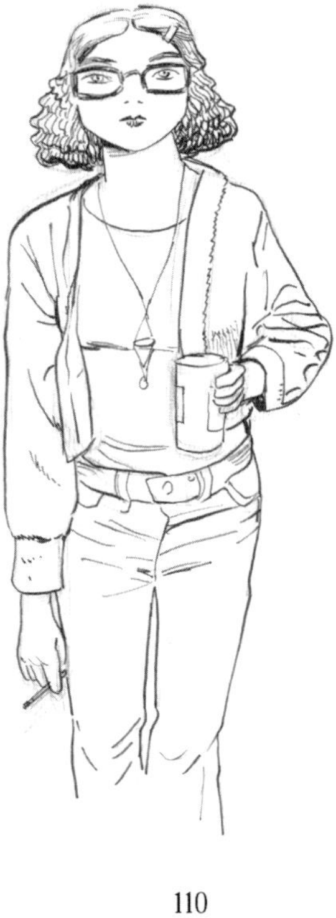
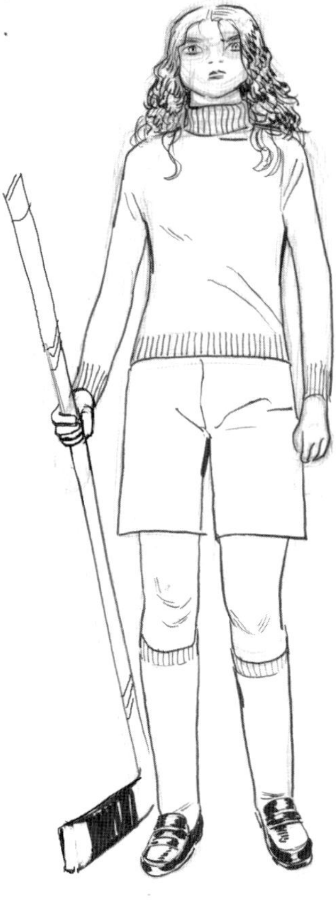

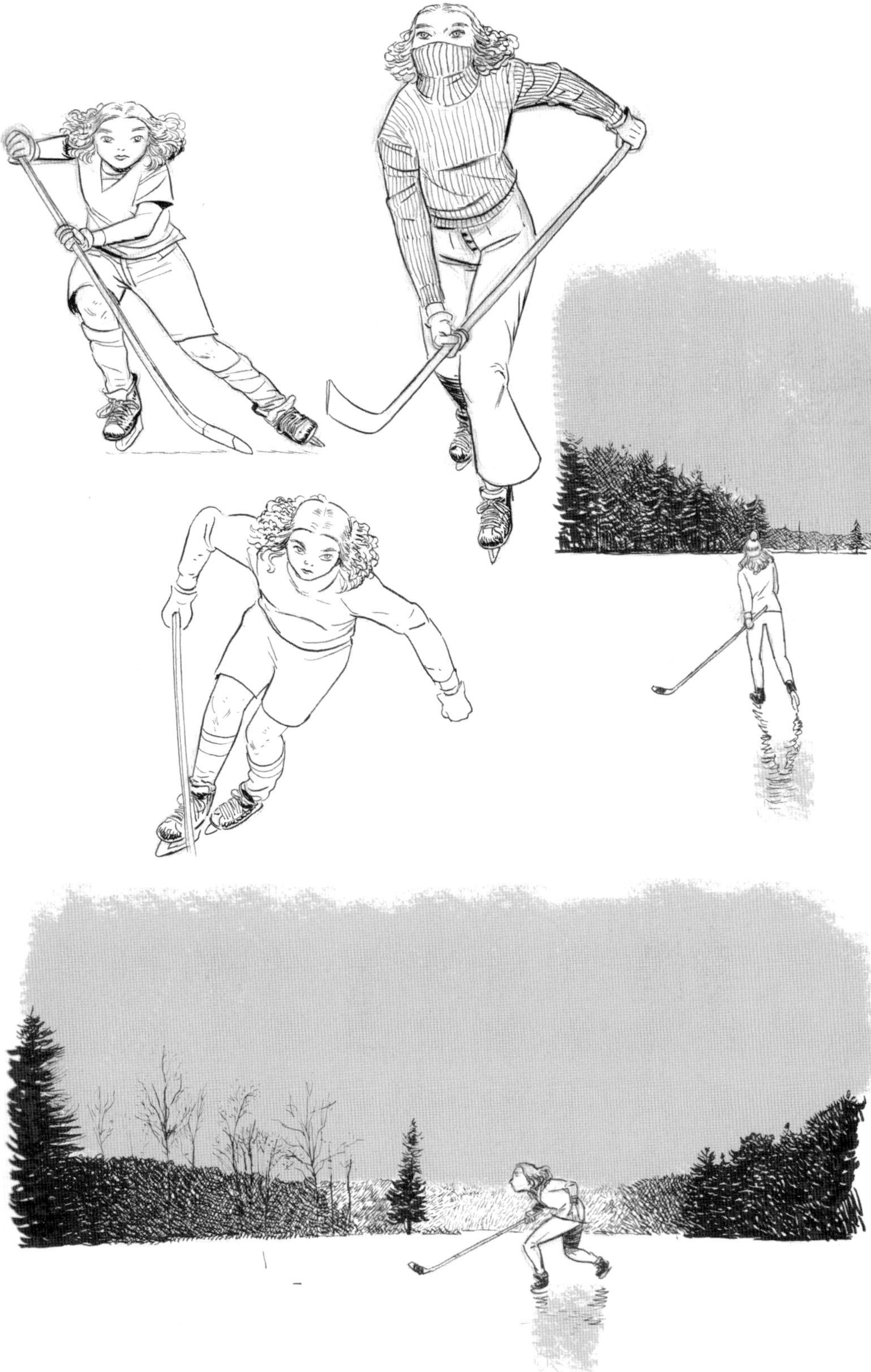

LANCELOT JONES

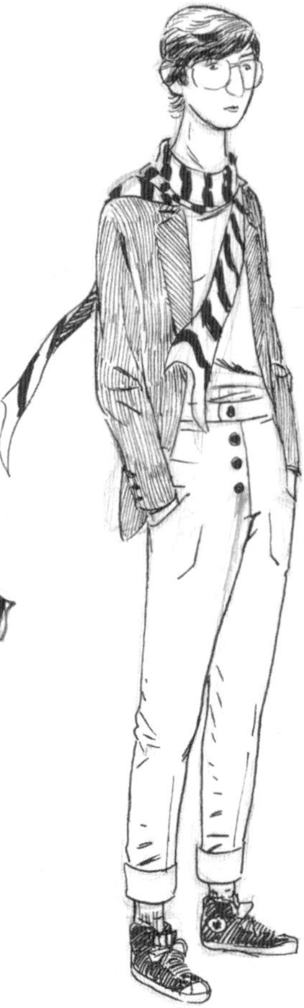

Lance is like a weirder version of Encyclopedia Brown or Young Sherlock Holmes or something. He's super well-read and remembers everything, and he's really intuitive. He dresses more eccentric than Friday, but not too much. A tiny bit gothic. Like maybe he'd have a scarf trailing behind him and she wouldn't. He's the Holmes to her Watson, but they're kids in the permanently early 70s world of their little town.
Lance should have glasses but not look like Harry Potter.

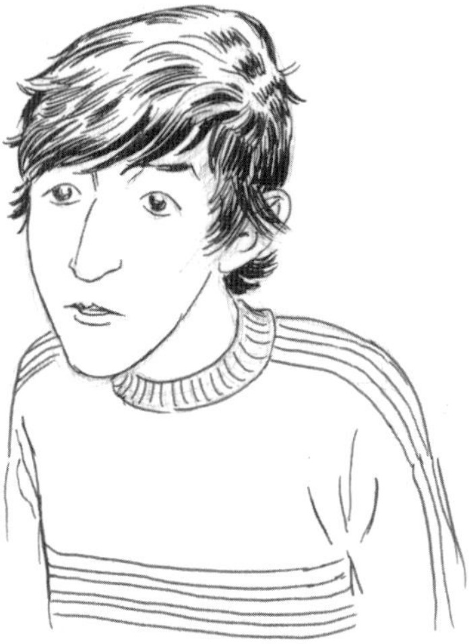

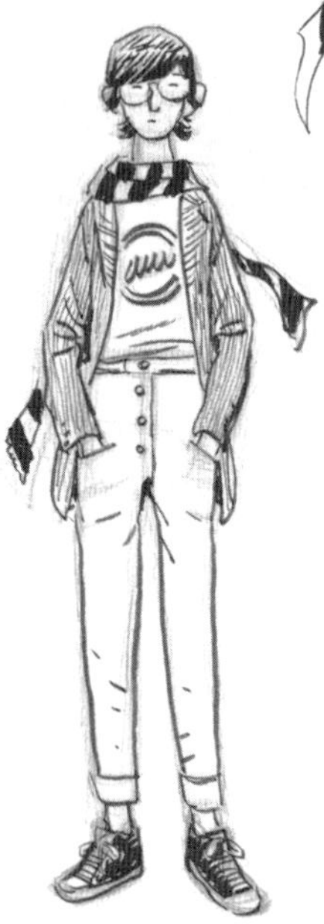

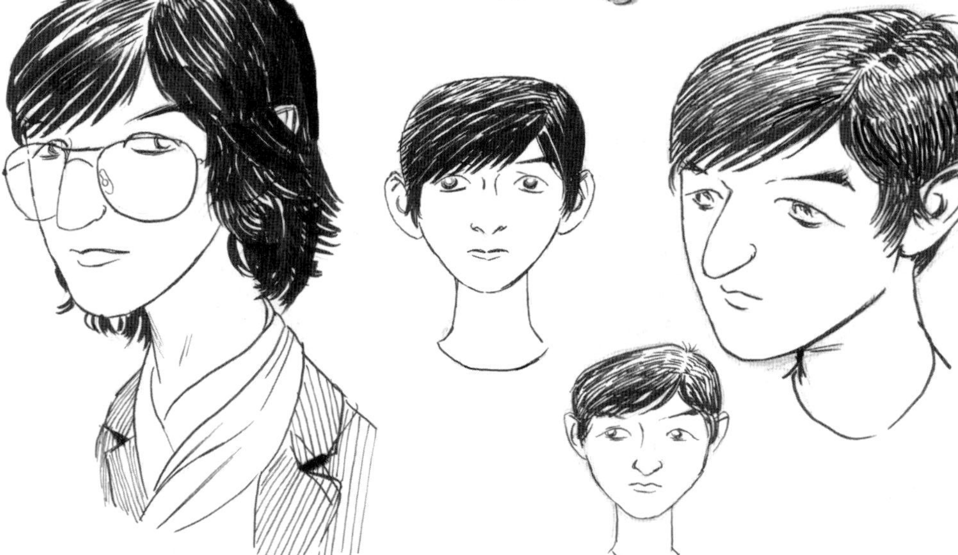

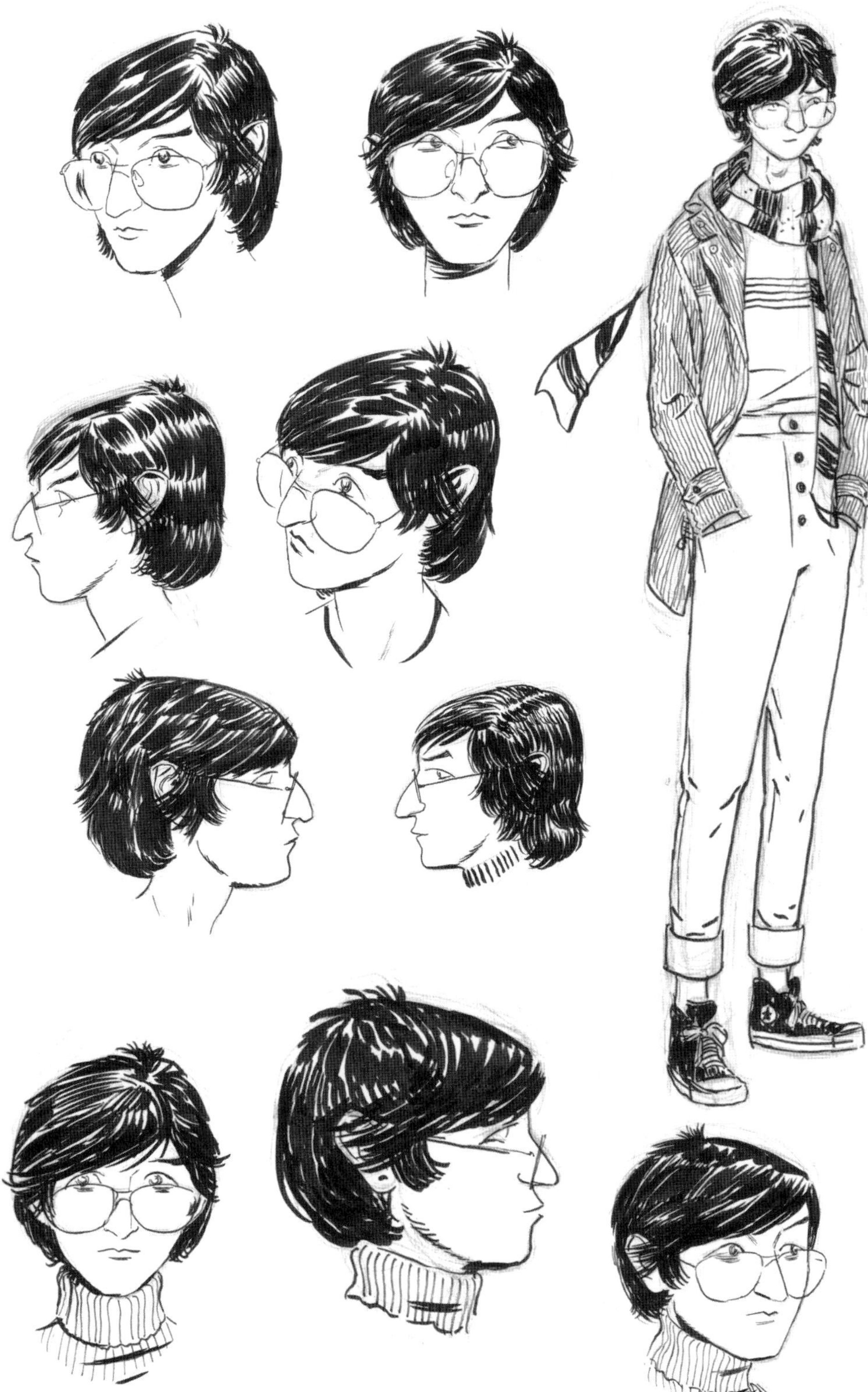

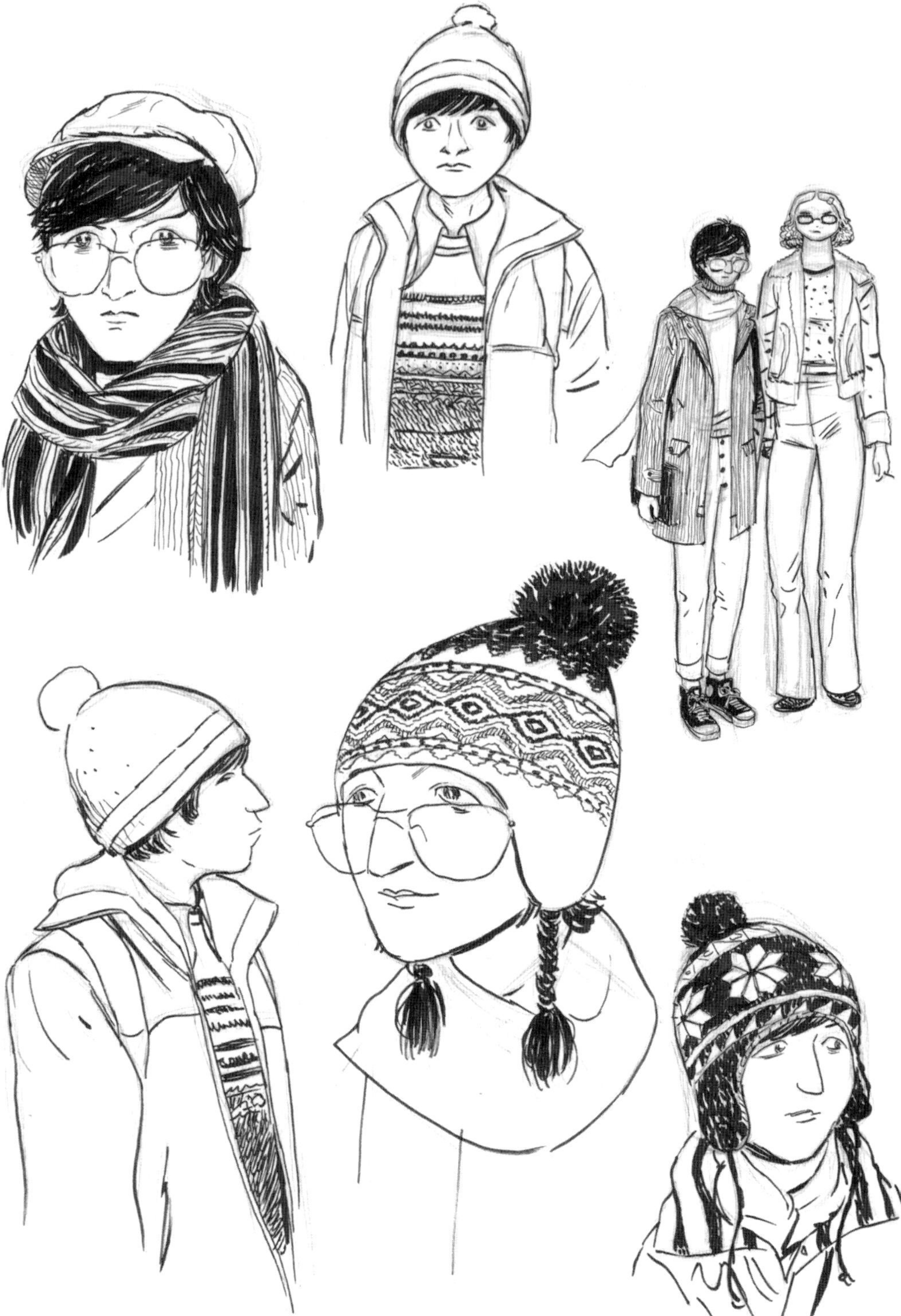

SHERIFF BIXBY

Bixby is tough, but not that sharp. He's smart enough to know that Lancelot is usually right, so he will sometimes accept Lance and Friday's help on a case. Bixby is like a bigger, more solid version of Roy Scheider in **Jaws**. Tough, an ex-soldier, busted nose. Maybe a mustache?

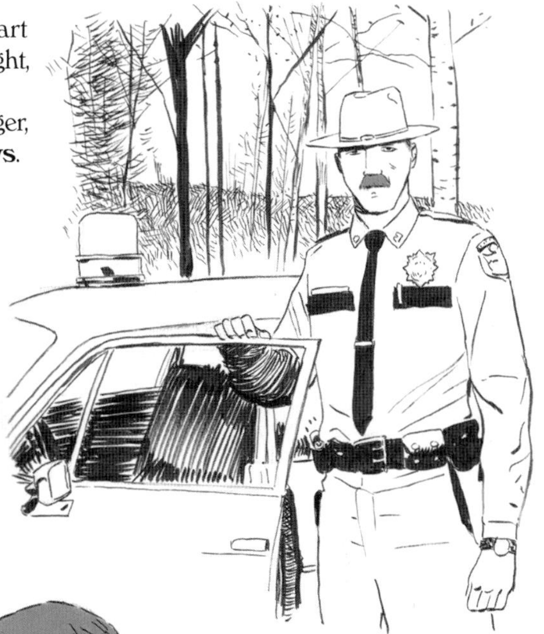

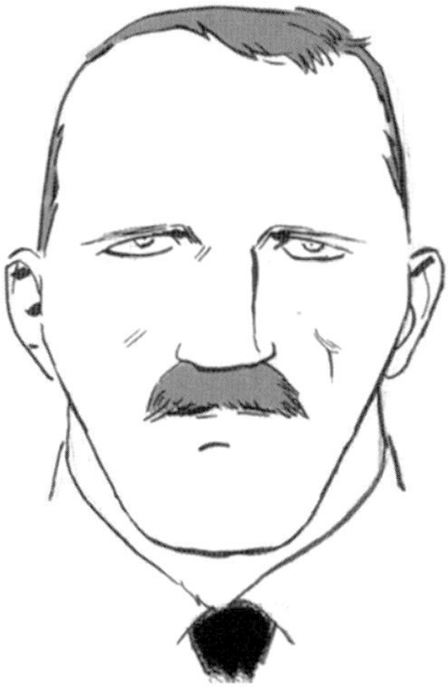

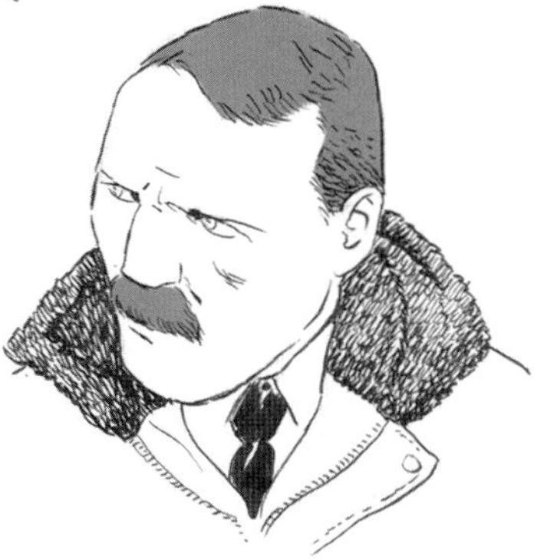

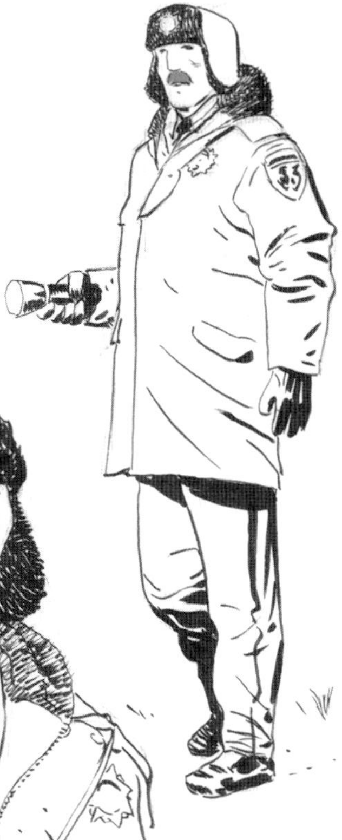

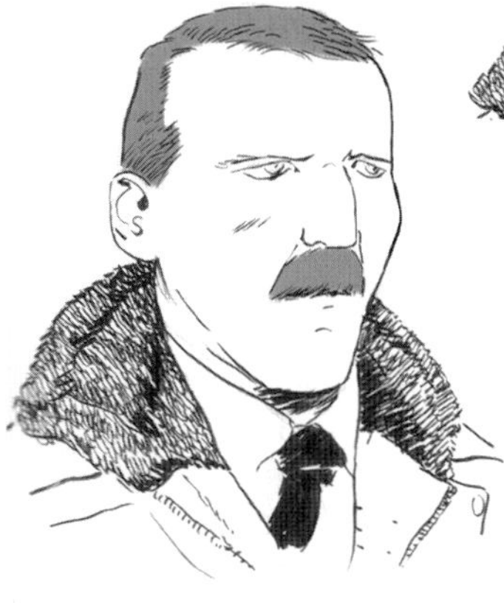

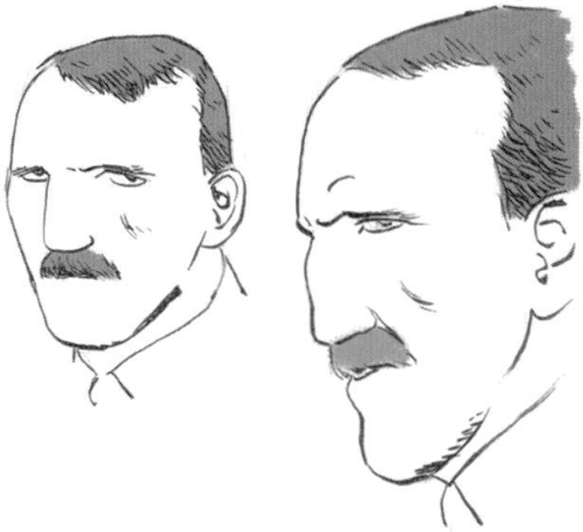

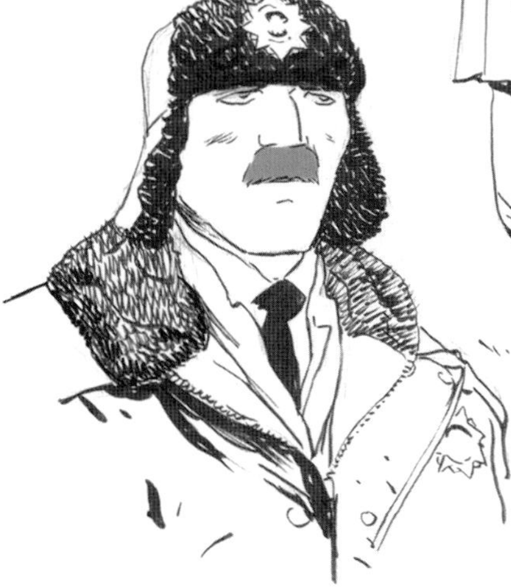

THE TOWN OF KINGS HILL

The town is in an unnamed part of a New England-looking part of America –probably 600 people live there. It's a port town, a fishing village on the coast with lots of fog and old buildings. On one side of the town is the sea, and on the other, once you get outside of town, you see mountains and hills and forests that go on forever.

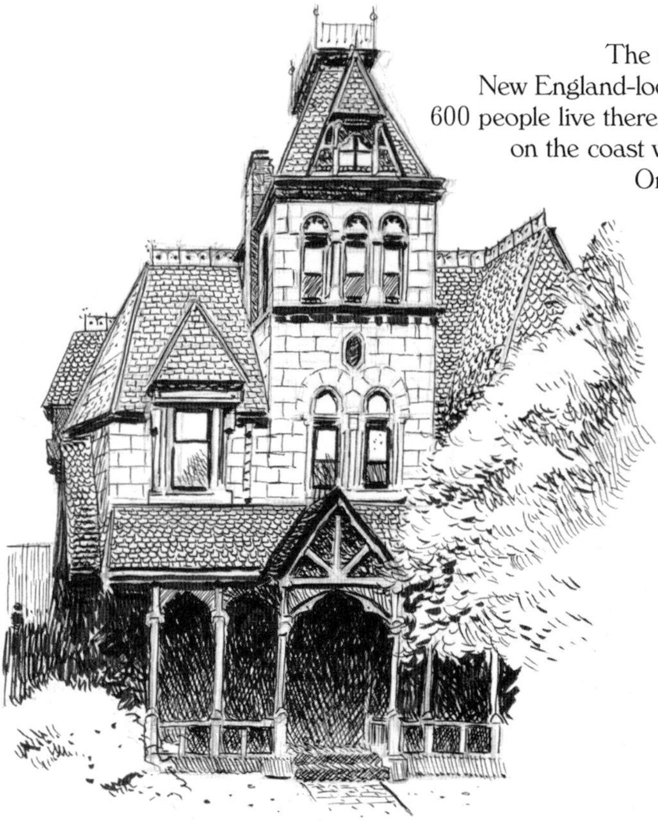

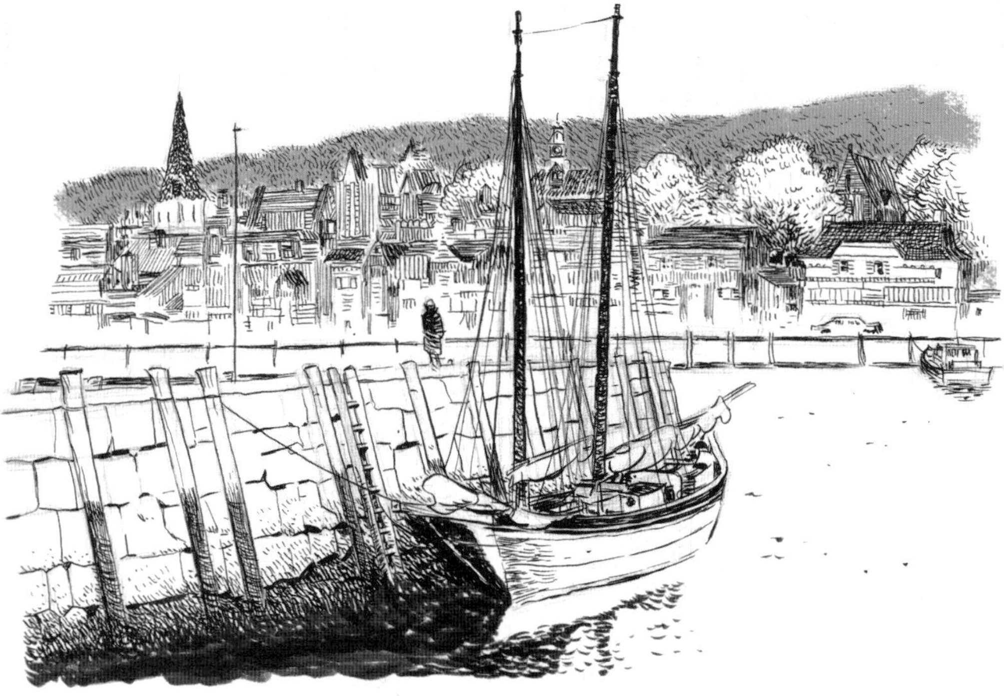

The town has a Lovecraft meets Gorey feeling, as we discussed. Lots of churches and gothic architecture. Victorian houses. A cool-looking old brick town library. In the town park there's the remnants of an old defunct insane asylum that is said to be haunted.

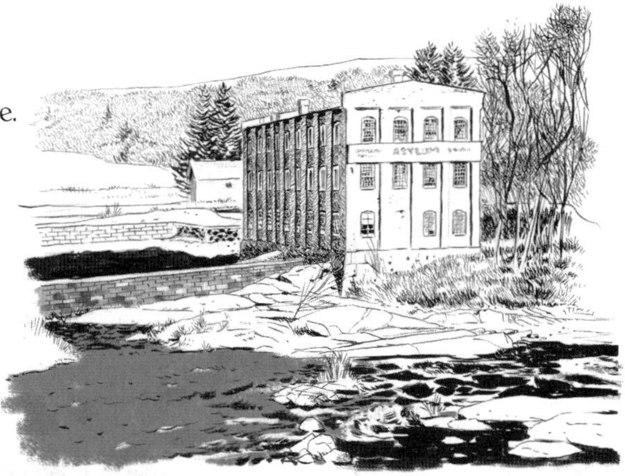
ASYLUM

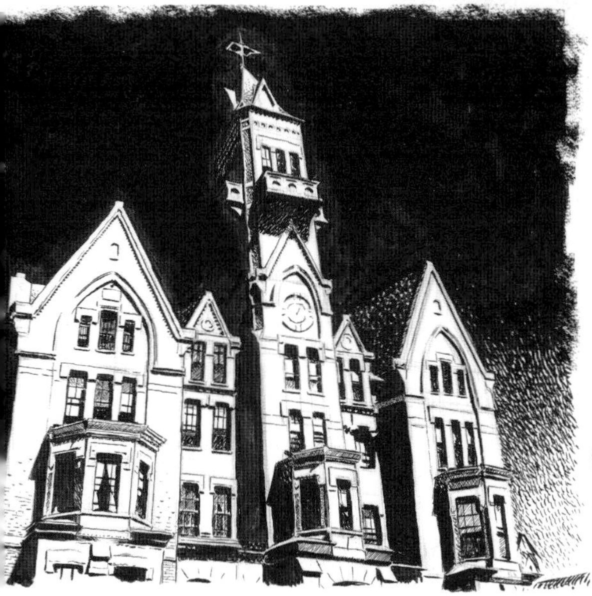

Kingswood University. The local college. Just outside of town is a university full of college students and their living quarters. Kind of like Exeter or someplace like that. Gothic old buildings, hundreds of years old.

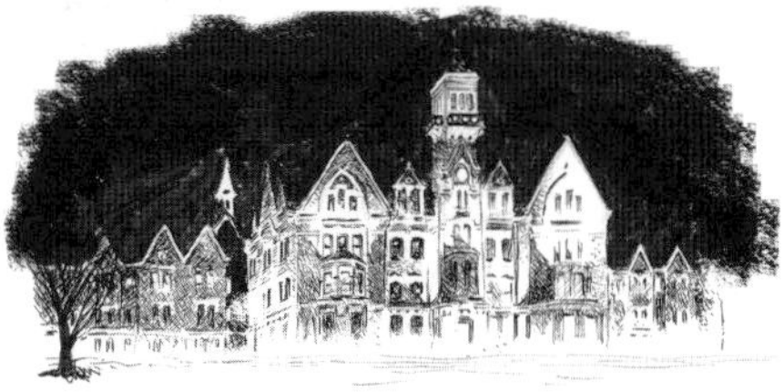

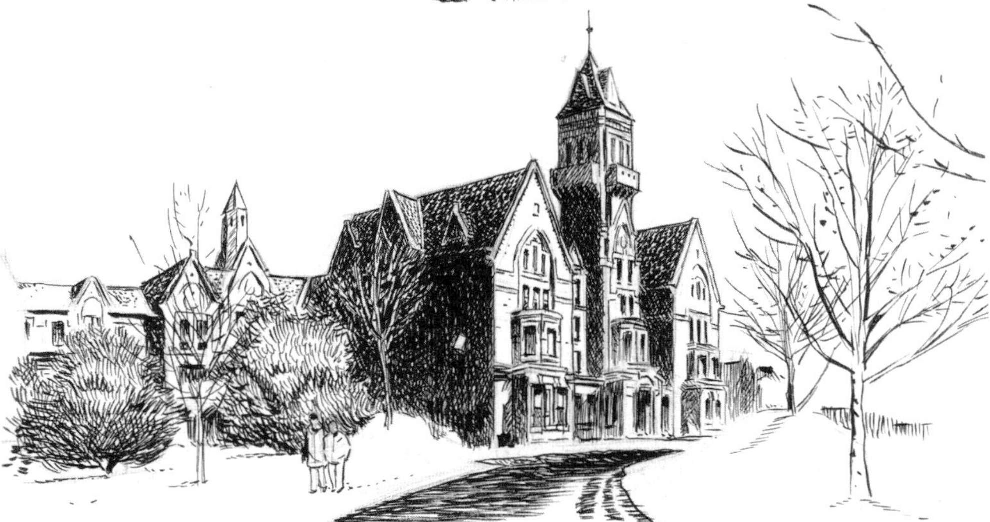

THE LIGHTHOUSE

Every stormy, fog-covered town needs a lighthouse.
Lance lives in the house that's right next to the lighthouse
and his father is the town lighthouse keeper.
His mother died when he was a baby.

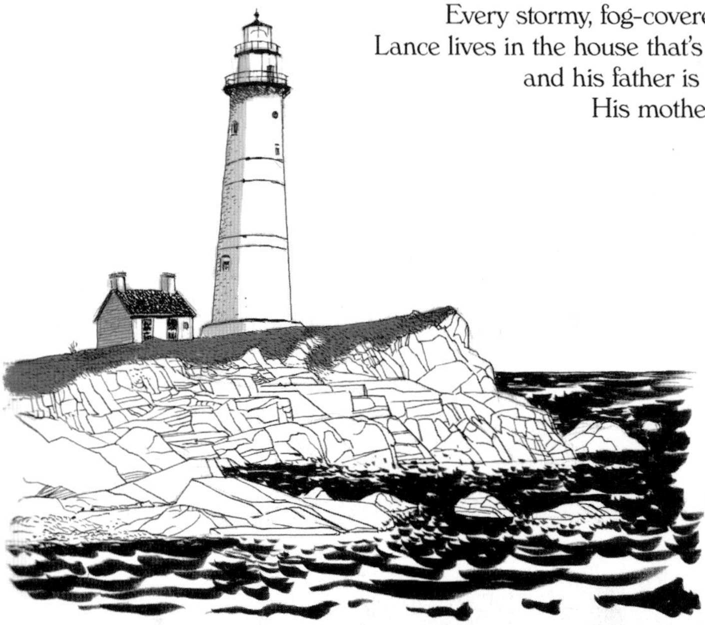

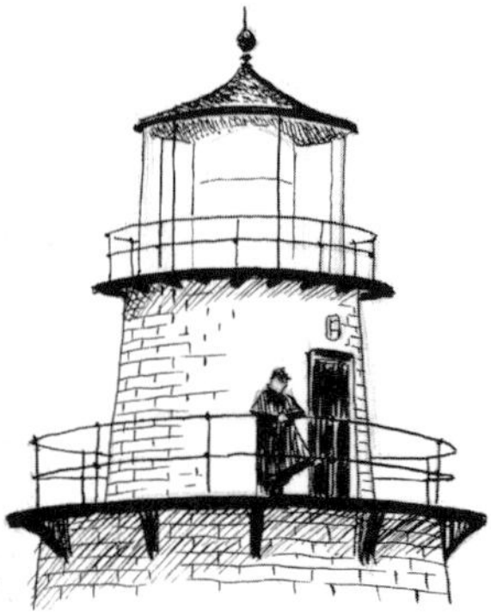

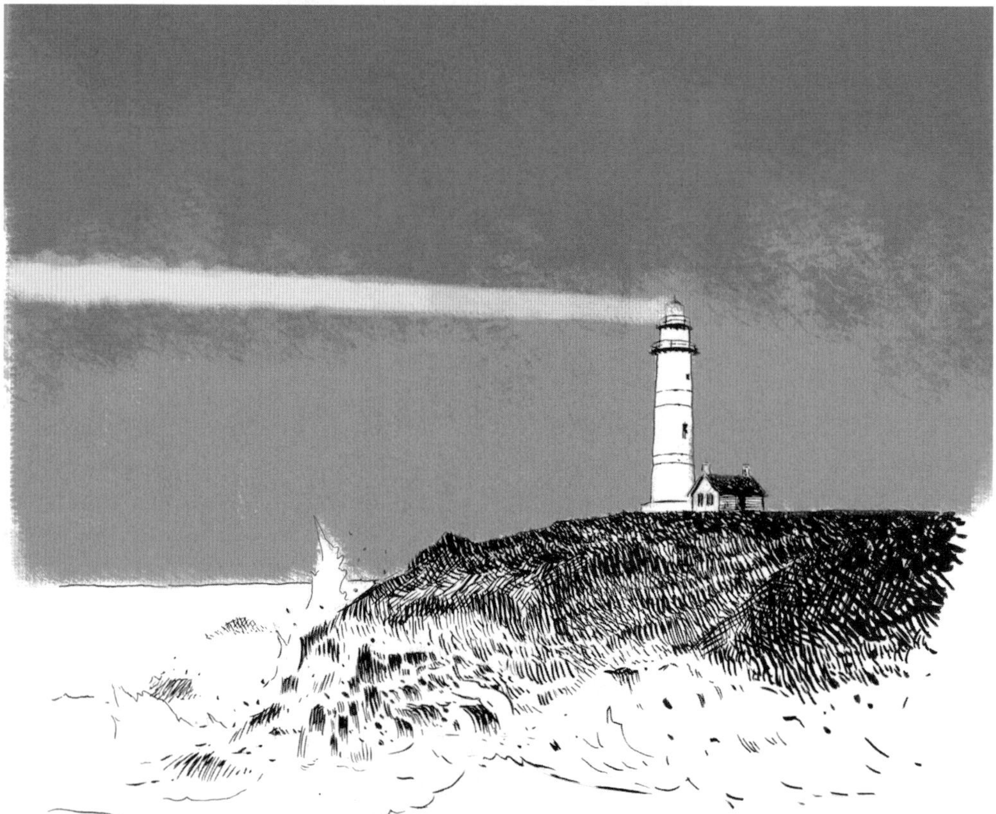

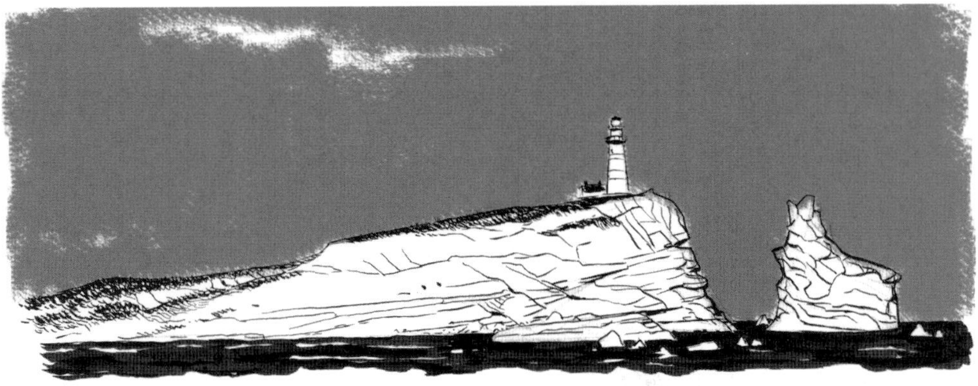

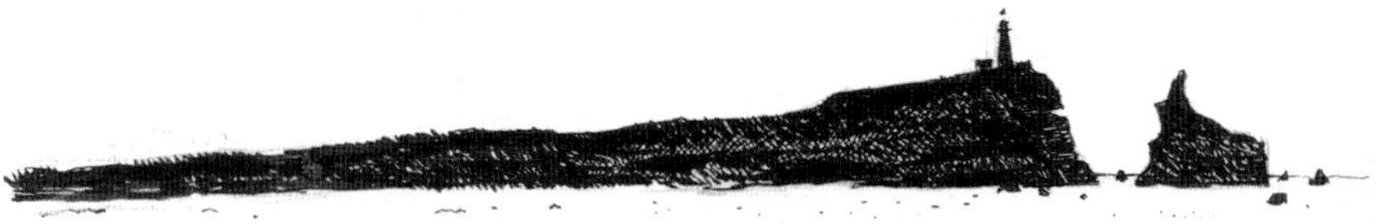

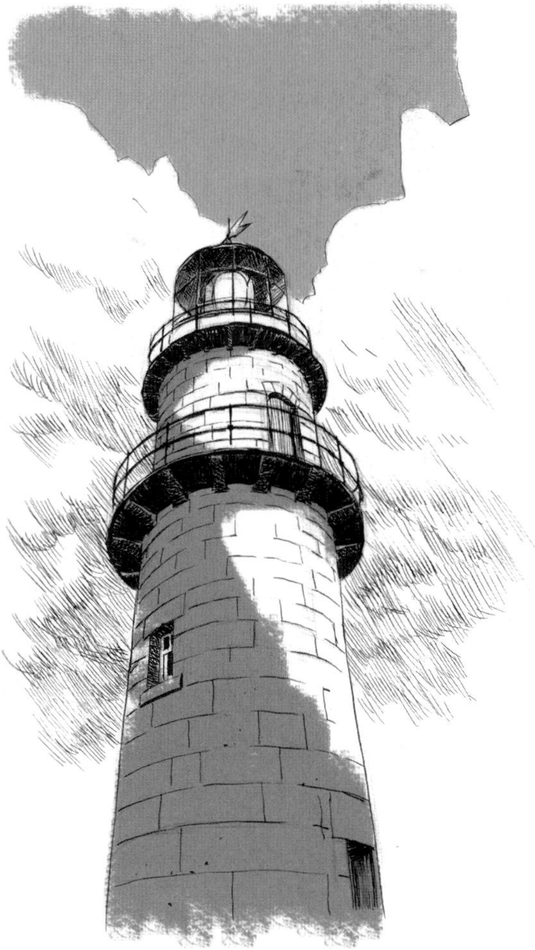

ED BRUBAKER South Burlington
DISCARD
Public Library

Ed Brubaker is one of the most acclaimed writers in comics, having won the Eisner and Harvey Awards for Best Writer five times, among others. His many graphic novels with artist Sean Phillips - CRIMINAL, FATALE, THE FADE OUT, PULP, KILL OR BE KILLED, and the RECKLESS series - have been published around the world in several languages. Moving into television writing, Brubaker first served as a Supervising Producer on HBO's WESTWORLD, and then with director Nicolas Winding Refn, he was co-creator and writer of Amazon's TOO OLD TO DIE YOUNG, the first streaming series to debut at Cannes.

Brubaker lives with his wife and dog in California, where he continues to work in film, television, and as always, comics.

MARCOS MARTÍN

Marcos Martín is a Catalan comic book artist whose work at Marvel and DC includes such titles as **Batgirl: Year One, Breach, Dr.Strange: The Oath, Amazing Spider-man,** and **Daredevil.** In 2013 he founded the online platform Panel Syndicate together with writer Brian K. Vaughan and illustrator/colorist Muntsa Vicente in order to distribute their creator-owned comic, THE PRIVATE EYE. The series went on to win an Eisner Award for Best Digital/Webcomic and the Harvey Award for Best Online Comics Work. THE PRIVATE EYE and Panel Syndicate have received critical acclaim and media attention for their role as one of the first DRM-free, pay-what-you-want comics and Panel Syndicate has continued to publish other works by the same team (BARRIER, THE WALKING DEAD: THE ALIEN) as well as opening up to other renowned creators like Jay Faerber, Ken Niimura, Alex de Campi, David López and Albert Monteys.

Image Comics has since published both THE PRIVATE EYE as a deluxe hardcover graphic novel and BARRIER as a deluxe five-issue miniseries in the original widescreen format.

MUNTSA VICENTE

An illustrator whose clients include **Elle Magazine**, Harper Collins and Vitruvio-Leo Burnett, Muntsa has recently applied her incredible color talent to several comic book projects. Besides being Marcos's colorist on all their Panel Syndicate series, she continues to work at companies like Marvel and DC Comics, as well as focusing most of her illustration work on children's books.

FRIDAY continues at panelsyndicate.com